IN THE SHADOW OF A VALIANT MOON

OTHER BOOKS BY STU JONES AND GARETH WORTHINGTON

It Takes Death to Reach a Star, Book One of a Duology.

OTHER BOOKS BY STU JONES

The Action of Purpose Trilogy

Through the Fury to the Dawn
Into the Dark of the Day
Against the Fading of the Light

OTHER BOOKS BY GARETH WORTHINGTON

The Children of the Fifth Sun Trilogy

Children of the Fifth Sun
Children of the Fifth Sun: Echelon
Children of the Fifth Sun: Rubicon (2020)

AWARDS

It Takes Death to Reach a Star

2019 IPPY Bronze Award Science Fiction
2019 Feathered Quill Gold Award Winner Science Fiction
2018 Cygnus Award First Place Ribbon Dystopian Science Fiction
2018 Dragon Award Nominee Best Science Fiction Novel
2018 New York Book Festival Winner Science Fiction
2018 Readers' Favorite Honorable Mention Science Fiction

Children of the Fifth Sun

2019 Eric Hoffer Award Honorable Mention Science Fiction
2019 Eric Hoffer Award Grand Prize Shortlist
2019 Eric Hoffer Award First Horizon Finalist
2018 London Book Fesitval Winner Science Fiction
2018 Killer Nashville Silver Falchion Finalist Science Fiction

Children of the Fifth Sun: Echelon

2018 Hollywood Book Festival Winner Science Fiction

IN THE SHADOW OF A VALIANT MOON

BOOK TWO OF
IT TAKES DEATH TO REACH A STAR

AWARD-WINNING AUTHORS
STU JONES & GARETH WORTHINGTON

In The Shadow Of A Valiant Moon

ISBN: 978-1-944109-96-7

VESUVIAN BOOKS

Published by Vesuvian Books
www.vesuvianbooks.com

Printed in the United States of America

10 9 8 7 6 5 4 3 2 1

Self-made gods with only the laws of physics to keep us company, we are accountable to no one.

—Yuval Noah Harari, *Sapiens*

For my father—a pillar of unshakable faith and fortitude, standing amidst the storm.
– Stu Jones

For Dominica—for the girl who holds the hand of this often-distant man.
– Gareth Worthington

NAMES FROM BOOK I

Bilgi [Robust, Logosian]. Mentor and father figure to Mila, Bilgi is also the stalwart and capable head of the resistance (see Opor).

Denni [Robust, Fiorian, deceased]. Resistance fighter and friend to Mila and Demitri. Killed four years ago in the battle for the Gracile Leader's rocket.

Demitri [Gracile, missing]. Former Gracile experimental physicist, tormented by another voice in his head: Vedmak. Demitri believed quantum entanglement allowed him to connect with Vedmak's 'coherent information' following the madman's death. Upon teaming up with Mila and the resistance to defeat the Gracile Leader, Demitri suffered a catastrophic injury that allowed Vedmak to take control of his body.

Evgeniy [Gracile, deceased]. A Gracile scientist and friend to Demitri. Killed by the Gracile Leader for dealing with the Robust resistance.

Faruq [Robust, Baqirian, missing]. Musul turned resistance fighter, stepson to Kapka and older brother to Husniya. Faruq is believed to have been killed four years ago during the battle for the Leader's rocket when he confronted Kapka on the launchpad. His body was never recovered.

Ghofaun [Robust, Zopatian]. A Lawkshaun monk turned resistance fighter. Ghofaun is one of the only Chum Lawk practicioners who can regularly best Mila. His fierceness is only matched by his wisdom and absolute composure under fire.

Giahi [Robust, Fiorian]. Resistance fighter and constant thorn in Mila's side. Strong-willed and capable, Giahi believes he should be leading the resistance and he's willing to do anything he can to see that goal achieved.

Gil [Robust, Velian, missing]. Drug addict and Mila's former information broker. No one has heard from him since the fall of the lillipads.

The Leader [Gracile, deceased]. Former head of the Graciles. Four years ago, he set a plan to accelerate the evolution of the Gracile kind by encoding their species information on the event horizon of a black hole—but not before orchestrating the genocide of all Robusts living in Lower Etyom. Conspiring with the Baqirian warlord Kapka, the Leader's plan fell apart when Mila and Demitri rallied the Robust resistance against him in a desperate struggle to prevent annhilation. Demitri killed him on the Asgardia space station.

Husniya [Robust, Baqirian]. She is the little sister of Faruq and daughter of Kapka. Rescued from danger by Demitri four years ago, she was found to share the biology that connected Demitri to Vedmak. Her companion spirit, Margardia, is benevolent who tries to shepherd and protect Husniya. Mila is currently her guardian and teacher. Now fourteen years old, Husniya, displaced from her people and angry at losing her brother, has grown into a troubled and defiant teenager.

Kapka [Robust, Baqirian]. Known as the Tyrant of Baqir, Kapka has long held the Musul people captive to his violent extremism. Kapka survived the blast during the battle for the Gracile Leader's rocket four years ago. Part gangster warlord, part terrorist, Kapka will go to any length to destroy his enemies. He has a particular hate for Logosians.

Mila [Robust, Logosian]. Tough and uncompromising, Mila is a true survivor. In the four years that have passed since the Fall of the Gracile empire, Mila has gone from reluctant freedom fighter to war-weary leader of the resistance. In a desperate bid to cling to her faith, she tries to follow the path of the Lightbringer and protect the people of Etyom. It is a task that keeps her from what she truly desires—finding and rescuing Demitri and Faruq.

Mos [Robust, Kahangan]. Resistance fighter, Opor's head of security, and long-time friend of Mila. Of all those who stand with her, few are more loyal than Mos.

Nikolaj [Gracile, deceased]. Demitri's neobrother. Killed by the Gracile Leader.

Oksanna [Gracile, missing]. Robotics scientist and former mate to Demitri's neo-brother, Nikolaj. She is missing along with all other Graciles.

Vedmak [Unknown entity, missing]. Believed to originally be a Bolshevik soldier who died during the Red Terror of Russia in the early twentieth century. His spirit/information became entangled with Demitri. Seizing a puppetmaster-like control of Demitri's body, Vedmak has only one aim: to bring back the glory of Russia and watch the world burn.

Yuri [Robust, Fiorian]. Bilgi's most trusted friend and advisor. One of the founders of Opor, he is known for his skill in the ways of deception and cloak-and-dagger tactics.

Zevry [Robust, Logosian, deceased]. Mila's older brother, who died attempting to sabotage the Gracile Leader's plan long before the Resistance knew of it.

TERMS FROM BOOK 1

Asgardia* – a project in the early 20th century to create an independent space nation.

Ax'd – an honorable death for Graciles who have outlived their usefulness to society.

Black Hole – a region of spacetime exhibiting such strong gravitational effects that nothing can escape from inside it.

Chiori – guinea-pig sized rodent commonly found in the slums of Etyom, it is the primary source of meat for most Robusts.

Chum Lawk – a martial art with roots in ancient Chinese Kung Fu. Mila, Ghofaun, and Bilgi are all master practicioners.

Creed – robotic, Geminoid, peacekeepers utilized by the Graciles, mainly to ensure the Robusts do not encroach on New Etyom. (See also Geminoid).

Enclave – one of seven walled communities in Lower Etyom: Alya (Musul), Baqir (Musul), Fiori (all religions), Kahanga (Musul and Tribal), Logos (Logosian), Vel (all religions) and Zopat (all religions).

Event horizon* – a region in space–time beyond which events cannot affect an outside observer, most commonly associated with black holes. of the Vapid.

Geminoid* – fully automated robots whose outer appearance is designed to replicate individual humans. Originally created by Dr. Hiroshi Ishiguro*.

Gracile – genetically engineered human, considered the epitomy of evolution, living in New Etyom.

Grov'ler – derogatory term for a follower of Yeos.

HAP – Habitable Aerial Platform. Nineteen HAPs used to sit 5 miles above Lower Etyom, before the war.

Ilah – the monothesitic god of the Musul Robusts.

Jacked – Adjective referring to a Robust's biology being enhanced with technology.

Jackbag – derogatory term for Robusts who have used dodgy modifications to emulate Graciles.

Krig – Thick, black, caffeinated drink reminiscent of strong old-world coffee.

Lillipad – slang for a HAP (see HAP).

Logosian – the term for Robusts who are born in the Logos enclave, but also used to depict those who follow Yeos the Lightbringer, a religion stemming from Judeo-Christian beliefs.

Lower Etyom – the collective name for the seven enclaves in which the Robusts live. Formerly a Gulag turned mining community called Norilsk in Siberia.

Musul – follower of Ilah, whose religion stems from Islam.

NBD – New Black Death; bacterial plague that wiped out most of humanity after WWIII. Outbreaks still occur in Lower Etyom.

Neuralweb – internet connected directly to the brains of all Graciles and some jacked Robusts.

Norilsk* – gulag-turned-mining town in Siberia.

Opor – the Robust resistance originally formed to overthrow the Graciles.

PED – Personal Electronic Device, used to communicate off the neural web.

Ripper – Robust humans. These criminals and outcasts have been exiled to wander the frozen wastes

Robust – non-engineered humans who survived the NBD and live in Lower Etyom.

Sard – vulgar slang used alone or as a noun or verb in various phrases to express annoyance, contempt or impatience.

Stim – drugs used by Robusts to elicit feelings e.g. relaxation (Easy) or intense power (Red Mist).

Vestals – the oldest organized remnant of Logosian faith, the wise and faithful sisters of this order can frequently be found offering relief to the weary traveler, the sick, and the wounded.

The Writ – also known as "The Holy Writ of Yeos". Given to Mila as a gift years ago by Demitri, this tome may well be the last known copy in existance.

VTV – Vertical Take-off Vehicle. Used by New Etyom peacekeepers, the Creed.

Yeos – the monotheistic god of the Logosians.

*real place, person, term or object as of 2019

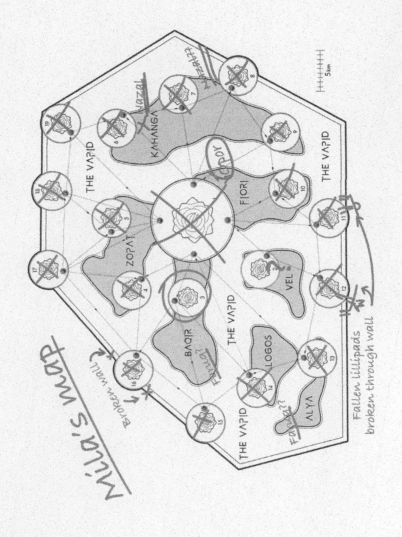

Mila's map

THE VAPID

THE VAPID

THE VAPID

THE VAPID

KAHANGA

Nazal

NERAZZ

FIORI

LOGDY

ZOPÁT

VEL

BAQIR

LOGOS

ALYA

broken wall?

Fallen lillipads broken through wall

5km

PROLOGUE

MOSCOW, MARCH 1938

In the darkness behind my eyelids all other senses are heightened. The murmuring of the witnesses seems deafening. Damp air clings claw-like to the nape of my neck. The stench of fear and evacuated bowels wafting from the other stalls, threatens to choke me. But above it all, the pain of betrayal, cold and fatal, stabs like the piercing edge of a blade in my heart.

I open my eyes to search for my accuser, but he does not make his presence known. He pretends he is too important to attend the last of these three trials. Of course, he *is* here. Hiding in the shadows, watching in silence as the charges are read. I'm accused of wrecking, espionage, Trotskyism, and conspiracy. These crimes are not mine. Just as they are not the crimes of the twenty men who stand here with me today. Nor were they the crimes of the men in the two preceding show trials *I* myself led for *him*. For this coward.

Twenty years ridding Mother Russia of the Tsarist regime, their pathetic White Army and every bourgeoisie man, woman, and child I could root out of hiding. His damn precious canals were built under *my* direction, with men—slaves—trained in *my* gulags. The Order of Lenin was bestowed upon *me*, a hero of Communism.

Yet, it was for nothing. His paranoia has driven him to madness. His power over the people is fading. I tried to tell the stupid kozel—to warn him. And for my loyalty, I—deliverer of the Purge—now stand trial. Stalin, you bastard, I know you are watching.

"I appeal to you. For you, I built two great canals!" My voice echoes around the great hall.

A flicker. The momentary flash of a match behind a muslin curtain in a window on the second floor. The outline of a pipe, now gone. The hall is eerily silent. My comrades in chains remain mute. Resignation carved into the pallid skin of their pathetic faces.

Stalin will not save me.

1

Not even Yahweh can save me from this.

And why should He? The blood of ten million souls stains my hands. White officers tied to planks and slowly fed into furnaces. Women and children, scalped and flayed. Dirty Christians given communion of molten lead. Filthy peasants buried alive or turned into living statues as ice-cold water was poured over their naked bodies in the winter-streets of Orel. Yes, death is my reward for these acts, for loyalty to the cause—but my soul will know no peace. And if that is my fate, then every dirty goat and pompous peacock will feel my wrath from the grave.

The bailiff pulls at my arm, leading me away from the podium to my doom. To be shot in the head. Perhaps, I deserve this providence. But what of Ida? Without my protection, my dear wife will be hunted down and murdered—or worse. I have confessed to all but espionage in hopes she will be spared. Yet, in my heart, I know this will not save her.

As I leave the court, some observers watch with disgusted stares, while others give pitiful sighs. They all should die. Every last one. Red. White. Tsar. Communist. It makes no difference anymore. No one understands. Only my Cheka brethren know what it means to be Bolshevik. To do whatever is needed.

I raise my gaze to the window where I know he is skulking and spit on the floor in defiance.

"*Menya zovut smert', i ad prikhodit so mnoy!*"

Yes, my name is Death and Hell follows with me.

CHAPTER ONE

THE RUINS OF ETYOM, NOVEMBER 2255

MILA

The young man in the brown jacket spins, arms raised high, a blood-curdling scream issuing from his lips. A few awkward steps and he falls, sprawling headlong across a pile of slush and rubble. A crimson fan spreads out under his corpse, staining the snow red. Another death, another friend of the cause, gone.

He was seventeen.

All around the pop-whizz of gunfire followed by deafening explosions from detonating grenades reminds us all the Kahangan stronghold of Nazal will not fall easily. I slide farther into the frozen mud of the ditch and scrunch into a ball.

"Mos." Where the hell is he? "Mos, you with me?"

"I'm here, Mila." The barrel chested Kahangan with midnight skin crawls up next to me, careful to keep his bulk below the rise. "Who's hit?"

"Mauricio."

"Is he dead?"

"He's not moving."

"Sniper?" Mos jerks his head in the direction of the building before us. *Politsiya* in faded Cyrillic letters adorns the ruined facade.

"Knows what they're doing too." I pull a small mirror from the arm pouch on my leather jacket and slowly raise it to get a better view. In the reflection is the form of a person, prone on the roof of the palace—if you can call it that.

A glint of light bounces off the glass.

I snatch my hand down and pinch my eyes shut as a chunk of earth explodes from the rim of the ditch, showering us with wet clods of cold mud. The lingering crack of a rifle follows. He's got a sarding scope and a good, stable position. Guy *definitely* knows what he's doing.

"There's a way up to the roof on the back side," Mos says. "I can flank his position and approach from behind if you can keep his attention." He cocks his head. "That's probably stupid, huh?"

"It's only stupid if it doesn't work."

Mos, already shuffling away, motions to a few others hiding in another ditch to follow.

"What are you going to do?" I ask.

"Wait for my call." Mos grins, revealing large, square, white teeth, then creeps away and seems to vanish into thin air.

The cold seeps through my clothing, stealing the fading warmth of the sun. My scarred Kalashnikov rifle feels like a cold, lead weight. I exchanged my bean-bag propelling weapon for a death-dealing one some time ago. I don't even remember when that happened. Like everything else in this forsaken city, it just sort of did. Yeos forgive me. I loose my canteen from my satchel and take a shaky swallow of the nearly frozen water.

A bark, much like a wild dog.

The signal. "Now!"

I drop the canteen, roll to the left, and rise to one knee. Three more of my fighters appear and the air ignites with the sounds of war. Dust and stone billow around the sniper's nest. Our suppressive fire has the desired effect: he's blinded by debris.

"Ceasefire!" I kneel again, the Kalashnikov pressed into my shoulder, watching as the dust clears. "Stand ready."

We wait in silence, a bitter wind snapping at our scarf-covered faces.

Another flash of light from the roof.

"Get down!" I flop into the muck.

This time there is no report. No exploding clump of earth. A cry of terror fills the air, followed by the sounds of a struggle. I chance a glance. Mos is standing tall and proud on the roof.

"Hold your fire!" I yell.

My comrades lower their weapons. Mos reaches down and plucks up a skinny Kahangan who drops a long-barreled rifle. The little man screams, flailing madly against my friend's superior strength.

"Traitor." Mos bellows loud enough to be heard, even from down here. With a single heave, the large Kahangan hurls the sniper over the edge.

The man's hollow scream is cut short as he strikes the frozen ground some ten stories below.

I force myself to peer down at his mangled corpse, twisted like a broken doll in the ice and mud below.

The Kalashnikov drops to hang from its canvas strap across my chest. My people follow suit, relaxing their guard, their eyes glazed over in a mixture of relief and stress. They're all good soldiers. Committed to the cause—peace in Etyom, the last city. The Kahangan civil war has been going on for too long. Kapka—who somehow managed to survive the RPG blast on the platform four years ago—continues his campaign against the followers of Yeos with renewed vigor, but has so far not managed to take this Musul faction. Instead, in this desolate place, power-hungry warlords fight over resources while the people suffer. Here, it's not Kapka who reigns, but Nazal.

Little is known of the origins of this despot. Some say, like all warlords, he simply rode to power on the broken backs of the Kahangan people. That there was nothing he wasn't willing to do and no one he wasn't willing to betray to claim the power he felt was owed to him. Others seem to whisper of his evil deeds like he's some sort of phantom—a terrible consequence of our own divisiveness. Whatever the case, Nazal is a plague. He's no Kapka, but the piles of corpses he's left in his wake can no longer be overlooked. The resistance will stop him because someone must.

The wind stabs at my cheeks. I hunch my shoulders to brace against the cold and trudge over to Mauricio's body. His empty gaze is locked on the sky, blood seeping from the corner of his mouth.

"He liked to sing." Husniya walks up, kneels, and places her hand on the body of the young man.

"You okay, Hus?"

A moment passes. She nods.

"You were friends?"

"Not really," she replies. "But he was always happy, singing songs in Fiorian. I couldn't understand the words, but I listened anyway. It was beautiful."

Husniya's compassion belies her age. Now fourteen, she is a far cry from the frightened child Demitri rescued from the suicide bomber in Zopat. But she is still young and has much to learn. Squeezing her shoulder,

I look back to the roof of the large, bullet-riddled building. Mos waves us over to a rusted, ice-encrusted ladder, which leads all the way up to where he stands.

Sard, really?

Exhausted, muscles aching, I reach the summit. The roof is littered with sandbags and sniper nests. "Nazal doesn't want to give this place up." Deep breaths of frigid air burn my lungs.

"No. He does not," Mos replies. The bulky Kahangan raises his head, his eyes great brown pools. "Ugly things are happening here, Mila. Kahanga needs us."

"Well, every warlord we take down brings us one step closer to peace," I say. "Get everyone together. We're not done yet. Nazal's forces will be waiting for us inside."

Mos bobs his head and motions everyone forward.

"Okay," I call out as the last few fighters make their way to the top of the precarious ice-covered ladder. "We're going to sweep the interior. Secure your gear. I don't want any unnecessary noise. Stay focused and stay ready. Keep line of sight with each other. We move in teams of four."

Everyone acknowledges, murmuring as they prepare for entry.

Husniya slides up to me, tightens her belt, and rechecks her rifle. "I'm ready."

"I know you are." I wink. "You stay with me."

***

The Kahangan warlord's abode is cold; a strange mixture of gaudy opulence and empty spaces devoid of life or comfort. Improvised bunkers and weapon caches litter the halls, and old Soviet-marked crates filled with grease-covered rifles lay stacked against the bare walls of the former police station.

Room by room, we clear the path. The resistance fighters follow my hand signals and silent direction. Their belief in me is strong but unwarranted. I'm simply emulating the tactics described in the war manuals I've read. *Entry point, deep threat, clear corners, collapse sectors of fire. Repeat.* Reading old-world instructions on tactics is no substitution for actual

6

instruction, but it's all I had, and it's already saved a life or two, including mine.

Ten floors and we've encountered no resistance. Can't be good. Armories, food stores, sleeping quarters. He's got enough here to stock an army—an army much bigger than his mercenary forces in Kahanga.

What the hell is Nazal up to?

Moving with caution, we clear through the stairwell and fan out onto the ground level.

Husniya presses into my shoulder as she works off my movements, covering my back. The girl is tough as nails, and yet there's still so much fear harbored deep beneath her capable facade. She thinks no one sees it, but I do. I know all too well what it looks like.

We move into the last room. From within the gloom, a man moans for death in a sharp Kahangan accent. As we move farther inside, it becomes clear this is the old jail. Inside a row of cages with thick steel bars, Kahangan occupants huddle together like corralled animals.

"It's okay," Husniya says and lowers her rifle. "We won't hurt you."

"Mos. Get in here," I call back to the main hall.

Mos acknowledges and navigates with heavy footfalls to our position. As he turns the corner, several of the prisoners stand to their feet and grab the cage bars.

A woman begins to sob. "Mosavva!"

"Mosavva. Praise Ilah, it's Mosavva!" the others chant.

Mos strides forward and produces a large ring with iron keys jangling from it.

"Mosavva?" I ask.

"My given name," Mos says and unlocks the doors. The people surround him, laying their hands upon him and calling out. The weeping woman is nearly inconsolable as she crashes into Mos' arms.

"You have come. You have come to make things right," she cries.

"I'm here, do not fear. Your troubles are over," Mos assures her. He looks to me. "Mila, this is my sister, Ayodele."

Sister?

Through the tears, she mumbles, "Mosavva is the rightful king of Kahanga. He has been gone from us for so long." From the safety of his arms, she looks up and touches his face.

"I was exiled," Mos says to her. "I had to wait until the time was right to return to you."

A sweet smile graces Husniya's face. It's infectious.

"So, what now? Mos?" I ask.

He looks to me, then Ayodele. "We must still confront Nazal. Where is he?"

"In the lower levels," she says. "Be careful, brother. He has allowed himself to become … deranged."

"All of you will stay here until it's safe. I'll come back for you." Mos turns, his friends and family wishing him a safe return.

We leave the freed captives with two of our men, who hand out rations and water as Mos and I move to the stairwell to gather with our forces.

"Nazal is fortified in the subterranean levels. I'm sure of it, now." Mos checks the cylinder of his .44 magnum revolver, *Svetlana*, counting aloud five mismatched rounds.

"Fortified?" I repeat.

"Yes. Definitely."

"For what purpose? What is he defending?" I ask.

Mos shrugs. "Your guess is as good as mine."

"And what's your plan to *un*-fortify him?"

Mos removes a bundle of red paper-covered rods from his shoulder bag.

Dynamite? "You may be the one who's deranged. Please don't blow us all up before we get there, okay?"

"No promises. Don't bump into me."

It shouldn't be funny, but I have to stifle a laugh. "After you."

Before long we stand, huddled together in a concrete stairwell, poised to enter the basement level and are faced with an old, thick, iron door. Mos shoves his bulk against it, but it doesn't budge.

"I don't like it," I say.

"What about it?"

"The books I read on tactics call this a *fatal funnel*. Even if we get this doorway open, one rocket-propelled grenade into this stairwell will end us all."

"Okay, what do you suggest?" Mos asks.

"Let me find another way in. I'll open the door for you."

"I'm coming with you," Husniya says.

A few of the fighters chuckle.

"What? I'm every bit as capable as any of you." She stares the men down. "I also happen to be a lot less stupid and undisciplined. Traits that come in handy when sneaking and fighting, if you didn't know."

Their laughs turn to scowls. Now it's my turn to chuckle. She's been around me too much.

"Fair enough, Hus. You come with me. The rest of you, stand by and wait for the door." We unsling our rifles and hand them over. Where we're going, they're not worth their bulk or the risk of knocking them against everything.

"Take this." Mos hands me the dynamite bundle and a small torch. "You might need it."

Without argument, I gingerly slip the bundle into my sling bag.

Back up the stairs and onto the ground-floor we go. Dust motes dance in the air. Gray afternoon light bleeds in through the glistening teeth of a few shattered windows. I close my eyes, take a deep breath in through my nose, and listen.

"What are we—"

I silence Husniya with a raised hand, straining to hear past the slight tinnitus in my ears. "There." I point across the room.

"I don't see anything," she says.

"You aren't *listening*. Use all of your senses." I move over to an ancient, padded sitting bench and slide it away, revealing a hatch in the wall. An old, long-since-used trash chute. I motion Husniya over, then crack the seal on the pull-down drawer. I'd bet anything it goes directly into the basement. We put our ears to the open hatch and from somewhere far below, hear the voices of men, Kahangan men, speaking in agitated tones.

"See?" I say, looking down the hatch.

She shrugs. "Sure."

"Now, let's hope it's not blocked up. I'll go first. You follow me. Stay close and stay quiet. When it's time to fight, you fight like a trapped animal. Understand?"

"Yeah." Husniya rubs her hands together in determination.

She holds the hatch as I slip in and position myself. Digging my heels into the angled walls of the chute, I inch my way down.

A clang above. It's Husniya.

She gasps, her boots squeaking on the walls, as she falls toward me.

"Stop." I hiss, screwing my eyes shut. There's no impact. I raise my head cautiously to find the toe of Husniya's boot a hair's breadth from my face. "Don't be so careless." I say. Breathe it out, Mila. She's still new at this. "It's okay, Hus. Just … be careful."

My legs quiver, the muscles shaking with adrenaline. A quick glance down and it appears to be clear, but there's no view of the rest of the room or what I'll encounter when we drop in. Gathering my resolve, I muster my courage and release.

My boots strike the floor and I pitch into a forward roll that carries me to concealment behind a stack of dust-covered crates. My hands fly to the sling bag, supporting the volatile explosive inside. After a few moments, breath held and chest frozen, it seems the dynamite won't explode.

In the square opening of the chute, the toe of Husniya's boot appears. She's ready to drop and waiting for my signal. I work my way to the edge of yet another tall stack of crates. They all have old, red Soviet markings—just like the ones on the upper floors.

Where did Nazal get all this?

Moving with extreme care, I peer around the stack in the direction of the voices. Ten men, maybe twelve. All of them are well armed and centered around one large Kahangan who appears to be giving the directives. Nazal.

There's a ruckus at the back of the storeroom. A huge man enters, barking orders with authority, and approaches the group.

My breath catches in my chest. His size. Those eyes. A Gracile?

Demitri …? No, it's not him.

I haven't thought about my gentle Gracile friend, or Vedmak, in so long. For more than a year, we searched for Demitri. Partly because I wanted to find my friend, but also because I was afraid of what Vedmak might do. My dreams, the omen, all pointed to him. Yet, in four years, the demon has not revealed himself. His potential threat has paled in the face of the very real Musul terrorist attacks, infighting between Robust gang

10

members and Ripper assaults on trading caravans in the Vapid. Eventually, with no indication Demitri, or his demon, had even survived, my search fizzled out.

Focus, Mila.

I have another look. Who *is* this Gracile? We all assumed those who survived went into hiding, unable or unwilling to fight down here in the slums. This one is nothing like Demitri or any other Gracile for that matter. He has a wild, animalistic look about him; his hair long and eyes predatory. His armor has a medieval appearance. There's a thick, snaking hose that leads from a small tank strapped to his back to a port in his arm.

He storms past a PM M1910 Maxim gun, bolted to the floor and pointed at the door—the one Mos and the others are hiding behind—and barks some unintelligible command. Whoever he is, he's learned to speak the Kahangan dialect.

From their pockets, the Kahangans pull out auto-injectors, each containing a bright red liquid, and press them to their necks. They drop the empty tubes to the floor, groaning and grabbing at their throats. One man howls. Another beats his chest, screaming as if suddenly driven to the edge of sanity.

A shiver of disgust streaks down my spine.

"Now, Hus," I whisper.

She drops from the chute like a cat and slinks across in the shadows to my position. Her eyes grow wide as she sees the Gracile and the Kahangans mad with vigor.

"Keep quiet and listen up," I whisper. "Make your way to the door, but stay hidden. On my signal, remove the cross bar and throw it open."

"What's the signal?"

"You'll know."

The girl steals a glance at the men. "And then what?"

"Then you find somewhere to take cover until everything blows over."

"Take cover? You said I could fight."

I grab Husniya's chin and hold her gaze. "Listen to me, Hus. In the field, things change. When we were up against Robusts only, it was one thing. Now there's a Gracile involved. And stims. I made a promise to your brother I'd try to keep you safe. That's what I'm doing."

11

She jerks her face free. "Just like you promised you'd find him?"

The old blade of helplessness cuts deep.

"I'm sorry Mila. I didn't mean—"

"Just do what I ask of you," I snap.

She says nothing more, stealing off in the direction of the door.

I reach into the crate next to me and pull out an old Soviet *papasha* machine gun. The smell of oily metal and wood wax fills my nostrils. I take care to check the action as quietly as possible and draw a full drum magazine from the same crate.

The artificial light, the sound of some old generator rattling in another room, the smell of ancient mold and rot. This oppressive place seeks to wound my resolve, to destroy the progress we've made. So much has happened since a simple information handler and a terrified Gracile led a woefully outmatched resistance against the tyranny of the Gracile Leader. But that was years ago.

Could it have been so long? Are we better off now than we were then? I have to believe so.

I touch at the edge of a faded photograph sticking from my breast pocket, and for an instant, remember the embrace of a mother, father, and brother. A reminder of those I've lost and of the hope that remains. Uttering a few words of an ancient catechism, I steel myself for the coming storm.

I sling the *papasha* over my shoulder, dip into my bag and carefully secure the bundle of dynamite and the lighter. The single large fuse, twisted together from six others, flashes to life as the flame makes contact. It's burning quickly. I stand and fling the bundle toward the other end of the large room and drop back down, covering my ears and pinching my eyes shut. The men scurry about, shouting in Kahangan.

Nothing. Sard. This *would* happen. Mos gave me bad dynamite.

The stationary Maxim gun swings in my direction and opens up, bullets shredding the fibrous crates in front of me in a shower of debris.

Crawling with the rifle, I charge the bolt and rise onto my elbows. "Now, Husniya. Now!"

The girl pulls at the crossbar, but it doesn't move. Bullets streak down the wall and she throws herself to the ground. Crates explode. Straw and packing materials puff up, hanging in the air.

Sard, gotta do something about that Maxim gun.

I rise from behind the crates, but my breath catches as I come face-to-face with one of Nazal's soldiers. His hands close around my *papasha*. There's an almost inhuman strength within him. He drives me back against the block wall. With a crazed look of furious confidence pouring from his features, he moves to tear the weapon from the grasp of what he surely believes is a defenseless woman.

Only, in his moment of unbridled machismo, he's got it all wrong.

I grab the back of the barrel and drive it with a satisfying smack against his face. Once, twice, three times. Leading with my knee, I drive up, delivering a stunning kick to the groin. His legs buckle as anything he's got between his legs smashes between my shin and the bone of his pelvis. I spin as he doubles over, grabbing his jacket and using his pitched angle to drive his face into the wall.

The Maxim gun pivots back in my direction. Nowhere to go.

"Sard." I grab the stunned soldier and pull him in front of me—a human shield.

The blinding flash and deafening concussion throws me back against the wall and to my knees as Nazal and half of his men disappear in a cloud of smoke and fire. My head spins, my ears ring. The dynamite. Finally. I cough and crawl for cover over the flayed body of the Kahangan soldier.

The heavy iron door bursts open. Mos and the resistance fighters pour in with a blaze of gunfire. In the smoke, the rest of Nazal's men collide with the ranks of my people. A second explosion rocks the room.

My head rings. Damnation. What was *that*?

There's now a hole in the back wall. Silhouetted against the stream of natural light and the swirling snow beyond is the massive form of the crazed Gracile. In one arm, he carries a crate and in the other, a fired RPG launcher. He drops the tube-like weapon, turns back to flash a contemptuous grin, and disappears into the whiteout of ice and wind.

Locked in a twisting melee, my fighters clamor with the drug-crazed Kahangans. Mos raises one man over his head and, with a shout, drives him headfirst into the foundation. Beside him, fighters scramble, parry and strike—taking out the Kahangans one by one. We have prevailed.

But, where's Husniya?

I scan the smoke-filled room and find the girl locked in hand-to-hand combat with a final, defiant Kahangan twice her size. My stomach roils and my muscles twitch. The desire to save her is overwhelming.

No. Let the girl earn her stripes, Mila. She can handle herself.

"Come on girl, don't try to fight toe-to-toe," I say under my breath.

The madman shoves into her and she pivots, isolating his right arm and leg just as I taught her. Swift and brutal, she strikes with an uppercut to his armpit, disabling the nerve bundle, followed by a downward stomp to his lower leg. The Kahangan screams and whirls on her. A knife flashes from a sheath on his belt. Husniya's confidence fails and for the first time, there's fear in her face.

My stomach contorts again. Come on, Husniya.

The Musul girl deflects the first knife thrust and parries the second. With his free hand, he punches her hard in the face. Stunned, she's open when he stabs again. At the last moment, she intercepts his wrist and strips the knife from his grasp, simultaneously punching him directly in the throat with all her might. Wheezing, but not injured enough, the man grabs her by the neck and pins her back against a crate. Husniya, eyes wide and exhausted, thrashes but can't release herself from his grasp.

That's enough.

Launching forward, I slam the butt of my rifle into the Kahangan's neck, sending him out like an extinguished candle. He crumples to the floor, dragging Husniya with him. She climbs out from under his limp body and sits up, rubbing her neck.

"I ... I had him right where I wanted him," Husniya protests.

I help her up and grab her shoulders in affirmation.

"I'm serious. I did just what you taught me."

"I know. You did great."

The battle finished, we make our way over to Mos, who is shaking the shoulders of our men in encouragement.

"We did it Mila. We've liberated Kahanga," Mos nearly shouts. "And it is thanks to you and the help of these good people."

"Come on Mos. Let's see what we can learn. I have questions."

As I walk amongst the crates to the other side of the room, the damage from the dynamite is noticeable for the first time. Dead Kahangans lay sprawled about. Some are missing limbs—others are piled like old loose clothes, jumbled against sandbag barriers.

Yeos, what have I done?

Mos studies me. "The dynamite?"

I nod, unsure of what to say.

My Kahangan friend puts his hand on my shoulder. "Mila, you saved our lives. You saved the lives of my people, hundreds of them. You had to kill a few cruel and loveless men to do it. It is a good and necessary thing you have done here today."

Before I can answer, a man coughs nearby. Mos and I step through the lingering smoke. There, resting up against the wall, is Nazal. The ragged stump that remains in place of one of his legs drools blood onto the floor. He's cinched his belt around his thigh to try to staunch the flow. It won't save his life.

Nazal's eyes flash with defiance. "The prodigal son returns," he wheezes.

Mos grunts. "I told you I would. I also told you I'd kill you the next time I saw you."

"You did, brother. You have made good on your word. Now you can be a despot like me. Like Father. All hail King Mosavva. Go become a selfish pig."

Mos bristles. "Get the name of my father out of your mouth, you dog."

"*Your* father? Oh, of course. I wasn't wanted. But you, you were the favored son. I suppose it's only natural you'd have such affection for the old bastard. Too bad you'll never get to tell him—wait, that's not true. I do still have his head."

"I'll keep a head for a trophy too—yours." Mos steps toward the broken warlord.

I slide in front of him and hold out my arms. "Give me a moment, Mos."

The Kahangan stares me down with an intensity I have rarely seen in him.

"Please, Mos."

After seemingly great internal deliberation, he steps back and crosses

15

his arms over his barrel chest.

I turn to face Nazal. "I'm Mila. You only just met me." I motion to his amputated leg. "I need some answers."

He looks me up and down. "Why would I tell a Logosian groveler anything?"

"Because you know something about this that's bigger than some old family feud. What is it?"

Nazal looks at the blood issuing from his ruined leg, "I'll die and you'll never know."

I shake my head with mock sadness. "Mos?"

My friend sets his boot on the edge of Nazal's severed thigh and presses—twisting his toe.

Nazal screams, his eyes wild with pain. He claws at the stone foundation until I motion for Mos to release. Chest heaving, and body quaking, drool spills from the warlord's lips. "Go sard yourself. Both of you."

The air is racked with screams of agony as Mos kicks the toe of his boot against the severed bone peeking out of the bloodied meat of Nazal's thigh.

My stomach churns and my own leg throbs in sympathy. I wave Mos off.

Defeated, Nazal hangs his head. Strings of saliva dangle like bloodied bands of silk from his mouth and nose. "No more. I'll tell you. I'll tell you," he whimpers.

"Where did the Gracile come from?"

"I don't know."

Mos kicks the stump, and the man jumps as though he was hit with electricity.

"I don't know, I swear. Stop."

"What *do* you know?" I press.

"We had an arrangement. The Gracile supplied stims for me and my men in exchange for crates of weapons and ammunition."

"What stims?"

"Just the red one. Red ... mmm ... something, I don't remember what he called it."

"Why did you want it?"

"You saw how powerful it made my men. Pure, adrenaline-fueled, rage. Resistant to pain. Why wouldn't we want it?"

Stims for weapons? Are the Graciles planning an attack? "The Gracile. He left with a crate. What was in it?"

"Something special." Nazal's eyes grow wide, but he slumps and a moan escapes him. "Don't ask what. It looked like junk to me. The Gracile wanted it. I don't know anything else. I don't know …"

"Where did the weapons come from? Nazal?"

"We've been gathering them from all over Etyom … Though, there's talk of a … silo …" He moans, fading from consciousness.

A chime goes off. My Personal Electronic Device.

"What silo? Nazal?" I press.

There's no reply. Nazal now wears the cold mantle of death.

Damnation. "So, Mosavva, the rightful king of Kahanga. Whose brother is Nazal the warlord, who also imprisoned their sister. I've learned much about you today. But what have I missed? Were the Kahangan's in league with the Graciles too?"

"He's not my brother. Not since he murdered my father for his crown."

"You should have told me."

Another chime sounds from the PED in my satchel. I reach into the sling bag and remove the old hacked piece of Gracile tech and the screen illuminates.

Mos tries to meet my gaze. "What is it?"

"Looks like it's headquarters."

"Oh?"

I show him the screen.

Mila.
Someone or something attacked us in the night.
Could be Rippers.
Return to base ASAP.
- Bilgi

Mos rubs his head. "When the old man rings, it's serious. Need me to come?"

"No. You've got a lot of work to do here. We can't let Kahanga fall back into enemy hands. If Kapka hears Kahanga is fractured, he'll come looking for more Musuls to add to his army. Just be ready if I need you." I point to several fighters. "You five—stay and help Mos. Whatever he needs. The rest of you come with me. We're heading out."

"I'm going to send a convoy to come get some of these weapons and ammo for the resistance. I'll leave the rest with you. Okay?"

"And what are you going to do?" Mos eyes me with curiosity.

"Figure out what the deal is with this attack back at base. Then try to determine why a stim-enhanced Gracile is dealing with Kahangan warlords. Something's wrong about all of this."

The Kahangan puts his hands on his hips. "You sure you don't need some rest before making the trek back to base in that?" He motions to the blizzard outside.

I zip my heavy leather jacket, sling the *papasha* across my back, and turn to leave through the blasted hole in the wall. Outside, the restless snowflakes whip and spin. "No rest for the weary, Mos. Not in this life."

CHAPTER TWO

VEDMAK

"Worthless—a failure from the start, like all the rest," I hiss. The pathetic youngling stares up with wet, almond-shaped, hazel eyes—Gracile eyes. I strengthen my one-handed grip around its neck, squeezing, cutting off the air to its lungs. The disgusting whelp doesn't even struggle.

You don't have to do this. There are other ways.

"Oh, there you are, little peacock. Just in time." The annoying Gracile, Demitri, who used to possess this corporeal shell is a constant thorn in my side. There seems to be no end to his perpetual interruptions, pleading for me to halt my work.

Please, let him go.

"Why? This creature is useless to me, to Russia." I rap on the youngling's head with the cane in my other hand. "Should I let it die slowly in the cold like an injured goat? No. We should all hope for such a quick release."

Why should he die at all?

"Without torture, there is no science," I rasp. "Its mind is like borscht. Malformed and lacking in the strength of its body."

Him, not it—he's a child, Vedmak. Not that it matters to you.

It's difficult to hold back the snarl of a smile spreading across these stolen lips. The Gracile lives in here with me. He knows my soul. My desires. I toss the runt into the waiting arms of one of my more successful ventures: Merodach—an enormous Gracile clad in armor—who does as I bid. The intravenous stim keeps Merodach in a permanent rage, yet under my control.

With powerful hands, Merodach holds the youngling's arms out, splaying it wide open. Vulnerable. It squirms in the dim light of the lab, throwing awkward shadows against the white walls.

Please, stop it. Stop.

19

"Silence, peacock. Always in my head. Always whining. Enough."

Merodach watches me, but he's not confused. He knows of the inner voice.

I stare through the round lenses in my modified Soviet gasmask and study the little creature—past its sad little eyes, and into the void of its feeble mind. Whatever dwells in there it's not what I wanted.

The laser-scythe ignites, screeching into life—my black walking staff now adorned with a crescent-shaped, cobalt-blue plasma blade that crackles and pops. I trace the edge across the youngling's cheek. The incision is instantly sealed by the white-hot blade. If it weren't for this mask, I could smell the burning flesh. Pity.

The pup's chest heaves rapidly, but still, no words come from its lips. As I suspected, its soup-like mind is useless. No ability to speak. If it can't talk, it will at least scream. I nod to Merodach.

Merodach's face breaks into a beautifully evil leer and he begins to pull on the arms.

The youngling shrieks.

"So, you can make a sound." I laugh, glee filling this chest.

For the love of Yeos, end it!

"Yeos? Oh, how delicious. Are we praying now?" My laughter fills the mask, and it's difficult not to choke on the stim vapor circulating inside. "Yeos doesn't exist. Neither do Yahweh nor Ilah. You as a scientist should know this best, little puppet. I am the closest thing there is to a god. Soon, the Logosians and the Musuls and all of Etyom will learn this."

The youngling is on its knees mumbling incomprehensibly; its face wet with tears. It bores me. I lift the plasma scythe into the air and slice down with a powerful strike. The youngling's head rolls off its shoulders and bounces across the floor of the lab—its wide eyes still staring off into space.

My Gracile demon is silent.

"Vardøger," says a deep voice from within the dark of the room.

Aeron, Merodach's twin, marches into the light, carrying a large crate in his muscular arms.

"Comrade Aeron. The task in Kahanga was a success?" I ask.

Aeron nods slowly, his powerful chest heaving with the Red Mistinduced adrenaline rush. "We obtained some weapons. There was resistance. The Daughter of the Star Breather was there."

Two quick steps and I'm upon him. The heel of my scythe catches him hard across the face. "I've told you not to call her that."

Aeron doesn't flinch. "*Da*, Vardøger."

The blood in these veins feels hot with anger. "Did you lose the enclave?"

"They killed Nazal. There will be no more alliance with the Kahangans," Aeron replies.

"*Blyat!*" I turn to lash out on my prisoner, only to remember it's already a headless corpse.

"Shall I send a team to kill her?" asks Aeron, sidling up to his brother.

"No, no. We wait." Damn that little *suka*. "Our forces are not strong enough yet, and her Opor is not to be taken lightly. Without the Kahangans, we must accelerate the plan. No one kills Mila but me, understand?" The air inside the mask is humid with my breath.

"*Da*, Vardøger," Aeron says.

Merodach grunts, as only he can do.

"Did you at least retrieve what I traded so much Red Mist and weapons for?" I ask.

The stimmed-up Gracile slams the huge wooden box onto the floor and rips off the lid, which he flings across the room. It clatters against the wall. Inside sits an ice-covered, metallic contraption: a skeletal cylinder with tubes, wires, and large discs. Across the edge of one of the skeletal pillars is a faded, painted word—TOKAMAK.

You found my brother's second fusion reactor?

I did indeed, little puppet. It will change everything. My plan is now closer than ever to fruition.

I don't think it is.

What are you whining about, little kozel?

It won't work.

You're lying.

No. I'm not. You know what I know. Look at it, Vedmak. Really look at it.

He sounds smug. I stare at the device, searching its exterior. How can

21

this wretched Gracile know it's broken from a glance? He's lying. I strain to pull the information from his consciousness. Normally he fights me, tries to hide his knowledge just as I hide things from him. Not today. Today he offers it freely.

His experience rushes into my consciousness. His work on extra dimensions and the collider, powered by this device, etches itself into my brain. It's the magnets—they're cracked and broken. The Tokamak uses a combination of electromagnets and electric currents to contain plasma, which is used to generate thermonuclear fusion power. Without them, it's useless.

"Fix them," I say aloud.

I can't.

"Fix them or I'll hurt *her.*"

Vedmak, I can't. Believe me. Search in my consciousness. You know I can't. Just leave her alone.

Searching his knowledge once again, I know it's true.

"Sard it all." The floor squeaks under my boot as I turn from Merodach and Aeron, leaving them to yank the decapitated experiment to pieces and feed it to the wild animals in my vault.

Where are you going? You said you wouldn't hurt her.

No, I didn't.

Stomping across the lab of the fallen lillipad, I make my way to my private quarters. This is probably the only Pistil that remained intact after that cockroach Kapka pulled everything down. But it is mine. And it has served me well.

When lillipad 17 on the northern edge of Zopat fell, the support balloons softened the impact, keeping the structure almost upright and intact. Still, the explosion melted the ice around it and formed a glistening and nearly impenetrable fortress. It couldn't have been planned better.

Despite Mother Russia providing me an icy hiding place, it wasn't enough. The pathetic Robusts and their sad little band of resistance fighters hounded me for more than a year. Something else was needed. My little peacock provided it for me—if not under duress. A Gracile invention that can bend visible light. They'd used them on the Creed strike ships as active camouflage. Draped over the lillipad, it—and the constant frozen whiteout—keep us hidden.

The door hisses open revealing the dim room.

I prefer the dark. The pain and torture from centuries of limbo have now become a comfort. Cloaked in the familiar gloom, my collection adorns the walls. Oil paintings amassed by the moronic Graciles who knew nothing of their worth. Works by Brodsky, Samokhvalov, and Neprintsev. Masters of the Socialist movement. The true Utopia. Most I found in the ruins of the Gracile fortresses. Mere trinkets to them, and of course of no value to small minded Logosians and Musuls. Now they serve as reminders of my mission. Bring back the glory of Mother Russia.

Past the makeshift bed in the corner, I step to the plate on the wall. The black glove slips off and I press a thumb against the onyx-colored glass. A confirmatory peep and a hidden panel in the white wall shunts back and to the side, revealing my prize: a Robust woman, naked on the floor. Her wrists are bleeding again, raw from a fresh attempt at escape, and her short black hair is strewn about her face. Her skin is smeared in dirt, but I don't care. I enjoy her this way.

Don't do it. Not today. Just give her one more day. Please, I beg you.

"But, you so enjoy this, peacock. I know what it is you want from her. I knew it from the moment we took her. Your desire. Your lust."

No, that's not it at all. You're twisting it. You're always twisting it. I won't let you do this. Not again.

"Let me? Oh, little puppet? You think I do not learn from our little tug of war? You think I would succumb to your influence again?" Twisting on the valve near the jaw of the mask, a new wave of Red Mist hisses through the hose and into these lungs. "The more you fight, the more I learn to tweak this cocktail."

Please. My demon's voice is barely audible.

The Robust woman looks up, just as she had done the first time I'd chanced across her path in the Vapid, Rippers attacking her caravan. It's amazing what is possible with a beautiful Gracile face. The instantaneous trust. The flicker of light in their eyes. Oh, to extinguish that light. Exquisite.

"Call out to him," I rasp.

The woman shuffles on the floor toward the back of the closet.

23

"Call out," I repeat. "To Yeos or whoever you think is going to save you."

Stop it! She knows what will happen if she calls out. She knows.

The Robust female climbs to her knees. "Demitri, please. I know you're in there. Please. You can fight him. I believe in you."

"Demitri? Oh, how deplorable. You put your faith in this whelp rather than your own god?"

"Yeos protects me. If that is through Demitri, so be it." She spits at my boots.

My back fist catches her across the jaw, sending her sprawling. "Yeos will not protect you. And neither will the pathetic child who dwells in this skull with me. He may have intervened before, but I learn from such mistakes."

The intense struggle of my cohabiting spirit to hold on to this corporeal shell is almost to be admired. His single-minded defiance, all to protect this flea-infested tart. But his fight is for nothing. These tests allow me to push the boundaries of his ability to reclaim this body—and thus tweak the stim that ensures my control. I place my boot on the Robust's chest and press her to the ground before shrugging off my heavy cloak.

"Demitri, please. Help me."

What would Ida say? What if someone did this to her?

The rage is instant, flowing from my innermost core into the balled fists of this Gracile engine. I lash at the walls, pummeling them until the knuckles of these hands bleed. "Just because you have learned her name, you will not speak it! Ever!"

The pathetic *kozel* says nothing.

"This pig is nothing like her. This is an animal for my use and nothing more. Let me show you."

Demitri's consciousness claws and pulls at me while the stupid *pizda* under this foot kicks and thrashes, but it is no use. It never is.

CHAPTER THREE

MILA

The storm whips and pushes, snow and ice stinging my cheeks as I squint. My limbs went numb long ago, forgetting the hot blood flowing in these veins. I try to step forward but my body is locked, frozen, not from the cold but rapt with anxiety. Is that a man out there? Was he lost in the storm? I will myself to see through the blizzard. The man shambles forward, his shoulders slumped, like a thing destroyed. The long lank hair and dark hollow eyes, it can't be *Faruq* … can it?

Snow swirls around, obscuring my view the same way it had the last time I saw him. The world spins as the memory floods my brain, drowning it. Once again, it's three years ago and I'm there. Always *there*. It plays out again, a lucid dream—a memory branded into my soul—I'm doomed to re-live over and over. My whole body is set aflame by a single thought.

It's him.

***

"What is it you want? Do not go against us, woman," the Musul guard says, his antique rifle poised at the ready.

They must not know who I am or they would have tried to claim my head already. Kapka's generous bounty on me, dead or alive, should be more than enough to force their hand. My teeth are clenched so tight they feel as though they might crack.

There are six of them, all armed with old Soviet rifles. At their center is a haggard prisoner, draped in rags and wrapped in cloth. The bent posture, ice crystals clinging to his beard, those terrible hollow eyes. There is no longer any doubt.

"Release your captive," I choke on the words.

The man raises his head, his face blistered red by the cold and his eyes near frozen shut. "Help me."

25

It must be Faruq. It has to be. The sudden dire stakes of this chance encounter now made clear. We all stand there, staring, locked in an awful stalemate midway along the Vapid road between the enclaves of Fiori and Logos.

"You do not know this man. He is not your concern," Kapka's man calls out. "Let us pass or we will be forced to spill your blood in this snow and leave you for the Rippers."

"Mila, let's think about this," Giahi says. "We've got nine orphans here and only five fighters to get them to the Vestals. Try to fight through these zealots and we're all dead. There is no strategy to be had here."

Eyeing the group, I try to find a way to do this that doesn't involve everyone dying. There is none. A wave of sickness passes, and I swallow it back. Maybe it isn't Faruq. Just another of Kapka's prisoners. Though, does it make him any less important?

"Last chance," the Musul transport guard calls out. "Clear the path, or die."

My fighters huff and stare in frustration, their feet sliding in the slush, searching for sure footing.

"Please, help," the captive groans.

"Mila, we can't save him," Giahi says.

"What if it's *him*?"

"It's *not* him. Faruq died Mila. On the platform, Kapka's RPG blasted him into oblivion. We're too few and you're still carrying that damn beanbag launcher. We're about to get a bunch of kids killed over one of Kapka's slaves," Giahi says, a hostile edge to his voice.

"Kapka survived," I say.

"Kapka's a cockroach."

I eye the prisoner and breathe out slowly. "Okay." Yeos forgive me for sacrificing this man.

"Good choice," Giahi says, bumping my arm.

"Don't talk to me," I snap. "Get the kids off the road. Walk wide to the right. Give these Baqirian Musuls plenty of room."

We herd the children off to the right and behind the concealment of a small snow bank, keeping the Musul transport group in sight. I lag behind, staring at the Musuls. Giahi and another fighter, Jape, shadow me.

The Baqirians start forward, shoving the withered shell of a man, his manacles clacking.

"Try anything and you're dead," the lead guard calls out. "The children too."

I release my launcher and let it hang from the strap across my shoulders, my palms raised as the men pass, their weapons trained on me. As they near, a sob breaks from the captive, the pitiful keening sound of total desperation.

"Mila. Please don't leave me," he mumbles.

My skin tingles hot. "Faruq!" I scream, lunging forward.

Giahi locks both muscular arms around me. "You're going to get us killed," he shouts.

The Musuls jerk to life, weapons shaking.

Jape holds steady, his Kalashnikov locked on them. "Easy. Just take it easy."

"It's Faruq! He said my name!" I shriek, clawing at Giahi's arms. "Faruq!"

"I don't care if it is. You're about to get us all killed. It's not worth one man," Giahi shouts.

"It is to me," I cry, struggling against him.

Backing away from the standoff, the Musuls continue to hold us in their sights. Faruq moans as he's dragged into the blizzard, a terrible wounded sound that cuts me to the bone. But, by the time I've struggled free of Giahi's vise-like hold, the small band has disappeared into the swirling white.

I sink to my knees in the slush. "I will find you, Faruq. I swear it!" I scream, the sound of my voice lost in the storm. "I swear it."

***

A hand grabs my jacket, jolting me back to the present.

"Mila, what is it?" Husniya asks.

"Uh." I shake my head and watch as the old man I'd first seen emerging from the storm shuffles past with a grunt of acknowledgment. "Nothing. It's nothing." My teeth chatter from the severe cold. "Come on."

Together, my party ducks beneath a few old planks of wood and follows the well-worn path below the surface to the entrance of the mine. I shamble forward, my feet numb and clumsy as though filled with lead. After what feels like an age, a heavy steel door looms out of the darkness.

The hollow sound of my knuckles rapping against steel resounds inside the torch-lit shaft of the abandoned mine. The cold has found its way inside me. It's possible I may not feel anything again. Waiting, the fighters lagging behind slump against the walls of the secret tunnel hidden deep below the carcass of The Forgotten Jewel.

"Keep your strength. Don't sit down. You may die here. They're coming to let us in." Again, I bang on the ancient door—the pattern jolting my memory back to a simpler time when I was just an information handler knocking on the door of my mentor. "Bilgi, open the door. The cold has nearly taken us," I say to the flat, oxidized surface at my nose.

"Who is it?" The familiar, and annoying, voice is muffled through the door.

"You know who it is, Giahi. Let us in."

"How many of our people did you get killed?"

Such a jackbag.

"Was the Kahanga mission a success?" he says, his voice dripping with sarcasm. "Did you save the Musuls there from themselves?"

Is he actually questioning me about this through the door? The cold flesh of my face tingles hot. "Let us in and I'm sure you'll hear all about it if I don't knock your teeth down your throat first."

"Mmmhmm. Just as I thought."

"We're freezing to death and we have wounded out here, Giahi. Open the door, now. That's an order."

The door unbolts. "Temper, temper, Mila. A leader should have more discipline."

I shoulder the door hard. Giahi stumbles back and raises his hands. Before he can adjust, I've grabbed his jacket and shoved him back again. "Sard off. If you weren't such a sarding jackbag, you could have been part of the leadership by now. But you're not. So help or get the hell out of my way."

I turn and loop a wounded fighter's arm over my shoulder. We hobble past the smoldering gaze of the now-silent doorman and into the torch-lit glow of the underground resistance headquarters. With a clang, the heavy door bars behind us.

Mercifully, the air is warmer here, thanks to the subterranean vents that provide us with our natural heat source. The torches placed at intervals cast a comfortable light throughout night without the generator. The inside of a long-abandoned mining complex shouldn't feel so like home, but it does. People run to meet us now, hugging friends and helping the wounded to the well bay.

I hand off the fighter hanging on to me to someone who can treat the nasty gash across his thigh. He mumbles a thank you, groaning as his arm encircles the neck of another and he hobbles off. War is an ugly business, and we seem to have been at it for far too long now.

"Are you okay, Mila?" Husniya strolls up, dropping a rucksack laden with weapons.

"Go get some rest, Hus. You've earned it."

"Hey, about what I said. About Faruq. I'm sorry—"

"Later. We'll talk about it later." I have no intention of talking to her about her brother, about my inability to rescue him. Persistent rumors of his being alive give Hus and me hope. But, after four years, my comrades grow tired of the search and my requests for help.

Husniya, whose face now seems childlike in the dim light, touches the sleeve of my jacket before she heads for her quarters. I'm not her mother or her sister. How should I know how to treat an orphaned Musul girl? Most days I don't even know how to take care of myself.

Shrugging out of my heavy jacket, I make my way down the main corridor with the others to the command room. Inside is the old man, his left shirt sleeve rolled up and tied below the elbow, where the stump of his arm stops. He turns, leaning on his cane for support. A smile spreads across his wrinkled face. "Mila!"

"Bilgi," I reply, and nod to the thin, hawkish faced man with long silver hair beside him. "Yuri. It's good to see you both."

Bilgi's most trusted advisor looks at me over his twisted wire spectacles. "Nazal gave you a hard time?"

"I should think so, Yuri," Bilgi interrupts. "Our people's purpose was to unseat the man. Warlords are not typically agreeable to such action."

Yuri inclines his head. "How many did we lose?"

It's difficult to look him in the eyes. "Eleven."

Bilgi grimaces. "That's a lot."

"I know. We had a tough time of it."

"But the mission was a success?" Bilgi asks.

"It was, though there's a lot more about all of that to tell."

Bilgi's eyebrows shoot up. "Oh? But should I not exhaust you on the details at this moment?"

"I'll tell you this—Mos is a Kahangan prince."

Bilgi and Yuri look at each other, their faces a mixture of confusion and amusement.

"I know," I say. "Supposedly, he's the rightful heir to the ruling seat of Kahanga. Nazal was his brother."

"Was?" Bilgi asks.

"Was."

"I see."

"That's not the strangest part, though, Bilgi." I ply my hands together. "Nazal was working with a Gracile, and when I say *working* I mean, they seemed to be exchanging arms and ammo for stims that made Nazal's men psychotic. I think the Gracile was using the drug too. It's bizarre. There's more to it and I don't like what it all could mean."

"Agreed," Bilgi says. "Yuri, dispatch runners across Etyom. Let's find out if the streets have any information on a Gracile collecting weapons or stims."

Yuri makes a note with a piece of sharpened charcoal.

Bilgi looks back to me. "You've had quite an interesting past few days, Mila. You must be exhausted. Take some food and rest. We will catch you up on what happened here when you wake."

"No. I've come this far. I won't be able to sleep without knowing. What is it?"

Bilgi gives me a look I know well. "I don't believe you will sleep after finding out, either."

"Tell me, Bil. It's been a long day."

"Very well." The old man shrugs. "It was twenty-four hours ago. We lost all communications. Not a hiccup, mind you. Everything went completely dark. It was … unusual."

"Okay."

"We initially thought it was an antenna failure. I sent three up to the surface to check it. They never came back," Bilgi says.

"A comms specialist and two security," Yuri adds. "As you well know, the antenna is hidden."

"You guys are killing me." I rub my face. "What happened?"

"The men we sent," Bilgi casts a look at Yuri. "When we found them hours later, half-frozen in the blood-splattered snow. They appeared to have been butchered."

"Butchered?" By manner of habit or some other frustration, I find my hands on my hips.

"Yes. Arms, legs, heads, all removed. Bodies flayed and gutted like fish."

"For the love of Yeos. Rippers got into Fiori. Damn them," I say.

"Maybe it is Rippers." Bilgi adjusts his cane. "Maybe it isn't."

"Bil, I'm too tired for cryptic answers. Tell me what you're thinking."

"I'm as perplexed as you, Mila. The attack was too precise, not reckless the way Ripper attacks are. Just when you get a chance, if you've got the stomach for it, look at the bodies. They're in the Mort chamber, ready to be shunted."

"Were the attack and the disruption related?"

"We assume so, but we don't know."

"So, we don't know anything."

"For now, girl. Just look into it when you can."

"Are we okay otherwise? Where's Ghofaun?"

"He's on an intelligence mission. We just got word from him. He should be back by the time you wake."

"Okay."

"Mila." My aging mentor winks at me. "I'm glad to have you back safe, girl."

I manage a weak smile and push through the door. Its rusted hinges squeal.

***

The hour grows late and much of the daytime activity of the resistance hideout is now quiet. Through the twisting red stone hallway, I pass bundles of tattered fighters huddled together. Some play a game of Ozzut, trading cards and trinkets and passing a jug of shine, while others lay where they can, resting with empty stares on makeshift cots and pallets. They've been through much.

A woman dips her brow. "Paladyn," she says with a look of admiration.

I force a smile and touch her shoulder but keep walking. Others raise their heads and murmur the word, gazing at me with hope in their eyes. Paladyn. A guardian. A defender of the people. The weight of the idea presses down, a sack of stones upon my shoulders that promises to bend my knees with each step. I just lost eleven of them. Eleven hopes and dreams snuffed out. I'm no guardian. I never wanted such a title or asked for any of this.

Slipping into the boiler room, I wink at Filly—the girl working the cauldron. She's young and spirited like her name suggests. It's here soiled and infected clothes are boiled for long periods to try to keep us clean and as healthy as reasonably possible. Filly talks about her mother, who works in the comms room, and hands me a bundle of fresh garments. She handpicks them, knowing by now the things I wouldn't wear. She also gives me a jug of warm water, a packet of herbs and a clean cloth for bathing. I thank her, promising to drop my soiled clothes in the morning, and head back to my bunk.

The lone candle ignites, throwing jagged shadows on the wall. The prospect of sleep offers both welcome relief and a deep-seated dread. Will I dream? Will I have to hear Faruq's screams as his captors drag him away? Will I have to bear witness as The Fourth Horseman steals Demitri's body and invades my dreams again? My eyelids are so heavy, but I'm filthy. Though bathing won't wash away the blood I've spilled—actions that stain my soul—I complete the ritual.

The candle nears the end of its life, brown wax spilling over the rim of the lid in which it sits. I slip out of my over-shirt, step out of my boots, then unfasten my cargo pants and let them slide to the floor, leaving me standing in my tank top and undergarments. I place a basin on the table beside my bed, crumble a handful of herbs into it, and pour it full of warm water that slides into it from the smooth ceramic jug. From the floor, I pick up a short plank of a clouded mirror. The smudged reflection of a survivor stares back. A person with so many more scars now. The oldest one running down my forehead and across my eye can almost be overlooked. Almost.

Wiping the mud and blood and grime from my face and body, the steaming herb-filled water reveals a woman hidden beneath the terrible remnants of war. A woman. What does that even mean? This vicious world doesn't care if I am male or female. It will chew me up and spit me from its mouth all the same. An equal opportunity for each of us to find death waiting at the end of a gun or knife inside the next dark alley at the hands of an elitist, a fanatic or a savage.

The toned muscles of my body tense as I carelessly brush the cloth across the edges of an open wound. Damnation. I gingerly touch the cloth to it. The faded strip of material collects flecks of dried blood. It hurts, but it's superficial. No one asked me if I wanted this wound, but I received it anyway. The same way I came into my position as a leader with this group. It just happened. Faruq, Demitri, and me, along with Mos and Ghofaun and Denni ... We were so full of energy and purpose in those days. By our passion alone, and guided by the hands of Yeos the creator, we won the war against the Leader of the Graciles. But the terrorist Kapka left his mark. Etyom, and the lillipads above, fell. Most of us lost something—or everything—for our efforts.

I drop the cloth into the bowl and return the mirror to the floor. I'm tired and my clouded reflection makes me think too much. Lying back, I pull the scratchy wool over my exposed skin and allow my eyes to fix upon one point in the stone ceiling—a dark patch like a bit of spilled ink.

"Yeos, merciful father," the prayer begins. Faith is all that remains of the old Mila Solokoff who went to war and became a leader of the resistance. I've tried so hard to not stray from the path of the Lightbringer. Yet, with every decision made, with every life lost, His guiding voice becomes harder to discern. Sleep creeps upon me, a drifting blanket of warmth and exhaustion.

Don't dream tonight, Mila.

I lean forward to the flame of the candle jumping from a wick grown too long and, with a puff of breath, darkness.

CHAPTER FOUR

DEMITRI

I t's black here, while he sleeps.

Behind the eyes once mine, I exist. In limbo. Alive, yet unliving.

Watching from afar every single movement Vedmak—or the Vardøger, as he insists on being called—makes. Every breath he takes I experience it as if it were mine, yet I am not in control.

Here in the recess of my own mind, I am a prisoner. He relishes it, knowing it pains me to feel my own body do the things he commands. Especially to sweet Anastasia, his Robust pet. It's the only reason he does it. Because he knows the torture it inflicts upon me. To feel her skin crawl, and see the absolute disgust in her eyes staring back, as Vedmak forces my body to penetrate her. I hate myself for being unable to stop him.

Next to me, here in the dark, I can hear her shallow breathing as she sleeps.

He used to take the mask off. To allow Anastasia to see my face, burned as it is. So she could despise me. It was a mistake. Without the stim, I was able to grasp control. She thought me, him, crazy—this body thrashing and crashing into the walls, arguing with seemingly no one, until I was victorious. Until I had control. She kicked and scratched as I released her bonds. I just kept repeating over and over that I was sorry, that it wasn't me. It was Vedmak, and I was Demitri. That he *made* me do things. I told her to run, to escape. She chose to hit me in the head with the steel of her restraints. The shock, the injury, had the opposite effect of what she desired. It loosed my hold on my own body and allowed Vedmak back. In her eyes, I could see the horror as she watched my face change expression—one minute me, the next him.

That was three months after he first captured her, out in the Vapid. She'd been attacked by Rippers and some other unknown assailant. We found her shaking in the stripped cart, muttering the word *ussuri* over and over.

Occasionally, when Vedmak sleeps, she talks to me; calls softly to me,

35

asking if I am here. If I can hear her. Telling me she knows I am strong. That I can save her. There are even moments when my will feels powerful and I can push words through the lips of my own sleeping body to her. I tell her that one day I will save her. But it is a lie. I can't.

After my attempt to free her, Vedmak keeps the mask on. I try so hard to fight. Sometimes I prevail, holding back his body. Holding back his lust. But mostly I fail. Fail her. I'm not sure why it matters so much—this one girl, this one Robust. Perhaps it is because she looks like Mila. He cut her hair short and sliced a wound into her face, using his laser scythe, to match Mila's scar. But Mila never searched my eyes as she does. Every time he punishes her, she searches for me—hoping against hope this time I will come to her rescue. In the three years he has kept her, I have grown to admire her strength, her resolve, but most of all her belief that there is still a good person somewhere in this engineered shell.

Perhaps what makes it worse is Vedmak doesn't even want Anastasia. It's Mila he wants to torture.

He knows hurting Mila would kill me. I'd probably fade away to nothing from the pain. But he can't let her know his whereabouts—he's not ready yet. She's been searching for him. For me. There have been times she has been so close and didn't know it. He's sat in the dark, breathing heavily behind his mask, watching her march by with her band of resistance fighters. I even screamed out, but of course she couldn't hear me.

The stim cocktail he's created, based on the Red Mist, and used to keep me at bay has been modified so often. Every time I feel I'm overcoming it, he changes it. Lately, the dose has been so strong I seem to have been dissolved for days. When I return, chunks of his plan have jumped forward. But the stim is imperfect. His Gracile warriors, attached to demons like him, do as he bids most of the time, but they have fits—psychotic episodes—where they are uncontrollable. Vedmak's workshop, the *poisons lab* he calls it, is dedicated to perfecting the stim, but so far he's still dissatisfied. I'm no biochemist, and of no help. But he knows what I know. And so, tomorrow, when he wakes, he plans to travel to Zopat and find the Alchemist—the Robust woman who sold me Red Mist all those years ago. Destroying the leader also destroyed me, the pain stripping away my hold on my own body, leaving it open for Vedmak to take complete control. And he's been in control now for four years. Busy the entire time. Plotting and scheming. Utilizing my knowledge to forge his plan—to continue what he started so many years ago in Revolution-torn Russia. He's so close, yet so far. The process is slow and his target will be hard to achieve. It will take many more years to fulfill what he plans to accomplish. Especially without the Tokamak.

This is what enrages my occupier most.

Many times I've tried to tell him. The process can't be accelerated. Not with the resources we have. He abused Anastasia for a week straight, believing I was holding out on him. Trying to make me tell him a faster way. There is none. But even if I did know, I wouldn't tell him. Even if he tortured her to death. Compared with what the Gracile Leader wanted, to create a black hole, the side effect alone of Vedmak's plan is far worse. But he's deaf to it. Thinks I'm only trying to dissuade him. I'm not. His plan is flawed. And if he's successful today, tomorrow, or in fifty years it won't matter.

Anastasia shuffles on the cold floor, the fingers of her bound hands brush against my back. She mumbles my name. If I had control of my own body, I know tears would now well and a stone would form in my throat.

Sweet Anastasia. Even if I could save you, we're all going to die, anyway.

CHAPTER FIVE

MILA

The touch of cool fingers to my shoulder jerks me awake. I twist, knock the hand away, and produce a knife from beneath my pillow.

"Mila!"

The blade is effortlessly torn from my grip. I jump from my cot, heart racing, my mind pulled from dark dreams of death and apocalypse.

"Mila, it's okay. It's me."

There's a silhouette—short with muscled shoulders. Slowly, the smiling features of the Lawkshan monk appear.

"Ghofaun?"

"Maybe you'd like to put some clothes on?"

Blood rushes to my face. "I'm … I was … Give me a second."

Without another word, he turns away. "I'm sorry, Mila. I only wanted to nudge you awake, not start a sparring match—with a knife, no less."

I quickly pull on my clean garments, check them for fit and function, and snap the light switch. The room flickers to life, powered by the clanking fossil fuel generators at the end of the complex. "Sorry about the knife. I'm a little on edge these days. You can turn around."

The monk turns toward me again, holding a tray in his hands. He's brought me something to eat.

"Where did that come from?" I say, motioning to the tray as I sit and lace my boots.

"I've been holding it."

The tray holds a plate of warm chiori with greens and a full steaming cup of krig, not a drop spilled. "You balanced a tray while standing on one leg and what? Used your foot to intercept the knife?"

He smiles.

"Incredible. You are something else."

He extends the tray. "Breakfast?"

"Please." I accept the tray, the smells of warm food and hot krig

38

making my mouth water. It's a pauper's meal but it may as well be a feast. I tuck into the steaming food.

"How was Kahanga?"

"Well, Mos is a Kahangan prince," I answer with a mouth full of greens. "Nazal was his brother. Stimmed-up Graciles have been trading guns for drugs there. We lost eleven fighters in the last few days. You know, just another day in paradise."

Ghofaun nods. "Well, Mos wanting that mission so badly makes more sense now."

"Mmm hmmm." I take a sip of my krig.

"What's that business with the Graciles in Kahanga?"

"I've got to do some more digging. Definitely not good."

"I can tell. I passed Husniya in the hall. She has a black eye."

"You should see the other guy. Twice her size. She did fine."

Master Ghofaun gives a sage bow of approval.

"What about you? Where have you been?" I ask, chewing another mouthful of meat and greens.

He fingers the Lawkshan beads on his wrist, a symbol of a lifetime devoted to the ways of peace through the disciplined application of foot and fist. "I just returned from Zopat late last night. The plague is resurfacing there too."

"Now that outbreaks have been reported in every sector of Etyom. It could get bad again. Real bad."

Not one for too many words, my friend simply bobs his head.

"What about Faruq? Any word of him?"

Ghofaun's lips tighten. "No, Mila. I'm sorry. There is nothing on Faruq. His trail has long since gone cold. We followed up on the rumor he was being kept in Alya by Kapka's governor, but nothing came of it. I fear we are now chasing Chinese whispers."

He's trying to spare my feelings. He believes, like the others, my continued search for Faruq is in vain. But I can't believe that—won't believe it. "Okay, thank you. Anything else?"

"Yes, one thing. Giahi worries me. The man seems to undermine the authority of Opor's leadership at every turn." The monk pauses, considering his choice of words. "Just be careful, Mila. He would benefit greatly if something happened to you or Bilgi."

"I appreciate that you care, my friend. Giahi is a big mouth and a coward, but I will keep your counsel in mind."

"I am glad to hear it, Mila." He turns to leave. "Will I see you for a sparring session later?"

"Oh? You haven't had enough already?" I laugh, gathering my tray and my soiled garments.

"Never." His eyes twinkle.

"Very well, Master Ghofaun. Husniya and I will join you later."

"I'll take your tray." The monk gives a slight bow and glides from the room.

***

On the way to the Mort, past the cavernous main room, the sharp bark of Husniya's young voice echoes off the walls. I pivot and move to the rusted door, pushing it open enough to hear the ongoing conversation in the large room beyond.

"We have to do something. Three of our people were murdered right outside our door. Doesn't anyone care?" Husniya shouts.

"We don't know anything about what happened," another voice in the small crowd calls out. "What are we supposed to do?"

Squeezing through the door, I do my best to remain unseen in the shadowed rear of the cavernous space. In the center, Husniya is up on a box addressing a group of about fifteen people.

What's she doing?

Giahi and a couple of his flunkies lean against an old piece of mining equipment. His face practically glows with amusement.

"We should send out scouts, start gathering information, root out the problem and neutralize it." The girl waves her arms dramatically. "Anyone who wants to kill us—we must kill them first."

The tone of the teenager's words is disturbing. She sounds so angry. It's easy to forget she's the cast-out daughter of Kapka himself. Somewhere deep inside might lie the same lust for blood, the same madness.

"You're just a girl," someone says. "And a Musul."

"Mos is Musul. You listen to him," Husniya snaps back.

"Not a Musul like *you*," says another. "We've heard enough. We need to know what we're doing and who we're looking for first—not run around out there chasing our tails."

"We need to talk to Mila or Bilgi first," says a woman near the back of the group.

"Yeah, that's right."

"Get down, Musul."

"Get down! Get down!" The group chants as a red-faced Husniya jabs an angry finger at them.

Enough of this.

Moving quickly forward, I reach up, grab her arm and pull her down from the box. The crowd laughs. Shame burns in the teenager's face.

"Listen up." I hold my hands up to quiet the crowd. "We're working on it. We've already dispatched scouts to gain more information. When we know something we'll take action, not before." I cast a glance at the furious teenage girl next to me. "But for the record, being a Musul has nothing to do with anything. The next time I hear someone carelessly dropping racial slurs, you and I are going to get to know each other better. Got it?"

More grumbling.

"Good. Until then, let's get back to work. We all have a part to play here." I clap my hands. "Let's go. Back to work."

The crowd complains but disperses, wandering out of the room back to their assignments. Giahi is the last to leave, a smirk plastered across his ugly mug.

I turn to Husniya. "Are you trying to start a riot?"

"I'm *trying* to take action. Which is more than anyone else is doing."

"Now is not the time to play hero."

"What is it time for, then?" she snaps. "We should be doing something, Mila. Not just sitting around." She pinches her eyes shut. "No, I don't need you. I'm fine," she mumbles under her breath.

"No one is sitting around, Husniya." I look at the girl long and hard. "We all have important jobs to do. We will act when the time is right. Leave the running of this group to the leadership."

"Fine. You're the boss, I guess." She grabs her bag from the floor and storms through the heavy doors, disappearing into the main hallway beyond.

Adolescents. Think they know sarding everything.

Still, Husniya is different. *No, I don't need you. I'm fine.*

It's easy to forget she has a voice too—Margarida. Her voice wasn't hostile in the way Vedmak was, but she's done such a good job of hiding it, I thought perhaps the spirit had left her.

Need to speak with her about it once she's calm.

***

The sealed door into the mort chamber pushes open and the stench of decay fills my throat. Don't stay too long, Mila, or you'll never get that smell out of your clothes. The portly attendant, who has dragged three large bundles to the edge of the chute, looks up. Covered in layers of heavy clothing smeared with filth, he wears gloves, goggles, and a mask over his face.

What's his name, again?

"Hang on a second, uh …" I say, holding up my hand.

"Beran," he says. "I was about to shunt these three."

He doesn't get many visitors in here, and for good reason.

"Yeah, hang on for a second, Beran. I need to look them over."

He scrunches up his face. "But I just got them bundled and they're starting to stink."

I gaze at the fat man until he gets I'm serious.

"Ugh. Okay," he says, grabbing the first bundle. "Hold on to your breakfast. It's bad."

Such an odd fellow. My eyes follow him as he works. "Do you like this? The bodies, I mean?"

"No. Feel like I could catch the plague at any moment."

"Were you told to do this job?"

"I volunteered. I don't have a trade and I hate violence." He works on untying the first bundle. "This keeps me out of the fighting."

"And instead has you dealing with the mess that follows." I peer into the body chute. A mine shaft leading down into some unknown chasm below.

42

"I suppose so." He unties the sheet and drapes it open, sending a fresh wave of the stench in my direction. I flinch, my eyes watering at the powerful odor of death, and bury my face into the crease of my elbow. He quickly unwraps the other two blood-soaked bundles and throws the sheets open.

"Sweet Moses," I gasp, trying not to turn away, unable to pull my arm from my face.

The remains can hardly be identified as human. I crouch to get a closer look, gazing upon the grizzly piles, searching for what I'm supposed to see here when Beran speaks up.

"Want to know what I think is strange?"

"Please." My words are muffled by the sleeve across my mouth and nose.

"Look at this here and here." He points to a neck no longer supporting a head. "A wild animal would tear it off. Even Rippers hacking with their weapons would leave a jagged cut. But on each of these, the line is straight, the wound bubbled over and smooth."

"What would do that, Beran?" I take a step back.

"Maybe a flaming blade, hot from the forge?"

"Out in a blizzard? That makes no sense."

"I don't know, Mila. I can only tell you what it's not. It's not an animal attack, and it's not a normal wound inflicted by the sort of weapons we use."

"Yeah." I cough. "That's what I'm afraid of."

CHAPTER SIX

VEDMAK

Before me, the ornate enclave gates loom from the swirling cold. Zopat—such a stupid name for an enclave. From where did the infantile Robusts gather such nonsensical nomenclature? Piteous fools. The huge double doors with iron banding tower even above this Gracile body. Why such waste and grandeur? The rodents that dwell here are short of stature. Despite professing to hate the Graciles, they attempt to emulate them—idolizing false gods. There are no gods. There is only me, the Vardøger.

I rap on the door with my cane, the hollow sound echoing through the thick walls of the enclave. A moment later, a slot in the door—perhaps large enough to allow a sizeable package through—shunks open.

"What you want, la?" a whiny voice asks.

"I want to enter, of course," I reply, my voice stifled by my mask. I glance back to my twin bodyguards.

"You have ID, huh? You have pass?"

Ah yes, the pass. I unglove a hand and shove it through the portal. There's a moment of silence as the guard inspects the skin.

"No pass here, la. You no come in."

"No pass? Oh, I must have shown you the wrong hand."

"No pas—"

I grab him by his tunic and pull. The guard's forehead smacks against the inside of the door. He manages a juvenile cry as he strikes the wood a second time. Repeatedly, I yank on the sad little man, smashing his distorted skull over and over. The *smack* of pulverized meat and breaking bone is satisfying.

That's enough, already, my Gracile demon begs.

Have you learned nothing, peacock? To protest only feeds my desire to make you squirm. I release the tunic but push through the slot to the shoulder so I can slip my arm around the guard's back. With a snarl, I pull

44

with all the strength this body will allow. The semi-conscious guard folds in two, a gurgle escaping his lips. There's a satisfying snap, his final scream—brief. One last jerk and I drag his entire body through the portal like a crumpled piece of human origami. The edges of the hole are adorned with chunks of bloodied flesh. The Zopatian's corpse drops to the snow and lies like a broken doll at my feet.

Merodach and Aeron laugh.

I hate you.

Not for much longer, Gracile.

I slide a hand back through the portal again and feel for the bolt. A quick flick and it's loose. The huge door creaks ajar. I push it open and storm with purpose along the path the peacock had taken those years earlier.

Now to find her.

The streets of Zopat are not as I remember them. The fluorescent lights are gone. Reveling commoners, alcohol in their hands, no longer line the streets. In fact, the ramshackle constructions appear more deserted than ever. It's reminiscent of Orel, a Russian city of old—potholed roads, doors to the aging buildings missing, plastic buckets lining the crumbling walls to collect what little rain falls. But she will still be here. The Alchemist.

Approaching the main drag, her dilapidated abode comes into view. The unlit electric sign that says *shop* hangs off-kilter, broken like everything else in this place. I look to the twins. They grunt their acknowledgment and storm the entrance. Calmly, I follow.

Inside, there is nothing but the stale air. Light streams through the cracks in the boards lining the only window. It illuminates the swirls of dust and particles that puff up as my Gracile warriors begin their search. Aeron flips the makeshift counter clean off the floor. Merodach disappears through a ragged curtain into a back room. There's a throttled scream and a moment later he returns, his face full of pride like a hunting dog that has fetched its master's prey. In his grasp is the arm of a Robust, though it's been dislocated at the shoulder and the crying man swivels about its loose axis.

The chest of this biological engine fills with pride. "Put him down, Merodach."

Merodach drops the Robust to the floor.

The skinny, rodent-like man rises to his knees, clutching at his limp arm, his eyes downcast.

"Where is the Alchemist?" I ask.

"Not know Al-keim-est, mah. You go now," the little man whimpers.

My exhausted sigh is enough for Merodach, who clamps a firm hand on the Zopatian's mangled shoulder. He lets out a blood-curdling scream as my soldier twists in the dislocated socket. A wave of a finger and Merodach releases his hold. The man slumps to the floor, sobbing.

"Where. Is. The. Alchemist?" I ask again. "The woman who worked in this place. Selling stims."

The Robust looks up with tear-filled eyes. Is that hope? He knows something.

"You, you mean Zlata." He shuffles back onto his knees. "She no here. Moved for safety, lah. Afraid of Musuls and Rippers after lillipads fall down."

Musuls? Rippers? She should be afraid of me. I drop to my haunches, my mask now inches from his face. "Where did she go?"

"Kon-is-teeva," he replies, his head bobbing with fervor.

"How poetic," I reply.

"I take you, and you let me live, mah," the skinny man offers.

"There is no need for an escort. I know the way."

I rise and turn away. Demitri remains silent this time. He knows his protests are of no consequence. As I push through the door, another brief scream fills the shop. Aeron and Merodach trot up behind, wiping their gore-stained hands on the walls and snow as we make our way along the ice-covered streets that lead us to the old factory.

The morning sky above is a dark gray, and snow begins to fall in large, heavy flakes that stick to the lenses of my disguise. Before long, guided by a sense of *deja vu*, I stand before the familiar façade of the ancient building. Where it all began.

Mila ...

What have I told you about using her name? Cultivate your silence, or you will regret it later.

No more words come from the Gracile.

Where in this corpse of the old world could the Alchemist be hiding?

The Creed destroyed it with their gunship. The bare scaffolding and crumbling concrete are all that's left. Only one corner of the derelict facility remains, surrounded by ancient mining equipment. A poor attempt at a perimeter, no doubt.

From within the dark gaps between the ancient contraptions, Robusts—with white hair and electric blue eyes—appear. Their coordinated clothing suggests some sort of gang affiliation. One by one, they creep toward us with caution and distrust in their eyes. Each holds an ax-like weapon. Is it fear or insanity that propels them to their doom?

"What you want, Gracile?" the lead Robust says. "You no welcome here."

"We're here for the Zlata, the Alchemist," I reply. This Gracile's voice is too soft. Too affable. Only the mask endows it with any form of menace.

"Who asking, lah?" the Robust fires back.

Aeron snarls. "This is the Vardøger, Robust pig. You will show respect."

Another of the white-haired gang waves his ax. "Why you want the Alchemist, Vaaar-dogger?"

"That's none of your concern," Aeron spits.

"Is our concern, Gracile. Zlata pay us good money for pro-tec-shun. You gostun, Gracile. Time to leave if you want all your parts."

Merodach steps forward, his hand already placed on the personalized weapon I gave him.

"You want to know why I am called the Vardøger, you ignorant *zalupa?*"

Vedmak, don't.

My demon fights for control, pulling at limbs that were once his, but he has not the strength for it. Wretched dog. The appetite comes with eating.

"We no care, mask man," a gang member says. "You go. Last time."

"The astounding thing about the Gracile body is its ability to be reprogrammed," I continue.

No, please no. The stim. It's too strong. I can't stop you.

"While many years of tinkering have made this biological machine near perfect, there are still things to be learned from other creatures. Like the humble fly." A mere thought switches on the neural-web link—the connection between the special lenses in my mask and the optical nerve in Demitri's head snaps on. Energy surges into the muscles of this body's limbs. I take a small step forward. "The fly can see many times faster than even a Gracile. The very hands of a clock tick leisurely. Time itself is slower."

The world before me moves in strange flickers, like a motion picture with too few frames. Each movement the Robusts take is slow and disjointed with the next.

"The stories tell that people feel they know of the Vardøger's arrival before they see him," I say. "A glimpse, a smell, a breeze."

"No more. Kill them," the lead Robust screams and launches at me, his ax held high.

Between his clumsy swing, I move with ease. A single frame in time captures the mask of horror on his face at discovering I am no longer standing in front of him. Catapulting forward beyond his comprehension of space and time, my laser scythe shrieks into life and slices him from balls to brains. His two halves separate and flop against the snow-covered ground. Spinning left, I strike the next one. He doesn't realize the top half of his head has left him and flown into the air until it's too late. By the time the third falls to the ground with a severed torso, I've already crashed into the fourth simpleton and slit his throat, the flesh hanging open like a great yawning mouth.

The neural link clicks off and the world returns to normal. Warm blood trickles from the left nostril of my Gracile host.

The remaining members of the Robust gang scream, falling over each other in terror. My scythe hums and crackles, the blue plasma flame lighting the dim corner of the warehouse.

"Kill them," I hiss.

The twins jerk to life, pulling weapons from holsters on their thighs.

Aeron's plasma broadsword bursts forth in a flash of blue-white light, dropping hard on the nearest Robust. The blade slices across his head and severs the right arm at the elbow in a flash of cauterized flesh.

Glorious. The heart in this chest beats fiercely with my pride.

Merodach swings a chain above his head, igniting the cannon-ball-sized plasma mace. The fiery sphere flies through the air and catches a Robust in his slant-eyed face. The impact disintegrates his features in a flash, vaporizing his skull into a mist of fluid and bone.

"*Otlichno!*" I cry.

Something flees from behind an old drill.

The Alchemist.

As fast as her tired old legs will carry her, she makes for the road. Aeron has already locked on to his prey. A powerful war cry and he pushes off into a sprint. In seconds, he's on her and with a backfist across her withered jaw, he's knocked her to the icy ground. Merodach joins his brother and delivers a brutal kick to her stomach. The twins howl in glee.

"Fools, I need her alive," I scream.

But they pay no heed.

Merodach pulls back for another kick.

The neural link clicks on. The world flickers and again adrenaline surges into the muscles of my Gracile shell. Before my warrior can strike, I've already intercepted him, grabbed his face, and shoved him back. Twisting, I drive a shoulder into Aeron's plexus and he buckles, confused. I stand, wide-legged and coiled—the laser-scythe crackling and spitting plasma—between the Alchemist and my creations. The scythe snaps off and the darkness returns.

"Simple minded kozels. I need her alive."

The twins stare back, genuine fear of my wrath in their eyes. Aeron mumbles, chattering nonsense under his breath.

I turn to the Alchemist, who lies in the slush—shivering, but breathing. "This is why I need you, old woman. This is why you are alive."

She lifts her head and pries her eyes open. "Who ... who are you?"

The mask unclips and slides off, the Red Mist hissing from the nozzle inside.

Her pupils dilate as she recognizes this Gracile's face—Demitri's face.

I'm sorry, it's not me ... Please, it's not me.

Oh, but it is, little peacock. But it is.

CHAPTER SEVEN

MILA

The unusual technique catches me by surprise. I'm only able to take a stumbling step out of the leg sweep when he plants both palms on my chest and shoves me back. Reeling, I struggle to regain my balance as the man seems to levitate, his fists above his head, his elbows tucked close. The spin wheel kick catches me across the jaw. A flash of stars breaks across my vison, and I tumble to the ground.

I roll to the side as his foot stomps where I was just a moment before. Rolling to my back, a shadow darkens the single light in the ceiling. The pressure in the air changes as the blow moves toward my face. At the last second, I intercept the strike meant for my nose with my forearm. A second punch lands against my cheek, followed by a third and a fourth. All composure gone, I gasp, arms flailing, as I lay on my back in the crunched position, the single dusty bulb above flashing as the shadow moves and strikes. The fifth punch slows and comes to rest gently against the sore spot on my face where the others landed.

"Why have you stopped defending?" Ghofaun pulls his fist back and crouches to look me in the eyes.

"I …" The words won't come. "I don't know. After I fell … I lost you and the light—"

"Do you need to see me to fight me?" His narrow eyes slim further.

He offers me a hand. I ignore it and stand for myself. "I have to see you to defend against your attack."

"Do you?" His question isn't a question. "Let me ask you this," he says. "How did you intercept my first strike once you hit the ground? Did you see it?"

"No, I …"

His eyebrows raise. "Yes?"

"I felt it," I say with a sigh.

"Exactly, Mila," Ghofaun says. "Trust your fighting instincts. When the eyes deceive, the body remains true."

"You never cease to amaze, Master Ghofaun," I say, touching my tender cheek. "What was that anyway? The series of movements where you first caught me off guard?"

The little warrior monk winks. "I call it the sparrow hawk."

I huff out a laugh. "Figures you'd kick my tail with a technique you named after me."

There's a shuffle by the ancient rust-covered door to the training room. Husniya enters and tosses her bag by the entrance.

"Husniya." Ghofaun spreads his arms. "Come in. We were just finishing."

The teen offers a small bow for her teacher, then cuts her eyes at me. Still miffed about being embarrassed earlier, no doubt.

"Thanks for joining us, Hus." I roll up my sleeves.

"What are we working on today, Master Ghofaun?" she asks.

"Fundamentals."

She lets out a sigh. "But master, we *always* work fundamentals. Why can't— "

Ghofaun holds up a single finger, drawing silence from his pupil. A stillness descends upon the room. He lets it grow bloated before he speaks, his tone even. "Fundamentals are everything. Master them and you shall master yourself, and thus, the art of Chum Lawk. There is no quick path to the top of the mountain. You must gain its summit with each and every well-placed and careful application of your body. Disregard this advice at your own peril."

Husniya stands still, listening to the words of her teacher. She doesn't have to like what he says to know he's right.

"Do we have an understanding?" he says, his voice firm.

"Yes, Master Ghofaun," Husniya replies.

"Good. Fundamentals. You will warm your core and limbs with a slow application of Mak Tow Chujin."

Husniya looks up, her mouth opens to protest. The monk shoots up a finger, causing her to swallow her words.

A little smirk forms on my lips. Chujin is painfully slow to start with

51

and he's going to slow her down even more. Just what she needs. I wait, arms folded, watching as Husniya composes herself and begins the form with long sweeping movements and deep stances. As she moves, Ghofaun swats her limbs with a short cane correcting her form.

"Bend knee. Back straight. Breathe," the warrior monk instructs.

Husniya moves slowly, her lips tight in her concentration.

"Straighten your back," he says, lashing out again with the reed.

"My back is straight, Master," Husniya gripes, standing.

Ghofaun looks to me.

"May I?"

He nods.

"Take your guarding stance again, Husniya. Make sure you're set."

She follows my direction.

Without a word, I step forward and shove her with one arm at a forty-five-degree angle to her stance. The girl stumbles, her feet tripping over each other as she tries to keep her balance.

"You see? The way you set up, you have no directional stability. Now set up again."

Husniya returns to her stance, clearly trying to master her frustration.

"Widen your stance a few inches, bend your knees, and lock your back in position," I correct her. "Now hold." I shove into her from a different direction. This time the girl holds firm.

"Good. Now, practice your form this way." I step back, catching a wink from Ghofaun, who takes over her instruction swatting her again.

She would never let me hit her with a cane like that, which is why Ghofaun is the one spearheading her instruction. Husniya has come a long way in the last few years—her body lean and strong, her mind more disciplined. At the end of the day, though, she's still a hot-headed kid. I smirk at the similarities between us and how Bilgi used to slap me in the face when I lost my focus or dropped my guard. Pain is a good teacher.

The thin cane snaps against Husniya's thigh and she grits her teeth but says nothing, making a tiny adjustment to the depth of her stance.

Good girl. I'll leave them to it for now.

***

The lights overhead flicker, a momentary reminder this place would be as dark as a tomb without the antiquated generators giving us what little electricity they can eek out. Our mechanics can repair them and have been doing so for many cycles, but we do not possess the materials to manufacture new machines. When the day comes, and the rattling junk that gives us our fleeting old-world resource does so for the last time, where will we be then? How will humanity take that next great and primitive step backward? Only time will tell.

An exchange of voices. Something about the tone doesn't sit right. I make my way toward the heavy steel doors at the front of the complex. Bilgi is speaking with a disheveled man, who has a rag draped over his nose and mouth.

"So you're going to kick me out, just like that?" the man says, the words muffled by the rag.

"Valen, you misunderstand me," Bilgi says, his voice calm. "We aren't kicking you out."

"That's what it feels like." Valen's quick breaths suck at the cloth.

"Listen, you're showing signs of infection. We can't treat you here. The clinics in Zopat are much better suited for that. If you stay you only risk infecting everyone else."

"*If* I have the plague. You don't know. It could be a cold."

"We can't take the chance, Valen. You know that." Bilgi's gaze is firm.

"You sarding son of a bitch. After all I've done for this resistance—"

"Return when you are well. I will say no more." Bilgi motions to the door.

"You don't have to worry about me returning. I'll die out there alone," Valen whimpers, the cloth trembling before his lips.

Bilgi says nothing and continues to hold his hand toward the door.

Valen hangs his head and steps forward. Bilgi stops him.

"Do I need to remind you of the importance of maintaining the secrecy of this location and our operation, in spite of your anger?"

The man shakes his head. "I know the rules. I'm not stupid."

"Farewell, Valen."

The man slips through the widening gap in the rusted steel barrier. It closes behind him with a clang and the crossbar is dropped back into place by a member of the security contingent.

Bilgi walks toward me, shaking his head.

"What was that about?"

"Valen drew ill. We don't know with what, but I feel like I need a bath just talking with him," Bilgi says.

"The plague is surging back stronger than I've seen it in my lifetime." I let a moment pass. "What was that about the rules? He said, *I know the rules* when you asked if he could keep our operation a secret."

"Our people believe if they defect or move against us, not only will we take their lives, but also the lives of those they love. It's a good incentive to stay silent."

My skin prickles at the words of my mentor. "Bilgi, you can't be serious?"

"I'm quite serious, my dear."

"They believe this because it's what you've told them?"

"Secrecy is of vital importance to our work." He measures my reaction. "What? Don't look at me like that. We've never had to kill anyone's family, Mila."

"I'm not sure I like that answer."

Bilgi puts his good arm around me. "Listen, girl, our world is no longer black and white—maybe it never was. The point is, we do everything we do for a reason. Our resistance to tyranny didn't end with the Leader. If we don't keep our protocols and protect our interests, we will cease to exist. Kapka or some other maniac will see to it. We can't afford for that to happen. We're still the best chance the people of Etyom have at being free."

"And once the people are free, Opor won't seize power and become the next tyrant?"

"Mila. Would we do such a thing? Would we become the thing we hate?" Bilgi asks.

"You and I would not, but someone else—someone like Giahi would."

"We will not allow such a thing to happen. Not as long as we draw breath."

"Yes, of course, you're right, Bilgi," I say and grab his wrist that hangs casually over my shoulder. "But in our effort to save Earth's last city, I don't want to lose sight of its people—or our humanity, for that matter."

My mentor squeezes me. "That's exactly why we have you here, my dear." He pauses. "By the way, did you get a chance to look at those bodies?"

"I did."

"And?" he asks.

"It's curious to say the least."

"That's one way to put it. Come, we received some information this morning you'll want to hear."

Bilgi shoulders his way into the command center and I follow on his heels into the warmth of the busy control room full of squawking radio chatter and overworked intelligence officers recording static-smothered transmissions. There's a sense of urgency here, the air abuzz with hushed whispers and relayed scraps of intel.

"Kapka's radicals are at it again. Just last night after you went to sleep, a group of his fanatics attacked the market district here in Fiori. Fourteen were killed, thirty-seven injured before one of our scouting patrols, aided by a few of the Fiorian guard, engaged them. Every last one of the bastards died for their cause."

I shake my head. "We freed ourselves from the Gracile's oppression, only to stoke the hate between ourselves. Kapka must be stopped, Bilgi. We've allowed this to go on far too long."

"He'll be stopped. Yuri and a small team have made their way to Zopat on an intelligence-gathering mission. I've got almost everyone else working to determine Kapka's location. Everyone but Dervy."

Bilgi strides over to one of the dusty tables and motions to a hungry-looking man with gray skin and only one functioning eye. The dead one, clouded and useless, is fixed on us in an unnatural, unmoving gaze.

"G'marnin' Bilgi," the man says in a musical accent. "Cun'aye dew far yah?"

"Mila, this is Dervy. He's one of our better radio operators." Bilgi pats him on the shoulder.

"Hello." How is this man, with his almost incomprehensible speech, one of our best radio operators? "I don't think we've met before."

The man snorts. "Dat's a cousin I ain't been round hair fer dat long."

Bilgi turns to me. "He means he was one of our best scouts until he lost his right eye. He asked for a transfer here to command to take a break from the danger. Right, Dervy?"

"Datsa roit, Bilgi. Meh body ain't whart it yeuse-da be. Tho I khan meek dew, when a purdy lady's aboot." He winks at me with his good eye.

A wave of disgust crawls across my skin. I have no idea where on earth this crusty old skirt-sniffer is from, or has been, for that matter. "Bilgi, can we get to the message already?"

Bilgi taps the table in front of the man. "Let's not be so eager to lose your other eye, my friend."

The skinny man grunts and flashes me another look, this one appraising me with caution.

"Tell us about the transmission you received from scouting party four this morning." Bilgi pushes a hand-scrawled note on the table toward him.

"Yah." The man casts one last shifty glance at me before turning to his notes. "Roit, so thissun came in earleh this marnin'."

Bilgi takes a breath, then smirks at me. "Dervy, do you mind if I read it for Mila? Just to avoid any confusion."

"By awl means, Bilgi," Dervy drawls, handing the note to him.

Bilgi clears his throat and holds up the note. In response, the room seems to quiet, the hustle and bustle slowing in anticipation.

"Go on," I urge.

"Scouting party four. Day six, third transmission: Logos was raided during the night."

"Logos," I whisper, dread welling in my chest. "What was raided?"

"Doesn't say. Just says: Numerous dead. Bodies found dismembered in the snow. Ripper attack possible. End transmission."

"Bilgi …" I mumble through fingers pressed to my lips.

"Yes, sounds familiar, doesn't it?"

"I want to check it out. See if it's connected to what happened here."

"I was hoping so," Bilgi says as I wheel for the door. "Mila," Bilgi calls after me, stopping me as my hands touch the cold hinged steel. "Take someone with you. I don't like the idea of you out there all alone."

"I'm not alone," I say, touching the starchy photograph in my front pocket. "I'm a lot of things, Bilgi, but never that."

* * *

After a short walk, the silence of my bunkroom greets me. I stop at my cot, grab my PED, bundle of writings, and a few other basic necessities. Kneeling, I pull the old sack from beneath my bag and tease the opening apart. Inside, the contents reek of leather bindings and ancient paper. I pull the old tome from the sack and study it, my fingers tracing the flaking gold leaf lettering on the spine. The Holy Writ of Yeos. A gift from Demitri. An original copy of my people's holy book—maybe the *last* copy. I've spent the last four years memorizing its every word, willing myself to understand the path of the Lightbringer. I pinch my eyes shut, utter a few sacred words, and tuck it into my satchel, taking great care to see it's positioned in a safe manner. It's time for me to return it to where it belongs, though it feels a little like giving up hope on my Gracile friend.

Slinging my shoulder bag, I exit the bunk and catch a glimpse of Husniya and Ghofaun stepping into the dim hallway from the training area. "Get your stuff, guys. Let's go."

"Sorry, Mila. Bilgi has another mission for me," Ghofaun says.

"Of course," I reply. "Are you at liberty to say?"

"Not at this time, Mila. It has something to do with your stimmed Gracile in Kahanga."

"I understand. Safe travels, Master Ghofaun."

"You two be careful," the monk says, bowing to me and Husniya.

"Where are we going?" Husniya asks, turning to me.

I pull a heavy jacket off the wall and push it into her arms. "You wanted to do something about the attacks? This is your chance."

CHAPTER EIGHT

VEDMAK

The old woman can't keep up—or won't.

She drags her clumsy feet, each step slowing our return to the poisons lab—risking our lives and my plan. Even with Aeron and Merodach alongside us, it is not safe here in the Vapid. The Rippers have become bold; their search for food and weapons, desperate. Forced to band together against the newly arrived Graciles from above and Robusts who have spilled out from their broken enclaves, the Rippers constantly in-fight like the animals they are. The spoils of their raids often destroyed in a spat between clan chiefs.

The Alchemist crashes into the icy ground and lays there, unmoving. The cold wind snaps and bites at her thin body, like a ghostly pack of wolves.

"Get up, old woman. Your attempts to delay us will only result in more pain," Aeron says, raising his heavy boot to stomp on her.

The fist of my stolen Gracile body catches him in the throat. He stumbles back, clutching at his neck, struggling to breathe.

"Fool. You think a decrepit fossil such as this would recover from a smashed hip? Use your head, stupid goat." I turn to the Alchemist and crouch to meet her gaze. "I may not break your bones here, but make no mistake, woman, I am capable of tortures that can last for days even on your wasted corpse."

Grasping her under the armpit, I pull her to her feet and sling her over one shoulder, before continuing the trek onward. It would be easier to use some of the vehicles I have restored over these short years, but the plan is too close to fruition. Can't risk wasting the fuel. So, we walk.

The wind howls as yet another storm closes in. With the lillipads fallen and the outer walls crumbled, there is little protection from Mother Russia's might. Ice-laden gusts push against this muscular shell. The sting of the cold is transferred from the perfect skin into my consciousness. It's a feeling long forgotten—physical pain. At least since the battle with the Ripper Chieftain at the launch pad some years ago. Before my Gracile demon's last stand.

Speaking of which, where are you, little puppet? You have been silent a long while.

I'm here, Vedmak. Where could I go? His voice is almost imperceptible.

There you are. It nearly felt lonely without your constant whining.

Lonely?

Who else can appreciate my greater plan? Who else understands the glory of being me? No one is as close, little Demitri. Our bond is special.

The Gracile doesn't respond immediately, but then says: *you need me?*

Do not be soft in the head, kozel.

Someone to understand. Someone to care about what you're doing. Otherwise, why do it? His voice has a renewed confidence.

Careful, peacock. Do not presume to abuse my good mood. I can still as easily pluck your feathers. Once more, and our pet will know pain like no other.

She's not your pet. She's a human being, and she deserves better.

Like you? You think she deserves you? Do not confuse a desperate whore's desire for escape for any kind of emotion, Demitri. She does not care for you.

It doesn't matter if she cares about me.

You forget, you cannot lie to me, little peacock. I can feel your pain. A hurt little puppy at the thought she is using you.

You're only frustrated because you can't get to her. Get to Mila. For all your power, your sarding army, her resistance is too strong.

Is that so? *Bez truda ne vytaschish y rybku iz pruda.*

Always talking in riddles. Without effort, you can't pull a fish out of the pond? What is that meant to mean, Vedmak?

Everything takes time. The plan is already in motion.

Plan? What plan? Something more than what you've been plotting?

Ah, naïve little Gracile. I was a master of deception long before your kind was grown in a glass egg.

I drop the old woman to the floor, rest a boot on her back, and pull back the sleeve of my heavy wool coat, revealing a taut, muscular forearm.

"Merodach, I wish to speak with the Rat."

What about Rippers? Do we have time for this?

To torture you? Always.

You can't even access the neural web down here. After the crash, the wireless chip in my brain was damaged. You have no range. You have to use a proxy, and that takes time.

All good things, Gracile.

My mute monstrosity lumbers over and kneels before me. His long hair parts between gloved fingers to reveal a cord. I pull on it slowly, allowing it to snake from the hole in the base of his skull. Then I grasp the end and force it through the skin in Demitri's naked arm and into the port.

Merodach twitches as our minds connect. In the recesses of the darkness, a voice—the former occupant of Merodach's shell—whimpers, but instantly fades away to nothing.

He is still in there ... in pain.

You should be concentrating not on Merodach's demon but on what comes next, Gracile. "Can you hear me, Rat?" I hiss.

There's a lasting silence until the image of a dimly lit underground cavern with rough rock-hewn walls illuminated by a few fire-lit torches comes into focus. As before, it is much like seeing the world displayed on one of the moving picture screens of old.

[Vardøger], a voice says. *[It's not a good time].*

Who is that? Who are you talking to? What am I seeing? Demitri asks.

"It is not for you to decide, Rat. You do as I command, or not only can you abandon all hope of ruling your pathetic band of misfits, but you can look forward only to evisceration at my hand."

[Yes, yes. My apologies, Vardøger], the voice replies.

I know that voice, Demitri says.

"Are things progressing?" I ask.

[Yes, of course. It's difficult, though. She has a loyal following. But I have a plan. Her attachment to Bilgi will be her downfall.]

Bilgi. You're talking about Mila?

[Who else is there?] the Rat says.

"None of your concern, Rat. Listen to me. Kahanga is lost. I have the Alchemist and the reactor. It's broken, but I will find a way. It won't be long now. It would be wise to be ready when the time comes."

[Of course. I will accel—]

[What are you doing out here?] a female voice says, the owner sliding in front of the eyes of my traitor.

You. There you are. She rests arrogantly on one leg, her hands on her hips, staring with those beady little eyes.

Mila! Sard it all, my demon cries.

She cannot hear you, peacock. You only serve to give our infiltrator a headache.

The window to the inside of Opor swirls as the Rat shakes his head, attempting to make sense of all the voices.

[You should be in the training room with everyone else,] Mila says.

The Rat brings his head up and once again her hardened eyes stare back at us. The pink scar cutting its path across her face. Her nose and ears full of metal. A streak of purple in her short hair. Disgusting. Not even remotely arousing.

The eyes of the Rat swivel left, his gaze falling on the slender form of a female with long dark hair and eyes like krig. She's younger than the frowning sow next to her, and there's something exotic about her. Not bad. Now this one I could make use of.

Husniya! Demitri squawks.

Ahh, the Musul girl you cared for—unnaturally so, I might add. But look at her now. Ready for my use. Can you imagine? How delicious, to see the betrayal on her face as the Gracile who cared for her now chooses to steal her innocence.

You're despicable, Vedmak, my demon cries. *That's a child you're talking about. Does your depravity know no end?*

Peacock, it runs deeper than you know. Now stop your endless braying.

[Well?] The disgusting sow asks again, prompting a response from the Rat.

[Yeah, I had to step out. I'm going back in now,] the Rat says. *[Sorry].*

Mila frowns. *[Sorry? You hit your head or something? When are you ever sorry, Giahi?]*

My demon's panic can almost be felt in the heart beating in this

Gracile chest. *Giahi. He's working with you?*

"Don't blow it, Rat," I say, ignoring Demitri.

My spy seems to gather his senses. *[Sard off, Mila. I said I'm going back in. Where are you two going all dressed up?"]*

[If I thought you should know, I'd have told you. Now go. You can use the training. You've gotten sloppy lately,] Mila fires back.

[Whatever you say, your majesty]. The view tips downward in a mocking bow and whirls one hundred and eighty degrees as Giahi opens a door and slips inside. Then, he whispers a single word before disconnecting: *[Soon].*

The images fade away and are once again replaced by the snow-covered landscape before me.

You have Giahi on the inside? How did I not know this? Mila has to get out of there. What are you going to do?

"I have been perfecting the Red Mist. Silencing you completely is almost possible. One of the many reasons I need the Alchemist."

Silence me?

Foolish boy, believing I need you.

A howl in the distance.

"Rippers," Aeron says, patting his brother on the shoulder. "Time for some fun, brother?"

Merodach grunts his approval.

"No." I scowl. "We move."

***

For several kilometers, the Rippers track us. Zopat only having one entrance on its south side means we have to trek the perimeter to make it to the lillipad. Our length of stride has kept us ahead until now. In shadows of the snowdrifts and outcroppings, they slink along our trail, gaining pace and closing distance. A fleeting glimpse as they dart between points of cover, but never seem brave enough to face us.

"They follow us still," Aeron says, throwing a glance over his shoulder.

"Keep moving. The snow is deep and we still have ground to cross before the Alchemist is secure," I say. "These weasels are too afraid to come straight at us, but they will steal her from us for the meat alone, if they are able. Isn't that right?" I shout to the swirling ice cloaking us in its frozen embrace.

The wind pulls at us, thrashing our tattered cloaks and cutting to the bone. The Alchemist groans, her frail body still hanging limply over my shoulder.

"The real horror is best left to those with the constitution to see it through. Don't you agree?" I shout again, raising a fist as we trudge along. "But not you, pathetic wretches. You lost your nerve ever since I took the head of your chieftain. So be a pack of good dogs and go along now. That, or make your play." My words disappear into the whipping of the growing storm. "See? What did I tell—"

The crack of a rifle is heard only an instant before the whining zip of flying lead buzzes past. I shrug the Alchemist from my shoulder, and she crumples to the ground with a grunt of pain. I drop low to the snow, eyes up, scanning. Aeron and Merodach follow suit.

Aeron groans. "I thought Rippers didn't use firearms?" There is a tinge of fear in his voice.

We are biological perfection, but a chunk of lead traveling at more than seven hundred meters per second still has the ability to rend each of us lifeless.

Get out of here. They're shooting at us! Demitri shouts, his shrill voice stoking the swarming feeling of total madness.

"I know that, fool. Just a single scavenged weapon. That was probably the only projectile they had anywa—"

Another crack echoes across the snow-swept landscape. A puff of crystalline powder pops from the ground between Merodach and my pilfered Gracile body, ice raining down and sliding into my collar. Sard. "Make for the lillipad. Do not stop for anything," I say, grabbing a fistful of the Alchemist's clothes and slinging the frail bag of bones over my shoulder again. In this powerful right fist, the unlit laser scythe stands ready.

Aeron and Merodach say nothing, rising and pulling their weapons from their thigh holsters.

"Run, but do not ignite. The glow of your weapons will make you easier to track in the storm."

With a grunt, Merodach shoves forward, carving a trench in the fresh powder with his heavy boots. Aeron and I follow, the Alchemist on my shoulder. Another rifle cracks, the zip of the projectile coming far too close.

Cowards. Come closer and see what fate has in store for you.

"Less than a half kilometer," Aeron shouts over his shoulder.

"Then get on with it," I say. "You both are supposed to be the pinnacle of human achievement. Show me something."

"Go, Merodach," Aeron says to his brother. "Let us show the Vardøger what we can do."

Merodach grunts, the grin on his face signaling his approval of the challenge ahead. With a movement built of sheer power, my titans blitz headfirst. I follow, forcing this body to its limit, these Gracile legs burning with the effort as they stab into the drifts.

Screams. They are coming for us.

Maybe there is war still in these pathetic savages. The Alchemist is all that matters. We do not need this fight right now. But I cannot help the grin that spreads across this face. Stop us if you can, urchins.

Something strikes Demitri's jaw with the impact of a war hammer. A perfect shot. I pitch forward, stumbling, the voice of my Gracile demon ringing in my ears. Demitri's body manages to right itself and struggles onward.

Another blunt impact strikes in the ribs and I spin around.

"Face me!" I scream.

A little masked gremlin covered in animal furs whoops and loads another rock in his sling as he tries to keep up. The rough projectile strikes me in the back with a spike of pain. Sarding primitives. I can't stop to engage him.

Aeron slows, the savages nearly upon us. "Vardøger …"

"I said stop for nothing. Form up and drive through them."

"Yes, Vardøger," Aeron says as he and Merodach step to the center a few meters ahead of me, creating an inverted wedge between the three of us.

"Let them feel your might," I order.

Aeron lets lose a savage battle cry as he and Merodach plow into the line of howling Rippers.

Another bullet whines past, passing with a sting through the flesh of Demitri's lower leg. This time I can see the shooter; a Ripper in a red mask with a painted skull covering his face, running away having taken the potshot.

My leg. They shot me! What are you doing? You're going to get me killed.

"I'll remember you, cave dweller," I bawl, the rage boiling over inside this body.

Ahead, at full stride, Merodach knocks three of them back with a swing of his unlit mace. A howling savage leaps at Aeron, but my titan grabs it and flings it back, knocking down a swath of its comrades. We power through their pitiful onslaught, leaving them to scramble after us like a pack of deranged children.

"Aeron, the tear is ahead. Cover me with a distraction," I call, these perfect lungs laboring for oxygen.

Reaching to his belt, Aeron spins off to the left, releasing a boomstick into the midst of our attackers. A deafening concussion echoes like the blast of a cannon across the hills, followed by the sustained strobing flash of its magnesium insert. The simple-minded kozels closest to the device fall prostrate in the deepening drifts. Others scramble over themselves, screaming of magic as they run for the hills.

I win. Again.

Merodach stomps off into the thickening wall of sleet that surrounds us, to find the fold in the cloaking material hanging over the entrance to the tunnel through the ice wall. A moment later, a sliver of light opens like a wound in the fabric of the atmosphere. Merodach's massive silhouette fills the fluorescent tear. I adjust the woman on my shoulder and power on, through the gap and into the safety of the tunnel. Merodach waits for his brother to clear it, then drops the material once again, concealing the entrance.

The slamming heart in this magnificent body slows as I shrug the Alchemist to the ground and slap the shoulder plates of each of my standards.

Nothing can stop me now.

CHAPTER NINE

MILA

The crunch of wet ice beneath the soles of our boots has a hypnotic effect, as one foot follows the other in a never-ending cycle. Head down, chin tucked, bodies hunched, we assume the position with which frozen beggars always seem so comfortable. The minutes drag on as we slog along the Vapid path in silence, our gazes flicking up from the icy road every so often to make sure we aren't being hunted.

I clear my throat and lift my chin from the warmth of the furry collar of my leather jacket. The words won't come. The cold wind burns. Just ask her, Mila. "Do you still have that voice? The one you used to talk to as a child?"

Husniya looks up.

"You know? You and Demitri had that in common. It was—"

"I know what you're talking about. No, I don't talk to her anymore." She adjusts the Mosin-Nagant bolt-action rifle hanging on her shoulder and lowers her gaze again.

"But, I saw you—"

"I said, I don't have a problem," Husniya snaps. "I grew out of that." She's lying.

"Tell me about *that* place," she says, deflecting.

In the distance, the high walls of the Vel enclave rise out of the ground like an alien fortress, dark and foreboding. Above the walls, a single column shoots straight up, penetrating the clouds and darkening the sky above. It supports one of the last remaining lillipads.

"That's Vel. It's always looked like that. Nobody knows what's inside."

"Nobody? Do the Velians come out at all?"

"Some do, but they're sworn to secrecy. Most of them became information brokers. They'd rather die than reveal their secrets. It became their primary source of income."

66

"Is that true? Do you know a Velian?" Husniya eyes me suspiciously.

"Yeah, actually, I do—or did." Gil. Whatever happened to you?

"There's a lillipad still standing in there. You think there's Graciles up there?"

"Maybe." I shrug. "Who knows?"

"How come Kapka didn't blow that one up? He brought down the ones not erected over Musul enclaves."

"The Velians fortified the enclave a long time ago. I imagine when everything went to hell, they locked the door and never opened it again." Only Yeos knows how they're surviving without trade.

"What do you think they're hiding in there? To bother fortifying it in the first place, I mean," Husniya says as we round the northern end of the dark enclave on our journey toward Logos.

"That's what everyone wants to know." I shove my hands deeper into the pockets of my jacket and watch hot breath lift away from my lips.

***

A good hour into our trek and we haven't uttered another word. As she grows older, the gap between us seems to widen. It's difficult to tell if it's due to her Musul heritage conflicting with my ways as a Logosian, or just the fact I have no idea how to handle a hormonal teenage girl.

A lone gunshot echoes across the Vapid. Husniya and I freeze, surveying the horizon. She looks at me with wide eyes.

"Let's go." I take off at a jog down the road.

"Wait," Husniya says, running to catch up. "We're running *toward* the sound of the gunfire."

"Yeah, Hus." My words come between drawn breaths. "That's what we do."

After reaching a bend in the road, we leave the path and ascend a short hill. Nearing the top, I move to my belly and crawl the rest of the way to the summit. It takes a moment for Husniya to reach my side.

Below, a group of pilgrims with their cart of belongings are lined up on the side of the road. They're on their knees, trying to control the sobs of the children. At the end of the row, one of them—a thin man with russet hair and plain clothes—lies face-down in the ditch, blood streaming from his head.

Surrounding the pilgrims, a group of Baqirans chant. Their faces are covered, and they're armed with long blades and a few assorted firearms. Kapka's radicals.

"Oh, merciful Yeos." I say, shrugging out of my extra gear and leaving it in the snow. For a moment I freeze, a breath captured in my chest. Is *he* there? My eyes desperately search the faces of the kneeling pilgrims, then those of the men forced into Kapka's service. No, Faruq is not among them. I'm not sure whether to feel injured or relieved.

"What are you doing?" Husniya asks.

I shake my head. "How many shots do you have for your rifle?"

"I, uh ..." The girl licks her lips.

"How many shots?"

She feels her pocket. "Four, I think."

"Have them ready and get a good stable position like I showed you."

"What are you going to do?" There's dread in her voice.

Already sliding down the hill toward the road, I whisper back, "Just be ready."

Upon reaching the road, I crouch and crawl between the low hills. Concealment is my ally here. As I move as swiftly as possible between the low barren scrub, the chanting grows louder. At the edge of the hill, I pause, raising myself up enough to get an eyeful. Fifteen meters of open ground stands between us. Gotta close the distance. Crawling low off the left side of the road, I can only hope they're not paying attention.

The men point to a sobbing woman who kneels next to the dead man.

"What about you? Do you worship Ilah?" A Baqirian jabs a knife at her.

"Yes." The woman shudders.

"Then you should be in the service of Kapka. What are you doing out here?"

She doesn't answer.

"You will come with us." They snatch the woman by the arm, dragging her to the side. The knifeman points to another woman holding a bundled child.

"What about you? Are you Baqirian or Alyan? Show us your brand."

The woman proudly lifts her head, her bottom lip quivering. "I am Fiorian."

The men converge on her, pull the baby from her arms and grab her by the hair. She screams and my blood turns to ice. Blood sprays from the woman's neck as they cut her. The baby squalls. It too is silenced with a cruel stab of the knife. The victims are pitched like trash into the ditch on top of the man.

"Are you a follower of the Great Ilah?" one of the attackers says to the next pilgrim, aiming the bloodied knife at him.

The man shakes his head. "We're just traders. Traveling together for safety. We've done nothing to you."

The radical steps forward, blade poised.

My body coils like a spring and I shove off, a scream of fury upon my lips. The criminals turn, their eyes wide with surprise. One of their gunmen sees me, raising his weapon to fire as I zig and zag toward their position.

The crack of a rifle.

I instinctively flinch and grab my chest. But a plume of blood rises from his head and he drops his weapon against the crimson-painted ice at his feet.

Husniya.

A second gunman steps forward, charging the action of the Kalashnikov in his hands. He aims not at me, but at the wailing travelers.

"No," I scream, my legs burning beneath a heart full of reckless abandon.

The weapon barks, stitching bloody holes across the backs of the travelers. They tumble forward into a jumbled pile in the ditch, still, like discarded dolls.

I collide with the first man, torque the knife from his grasp and bury the blade in his heart. The man with the Kalashnikov turns on me, the weapon burping fire. I dive, rolling at an angle as he tracks me. A bullet whistles past the gunman's ear and he flops against the ground, scanning the hills for the sniper he can't see.

Stay low, Husniya.

Another crack of her rifle. Another knife-wielding thug goes down off to my left. I rise and sprint toward the next gunman. He draws himself up to a knee, but I intercept the weapon at the muzzle. The hot steel sears through my glove and into my palm as I force the barrel up and drive it against the bridge of his nose with a wet smack. I twist the weapon from his grasp and clench the trigger. Fire blazes from the barrel. A stream of bullets thump against meat and bone until the weapon runs dry and silence reigns.

Ears ringing, I struggle to catch my breath. My lips peeled back in a snarl, I throw the empty weapon against the frozen turf with a curse.

"*Sard it all.* So much death—for what?" When did you become such an efficient killer, Mila? I turn my blood-splattered face toward the gray, snow-laden heavens above. Was this right? Will Yeos forgive me? A single guilty tear streaks down my cheek and off my chin.

Husniya approaches. I wipe my face.

"Mila!"

"I'm okay."

The girl runs up, and the Moisin-Nagant clacks against the ground. "No, stop saying that, you don't understand me," she mumbles grabbing her face.

"What are you talking about?" I ask. Is she speaking to her voice?

Husniya continues to mumble, ignoring my question. "These men are Musuls. They look like my brother. I didn't want to kill them, but I had to." She cringes at one of the dead men, his head opened like a ripened melon.

"Husniya, they were murdering innocent travelers." I take a deep breath. My hatred for their kind spills over to her. It shouldn't. Talk to her, Mila. Find the words. "We killed them, the same as we would a pack of Rippers or a Kahangan war party. It doesn't matter where they come from."

"So, we have to kill people to try and stop them from killing people?"

"Sometimes."

"But we didn't stop it, Mila. We made it worse."

I turn from the piles of bodies. "I don't believe that. These travelers were slaughtered for their beliefs and we killed their murderers for acting like animals. Ignoring it wouldn't have saved them. We did the best we could."

"These Musuls …" Husniya clutches her hands to her chest. "I don't understand this. I can't be like them. I refuse to be ..."

"Just like your brother, Faruq." I wrestle the words and squeeze her shoulder. "And Mos and every other Musul who refuses to bend to Kapka and his thugs."

Stepping toward the ditch, I pull off my burned glove and use the fresh snow to cool my blistered hand. Then, on the breeze, a faint whimper. It's coming from the ditch. Scrambling over on all fours down the embankment covered in gore-drenched snow, I find a petrified child, wounded, but alive, half-buried by the lifeless corpses of her family. She's in shock.

I don't have to call for Husniya. She's already pulling the child from the trough and applying a compress to the bullet wound in her shoulder.

"You stay with her," I say, standing and doing my best to compose myself. "I'll do a quick sweep of the dead and see if there's anything of value to us."

The child looks up at us, eyes wide, mouth opening and closing, but no words come.

"She's going to live," Husniya replies, looking up at me. "I can stop the bleeding. It's not a vital hit."

"Wrap it and get her ready to move," I say, standing and scanning the numerous corpses of friend and foe alike. "This will have attracted the attention of other scavengers, and we don't want to be here when they arrive."

CHAPTER TEN

VEDMAK

State your floor, the computer says.

"Ten," I say.

I'm sorry, please repeat, the mechanical voice replies.

The damn mask. "Ten!"

Thank you, the computer answers.

The elevator ascends. Inside the cramped box, the twins' breathing is loud and labored. They will need to replenish their stim soon. I shift weight off the injured appendage. An oozing wound. Not immobilized, but I'll have to dig out any remaining bullet fragments if it will ever heal. Sarding animals are using firearms now. That changes the game.

The old woman squirms on my shoulder, so I lock her into place. Seconds later, the sleek doors slip open again. We step out onto the gangway and into the corridor, marching forward until the lab stands before us. A press of a thumb to the scanner and we're granted access.

It's dark inside, save the faint light emanating from each of the glass eggs, suspended in the air, illuminating the path to the other end. Inside these artificial wombs, my creations float in their nutritious fluid. The EYE passes overhead, scanning the fetuses as it goes. Satisfied there are no anomalies, it disappears into the dark again. Just as with Demitri, it has no idea what secrets these fleshy forms hold.

I dump the old woman on the floor.

She gazes, wide-eyed, at the rows upon rows of immature Graciles in various stages of development. "You are farming Graciles?" she asks, a frown creased into her aged forehead.

"The pathetic weak-minded sheep brought to life by the Leader were not worthy to own such biological machines. I'm giving divine souls a second chance in a new body—a Gracile body."

The old woman stares, confused. "Growing an army?"

Divine? interrupts Demitri. *They're not divine. You're only keeping those*

72

souls who were killers, rapists, and sadists. Every one that isn't, you murder the host.

And so, the process is slow. Too few valuable souls, kozel. Too few, and none like me.

You don't want them like you. If they were, you couldn't control them.

"Hence the Alchemist," I say aloud.

The fear in her eyes is palpable. "But it would take years to grow them to adulthood," she says.

I grab her by her thin arm and drag her to her feet. "Shall we go?"

We continue past the glass wombs until we reach the poisons lab. In one corner of the stark white room is a desk littered with conical flasks, beakers, and makeshift distillation apparatus. Red liquid-filled vials are stacked on a nearby shelf. The three-dimensional image of a chemical compound spins on the only monitor. In the other corner sits a table covered in a white cloth stained pink and red and encrusted with dried blood. Various tools and glass plates are scattered across it. A single microscope and incubator are placed at the farthest end.

But the lab is missing one thing. "Where the hell is Sergei?"

"I'm here, Vardøger. Sorry, I'm here." The hunched-over Gracile enters through the sliding doors, limps back to his desk, pulls on two fresh gloves and resumes his work.

"Alchemist, meet Sergei. You'll be working closely together. Tell her what you're doing, Sergei."

The Gracile turns his head but refuses to make eye-contact with me. He twitches and refocuses on the Robust woman at my feet. "Immunosurgery," he says. "I'm removing stem cells from embryos to be implanted in the brain of adult Graciles. We thought it was only a protein that allowed connection to the other place, but it's a micro-area of the brain. Like an organ. *In vivo* gene editing didn't work. The whole cellular structure has to be there. I have to separate the cells from the embryos, using antibodies and mechanical dissection—"

"Stop flapping your lips. She doesn't need to know the details, imbecile," I hiss before turning to the Alchemist. "He takes the best bit of the embryo brain and puts it in the head of an adult Gracile."

You're growing clones of me, only to murder them.

Not all of them, Demitri, my boy.

You're a monster.

Ignoring Demitri, I continue talking to the Alchemist. "We filter out those Graciles with connections to souls—*dushi*—of which I approve. You create the stim to ensure those souls stay in control of the body. Understand?"

"That's why we don't see them anymore, the Graciles. You have them." the old woman says, her eyes wide.

They had no idea how to survive in Lower Etyom. You tricked them here with promises of safety.

"Yes, I have them." I huff out a laugh. "They are the beginnings of my *Einherjar*—those who have died in battle and have been waiting for the right time, the end days."

"Why?" the Alchemist asks. "Why do you need an army? To fight Opor? But then what? What about the other enclaves? The Rippers? You don't have enough Graciles."

"The captured Graciles suffice as a militia until my army has grown. Sacrificing some of the embryos for their stem cells is worth it to have an immediate force. Besides, accelerated growth of the embryos shortens the time to adulthood significantly. It will not be so long before I have my legion."

"Do you think this old mind frail and feeble?" the woman asks. "I saw the room of embryos. You have a few hundred at best. Not nearly enough to conquer Etyom."

Not to mention the fact half the souls you pull across aren't evil enough.

"Do not mock me, old woman. You think I have not thought of such things? I have the capacity to grow many more, I just need more power. Then, I can grow thousands."

You know what will happen if you do. The embryos you're creating are already attached to demons. If you pull too many through at once—

Be silent, puppet.

"What if I not help you?" the Robust woman says, folding her arms defiantly.

A curt nod and Merodach drags her to her feet and, with her in tow, storms from the poisons lab.

"Wait, wait," the little woman cries, her feet dragging on the floor. "I never said I not help. I just ask—"

"He won't answer," I call after her. "Poor Merodach is the result of my earliest trials. Implantation of the stem cells left him mute. His frustration at not being able to speak vents through unbridled violence. An exquisite side effect."

***

Past the glass eggs, across the gangway and into the lift. We descend to the lowest level of the pistil and exit through the north-facing airlock. The pressure door pops open to reveal a cobbled-together structure covering a cavernous hole into the lillipad platform. A ramshackle staircase leads down into the dark, past the concrete of the lillipad and into the frozen ground beneath.

I lead the way, Merodach still dragging the Alchemist and following close behind.

We drive farther down beneath the permafrost and into a tunnel dug by my own hand—at least until I had slaves to do it for me. The walls are wet with frozen water, glistening in the light of a few burning torches. We push through a heavy, iron-banded door and into a large cavern with three alcoves enclosed in thick bars.

The torches illuminate little, and my mask only attenuates what light is left, so I slide it off and throw it to the floor at the feet of the Alchemist, who now kneels wide-eyed at the scene before us. In one alcove, the Gracile children I have grown to maturity stalk about the cage, foaming or drooling from the mouth. Though only two years in age, accelerated growth means they are physically closer to ten. Yet their minds never seem to keep pace and so they remain intellectual infants, defecating where they stand and unable to communicate. It matters not. They do not need to speak. To have little control of their bodies is advantageous—there is no fighting my brethren for the shell.

They all look like me, Demitri says.

Of course they do—they are your clones.

I step forward to admire my young Gracile army. One of the clones bumps into another. He lashes out, tearing out the throat of the boy with whom he collided. Blood sprays across the floor and the defeated Gracile slumps to the floor like a sack of rotten vegetables. I can only cackle in glee.

"You'll have no army if they kill each other," the old woman says.

I turn to face her. "Your stim will fix that. The *dushi* need to be in control of the body, but I only need to control the dushi. Understand?"

The woman says nothing.

Whimpering draws our attention to the middle alcove, some two hundred feet in length and fifty feet deep. Here, the adult Graciles I have collected sit, pathetic and scared, waiting to be bonded with a soul. Unmoving and catatonic like caged cattle, they stare into space, all hope drained from their eyes. Like all good heifers, they cluster at one end of their prison, as far from the third enclosure—full of sleeping Rippers—as they can be.

Another door to the far-right swings open and three of my *Einherjar*—Heimdall, Balder, and Dagr—power in dragging with them a fresh catch of Robusts. Two men and a woman.

Oh, Yeos, not again. You have to stop this.

You're such a child, Demitri. Why would I stop it?

The muscles of my stolen body tingle again.

"What will you do with them?" the Alchemist asks, her eyes glassy with fear.

"All dogs must eat."

You drive them to this, the Rippers. Starve them for weeks then feed them a person. You—

Yes, yes. A monster. Perhaps I should feed your sweetheart to them?

Heimdall jangles a set of keys in the lock of the cage to the Rippers. Inside, they stir from their slumber. The Graciles in the neighboring prison, though unable to see, know what will happen. They cling to one another, sobbing quietly. The first Robust male is lifted by his garments and tossed screaming inside.

The Rippers howl and shriek and within mere seconds, the Robust man is torn to pieces, no more than a blood-stained smear on the rocky ground, chunks of flesh hanging from the mouths of those nearest to the door, while others go hungry.

What would she say if she could see what you have become. This is beyond even your evil. She would never condone this. She'd hate you.

Silence, peacock.

You know I'm right. She'd detest you.

The piercing pain in the mind I occupy is intense. White hot and so very sharp. Over and over, it stabs at the back of the Gracile eyes through which I see. I screw them shut to block out the torture, but drop to the ground, panting. The pain spreads through this biological machine, tightening the stomach.

The room spins and the blurred figures seem to divide into two or three. Then everything snaps into focus. Like a circuit breaker, the world is alive with color. Vivid and clean.

And then she stands before me, chestnut hair neatly gathered together under her favorite hat. The same overcoat she always wore, the one with the broach. Her eyes bore into me, full of pain and disappointment.

Ida. No …

It's her. It's Ida. Am I doing this? Demitri says.

A single trickle of red slides down her perfect porcelain nose, across her pointed chin, and drips onto her polished shoes. The bullet wound in her forehead slowly opens like some wormhole to the past, the glint of the bone and brain within.

"Arggh! Enough of this." I shake away the hallucination and return to the dim light of the cavern. "Throw the next one in," I command, standing once again.

Heimdall does as ordered.

More raucous howling ensues, followed by a blood-curdling scream.

Damn you, Vedmak.

I'm already damned, little peacock. You of all people should know this.

"Please stop, stop it," the Alchemist begs.

Crouching down, I meet her terrified gaze. She searches Demitri's eyes.

"Who are you?" she asks. "Where is the young Gracile I met?"

The lips of this face curl. "You should be worried more for your own life, Alchemist. You will help me or you will become the next meal for my dogs."

Her gaze darts from the cage and back to me.

"You need another reminder?" I turn to Heimdall. "Throw the last one in."

"No! Okay, I'll help." She sobs into her hands.

"Good," I say. "Well, Heimdall?"

My *Einherjar* soldier grabs the last Robust man by the throat. "In you go."

Protests spill from the whelp's lips like water from a faucet. He kicks and screams and cries. His girlish shrieks pierce these enhanced eardrums. "No, please. I can help you, I can be of use. I know things. Important things!" he says, in between wails.

"Wait," I hiss, stalking toward the now-still man. "What *things* could you possibly know that would help me?"

"If I tell you, you let me live, yes?" he whimpers.

"If you tell me, you may not die today."

He seems to consider this before speaking. "There's something in Vel. Something that would give whoever possessed it the greatest power in Etyom."

I study his piggy, fearful eyes. "If it is in Vel, why do the rodents who reside there not wield this power?"

"The Velians are secret keepers."

"What secrets?" I press.

"The rumor they have a nuclear stockpile. Weapons. Left over from the Soviets of old."

You can't use nuclear weapons to destroy Opor. You'd kill everything inside Etyom and contaminate the area for a hundred years. This is insane.

Perhaps this is a good idea, no? Kill everyone?

You don't want that. You've worked too hard to stay in this dimension.

Perhaps, little peacock. "What good are weapons of such destruction? It would only serve to kill us all."

"But," the man stutters, clearly wracking his brain for a better answer. "You don't want others to have them, right? The Musuls. Or Opor? They could be used to generate power, to fuel ships and lillipads or whatever else you need."

Power? Fuel for the Fallen Creed gunships. Power for the lab, more Gracile embryos … More souls. Peacock, is this possible?

There is no response.

Demitri, can it be done? Do not test my resolve or the frailty of your Anastasia.

Maybe, he says. *In the latter half of the twentieth century, there was a movement to disarm nuclear weapons and use the material for fuel. The main weapons material was highly enriched uranium. It can be blended down and refined to produce low-enriched uranium fuel for power react—*

Can it be done? Yes or no? Don't waste my time, *kozel.*

Yes, in theory. But I've told you before, what you will cause if you keep bringing souls across this quickly.

That, I can control. Do you know how to do this refining?

No.

He's a blithering fool and coward, but perhaps no amount of torturing the Robust hostage will convince him to do this. However, he is not the only sheep here. There are many more who fear for their pathetic lives.

"You. Graciles." I drag a gloved hand across the bars of the middle alcove, the metallic rattling ringing out. "Who wishes to live? Who can build me the means to refine weapons-grade uranium into fuel?"

They murmur among themselves.

"Come, now. Some of you are highly educated. You mean to tell me you all wish to die? Perhaps I shall feed all of you to your neighbors."

More snivels. Yet, there—a hand. And another. I motion to Aeron, who snatches the keys from Heimdall, unlocks the alcove and pushes through the huddled Graciles until he reaches the first raised hand. Aeron grabs the wrist, then surges further into the flock and grabs the second raised arm. With a grunt, he drags them both out into the cavern and dumps them to the ground. Two sets of wet, female, Gracile eyes stare up at me.

I can't even say I know them. Was I so isolated?

"Women? You believe you have the knowledge to help me?"

The first nods with fervor. "Yes, yes we can. I'm Nadezhda, and this is Alyona. We're engineers. It wouldn't be so difficult."

"If it is not so difficult, do I need you both?"

"Yes." the second blurts, shuffling closer to the first. "We worked in the same lab."

"We shall see, sheep. We shall see."

CHAPTER ELEVEN

MILA

Evening descends, the cold ever deepening. It's a foe that never seems to concede. The familiar numbing ache attacks the limbs first, but quickly penetrates the psyche leaving an icy resignation that steals any joy from life. I should be used to it now, after all these years. I'm not.

I lift my chin from the fur-lined collar of my jacket and flash the Logosian enclave brand on the back of my hand to the sentries standing guard at the enclave gate. They barely acknowledge it, but perhaps more surprising, say nothing to Husniya. Do they recognize me and know I wouldn't bring a radical in, or do they simply no longer care? No wonder Logos is having problems with attacks by outsiders.

We pass through the brass-crested gate and into the cluttered streets beyond. The ramshackle, stone and rusted sheet metal favelas of my home enclave lay ahead. People shuffle to and fro with a distinct familiarity, yet there is a weariness I don't remember. How long have I neglected my home?

"Oh." Husniya pinches her nose. "What is that?"

The smell of spices and the smoke of sizzling chiori fills the cold air. My mouth waters. "Chiori with Logosian spices."

"No, that *awful* smell." She shakes her head.

"Oh, the fires," I say without turning.

"Wood fires don't smell like that." Husniya grimaces and covers her face.

"I know. The fires are the only true way to sterilize the infected dead." Husniya moans in disgust.

We shuffle past the old street where Clief's bar used to be, the place where I'd held my friend for the last time. My people have done a good job of rebuilding in the wake of the Creed's attack on Logos, but it still hurts deep down to know I was the cause of such ruin; that because of me, a good friend and countless others died when the Gracile's robotic puppets came to end me. My chin drops back into my collar which is still moist with the steam of my breath. Freedom from the Gracile Leader came at a great cost.

Ahead, up several winding flights of steps carved into the rock of Zhokov mountain, lies my reason for coming here at all: The Covenant of The Holy Vestals of the Word. We climb slowly. The sling bag with the ancient tome inside is snug against my back—the heavy binding presses into my spine through the thick lining of the jacket. This slight pressure feels almost symbolic—the weight of my beliefs.

We reach the top of the staircase, huffing and wheezing in the cold. Against my chest, the injured child lies limp, passed out from the pain. Her bleeding has slowed but she will need the Vestal's intervention if she is to retain the use of her arm. Husniya pulls on the two large metal rings of the covenant doors. They don't budge. She leans back and, with considerable effort, drags open a small gap. I'm not even through the threshold before I'm approached by two young women wearing the signature crimson and cream-colored robes typical of their order.

"Sister Vestal," I call out. "I have an injured child here. Her family was murdered along the Vapid road. Please help us."

"Of course, dear, give her to me," the Vestal says, wrapping the child in a wool blanket and passing her off to the attendant behind her. She turns back to me, craning her neck to see over my shoulder. "Will your friend come in?"

Husniya is still hovering outside the threshold.

"What's wrong, Hus? Come in out of the cold."

"I'm, ah," The girl looks around then down at the snow at her feet. "I don't feel like I should."

"Come in," I say, trying to keep my voice neutral. "The temperature is dropping. You can't stay out there all night."

The Vestal steps beside me with her arms outstretched. "Come in from the cold, child. Every son and daughter of Yeos is welcome here, no matter their beliefs."

Husniya hesitates still. Though never as religious as Faruq, she holds to her faith in Ilah.

"Please," the Vestal says. "We would love to have you with us, even for a short while. I have a blanket and a hot cup of soup for each of you."

The mention of hot soup does it. Husniya slips through the gap, pulling the door shut behind her with a hollow clang.

"Okay, but I'll just stay here in the entrance if it's all the same to you," Husniya says.

"Oh, yes, child. Yes, that's fine." The Vestal drapes a wool blanket over her shoulders. "Whatever makes you comfortable." She gestures to a bench. "You can sit here while you wait for your soup."

A blanket slides over my shoulders followed by the strong hands of the sister Vestal, who begins to rub the chill from me.

"Thank you, sister."

"Oh no, thank you, Mila," she says with genuine warmth. "It is so good to have you with us again."

"Yes." She knows my name? "It's good to return."

"Will you come with me? We'll take good care of your friends."

"Okay, thank you," I say and give one last glance at Husniya, who now sits on the floor cocooned in her blanket.

I follow the young Vestal down the curving candlelit stairs lined with pale sculptures meticulously cut by hand from the living stone. As we walk together, the sculptures are replaced by tapestries, relics, and tributes. Some are items from the old world so rare and valuable, it would be impossible to calculate their worth—much like the tome in my bag. It may well be the greatest treasure I have ever possessed. A gift from Yeos via Demitri. And now I must find a way to let it go.

We exit the stairs, pass through the arched hallways of the catacombs, and meander to the simple underground chapel. It's beautifully adorned with flickering candles, hanging cloths of the deepest crimson, marble effigies, and elaborate frescos. Here the air is warmer, the musk of incense and mountain herbs a pleasant bouquet that lifts my spirits. Extending my index and middle fingers, I touch the founder's stone, then my bowed forehead. The plea for mercy spills out, a prayer rehearsed and recited thousands of times before.

It was here, some four years ago, the Mother Vestal cared for me and shared with me her wisdom and strength. A moment that helped me to carry on. "*You were fashioned with love by your creator to do one thing,*" she'd said. "*You have a destiny even you do not yet fully understand. No matter how dark the path, you are destined to carry the message of the light.*"

At that time, I'd thought I had lost everything. Little did I know I would lose much more.

The sister Vestal directs me to a padded bench where I sit and am given a hot mug of broth by another attendant.

"Thank you." The delicious warmth seeps into my fingers and I cautiously take a sip from the steaming mug.

"You are most welcome, Mila." The Vestal smiles. "My name is Katerina. What brings you and your friends to us today?"

"Several errands, one in particular, which is long overdue." I swallow another large sip of the herbal soup then set the mug aside.

Might as well get this over with.

I pull the bag open. My heart beats faster in my chest. The longing to cling to something that is not, and never was, mine alone grows stronger.

Sister Katerina waits patiently, her hands clasped in her lap.

My face tingles with heat. "I'm sorry. I didn't intend to make such an ordeal of this," I swallow and continue opening the bag. "This is difficult for me."

In one swift movement, I pull the heavy tome from the bag and rest it in my lap.

Sister Katerina's eyes grow wide, and her hands fly to her lips.

"That can't be what I think it is."

"It is."

"Sisters." The Vestal calls at the top of her lungs, her voice high and shrill. The outburst catches me off guard. It takes a moment, but the rapid shuffling of feet greets my ears as women dressed in flowing crimson and cream round the corner and pour into the chapel.

"May I?" the sister says, turning back to me with wonder in her eyes.

"Of course, Sister Katerina."

She receives the tome tenderly, the way one accepts a baby into their arms, and turns it so she can marvel at the ancient leather bindings and flaking gold lettering. The others gather in hushed whispers of praise. The sister Vestal opens the cover and appears to wonder at the faded handwritten script inside, stroking the page with reverence.

"I came into possession of this some time ago," I say, unable to divulge it's been four years since Demitri gave me the Writ. "I knew it had to come here, especially since it might be the last one. I meant to do it before now—I couldn't bring myself to let it go. It was selfish of me, I know."

"Dear." Sister Katerina's voice is gentle and without judgment. "Do not be hard on yourself," she says and pats me on the arm. "Which of us would have had the strength to let go of such a priceless treasure?"

"Thank you, sister."

The sister stands and holds the tome up for all to see, the room now full of the resilient ladies of this ancient order. "The Holy Writ has returned to us."

The small room echoes with cheers and the sound of applause and shouts of joy. She waits for the jubilation to subside before continuing.

"I know you are all as anxious as I to see more, and we will each have our turn to study the words of the Lightbringer, but for now, please return to your duties. Those who do not have pressing matters may sit and listen to Mila's tale."

Without protest, most of the graceful women file from the room with beautiful smiles, hugging one another and giggling.

There's a smile on my face too, a big one. I tell the sister my tale, sparing no detail. How the Writ had previously been held as part of a Gracile collection of old books. How Demitri had brought it to me as a gift before we together took on the Gracile leader with hopes of saving Etyom, and how it had stayed safely with me since. The Vestals listen, awestruck, hanging on every word like children receiving a bedtime story.

One of the young women raises her hand.

The senior Vestal nods to her. "Yes, sister?"

"Miss Mila, would you say the Holy Writ empowered you through the dangers you faced?"

I consider the earnest question of the girl who looks so young in the flickering light of this place. It's easy to forget some of these young ladies took their vows of service at a young age and have seen little of the terrors that lie in wait right outside the doors to their sanctuary.

"Well. It didn't give me inhuman power, if that's what you mean, but it did give me strength in my heart. To know one is not alone, even when the days grow dark. You can't put a price on that." My fingers graze the

85

frayed edges of the crumpled photo in my pocket.

The young vestal bobs her head vigorously.

Why do my own words feel hollow? Have I strayed so far from the path? Why does Yeos no longer speak to me, in dreams or otherwise? I try to stand for the weak and oppressed, to search for Demitri and Faruq. Yet these days I can't help but feel so distant from the Lightbringer.

"And um," another Vestal starts, only raising her hand when the Vestal Katerina shoots her a scolding glance. "The Gracile man, was he as handsome as the stories tell?"

"Sister Eugenia," Katerina admonishes. "That will be enough of that."

The young Vestal blushes.

"I don't begrudge your curiosity." I wink. "He was handsome, perfect in appearance some might say, but he was also troubled. A demon was at war with his better nature."

"What happened?" the girl blurts, not even bothering to raise her hand this time.

"His demon stole him from me." I turn my gaze down. "I tried to find him, to help him overcome it, but he was gone."

"Is the will of Yeos to help Graciles, too?" another young Vestal asks.

"He was my friend. In the end, that's all that matters."

The chapel grows quiet, the flickering candles throwing dancing shadows on the walls.

Sister Katerina clears her throat. "I think it's time you all return to your duties. I will see to our guest."

The young women acknowledge their senior and leave the small room with grace.

Sister Katerina moves to the floor, pulls a basin from under the bench and fills it with crystal clear water from a nearby ceramic jug. I protest, but know full well it will do no good. The washing of a weary traveler's hands, feet, and wounds is a servant-hearted practice the Vestals have engaged in for as long as their order has existed.

In an instant, the weariness of my trials slips away as the sister's sponge strokes from my calf down to my toes in a cleansing process as much for the soul as it is for the body. A few quiet moments pass. I take a deep breath of the scented air through my nose. But this is not why I came.

"Sister?"

"Yes?"

"I am also here on an errand to investigate the attacks in Logos last night. Do you know anything of this?"

The Vestal does not raise her eyes. "I know several Logosians were murdered, but not by fanatics. Their bodies were dismembered. At first, people said it was a Ripper attack, but I have seen the results of such an end and this was not that."

"Then what?"

She shrugs. "I gave the final blessing over the remains. The wounds were clean, the flesh cauterized as though by fire. It was unusual. And we did not find everyone. Some must have been taken."

"We experienced something similar in Fiori. People dismembered in an almost surgical fashion. I'm struggling to understand who or what could have done this."

"Some mysteries are not so easily answered." Katerina sighs. "Be careful how hard you pull on such a thread, Mila. The perpetrator of this ugliness is not to be taken lightly."

"Of course, thank you, sister." We sit for another moment in silence. "When I came here last, I had the fortune to speak with the Mother Vestal. Is she here?"

Katerina hesitates. "Our good mother passed from us into the arms of our creator almost two years ago."

"Oh." My heart aches at my ignorance of her passing. "She was so good to me at a time when I needed it."

The Sister Vestal smiles. "That was her way and how she shall be remembered."

"And who is the mother now?"

Another small sigh from Sister Katerina. "None has taken on this great responsibility as of yet, but I fear it will soon be mine to bear since I am senior."

I touch her arm. "You are well suited for it."

She bows her head but says nothing. Several moments pass in silence, and I inhale deeply the fragrant aroma of spiced incense.

"May I ask you something about the end of days as spoken of in the

Writ?"

The good Sister dries my feet with a clean cloth. "Of course. I will try to be of assistance."

"Well, uh." Come on Mila. You can tell her. "I have dreams. Terrible, prophetic dreams that come true."

The sister gives a dip of her head but doesn't seem surprised.

"Years ago when I was a child, I dreamt of the New Black Death ravaging the people of Etyom. Not long after we had the worst outbreak we'd ever seen, at least until now. My father was lost to it."

"A pestilence," the sister says. "The plague."

"Yes, exactly. Then years later, Kapka rose to power over the Musul nation and my visions turned to war. With the Gracile taking most of the resources, we were forced to fight for what scraps remained."

"War and famine. It is the four horsemen you dreamt of," she says.

"Yes," I whisper.

The sister begins cleansing my hands and face with the sponge. "And now, you dream of Death?"

My throat seizes. "I did, though the dreams have stopped."

"And what causes such fear of Death? Your faith in the Lightbringer ensures you eternal life in heaven, does it not?"

"Yes, sister. It does. But my faith in the unseen sometimes wavers when it shouldn't. I fear this final horseman the most, because ... I know him."

The sister is quiet, now stroking my face with the cool sponge.

"Remember the demon I mentioned? The one who stole my friend from me?"

"And you believe this demon will usher in the end days?"

"Yes." My voice is but a whisper. "He is planning something terrible. I can feel it. I don't know when, but he is coming and when he does, he will watch this world burn. How is it possible to defeat such evil? Must I sacrifice my friend to save everyone else?"

The sister's face softens. "With love." Sister Katerina sets down her sponge and holds my face in both hands. "You carry the weight of the world on your shoulders, dear Mila. Remember the saints? Remember the prophets, and the martyrs who came before you? Did they carry their burdens in despair? No, they did not. They knew the weight and instead of continuing on with their chests out, they humbled themselves choosing a life of service. They understood it was not about them, but about the giving of themselves so others may find the light. That is called sacrifice."

Her words ring true but are quickly clouded by my own faithlessness. I fear my path has strayed so far even Yeos cannot see me.

"There is one way to endure the path of the Lightbringer," she continues. "Every step, every single act must be one of love. Not pride, nor strength, nor self-righteousness. Love and faithfulness are the only weapons that will defeat such evil."

How am I to fight the harbinger of death with love? Fight Vedmak with love? From what Demitri told of him, he is a wicked creature, incapable of remorse. And even if I do succeed, what will become of my Gracile friend? Unable to find the right words, I simply bow my head.

Sister Katerina touches my shoulder and I meet her gaze. She knows the weight of my calling.

"We are not the Lightbringer, you and I. Our light is not perfect and untarnished. But we are called to reflect the light in times of darkness so others may feel its touch. Be a reflection of the truth you already know." She pats the heavy Writ. "The word came to you first for a reason, my sister."

Her calling me *sister* causes a readied tear to streak down my cheek. My heart hurts with self-loathing and regret. "If Yeos will lend me his strength to see it through, I will try, Sister Katerina."

The words taste bitter, and I hate myself just a little more for how easily the lie rolls off my tongue.

CHAPTER TWELVE

VEDMAK

The permanent night sky is obscured by the thick clouds laden with snow. No stars to guide us through the Vapid. The path ahead gradually fades into the rest of the powder-white landscape. But it matters not. Our prize is marked clearly in the distance by the tall stem of one of the last standing lillipads, protruding from within the walls of Vel.

Aeron and Merodach trudge through the knee-high drifts beside me, their fists holding tight to thick chains leashed to Rippers doped with Easy. The enslaved Vapid roamers sniff the ground and keep sharp eyes for potential attackers. A contingent of ten *Einherjar*, led by Heimdall, Balder, and Dagr bring up the rear, dragging a large wooden cart with an enclosed metal housing. Traveling with too many makes us a target—too few and we'd be slaughtered. We're unable to move as fast as we did when we were only four in number. A good thing there are no signs of any further Ripper activity, so far at least.

The leg feels stable if not fully recovered. A few moments of digging and Sergei was able to pull a shred of copper jacket from the wound. Disinfected and sealed shut with accelerant foam, it will not cause me further trouble, for now. Still, the cold bites through the thick clothing and into the skin of my host, while a slashing wind cuts against these tired muscles—as if Yahweh himself wished to prevent me from reaching my goal. But nothing will stop me. Not even the whining fool occupying this skull, constantly battling me for control.

Yet my sway over this biological engine is waning. Demitri's consciousness creeps in. Like a cancer, his soul penetrates, forcing aside my own. Until the Alchemist can perfect the stim, I must use other means to maintain control. The most effective being his affection for my pet. I yank on the chain and the beaten Robust woman crashes into the snow again.

"Keep up, *dear*. We cannot afford to loiter in this wasteland."

Leave her alone. She's tired, and hungry.

All who struggle should be hungry, peacock. It keeps the fire burning inside.

Just let her go, I won't fight you if you let her go.

"You think me a fool, Demitri?" I say aloud.

The Robust whore at my feet looks up at me, her eyes wet with disgusting hope.

"Vardøger," Aeron calls over his shoulder. "There's movement ahead."

Dragging my pet along, I stand beside my warrior and survey the horizon, hot breath fogging the lenses in my mask. "Rippers?"

"No, I think not, Vardøger. It appears to be a small convoy of Musuls."

"Should we prepare for battle?" Heimdall asks, tying back his long, dreadlocked blond hair.

The neural link with the lenses in the mask activates and I am momentarily endowed with binocular vision. Yet before me are not Musuls. Instead, *Ida* stands there, her porcelain skin pink with the sting of snow, her beautiful coat clinging to her, wet and frozen, her lifeblood ebbing from the wound in her forehead.

Pain deep and swelling aches within.

She judges you. From wherever it is you come, from wherever your soul existed before you found me. She judges you from there, Vedmak. You failed her.

Silence, petulant child. You know nothing. You elites are all the same. Passion in any form is not within you. You are but an empty husk, ready to be controlled.

Yet she haunts you.

I said silence!

"Vardøger, what are your orders?" Heimdall demands.

My laser scythe screams to life, slicing in a sweeping arc through the meat of his chest, and is extinguished before my soldier can utter another word. He clutches at the bubbling wound, a look of betrayal set into his anguished face. He stumbles backward, tumbling into the snow.

"This is the fate of those who think they can press me."

Merodach grunts and Aeron snorts out a laugh.

Ignorant pigs, all of you. "Do not interrupt me while I think."

I turn back to the icy view. She is gone. In her place, hazy figures

91

stand. A few adjustments and they enlarge across my field of vision, their features somewhat sharper. Five Musuls march in full regalia. Kapka's men. But there's a sixth, traipsing clumsily between them, bouncing off the shoulders of his captors. His face is drawn and sickly, his hair long and unkempt.

Why five Musuls to guard this one man? Kapka wouldn't waste resources unless he was important. He may be an asset or at the very least, leverage to be used against them. "Stay here. I will investigate. Do *not* make yourself known. I will hail you should the need arise."

I hand the leash of my pet to Aeron, pull off the mask and stuff it into the satchel slung across the broad chest of my Gracile host. Slipping on the heavy hood of my cloak to ward off the cold, I trudge toward the Musuls.

The short distance to the band of extremists takes longer than I'd hoped. The snow deepens with every step, and my host's legs become inefficient, already tired from the day's exertion. And with each exhausted step, my Gracile demon gains a droplet of control. I scan the horizon. It would take too long for my militia to reach me should the worst happen, but as I draw near, it is clear there are no Musul reinforcements and nowhere for more of Kapka's dogs to hide.

What do you want to achieve with this? Why do you care about one Musul man?

Details, peacock. Details. The world runs on the minutiae of men. The smallest of details can set a chain of events in motion that change the world beyond recognition. And often they are the petty personal things precious to a moron in power.

Like Nicholas Romanov?

Of course like that goat of a Tsar. The fool led Mother Russia into loss after loss at the hands of the enemy, even leaving his slut German wife to rule in his absence. No doubt opening her legs for the charlatan Rasputin. So, the revolution and my purpose began.

And what about Stalin?

Choose your words wisely, puppet.

His petty actions led to your execution, didn't they? You and your wife, Ida.

I claw at this Gracile face, the unkempt nails on these fingers gouging out chunks of flesh. Repeatedly, I beat the skull in which I reside, the ringing loud inside.

Stop it! Demitri screams.

You will remain silent if you want to keep this face remotely pretty, Gracile.

The Musuls stop in their tracks. They must have seen my outburst. They hold their melee weapons high. Three have automatic rifles—two *Kalashnikovs* and a *papasha*. How amusing to be threatened with firearms designed by my countrymen. Putting both hands in the air, I approach slowly and steadily, trickles of blood working their way down Demitri's cheeks.

"It's curious. Five Musuls out here in the Vapid, escorting one disheveled, sad little man. How does this come to be?"

"Back off, Gracile, or we'll kill you," the nearest Musul spits, jerking the machine gun in his hands.

The prisoner's head rises slightly at the identification of me as a Gracile, his tired black eyes staring out from underneath a mat of frozen hair.

"Musul dogs, you would already be wandering the afterlife searching for your false god if I'd only wished it. Tell me, who is this man? He must be some precious cargo, or you would have already risked attacking me and losing him."

The Musuls glance at each other. None respond.

"Are you now dumbstruck? Have your tongues become lead in your mouths?"

"It's none of your business, Gracile. Last warning. Sard off—"

His head leaves his shoulders and rolls into a snow drift. His eyes are fixed on me in terror, the lids blinking involuntarily. My laser scythe hums and crackles, its blue flame illuminating the color-drained faces of the remaining four Musuls. The one with the *papasha* is shaking so badly he can't even raise it to point it at me.

"Do I need to ask a third time?"

They stutter but no meaningful words fall from their lips. The heavy snowflakes stick to the metal of the Musuls' weapons. Bored of their incompetence I shut down my weapon, grab the prisoner by his hair, and yank his head back to reveal a gaunt face—a familiar face. The angled jaw and Roman nose spark a tingle of recognition in my host.

No, it can't be.

Should I know this lame goat? I release my grip on his hair.

What have they done to you?

You *do* know this mongrel. He is important to you. Tell me how.

Demitri is silent.

No, not to you. To someone else. To Mila, perhaps?

I don't know him.

Lies, Demitri. Too little too late, your effort to conceal it—

"Demitri?" For a moment the hollow eyes liven.

Is that hope? How deplorable.

"And still mumbling to yourself I see," the man croaks through cracked lips. "Help me, please."

It's not me. It's Vedmak. I wish you could hear me.

I stare into his eyes, willing the memory to come, to be pried from Demitri's consciousness. Those eyes, that stalwart expression. "Faruq. You are Faruq."

"You barely remember me. The past means nothing to you?"

A wicked grin spreads across this face. "Oh, this is delicious. Kapka has had you all this time? I could not have planned it better myself." I turn to his guards. "You're keeping him moving, aren't you? So that little *suka* won't ever find him."

The Musuls acknowledge sheepishly, their weapons still poised, while Faruq stares at me—his face full with the resignation of a man who has accepted death and only waits for its sweet embrace. But he will not receive it this day. At least not from me. I lean into him, these Gracile lips near brushing his ear.

"She gave up years ago, you know. Stopped looking. Stopped caring. You were but a fleeting distraction. Now she busies herself with other menial tasks she deems more important than your life."

He doesn't flinch.

Don't listen to him, Faruq. You know Mila better. She's been looking for us both.

"Oh, and I hear your sister is with her ... or at least beside her like a loyal Musul dog. I'm sure she begs and rolls over like a good pet for her Logosian master. In fact, I'm sure she spreads her legs for every man in Opor, like a trained whore."

The Musul doesn't respond—his features unmoving. No anger. No pain. Nothing.

My own rage boils to the surface. The cane of my scythe strikes across his jaw and he crashes into the snow. There's no defiance. No retaliation. He just lays there. "Get up. Are you so pitiful that you no longer stand for yourself? Have you no courage, no honor?"

Can't you see he's broken? Just leave him be, Demitri whines.

"Fine. Lay there like the beaten dog you are. To kill you would only free you from this tortuous world. Oh, but do I wish that *sow*, Mila, could see the miserable derelict you've become. That would be worth my time." I turn back to his captors. "Take him. Make him suffer. I have no further interest."

A scream in the distance.

I spin aboutface.

In the dark, behind the intensifying snowdrift, the clang of metal against metal rings out. Barely visible silhouettes of near thirty Rippers thrashing machetes and thrusting spears mingle with the shouts of my militia.

They're under attack.

***

My hoarse battle cry rises above the melee but is muted against the snow-laden wind. These lungs heave and gasp in pain, the price I pay for having returned in such a short time.

The nearest Ripper's head cleaves in twain, his skull sliding apart. Thick red matter falls in globs against the fresh powder at his feet. With the neural link engaged, and the world slowed, the massacre plays out in a creeping dance of death. My *Einherjar* fight with vigor, but the sheer number of Vapid roamers is overwhelming. Their attack coordinated, like pack animals, while my soldiers thrash out, all brute force and little training in the art of war.

Another slam with this armored shoulder and a Ripper tumbles into the snow. My scythe opens his belly before he can rise. There's a popping sound as his gut bag releases and the plasma blade seals his innards into the wound. He cries out in anguish. I stomp on his head to finish him.

Aeron and Merodach liberate our pet Rippers, now stimmed up on Red Mist. Breaking free, they scream and howl, clawing and biting anything in their path. Some of them grab up the weapons of the fallen, only to be cut down by their own kind. Wave after wave of new foes appears from within the snowstorm. They must believe the cart is laden with goods. But their attack will yield nothing. The cart is to be loaded with the nuclear stockpile we seek.

You'll never win this. You have to run. Do it, or we both die.

Your answer to everything, *kozel*. I run from nothing. I would rather die here and take your wretched soul with me.

A shadow descends upon me. I grab the attacker's arm and draw it over my Gracile host's shoulder. The Ripper's arm snaps at the elbow, a childlike scream sings from his yawning mouth.

This is insane. Your people are being butchered. Tell them to run.

Never! Do not believe they are your Gracile siblings, puppet. They are but shells with my brethren inside. We will prevail against this filth. But where is *she*?

I scan the battlefield, searching for her skinny frame. There. Hiding behind the wheel of the cart, hoping to escape.

Just leave her be. What is wrong with you?

I power through the scrum of fighters, past their grubby, clawing hands. In a single lunging stride, Aeron intercepts the cabal on my left, cutting through them with a buzzing flash of his plasma sword. On my right, Merodach clears a bloody path so I can make it to my quarry. But the limbs of my host fight back, refusing to obey my command. These legs are like lead, anchored against the earth itself.

Puppet, do you fight me?

I won't let you hurt her.

You have no choice, boy.

Yes, I do.

My host's legs stop moving altogether. The lower half of this organic machine shuts down, my control gone. The muscles tingle with pins and needles, as if the life blood has been cut off.

"Let go, peacock, or you will regret it," I say aloud.

I can't regret more than I already do.

"Foolish child." These hands still work.

From the inner pocket of the cloak that shrouds these huge shoulders, I pull a syringe of Red Mist, the latest version before the Alchemist was captured. It's unstable but powerful. The red liquid sloshes about inside the glass cylinder. Before Demitri knows what's happened, the needle slides into the jugular vein of his neck. A hissing shot fires the liquid into the bloodstream and immediately my control returns—tenfold.

No . . .

Muscles afire, I force this body forward.

The sound of gunfire close. I register a snap of pain like the bite of a serpent in Demitri's shoulder, but it doesn't slow me. These eyes lock on the shooter, the red-masked savage from before. You. You're dead. I cross the distance in the blink of an eye, crashing into the shooter. Still clutching his rifle, he is unprepared for death as a closed fist folds his jaw flat against his neck. I slam down, obliterating his skull.

As I approach, she cowers. I grab the heavy chain attached to her collar and lash it to a metal ring on the wooden cart. My scythe screams open and with a blaze, the chain is soldered to the iron peg. I crouch down to Anastasia's level. The crackling, spitting scythe illuminating her gaunt features and pink scar. "You will never escape. There is no hope for you."

"Demitri will save me," she stutters.

"Your faith is misplaced." Her throat feels fragile, like glass, within my one-handed stim-enhanced grip. "He is but a boy. A coward. You think he cares for you? *Loves* you? You are beneath his kind. A plague-infested rodent. For now, you are a mere distraction from the torment of living in limbo—"

A crushing blast of pain pierces my host, slamming into his skull from behind. I feel the rippling agony just as he would. Demitri's body takes far too long to steady. A trickle of blood runs from the gaping head wound and my scythe drops to the ground. Rage boils from the depths, from the hell in which I was reborn. Standing amidst sickening vertigo, I force Demitri's body to fight back.

You're killing us both. The voice is distant. Dreamlike.

I ignore him, turning to my attacker.

The little gremlin wearing animal skins loads another stone into his sling. This cave dweller is somehow able to badly wound this body with mere rocks. The rage inside deepens. I take two steps toward him, a stream of vomit spilling from the mouth of my host. The second fist-sized rock strikes center mass. Demitri's body fails, stumbling to all fours. I force these fingers to grasp the hilt of a short sword. Crude but functional. Rising, I am upon him. His eyes are wide with fear as I drive the barbaric weapon through his gut.

"Primitive dog." I yank the sword from him and throw it away. He falls back into the white powder, a dying gasp on his lips.

Using the extinguished scythe as a crutch, I stumble toward the cart. The familiar chaos of battle fills these ears, the once perfect vision I enjoyed is now blurred. Blood continues to leak from Demitri's head, soaking into the garment at the neck. I drop into the snow, panting, hot breath mixing with the falling snowflakes.

We're both going to die, Vedmak. Here in the Vapid. Our time has come. Your plan will never come to pass.

"I will not be beaten."

Death comes for us all, whether we want it or not.

"I am Death."

Staring up at the large flakes of snow dancing their way slowly from the dark sky above, her face slides into view. A strange apparition. Her features are blended, a ghostly concoction combining my Ida with the revolting morphology of Anastasia. A pink scar carves its way through the perfect skin of my wife's face.

"Demitri," the woman says, her voice a whisper. She raises my own scythe high above her head to finish me. "Demitri, tell me you're in there."

Aeron steps in, shoving the woman back, shattering my hallucination. "Vardøger. We are lost. There are too many."

"You have to seal my wound." I point to the injury.

Aeron ignites his broad sword and presses it against the bloody gash. The flesh and hair sizzles and burns, the pain searing through into both my and Demitri's consciousness.

We both scream in anguish.

The world becomes dark, my grip on this corporeal shell and this world melting away. "Take me ... back to the lillipad ... We need more soldiers."

Aeron seizes hold of this heavy body and lifts with all his might and drags me back into the fray, away from my pet still chained to the cart. The smell of gunpowder, blood, and feces drifts on the cold air. Bullets whistle past, the sound of metal on metal clanging out in violent repetition.

Aeron's temple explodes, fragments of brain spattering the ground. He slumps forward into the snow and I fall from his arm into a slush-filled ditch. The gentle snowflakes kiss the skin of my host's face, as if Mother Russia herself had sympathy for him. Aeron's feet twitch and spasm, the nerve endings of my dead standard firing without control. What a waste. My gaze falls on Merodach as he charges into the rifleman who felled Aeron. His glowing mace eviscerates the shooter in one strike. Merodach turns back to me.

"Go," I hack. "Get back to the lillipad and activate one of the Creed's strike ships. Use Demitri's DNA to isolate this body and find me."

He hesitates, perhaps not wanting to leave me out here.

"Go, you simple-minded *kozel.*"

Merodach gives one last look to his brother's corpse before dashing off into the blizzard.

The battlefield now has few players, only bodies piled atop one another. My Ripper dogs have been put down, and those *Einherjar* who may still be alive must have fled.

My reign is cut short by mere animals.

Through the wall of sleet and snow, she appears, her long coat floating in the breeze. Her stare is devoid of emotion, as cold as the ditch in which I lay. She reaches out for me, beckoning me to follow. Ida, my love.

"No. I must stay in control." I try to stand, but instead roll to the side with a groan.

Time for us both to die, Vedmak.

The stygian nothingness tears at my mind, rending my soul asunder.

CHAPTER THIRTEEN

FARUQ

The power-hungry slave-driver shoves me from behind again. I manage two stumbling steps to right myself, though my emaciated legs quake with the effort.

"Get a move on. We want to get there before nightfall," he says. "Take too long and we might leave you out here for the Rippers."

Being disemboweled by Rippers might be preferable. To feel something, anything. The thought is intriguing enough that I've stopped walking, soliciting another vicious shove from behind. This one sends me face-down into a pile of wet snow. Curses spit from my cracked lips.

"I said keep moving," my handler shouts, dragging me halfway up by the arm. Crystals of ice cling to my face and beard.

The rear guard swivels back and forth, his *Kalashnikov* at the ready, searching for Rippers. "Stop shoving him, Sabri," he says. "You're only slowing us down. Kapka said—"

"I know what Kapka said. Do not try to lecture me, Tareq," Sabri snaps.

"Oh?" Tareq says, motioning to me with the rifle. "So, screwing with him is more important than our lives? Because I can still hear the screams of Rippers fighting with that deranged Gracile's crew back there. We're already down one soldier from our encounter with that psycho."

"Speaking of which," Sabri says, jerking me to my feet. "Why didn't you shoot him for what he did? Kapka will hear of your cowardice."

"*My* cowardice?" Tareq replies. "You were right next to him when he lopped off Barad's head. Why didn't *you* do something?"

"You had the rifle, incompetent fool."

"Did you see him? He looked crazy."

Their argument melts into white noise. Sabri and Tareq always squabble. Day after day. Month after month. It's all I ever hear—being dragged around by these brainwashed idiots—besides their constant threats.

They enjoy keeping me on edge. The bags on my head, the taunts, and the broken fingers or toes. Being left in the cold just long enough I don't starve or freeze. Never knowing if today is the day I will meet Ilah. But in the end, it becomes normal. Perpetual fear is exhausting. Eventually, it fades away and is replaced with ... nothing. Another torn ligament. One more shattered rib. It doesn't matter. Physical pain means nothing, and that is all Kapka's men know how to deal.

They could not break my spirit ... until today.

Mila's face, the launchpad, Kapka's leer—they all flash through my mind, over and over. The smells of that war fill my throat as if I were still there. Sprinting for the rocket. Her hands grasping the sleeve of my jacket as I turned to confront the tyrant of Baqir who was pointing an RPG at *her*. Struggling, clamoring for the giant weapon before it fired against the platform—and then, there was only darkness.

I should have been delivered to the Kingdom of Heaven for my great sacrifice. For saving my friends, and the rest of humanity. Through my actions, the Earth must have been protected, as four years later it still spins. This is only possible because I gave my life to help Mila and Demitri escape. Yet even Ilah rejected me and sent me back to this broken world—alone, in a haze of pain and confusion, lying trapped beneath the collapsed launch pad. No one came to my aid. Not Mila and Bilgi's resistance, Opor. Not Husniya. Instead, Kapka and his men dragged me away with promises of a slow death.

For so long, I told myself perhaps Mila and Demitri had died stopping the Leader. That was why I had not seen them. Or perhaps they believed me dead from the explosion. Then I'd seen her, that day on the Vapid road, as Kapka's men herded me along like a beast. I'd been so sure she would act, that she would recognize me, hear my voice and set me free. But she had not, instead choosing to protect the children with her. I'd believed it a noble choice. Believed her last words as I was dragged away: an oath she would find me. It was the only thought that kept my heart beating.

But she never did, and now I know the whole truth.

Demitri was here. Right in front of me. And he did nothing. My guards were paralyzed with fear, easy to dispatch. He handed me back as if I were some diseased animal. He cared not for my life. Maybe even took joy from my suffering. He'd pretended to be so gentle, so kind, but no one is kind in this world. It has its ways of destroying us all—tearing us down until we're nothing, then building us back up in its terrible image. Demitri is no different.

Neither is Mila.

She is alive and well alongside Husniya, and neither has come for me. My life debt to her was given based on a lie. I'm sure she hadn't intended to intervene and stop Kapka's men from raping my sister or killing me. She'd stumbled upon us while on a job to make money. Those men had simply been in her way. Demitri, he'd said she had better things to do than search for me. Why would he bother to lie? Maybe she'd never cared about me to begin with.

I'm such an idiot. My childish hunger for family. For love.

I trudge on into the swirling blizzard, shoved now and again by my captors. My body moves with autonomous Creed-like robotic precision, each leg performing its sole duty over and over in mindless repetition, driven by some primitive instinct to survive. Raise, reach, stomp, repeat.

After what feels like an eternity in this frozen hell, the outline of wooden stakes protruding from the ground comes into view. Snowflakes glue to my lashes, obscuring my vision. Yet it's clear this place is different than the others. Sometimes they hood me when we move, sometimes they don't bother. But I know with stinging clarity I've never been here before. It's an outpost of some sort, far down a road that seems to go on forever. The Road of Death, I heard Sabri call it. I have no idea where it leads, but what I do know is we are out in the Vapid far beyond the walls of Etyom.

Why the effort to move me out here? Before, I was only carted back and forth between Baqir and Alya. Always moving, never anchored in one place for too long. Kapka was insistent upon it.

The pikes jut from the ground like a row of jagged teeth. A deterrent to the beasts of the wild or roving bands of savages, though I can't say for certain Rippers even come this far out. No one knows what lies beyond the walls of the last city.

We pass through a simple gate manned by two of Kapka's brainwashed fools, past the campfires and the men who stare with curiosity and hatred. We walk until finally stopping before a row of simplistic cages. They're wooden with iron bands at the seams, covered with an awning. My home for who knows how long.

Kapka's men do not give me a roof because they care about my wellbeing. They give it because in my current condition, further exposure would finish me. They can't allow that. Kapka must have his whipping boy.

"Get in the cage." The guard gives me a shove.

Unable to stand any longer, I crumple forward, crawling on my hands and knees into the small square enclosure. The men laugh and make barking sounds. The hatch slams shut, a bolt inserted to hold it in place. My daily meal, a piece of molding hard tack, is dropped outside the bars. The men continue to laugh as one steps on it and grinds it into the muddy slush.

"There's your food, if you still care to have it, mutt," Tareq says. They laugh and shuffle away toward the warmth of one of the fires. The flickering oranges and yellows a majestic tease, a comfort to my eyes my body cannot share. An involuntary moan escapes my lips as my hand scrapes beneath the wire of my prison, reaching for the old bread.

A boot crushes my hand into the slush, the pain excruciating. I scream, jerking back, hoping to free it, but it will not move from this vise. Another moan. I slump forward, mumbling for release. A shadow darkens my cage.

"Faruq, my favorite stepson," Kapka says, his voice a strange blend of hate and false warmth.

"Please," I manage.

"I'm sorry? Did you speak to me?" A single gold tooth glints in the light of the fire.

"My hand," I whimper. "Please."

"Oh? How careless of me." He twists the toe of his boot, causing me to scream out again, then steps back.

The old bread is now ruined and inedible. I pull my hand through the rough wire of the cage and examine the scuffed and bruised flesh. My gaze flicks up only for an instant, taking in the leering bearded face and broad shoulders of my oppressor. He's still dressed in his ridiculous old-world style with a layered, fur-collared, sand-colored suit complete with expedition boots. There is scarring across his neck that disappears into his collar, but it seems his square face was spared damage from the blast of the RPG.

"Oh Faruq, you look especially wretched today. Are you being treated well?" He squats to peer into my cage. "I will speak with someone about this, do not worry. Only the best for the son of one of my favorite wives …" He rubs his beard with a gloved hand. "I'll remember her name, give me a moment."

It takes all the resolve I can muster to spit across his shoes. A flash of movement and he grabs a bucket from the icy ground. Before I can protest, a stream of frozen water drenches me from head to toe, soaking through the fibers of the burlap smock I wear, killing the last shred of warmth. An involuntary shivering takes me, my body quaking as I gasp and sputter.

"You are a worm. You are less than the sard beneath my boots and I will scrape you from the soles just the same." He leans closer, the distant light of the campfires casting shadows on the side of his face. "You think you know pain? Loss? This is what is left of your miserable life, boy. This is what happens to those who rise against me. I'll do it to you, to that Logosian whore, even your dear sister who betrayed me. I can make this vendetta last forever."

My teeth chatter, chomping with rapid clicks as the awful cold deepens.

"I'll see you soon." Kapka grins. Then with a wink and a laugh, he turns away, pulling his jacket around him and heads off to his private tent.

These disgusting imposters of my faith—fanatics, deranged by promises of power and ecstasy. Why have they been unchecked? Why has no one stopped this? Even Ilah seems not to see, for I am suffering and they are free to push their terror on the world. It is madness.

I now know with absolute certainty there is nothing left for me in this world. No friends. No family. No hope. Once upon a time, there would have at least been vengeance to cling to. Now, only death remains. If Kapka won't give me that release, I will have to take it with my own hand. Burning in the fires of Hell is still better than living another day in this place.

CHAPTER FOURTEEN

MILA

Back out in the frigid wind, I shudder and push the temple door closed behind Husniya. The storm has subsided for the moment and I can almost make out the blue sky beyond the wisps of threaded clouds. Down the uneven snow-draped rock steps, Husniya and I do our best to not slip on a patch of ice and tumble to our deaths. The journey is precarious and slow. I've only just reached the bottom of the stairs when a young boy runs toward us from across the way. Not older than ten years, he's disheveled and scrawny. It's all too familiar. Criminals use kids like this to distract—right before a guy with an iron bar lays you out and lightens you of your belongings.

Eyes up, Mila.

The market, the entrance to the mines, the men gathered around a nearby burn barrel. All clear. I scan the boy for an explosive belt, guilt in my chest rising over deeming him a possible terrorist threat.

Husniya, oblivious, talks without reservation.

"Hang on, Hus," I say, holding up my hand. "Be ready."

"For wha—"

"Just be ready."

The boy pulls his hand from his jacket. In his grasp is a small folded piece of paper.

"You're Mila?" he says, his breath huffing out in small clouds of steam.

"No, you've got the wrong person, kid."

He stands there, bewildered, hand outstretched. "But she said Mila would be coming out from the Vestal sanctuary. She described you."

"Who's she?" I pluck the note from his little fingers.

"The beautiful lady. She gave me three copper coins to run the note to you. That's all. Honest."

I unroll the bit of parchment, brow knitted.

Outside the East entrance.
Turn left. Five minutes.
Tell no one.

The intrigue alone has me, but there's no way I'm going. Not like this. I crumple the parchment and drop it to the ground. The sour look on the kid's mug deepens.

"Go find this beautiful lady and tell her I don't do clandestine."

"Clay—what?"

"Just tell her I'm not coming, okay?"

The kid squirms. "No way lady. I'm not going back outside the wall."

I pull a wad of old soggy dollars from my pocket and refold them. "No?"

The kid's eyes widen and he rubs his hands nervously. "Um, yes, I mean. I can try to find her for you."

"I don't want to trouble you."

"Oh no, you're not troubling me, honest." The kid licks his lips, no doubt thinking of all he could have to eat for a single Etyom dollar.

"Then make it happen." I unfold two dollars and extend them.

He grabs for the cash. "Yes. I mean, yes, miss. I'll take care of it. Thank you, miss." He runs off, little shoes stabbing into the snow and slipping on the ice.

"Let's go, Hus. We're being watched. Keep your eyes forward. We're just two people leaving town."

We trudge through the ramshackle streets full of garbage and ruin, past the rows of fragile shanties, until nearing the main gate I veer left, pulling Husniya down a cramped alleyway.

"What?" she protests.

"Just be quiet and follow me."

At the end of the alley is an abandoned two-story sloop bar. For a moment, I'm back at Clief's place, bouncing drunken miners or helping the old man wipe down the tables. It wasn't much but it felt like family, like I belonged somewhere—for a while.

This one has been closed for some time.

"What is this place?" Husniya says, following me to the door. "It looks

106

terrible."

"It's a sloop dive—or was."

"What's sloop?"

I jiggle the doorknob. "Fermented mash of beetroot and midget potatoes. Dangerous stuff if you don't make it just right." The door jerks open with a sharp shove from my shoulder. The mustiness of the dank interior seeps out. I slip in and make a beeline for the stairs and traverse them one rickety step at a time. At the top and down a dust-laden corridor is a wooden window hatch looking over the East side of the outer wall. We prop it open. Below, where the note said to meet, a small armed contingent waits. They seem to be led by a woman. She has a familiar aura, standing tall and regal, her arms crossed.

"A trap. I knew it," I say, searching for other threats.

But there's something different about this little militia. The realization like a slap in the face. She's a sarding Gracile. The others aren't though. They're so frozen in place it's unnatural. I've seen that before as well. Creed.

"That's a Gracile isn't it?" Husniya's voice is only a whisper.

"Yep."

"And Creed soldiers," she says, shaking her head in disbelief. "Tell me we're not going down there, Mila. I don't want anything to do with them."

I say nothing and analyze the small group. The tall woman with the proud face and sweeping garments is the leader. But who is she? Nothing makes any sense since the lillipads came down. It used to be for better or worse everyone knew their place and what they could expect from certain factions. The falling of New Etyom and my meeting Demitri changed all that. Now I don't know what to expect from anyone, much less a Gracile.

When was the last time anyone even saw a Gracile—or Creed for that matter?

The messenger boy rounds the edge of the wall. The Creed's plasma rifles rise from under their cloaks. The boy slows, his eyes wide with fear. The woman raises a hand and the sentries lower their weapons. She motions the boy closer. He comes to a stop, looking like a baby's doll compared with the massive soldiers around him. The woman bends and they exchange words, the boy shaking his head as he tells her I'm not coming. She takes it in, saying nothing, then stands. Her shoulders slumped, she motions for the boy to leave. Needing no further inspiration, the little lad spins and flees in the opposite direction, back to the relative safety of the enclave.

That wasn't annoyance. She was disappointed. But why?

"Husniya, do you have any rifle rounds left?"

"Just one," she grabs a fistful of my jacket sleeve.

"What?"

There's fear in the girl's face. "Mila, I don't want to kill anyone else. Please."

I meet her tearful gaze and give her a pat on the back. "If everything goes right, you won't have to. Just let them see you up here when I point."

"They could kill you," she says as I pull a Makarov pistol from my sling bag and shove it in my waistband.

I turn from the window with a shrug. "Yeah, they could."

***

My hands are in the air as I round the enclave wall. The Creed notice me first, their bulbous metallic plasma rifles leveling in my direction. In sync, their hollow robotic voices call out.

"Identify Robust—Mila Solokoff, resistance leader, dissident. Female is armed with a semi-automatic small caliber pistol and may have hostile intentions. Standing by for orders to initiate deconstruction."

Deconstruction. Hearing the word spoken by a Creed this many years later still gives me the creeps.

"Not at this time. Thank you," the tall Gracile woman says.

The Creed drop their rifles to a low ready, but I'm no fool. They're still locked on me. Any sudden moves and *poof*, I'm pixie dust.

"Not at this time? When then? In thirty seconds when I don't like what you have to say?" I lower my hands slowly.

"That depends on how you choose to behave," the woman says.

"One might say that lane goes both directions," I reply, motioning to the open window. The woman shifts to see Husniya two stories up, supporting a long-bolt action rifle. Half of the Creed contingent raise their rifles toward Husniya.

"Identify Robust—Unknown Musul female, possible resistance

member, armed with a—"

"Yes, I can see her. Standby," the Gracile female says, irritated.

The Creed soldiers stand fast.

"Deconstruct me if you wish. But you're the one who called me out. You'll never learn what you needed to know, and your Creed won't be able to stop my sniper before she blasts the contents of your skull into the snow."

A moment passes. The Gracile woman gives a wave of her hand, and the Creed lower their rifles.

"How poetic. Spoken like a true survivor," she says.

The Gracile puts one hand on her hip, shifting her weight to one foot. Just beneath the hood of her heavy cloak, picturesque chocolate-colored ringlets of hair encapsulate the perfect features of her face. The overly long legs, the flawless feminine features. Did I always hate Gracile women this much?

Get on with it, Mila. "What do you want? I'm a busy person."

"I need to speak with you. I need to know something." Her face is cold and calculating, but her voice seems earnest.

"Let me stop you right there." I raise a gloved hand. Graciles are all the same. Always speaking in florid riddles. "Whatever you've got to say, say it. Stop wasting my time and get to the point."

The wind picks up, whipping dusty waves of snow across the Vapid.

"My name is Oksana. I need to find my mate's neo-brother, Demitri. I understand you knew him before the fall."

In an instant, the entire tone of the meeting shifts. The skin of my neck tingles with a chill. I hold up my fist and from the corner of my eye see Husniya lower her rifle. Casting a glance over each shoulder, I turn back to the Gracile woman.

"Why should I help you find Demitri? For all I know, you want to kill him. Just like every other Gracile did."

She eyes me, confusion etched into her face. "I need to know what happened. I need to know why Nikolaj died. Demitri can tell me. The word is you were the last person to see him alive before everything fell. In exchange, I have information you might be interested in."

"What could you know that I would care about?"

"I hear you're looking for a Musul Robust, a man by the name Faruq?"

The already cold air seems to freeze solid. My breathing stops and my heart falters. Could she know something? Can't risk losing this lead. "We should discuss this in a more secure location."

"I agree," Oksana says with a slight bow.

"I know a place. Follow me and keep out of sight."

CHAPTER FIFTEEN

DEMITRI

Deep, throaty growls fill my ears. What is that? The snow seals my eyelids together and the cold stabs at my face. Is this purgatory? Is this Hell? More growls and aggressive huffs, closer this time. I force my eyes open, but I still can't see much. My whole body aches and my insides feel as if they are on fire. But unlike when Vedmak's asleep, this is very present. As if ... Vedmak?

Silence.

Vedmak?

He's gone. I'm in control again? That last blow to the head must have done something.

The hostile sounds grow louder. They're like nothing I've heard before.

My tired legs manage to push me into an awkward sitting position, but a fresh streak of pain shoots across the base of my skull and my skin burns from more slashes than I can count. Propped against a rock, I survey my immediate surroundings. The battlefield is stained pink with blood, though a fresh layer of snow covers many of the bodies. Why was Vedmak—was *I*—left alive? Why didn't the Rippers kill us?

In the dark, a shape lumbers on all fours from one snowdrift to the next, its hoarse huffing becoming louder. The snow puffs up in large billows as it pounds the ground.

What the hell is that?

It rears up onto its hind legs. A break in the cloud cover ahead reveals a large, yellow, full moon, providing a shaft of light that illuminates the creature in the gloom. It stands taller than any Gracile and has shiny black fur, dead eyes, and a gaping mouth baring saliva-covered, fangs. Its club-like hands are adorned with long claws.

Images from my old books rifle through my brain. Can it be? Am I looking at a bear? They were thought all but extinct. Yet here it is. With the

111

walls of Etyom breached, anything could enter. The world outside is not as dead as perhaps we thought.

Is this why the Rippers fled? Is this why I'm still alive? Despite having control of my own body, it fails to move as I want. All I can do is stare, transfixed by this enormous animal. Don't think it's seen me. Here, covered in snow, my breathing shallow, I'm just another body. Still, was one bear enough to frighten off all those Rippers? Despite knowing I'd read the books, the information eludes me. Without Vedmak, it's like half of me is missing. So hard to discern which memories are mine and which are his.

It snaps its attention in my direction. Sard. Did I move?

The beast drops to all fours again and lumbers forward, huffing out its deep voice. What did it see? Was I talking out loud again?

The chink of metal on metal.

I strain to see the source, close behind me. It's the cart, half-covered in a drift—and chained to it, Anastasia. She yanks on her shackle again in frustration as the bear approaches. Each loud clank only angers the animal.

"Anastasia, stop." My voice is but a whisper.

She doesn't hear me.

"Anastasia."

The bear trudges past, ignoring my broken form, fixated on the panicked Robust woman.

Vedmak's laser scythe lays a meter away, just out of reach. Move, Demitri, do something. My painful crawl to Anastasia is worthless, the animal already upon her. It rears up again and bellows, spittle raining down on her. She screams and covers her face, awaiting the inevitable.

"Come on." My fingers curl around the staff, but it's too late.

The bear cries out in anguish, tumbling into a drift. Blood spurts from its side. A flash like fire streaks across the bear, tearing a chunk of its body away. The black beast howls. Anastasia clings to the hub of the wheel closest to her, too scared to sob, her pants wet with urine.

From within the gloom, two green eyes shine like gemstones. Their owner prowls from the dark, its growl low and purposeful. It's another fiend. But it's no bear. Orange and white fur is adorned with splashes of black. It has a large head and a long tail. Each movement is calculated and majestic. Every step carefully placed as it stalks the bear.

"Ussuri! Ussuri!" Anastasia cries.

Without warning, the orange beast launches forward and collides with the bear. The bear swipes and gouges the shoulder of the fire-colored monster. But it's not slowed. It pulls the bear over and to the ground, then clamps its huge mouth around the bear's lower back, piercing the flesh with long yellow fangs. A final scream, followed by a nauseating crunch. The bear does not rise again.

Silence falls over the battlefield.

The auburn behemoth drags the bear away, leaving a trough of snow filled with blood in its wake. The gloom closes in around them, and only the dancing snowflakes can be seen in the dim evening light.

Anastasia whimpers the same word, over and over. "Ussuri, Ussuri."

Is it gone? Should I move?

An eternity passes, only the constant snapping of the wind can be heard.

Can't stay here. It's a miracle I haven't frozen already, let alone Anastasia.

I roll to my side and manage to climb to my feet. Dizziness envelops me and the world spins. It takes a minute to ensure I'll not fall back into my resting place. Grabbing the scythe to use as a crutch, and reaching out with my other hand as if the air will support me, I stumble forward toward Anastasia.

She screams ferociously, spitting and hissing like a wild animal.

"Anastasia, it's me, it's Demitri." I lay the scythe against the cart, out of her reach as a gesture of peace.

The Robust woman lashes out, her ragged nails catching me across the brow.

"Sard, ah, son of a—" I cry, clasping a hand to the stinging wound, but thankfully, it's only a scratch.

Anastasia shuffles back and stares up.

Wiping a drop of blood from my face, I drop to my haunches, which sends yet another wave of nausea and pain from the pit of my stomach into my vertebrae. Somehow, I don't collapse. "It's okay," I say. "It's me."

Anastasia's eyes well up. "Demitri?"

"It's me. I promised you. I promised I'd free you," I say in the softest voice I can manage. "We don't have much time. I don't know when he'll have control again. Stay still. I need to get this chain off you."

She searches my eyes for truth in my words.

"You're a follower of Yeos, right? You need to get back to Logos.

She shakes her head. "I'm not from Logos."

"You're *not* from Logos?"

"My people are wanderers," she manages, still studying my face. "The Logosians believe Yeos is found only through their ways. But we believe He is everywhere, in everything—"

"In the Vapid? I thought only Rippers lived outside the enclaves?"

She seems irritated by her sermon being truncated. "Inside, outside. It makes no difference. There is only Etyom."

There's a painful truth to her words. Now more than ever. With the HAPs fallen and Graciles all but captured, New Etyom is nothing but a memory. Even the enclaves offer little in the way of protection anymore. This place is hell, and we are all in it together.

This isn't hell, kozel. But I will show you of it.

"Vedmak? Oh no. Not now."

A fresh wave of fear ripples over Anastasia's face and she yanks on her chain again in an attempt to break free.

For a superior species, you are not clever, stupid goat. You can never escape me.

A knot forms in my stomach and my limbs begin to tingle. He's coming back, regaining control. I'm not strong enough. Haven't been in control long enough. His will is too powerful.

"Anastasia, you have to listen to me. You have to find the resistance. Find Opor. Ask for Mila Solokoff. She'll be in Logos. Or maybe Fiori, I don't know for sure. But you have to find her. Tell her... tell her—" I stammer, searching for the words.

The Robust woman's face expresses only the primal desire to get as far away as possible.

Yes, puppet what to tell her? What could her simple mind understand about the plans of a god?

114

Keep it simple, Demitri. "Tell her I'm alive, but trapped. Vedmak is in control. Tell her the Gracile Leader's plan pales in significance to what Vedmak is doing. He's making an army of Graciles like me. That's important, okay. Like *me*. But it'll trigger a VME. Tell her to find a scientist. You have to remember *VME*, that's also important. Okay? And she has to get to Vel. To the nuclear stockpile—"

Vedmak's cackle is deafening. *Stupid peacock, look at her. Do you think she understood any of that? You know what she remembers, puppet? You. Penetrating her. Punishing her as she sobbed. She doesn't care for you. She only desire's release—*

"Sard off, Vedmak. It wasn't me. I never wanted that."

My muscles tingle hot, limbs coming alive with electricity. It won't be long. I'm rapping two fingers on my forehead, again.

Anastasia slowly reaches out a hand and touches my face, tracing the burn marks left by the explosion on the space station four years earlier. Her gentle fingers, the feeling of another person's skin on mine, and her soft eyes searching my innermost being, makes a stone form in my throat and my eyes well.

"I'm so sorry, Anastasia," I manage, choking back a sob. Tears streak a clean path through the dirt on my cheeks.

"My people have a saying. The snow is an open book, for those who know how to read."

"I don't follow," I say between sniffs.

"Yeos shows us the answers. We have but to open our hearts and learn how to see them. Sometimes they are written in the snow at our feet. Others are within us."

She sounds so much like Mila. The irony.

She holds up the chain. "Free me, Demitri."

Enough of this.

My hand shoots out and grabs Anastasia by the throat.

"No, Vedmak."

Her face turns red as she gasps for air, her eyes bulging. She claws at my hand, but I can't let go.

"Let her go!" I scream.

This whore should have died long ago. I allowed my own desire for

115

pleasure to keep her alive. Time to remedy that mistake.

"I won't let you."

You already did.

Anastasia's limp, her fragile neck all but crushed in my fist.

My free hand grabs for the laser scythe. It ignites with a shriek and before another thought can enter my head, the burning blade has sliced through the chain and back up through my forearm. For a moment, it doesn't hurt. Anastasia goes tumbling into the snow, my severed hand still clasped around her throat. She chokes back to life and flings the appendage away.

You fool! You would do this to us?

The searing pain stabs and spreads from the already-cauterized stump up my arm and into my spine. It's too much. I no longer have control of my limbs. Awkwardly, my body jerks and thrashes as Vedmak fights for control. The world spins and darkness claws at my consciousness, sucking my identity back into the void. I crash into the snow, writhing like a wounded serpent.

A growl. Long and loud, it calls out, filling the evening air.

The flame-colored beast glides forward.

Vedmak fights me for control again, screaming in my skull.

A heavy paw presses on my chest as if a lillipad had fallen on me. I sink into the snow. My ribs groan and pop under the pressure. Unable to breathe, I stare up at the drifting flakes that seem to appear from nowhere. The massive head of the fiend enters the frame. It glares at me, its hot breath tainted with the metallic smell of blood.

A damn tiger? Vedmak scoffs, disappointed this is how he is to die.

"A tiger," I wheeze. "That's what it is …"

"Ussuri," Anastasia says from somewhere nearby.

It's hard not to laugh. Even in this state, like a child, I'm curious about another animal few have seen. What's wrong with me? Shouldn't my life flash before my eyes? I hack up a mouthful of blood, half laughing, half coughing. "I see now. Ussuri is Russian for tiger."

"No," Anastasia says stepping into my field of view. She stares down at me, short hair hanging about her face, and slides a hand into the tiger's mane. "Ussuri is his name." Tears streak down her cheeks, as she mouths three silent words: I love you. At least that's what I hope she said. Her lips are obscured by blustering sleet, and I can't be sure my tortured eyes do not betray me.

Yes, Anastasia, I love you too.

She drops the heel of the scythe into my nose and the world goes dark.

CHAPTER SIXTEEN

MILA

With a shove, the ramshackle wooden door groans on ungreased hinges. Dust hangs in the stale cold air, motes drifting across shafts of light emanating from a crack in the wall or a hole in the collapsing roof. Still, this abandoned sloop joint should provide us with the privacy we need.

"Here we are," I say.

"This is your meeting place?" Oksana can't hide her disgust.

"It's not *my* place. It was all I could do to get your clumsy footed group into Logos undetected."

"And next I suppose we will have to crawl on our hands and knees through the filth to get to the secret room behind the wall? That's how the rodents do it, correct?"

My skin prickles hot. I'm going to break her perfect Gracile nose. "Lady, this isn't New Etyom. This is the real world. We make do with what we have—a concept you're going to have to climb down off your high horse and get used to."

"Thanks to you and Demitri, if the rumors are true."

"Rumors have a habit of warping the facts. You left out *your* benevolent Leader with his glorious plan to dissolve us all into a black hole. Oh, and let's not forget Kapka and his radical idiots, and—"

Oksana holds up a slender gloved hand. "As I said—rumors."

"They're not sarding rumors. I was there, Gracile. Your Leader tried to wipe everyone out before preserving your kind onto a black hole forever. It's only because of the Robust resistance and Demitri's courage you're still breathing."

"That's insanity. The Leader wouldn't do that."

"But he killed Demitri's brother, didn't he? Your mate?"

Oksana is silent, her eyes glazed over.

"You tell me what you know about Faruq and I'll tell you everything

I know about what happened."

"Mila?" Husniya's voice drifts down from the floor above.

"Come down, Husniya. You're going to want to hear this."

Husniya descends the stairs, leaning her rifle against the banister.

Oksana clears her throat. "The Musul Faruq is alive."

Husniya looks at me, her pale face a terrible mixture of hope and fear. "Mila, is that true?"

"Grab a chair, Husniya," I say, turning my focus upon Oksana. "Listen to me now. This is not a game. If you're making this up—"

"Making it up?" The Gracile screws up her face. "Why would I waste my time?"

"You need to know how serious I am about this."

Oksana seems to swallow her instinct to insult me and instead simply tilts her head. "I understand."

"So?"

"This is an exchange, remember? You tell me what I need to know first. Then I tell you what I've discovered," the Gracile says.

"Hang on," Husniya starts. "You can't lead us on like that. I want to know about my brother."

The Creed shift, their lifeless eyes falling on my protege.

"Hang on, Hus." I motion for her to stay sitting. "Let me do this."

There's a breathlessness inside me that seems to pull at my insides. I compose myself. "All right, I'll tell you what I know. But first, you need to give me some space to breathe." I look to the Creed standing two steps to my right and shoo it away.

Oksana barks out a command in a language that sounds like old Russian. In response, the Creed chant, "Acknowledged," in unison, take a few steps toward the outer edge of the room and slump into some sort of hibernation mode, their processor fans still whirring softly.

"Thanks."

Oksana waves her hand. "Please continue."

"So, you're what to him? A sister-in-law?"

"Who?"

"Demitri."

Oksana sits forward. "I thought I was asking you the questions?"

"You did." I scrunch my brow. "But I need to know the context and how you fit into all of this. It's important."

Oksana smirks. "It's irrelevant, and I don't make a habit of telling Robusts my business."

The old heat warms in me again. Breathe, Mila. "Listen, this is going to come as a shock to you because you like to think you don't associate with my kind—but Demitri wasn't just some guy I ran into. He was my friend. The kind of friend you risk your life for, and I don't talk about my friends unless I know what the purpose of such talk is."

Oksana smooths down the pleats on her coat. "I guess you could consider me a sister-in-law of sorts. I was mated to Demitri's neo-brother, Nikolaj. And as you've already pointed out—quite coldly, I might add— the Leader murdered him." Her gaze lowers, her voice is neutral but deep inside, there's real pain. "I want to know why. What the hell happened? Was the fall of New Etyom actually connected as the rumors suggest? I hate not knowing."

A strange sympathy for this woman stirs. For a moment, she actually appears human. "It haunts you, not knowing what he died for."

Oksana meets my stare. "It does."

I let a moment pass in contemplation. "Demitri was troubled. He had a voice in his head that plagued him for years. A demon whose only purpose, it seemed, was to torture him. He knew he couldn't tell anyone, that in your world up there, such brokenness was a fatal flaw. He would have been Ax'd."

"Hold on," Oksana says. The sound of two men laughing passes the front of the old dive. She waits until the voices dwindle before continuing. "What was it you said about a demon? Is this based on some superstitious old-world belief system?"

Don't take it personally. "Yes. That shouldn't surprise you. I'm Logosian."

Oksana regards me with questioning eyes.

"Maybe you would feel more comfortable with Demitri's theory on his condition?" I continue. "Demitri said he discovered a genetic flaw in himself. I didn't really understand everything. Something to do with a protein, information never being destroyed and quantum entanglement.

Basically, he was connected to something, or someone, long dead who still existed in another dimension. Anyway, he was so afraid of you people that he took drugs to suppress his condition. Drugs only made in Lower Etyom. His dealer in New Etyom was also an informant for the Robust resistance. And they knew what your Leader was up to—trying to give Graciles eternal life by making you a permanent feature on something called the event horizon of a black hole."

The Gracile woman is looking at me like I'm crazy.

I continue anyway. "During a trip down here to get more of the narcotic that silenced his demo—em, voice—he got caught up in the resistance plan to stop your Leader. He met a young Musul girl and rescued her from a bombing in Zopat. He found she, too, was entangled with another. He figured if he could find out what they had in common, he could silence his voice forever."

"So that's what was happening that day? I remember the girl. He escaped with her in a VTV."

I motion to Husniya, who is sitting still as a statue, an unreadable expression on her face.

"Oh?" Oksana replies, intrigued.

"Using a comparison of her DNA with his, he isolated this genetic key. But, as he tells it, he inadvertently gave the Leader the final thing he needed to create a sustainable black hole."

"The ability to prove and contact extra-dimensions ..." Oksana says, though seemingly more to herself.

"When the Leader found that Demitri knew his plan, he had to try and stop him. He tried to capture Demitri, but when that failed, the next easiest way was to murder Nikolaj, crippling Demitri mentally."

"That's why my mate was murdered?"

"I'm afraid so. Then began our desperate bid to stop the unstoppable. All hell broke loose. The Leader accelerated his plan to kill everyone except the Graciles, Kapka and his fighters took it personally and we ... Well, we did our level best to stop it all. Even went into space to do it. Sounds crazy when I say it out loud."

"So, *you* stopped the Leader from completing his plan?"

"Me and a whole bunch of my friends, including Demitri. A bunch of them died."

Her eyes widen. "And Demitri? Did he survive the ordeal?"

"Yeah, he did, and he didn't." I pull on the back of my neck.

"What does that mean?"

"It means he physically survived the crash landing as we fled from the Leader's collapsing space station, but … He wasn't Demitri anymore. The stress, it was too much for him. Vedmak took over."

"Vedmak?"

"The name he gave his voice."

"I see. And where is this Vedmak who controls Demitri's body, now?"

"I wish I knew. Never could find him, but he's out there. I know he is. I must find him, too. Vedmak is planning something terrible."

"Such as?" Oksana's eyes search mine.

"I don't know, exactly. But it's bad."

Silence fills the room, the muted cold seeping into my clothing.

"Sounds like more Robust hocus pocus to me," she says finally.

"All right, *Oksana*. Your turn. Tell me everything you know about Faruq and where he is. I mean everything."

She rights herself off the stool. "After the HAPs fell and our world was torn out from under us, those of my kind that survived had nothing left. No semblance of the life we had known and no one to lead us out of this hell. I did the only responsible thing I could and took charge."

She looks distinctly uncomfortable as though this sort of sharing is not in her nature. Keep your thoughts to yourself, Mila.

"With nothing left of our world and no desire to live in yours, we tried to find a way out. Maybe a better life existed out there beyond the walls of the last city." Oksana hangs her head.

What is that look? Failure? "Go on," I urge.

"It's called the Road of Death. The only way in from the outside world established long ago when this place was a mining colony." Oksana raises her wet eyes to meet my gaze. "We were not fighters or survivors and were ill-equipped. Between fending off hungry savages and fighting the elements, we lost almost everyone. Those who did survive scattered. I don't know where they are."

Silence ensues for a moment as I wait for her to continue. The air in this dive is heavy and cold, stinging the warm tissues of my lungs with each breath and completing the desolate mood.

"I've tried to get out four times," Oksana says. "Each and every time more prepared than the last, but it's never enough. I don't have the resources or the help to do it."

Get on with it, woman. "How does this connect with Faruq?"

She holds up a hand to stay me. "This last attempt, I tried a different path and came across a Musul encampment far beyond the walls of the city."

I sit up. "What? When was this?"

"Just a week ago."

I'd never considered looking *outside* the walls. "What do you mean encampment?"

"Just as it sounds. A place where they're keeping things they don't want others to know about. Stockpiled weapons and special prisoners to be exact. The madman, Kapka, is frantic. Searching for something that will turn the tide against his enemies, a weapon of mass destruction. The word is he's found it. A nuclear missile stash in the Vel enclave. Apparently, the Soviets buried it there hundreds of years ago."

No way. Is that what they've been hiding all along? Without a word, I fish into my sling bag and grab my old PED. Hardly ever use this thing anymore but it's worth a try. I fire off a message to Gil, my old information broker. He's from Vel. Maybe he's heard something.

Oksana sees my distraction and stops talking. Husniya hasn't said a word but I can tell by the anguish on her face, she's dying inside. To this day, she still doesn't know about my encounter with her brother on the Vapid road those years ago—how I'd had the chance to save him but hadn't. I couldn't bring myself to tell her.

"Yeah, I'm listening. And Faruq?" I say.

"While trying to determine the best way around, my team intercepted a runner bringing information from Baqir."

"I'll be surprised if he told you anything," I huff.

"He did not. My Creed were forced to silence him before he gave away our position, but he was carrying a message to the encampment. I had Zaldov here translate it." She motions to a Creed soldier that has a strangely familiar look to him. For the first time, it occurs to me this particular

Geminoid hasn't left her side since we first met.

"A pleasure to make your acquaintance," Zaldov starts in a hollow robotic voice. "The information we gained was quite informative. We were able to adjust our tactical planning according—"

"Okay, this is new." I chuckle, waving for him to stop. "You've named them? What are they, pets?"

"Just this one." She gives Zaldov's synthetic arm a pat. "He's special."

"Well, I don't trust it."

Oksana smiles, the gesture loaded with an irritating amount of contrived emotion.

"So, what did it say?"

Oksana motions to Zaldov who recites the message.

"'The criminal traitor Faruq will be transferred to this location in two days' time. I will arrive to personally receive him. Have my tent ready. Spare this traitor, Faruq, no pain or injustice—but keep him alive. The Logosian and her band of heathen dogs must *never* be allowed to find him. Failure in this will be punished by death. Sworn this day—Governor Kapka, Savior of the Chosen People and Rightful Ruler of the Musul Nation.'"

It's all I can do to keep from spitting on the floor in disgust.

"Did you verify Faruq was moved there?" Husniya pipes up.

Oksana scoffs. "Why would I do that? Your friend. Your problem. I'm simply trading information."

"So, if I ask for your help in showing me where this encampment is, you're going to tell me to get lost?" I cross my arms.

Oksana rises from her stool, motioning for her Creed, who spasm to life and step forward. "I'm not in the practice of babysitting Robusts."

I stand, my face hot. "Listen here, you uppity sarding church bell. You think you're better than me, but you're not. You're just like the rest of your selfish kind—like these Creed—cold and dead inside. No wonder you're alone with only robotic puppets to keep you company. Demitri at least reconciled with his humanity." I motion for Husniya to grab her rifle. "You can find your own way out of Logos. Come on, Husniya."

I've taken three steps toward the door when the Gracile speaks.

"Mila."

"What?" I stop but let her speak to my back.

"The Road of Death is to the southeast. Once you are on it, bear right at every fork. That path will take you to what you seek."

I nod but still don't turn around.

"Zaldov, come," Oksana says.

"Good copy. Contingent fall in. Stealth movements only," Zaldov says.

Without another word, Oksana leads her group out. Husniya and I stand aside, watching the strange troop move past.

Zaldov stops beside us. A bizarre toothy smile spreads the lead Geminoid's lips apart, showing perfect white dentures. "Mila—"

"Nope. No, thank you. Whatever it is—I don't need to speak with you."

His eyes move rapidly as he processes my words. He rights himself and turns to Husniya, fake smile still stretched wide. "Husniya, I greatly enjoyed our meeting today. My hope is that fortune will bring us together again soon."

Husniya appears stunned but smiles in return. "Thank you Zaldov. Yes, that would be nice."

That would be nice?

"Zaldov, come," Oksana says, and cracks the door and peeks out into the swirling snow.

Zaldov gives a slight bow to Husniya, then follows Oksana.

Husniya is still smiling as the strange group exits. She looks at me and shrugs. "What? He seems nice. Reminds me a little of Demitri."

I shake my head. "Don't put your trust in those abominations. They're wholly unpredictable."

Husniya crosses her arms, scowling. "You're a miserable person sometimes, you know that?"

"Yeah, I do." I grab the flimsy door and glance back at the teen who hasn't moved. "Let's go. Do you want to rescue Faruq or not?"

"What sort of question is that? Of course I do." She steps toward me.

"Then we better get back to Fiori before nightfall."

CHAPTER SEVENTEEN

VEDMAK

Dawn is breaking. A chilling wind snaps across the barren landscape, though the snows have subsided for now. That little *suka* didn't kill me after all. All to save the whining child inside this head? Her mistake. It will be a special pleasure to remove her bowels with a blunt instrument.

A violent cough shudders from within, sending a wave a pain through every fiber of muscle, tendon, and bone. This Gracile shell is broken. The skull feels cracked. Dried blood crusts the skin. Deep slashes flay the body. One hand is now missing, though the severe injury seems to have been cauterized by the scythe. Yes, this body is broken, but it is not yet dead. At the lab, I can heal it. Then I can hunt my pet down and eviscerate the little bitch.

Just not yet.

Now is the time to move forward. So close to Vel, I cannot give up the prize.

I search for my mask, but it is nowhere to be seen. Not that it matters—the supply of Red Mist in the tank is likely depleted, anyway. I must maintain control by the sheer force of my will alone. With a loud groan, I roll to the side and push with the remaining hand until I'm standing. The world shifts and moves out of sync with the swivel of this heavy head. After a few moments, everything rights itself. The muscles of this Gracile machine feel weak, atrophied. To make it to Vel, I will need sustenance.

There's nothing to eat out here, Vedmak.

Foolish boy. You were never a soldier. You know nothing of true survival.

My laser scythe lies in the snow. She didn't take it either. What kind of idiot is she? Some earth-worshiping child of the Vapid? And to be roaming around with a damn tiger. A pity it did not come for me when I

126

was at my best—it would have made a good cloak. I snatch up the scythe and use it as a prop, hobbling a step at a time in the direction of Vel, all the while scanning the environment for threats.

The going is slow, the deep drifts impeding my advance, sucking at the boots as if to hold me back. The rumble in this borrowed stomach is more urgent than any of the wounds suffered so far. The bodies of the fallen have all been buried. Sustenance in their flesh is not an option. Yet, not more than fifty meters ahead, the frozen corpse of the bear pokes from the snow. Its innards have been devoured. Liver, heart and lungs gone—the most nutritious organs taken by the flame-colored fiend. But, it had left behind the meat. And meat I can use.

A swift slice with my laser scythe and a hairy chunk of flesh is removed from the bear's hind quarter. I drop beside the carcass and throw away the extinguished cane in favor of the meaty morsel.

Are you at least going to cook it?

No need.

Holding the frozen meal by the fur, I bite into the frigid flesh. Crystals of iron-flavored ice melt in the mouth. The meat is tough and cold, but satisfying. My stolen body convulses in disgust, the tongue recoiling, but I force the nourishing mouthful down anyway. It plops into the void of an empty stomach.

Disgusting.

Life, little puppet. Life.

Immediately feeling satiated and stronger, I slice off a few more chunks of flesh and stuff them into the pockets of my cloak. Then I continue to hobble along, the cane supporting the full weight of this muscular frame.

In the distance, the last standing lillipad protrudes into the sky from within the walls of Vel. A metallic flag signaling my journey's end. Once I'm there, Merodach will come with a ship and collect both me and my prize, enabling my plan to accelerate—

Why?

Why what, pathetic creature?

Why do this at all? For four years, Vedmak, you've been plotting and scheming to build your army and take Etyom for your own. Maybe to take back

Mother Russia, if it even exists beyond the ruins of the old world. But for what? Why does it matter to you?

"So many questions. Such a child. Always whining. Slapping your lips together like an old woman," I say, trudging on.

Insulting me can't hurt me, Vedmak. You don't have Anastasia to torture. We're alone. It's just you and me."

Another gust of wind nearly topples me over, but with the scythe dug into the snow, I'm able to keep balance. "A simpleton like you would never understand."

I understand well enough, Vedmak. Or do you prefer Genrikh?

"That name should never pass your heathen lips."

I don't have lips now, you do. I only exist in your head. Just as you did in mine, Genrikh. That is your name, isn't it?

"It holds no meaning for me anymore."

The wind stabs through the soiled cloak. Another step forward, and another. This babbling fool will not slow my progress.

I disagree. I think it holds much meaning for you. Living in your consciousness has given me insight I'm sure you never anticipated. Before, I tried to block you out. Hide from you. But now, after four long years, I know who you are, Genrikh Yagoda. Commisar of Internal Affairs—the Narodnyi Komissariat Vnutrennikh Del. Tasked with Stalin's Great Purge. Who knew I was playing host to a war criminal of such notoriety?

The frigid air seems to clamp around the limbs, halting my advance. The muscles fail to respond to my desires as if he were taking back the body for himself. "You think you're clever? So, you read a history book. Books don't make a man. Life does. Sacrifice does."

And you would know sacrifice, wouldn't you? Serving Stalin and the Bolsheviks. Building his canals. Murdering all the innocent souls who did not follow your philosophies. A fool, blinded by loyalty. Until in the end, like so many Soviet officers who conducted political repression, you became a victim of the purge.

"Shut up."

Demoted from the directorship of the NKVD and arrested.

"I said, shut up." These teeth grind together.

Charged with murderous crimes and tried at the Trial of the Twenty-

One.

"I'm warning you, *kozel*."

Found guilty and shot.

"Enough!" This Gracile's scream is sharp but fades fast in the whipping wind.

It's not enough, though is it? Because I know what happened. Things perhaps even you don't know.

Forcing the legs to move, I slog forward again, holding the cloak close to shield from the numbing cold.

The others were pardoned. You knew that, didn't you? The other twenty from your trial? Posthumously, of course, but pardoned all the same. You weren't. Deemed too much of a monster, even by your own people.

"It matters not. None of it does."

And Ida? Did she matter?

"Sard off, you insignificant insect. You know nothing of her."

I know she was shot. Right after you. Executed for your selfishness—your mistakes.

I've stopped again, anger like a wave of old ugliness rising to the surface. Toxic raging heat bubbling up. "You don't know that."

Why do you think you keep seeing her that way in your hallucinations? I see her too. And you see her like that because I know what happened to her. Your consciousness feeds off my knowledge. She was unceremoniously shot in the head, Genrikh. Your wife was murdered because of your misplaced loyalty.

Dropping into the snow, I force a strained roar into the morning air. It seems to go on forever, these Gracile lungs heaving out steaming air until I can scream no more.

Quiet once again fills the barren landscape.

Is this why, Genrikh? You wish to kill and maim and destroy because of your guilt? Because you couldn't protect her? Or is this your revenge on the world for being betrayed by those you trusted? It doesn't have to be like this.

A break in the clouds allows a shard of sunlight to slice across this pilfered face. Its warmth contrasted by the frozen zephyr. I soak in the sensations, the duality of it. Then, a chuckle rolls from deep inside, working its way into the throat until a full raucous belly laugh empties into the air.

"Guilt? Revenge? Such a petulant child you are, Demitri Stasevich.

Not worthy of the Russian name with which you were bestowed." I climb back up, my purpose swelling again. "Do you still not see? I had everything taken from me, including my life, so I may see my destiny clearly. To purge this world of every damn man, woman, and child and replace them with the worthy. I was not an *instrument* of the purge. I *am* the purge—this planet's answer to the disease that is humanity. I am Death, and Hell follows with me."

But Ida …

"Ida knew what it meant to be a Bolshevik. To have a purpose greater than herself. I do not mourn her. She would not disdain my actions. You are simply not fit to speak her name."

My Gracile host cries no further, and so, I continue onward in beautiful silence.

***

It's taken nearly the whole day to arrive at Vel. The last standing lillipad is silhouetted against the cloud-obscured, blood-red sunset. The walls of this enclave are not like the others. Here, the high ramparts are metal. Barbed wire adorns their top, which occasionally crackles with an electrical charge. The Velians wanted to keep even other Robusts out. Of course, now it is clear why—a nuclear stockpile.

Yet, even from the outside, something feels dead. As if cutting themselves off from the world resulted in their slowly rotting away until only the shell remained—inside the putrid vestiges of Robusts lining the streets. Are the Velians dead? Should it be so easy to enter and take what I desire? Another scan of the fortress-like enclave suggests otherwise.

How to enter? There is no main gate like the other enclaves. They would not have built such a bastion without some way in and out. At least an escape route would be needed. The monstrous alien barrier seems to have no end, and no door of any kind. I rap on the metal. Only a dull thunk sounds back. It's anything but thin, or hollow. There's no telling how dense this great barricade is. Once again, the heat of fury boils within. Thrashing out, I beat on the wall in frustration with the only hand I have left. It serves no purpose. Even with this Gracile engine, not even a dent is made.

It's no use, Vedmak. You're never getting in. Forget the stockpile. Forget it all.

Never, wretched weakling. That has always been your folly. Defeated before you begin.

The sky darkens with heavy clouds. The wind howls, the tempest growing as the snow begins to swirl. Another blizzard will soon be upon me.

There's nowhere to go. Nowhere to hide. Just let us freeze out here and it will finally be over.

I think not, boy.

Through the ever-heavier snowfall, the outline of a bunker appears, some two kilometers from the wall's edge. No larger than an old dacha, it can't hold much of importance—except, maybe …

I quicken my pace, hobbling toward the shelter.

While small, it appears to be made of the same thick metal as the enclave wall. Even the tiny porthole, just large enough for an average Robust, is heavy and apparently impenetrable. Even more reason to know the true contents of this metal box. There is an empty thunk, lost to the powerful storm now blustering around me, as I rap on the door with my scythe. Nothing. I tap again, harder this time. There's a clunk from the inside. Scuffling. Then, through an old speaker in the wall, a tinny voice speaks.

"Password?"

Password? Their primitive games are annoying. "Please," I say in the feeblest voice I can muster. "Rippers attacked me. I've been beaten and maimed. They took my hand. I'll die out here. You have to help." I wave my cauterized stump in the air at an imagined camera somewhere overhead.

"You're a Gracile?" says the voice over the speaker.

You're deplorable, is what you are.

He can see me. "Yes. Please, I barely escaped with my life. You have to let me in." I drop my hood so the scars and lacerations can be seen. "I'll freeze or be eaten alive. I need shelter."

Don't let him. Whoever you are, don't let him in.

No use, kozel. He can't hear you.

"Are you alone?" the voice says.

"Yes, I'm alone. But I have things to trade. Please … I even have stims. Easy, Swole, you name it."

That did it. The locks on the inside clunk and the portal cracks open. Before it can be shut again, I push-kick it with all the might left in this engine. The heavy door swings inward, knocking the skinny Robust to the floor. He scrambles for a wheel gun nearby, but I kick it away and stand on his wrist. The runt screams out, the pathetic goat-like cry melding with the storm that has followed me in.

"No, please don't kill me," he whimpers.

Long, lank hair sticks to the scrawny man's features. His sunken eyes are full of fear, though his shaking is so violent and arrhythmic it's probably more due to lack of stims than terror. The temptation of more drugs must have driven his opening of the door.

I release his arm, close the portal behind with a clang, then turn back. "What are you hiding in here?"

"H-h-hiding?" he stutters.

"This place is too heavily fortified to have nothing of worth inside."

Scanning the interior, it's barren save a small table and chair, and an old-fashioned stove with a cooking pot hanging above. It hasn't been used in an age. Such meager furnishings for such a large space.

"There is nothing. Really. I'm alone and everyone is gone. I j-just need something to help me sleep."

Under the table sits an insect-eaten carpet. A clean perimeter of at least two inches surrounds it. How cliché. I grab the table and flip it away. It smashes into the wall. Then, I use the cane of my scythe to lift the rug and flick it over. As suspected, another metal doorway. One with a keypad embedded into it.

"Open it," I command, turning back to my prisoner.

"I can't. I mean. I'm not supposed to. But you don't want to go in there, anyway. There's no one left in there. No Robusts, anyway. Rippers came. They got in and my people were forced out. They fled for their lives."

"Everyone except you."

"There was nowhere to go." The man presses his back up against the metal wall and pulls his knees close to his chest.

In two hobbled strides, I'm upon him. I drop my scythe and, using his scabby tunic, lift him clean into the air. Pain streaks through this body, spiking into the spine and brain, but I cannot let him know of my weakened state. The clickity-clack of something small falling from his jacket pocket onto the floor breaks the silence. It's a cobbled together PED.

I drop him to the deck. He cries out and once again huddles into a ball.

I grab up the PED and flick it on. There's a message.

Oh, sard no. Of all the luck ...

Luck? A wolf's legs feed him, boy. And I am a wolf who has walked a thousand miles. "You know this woman?" I hold the PED close to his eyes.

"M-Mila? Sure, she's an old handler of mine. I mean, we haven't talked in a while, but ..."

Oh, come on, you fool. Be quiet.

"'Urgent. Gil, do you have intel on a nuclear stockpile in Vel? Kapka wants it. Contact me ASAP. Mila,'" I read aloud. "I'd say that was pretty recent, wouldn't you?"

"Yes," the Robust named Gil mumbles.

Can't let her or that animal Kapka claim my prize. There must be a way to stall until Merodach arrives. "You say there are Rippers inside?"

Gil nods feverishly. "Yes, lots. If you go in there, they'll murder you."

I drop to my haunches and meet his gaze. "I thank you for your concern. Perhaps we should send our mutual friend Mila a message, warning her too. What do you think?"

Confusion and fear knit the man's brow into a crease.

Vedmak, no. I know what you're doing.

"Of course you do, little Demitri," I say aloud, confusing the Robust even more. "But *she* doesn't."

CHAPTER EIGHTEEN

MILA

There's no music drifting on the wind today. No children running this way and that, or jovial laughter from those perusing the narrow vendor's alleys. Since the lillipads fell, the Fiorian market is but a shadow of its former self. Faded tattered banners hang, drifting in the light breeze above rows of handmade wooden tables—some with awnings to shield vendors from the nearly constant falling snow. Only a handful of merchants peddle their goods here anymore and even fewer are still out at this hour. Most have already packed their wares in preparation for the long, cold night.

The old man behind one of the wooden tables seems restless, his worried gaze flicking to the other vendors. He's cold and hungry too. I point to two midget potatoes as well as a packet of herbs and spices. *"Dui patate è un paese d'arbe."*

"Sì, Madame." He gathers the items and pushes them forward.

"And the carrots," Husniya says from over my shoulder.

The little hunched man looks from Husniya back to me.

"Okay." I sigh. *"Tutti dui carroti."*

He bobs his head, snaggled teeth hanging precariously in swollen pink gums. *"Bona fame. Ancu qualcosa?"*

I know he doesn't have any meat left, but I'll ask anyway. *"Chiori?"* My famished stare roves across his meager selection of items.

The little man shakes his head and holds out his hand. I deposit a dollar and wait as he fishes two crudely stamped copper coins from his pocket.

"Ringraziu," I say with a wave, handing the items to Husniya to shove in her bag.

The vendor mumbles a reply, shuffling back and forth, raking his remaining foodstuffs into a plain burlap sack. He pulls his fur hat down around his head, then hurries away to find someplace warmer.

As Husniya and I head for the alley that will lead us back to base, a squad of the Fiorian guard march in the opposite direction. Their colorful blouses swish with their arms and legs. *"Unu, duie, trè, quattru,"* the squad leader calls in cadence with the rhythm of the march. He bows his floppy hat as they pass.

I return the gesture. These men still hold to their duty, however ineffectual. It's good for the Fiorian people—for all of us. The appearance of safety is something at least.

We trudge along, the toes of our boots gouging muddy brown furrows in the pristine powder. To our left, the remnants of a fallen lillipad jut from the snow. Beneath the massive structure lies the decimated northwest sector of Fiori, including the destroyed enclave wall. There's no telling how many died when the elite's towers came crashing down without warning.

The years beneath the cloud line have taken their toll and the Gracile structure looks like everything else in Etyom. Seeing the thing, something so perfect in its design lying there so broken, always reminds me of Demitri.

What happened to you, friend? What madness are you caught up in? I know you're out there.

"So, what's the plan?" Husniya says.

"Hmm?"

"The plan. How are we going to go about helping Faruq?"

"Oh." I tuck my chin into my collar. "I'm working on that. We've got a lot to brief Bilgi on and then we have to prep gear. Then there's always the issue of volunteers. A lot of people don't think we should use our resources to search for one man. Just let me handle it."

"If you say so," Husniya mumbles.

I swallow back my irritation. "Hey." I give the girl a nudge and point to the snow-covered ruins of the Forgotten Jewel. "The first time your brother and I came here together to meet the resistance, back before the Creed dropped in here and laid it flat, we met Mos for the first time, got sacks thrown over our heads and—"

"Were taken down in the mine where you thought they killed Faruq at which point you beat up a bunch of their guys. Yeah I know. You told me that story a thousand times," Husniya says, rolling her eyes.

"Okay, smarty pants. But because you've never known different, you

135

don't understand what a big deal it was back then for me to be traveling with a Musul."

Husniya shrugs. "Yeah? Isn't Mos Musul?"

"Yeah. I guess he is, but he's from Kahanga. The Kahangans kinda kept their war to themselves. But you and Faruq? Well, you were from Baqir. Kapka's enclave. And Kapka's Musuls, well, violent Musuls brought the war outside of Baqir."

"So, you were fine with Mos because his Musuls only killed each other?"

"No, no. It's not that. I didn't even know Mos back then. I met Faruq first." Sard it all to hell. "You're twisting my words."

Husniya bores a hateful stare into me for what feels like an eternity—then bursts into a fit of laughter. "You're so easy to mess with. Bring up religion and you get your pants in a twist."

I give her a semi-playful nudge with my shoulder. Just hard enough she has to take a couple of steps to regain balance. "Your brother was the most genuine person I'd ever met, Musul or not. I knew it right away. He was who he said he was." I cast a glance at Husniya. "That's a hard quality to find in people these days. The only thing I knew was I wanted to be around him. That he was someone worth fighting with and ... for."

We wind down through the maze of debris to the hidden entrance beneath. The cold is becoming unbearable. Hopefully, someone is waiting by the door. I bang on it with my fist, hammering out this week's code. From within, the rusted crossbar squeals as it slides free. The hidden door cracks open and Husniya and I shuffle inside.

A shadow darkens the already dim light of the room, broad shoulders blocking the single bulb dangling from the ceiling.

"Look who's back," the familiar voice says. "How was your trip to Logos?"

"Mos." I embrace the Kahangan, slapping his shoulder. "We almost got killed by a bunch of radicals in the Vapid, but my little sharpshooter here saved us."

"Of course she did." He opens his arms to Husniya, who crashes into him and squeezes as hard as she can. "All that training. All those hours of trigger reset drills and breathing control—it's all worth it when the chips are down. Good job, Hus. I'm proud of you."

"Thanks Mos," she mumbles into his chest, her thin frame dwarfed in the safety of his meaty embrace.

"And Kahanga?" I shut the door and draw the bar back across. "Your family? Is everything moving forward with the rebuilding?"

Mos guffaws, the sound clipped like a bark. "It's coming along, though I'm afraid to leave my home enclave for too long. The setbacks have come hard and fast for us. Nature cannot stand a vacuum. With Nazal out of the picture, every power-hungry fool with delusions of grandeur has come to grovel, steal from, or even attack us. A few of these warlords affiliate with Kapka, which means they have access to weapons and supplies. That makes them more difficult to root out and eliminate."

"Do you have what you need? From us, I mean?" I say, slipping out of my heavy jacket.

"Support, yes. Supplies, no. It takes a lot of resources to rebuild something so fractured."

"In time, Mos, under your leadership, Kahanga will thrive. You'll see."

I rub my hands together, hoping friction will bring my fingertips back to life. "Hey, have you seen the old man? I need to talk to him."

Mos gives a shake of his jug-like head. "I was told he's resting. Hasn't been feeling well today."

"Mmm, tomorrow then. It's just as well. I'm smoked."

Husniya holds out her hand. I unload my pistol and hand it to her.

"You've got dinner?" I ask.

She pats her canvas bag. "I'll drop this stuff with Gus in the kitchen. It'll be ready shortly."

"Okay. I'll see you there after I drop my stuff. Tomorrow, we'll gear up and plan for that other thing."

"Yeah, Mos, guess what? We know where—"

"Not now, Hus. Tomorrow okay. I gotta pitch this right."

"Okay," Husniya says, swallowing her excitement. "G'night Mos." She heads off to check our weapons back into the armory and take the food to Gus.

"Goodnight, my little Baqirian princess," Mos calls out.

Husniya grins over her shoulder as she retreats.

"Where what is?" Mos says, staring at me.

"Tomorrow. I'm exhausted."

My dark-skinned friend puts a massive paw on my shoulder. "Sure. Then how about you join me for a drink after you eat?"

"You know I don't do sloop, Mos."

"Not sloop. Ghofaun is breaking into a bottle of his unfiltered rice wine. He calls it Dreamy Clouds. Makes it himself," Mos says with a wink.

"Dreamy Clouds, huh?" I shrug, my body heavy. Perhaps it'll help me sleep. "Yeah, I suppose I could go for some of that."

***

"Mila ... Don't leave me ... Please."

"Faruq!"

My body wrenches awake from the alcohol-driven blackout. My chest heaves, my mind clouded with the fading of painful memories.

Sard. What time is it?

I sit up on my narrow cot still dressed in yesterday's clothes. A groan escapes my lips. This is what I get for being talked into drinking with a Kahangan and a Zopatian monk. The hangover amplifies my exhaustion, sending a flotsam of failure and jetsam of regret floating upward into my consciousness like trash rising to the surface of a scum-covered pond. I'm so tired. So many things remain unresolved. So many friends lost, missions failed. Months and years of tireless pursuit of the impossible. How long can I continue like this before I'm all used up?

The door to my chambers cracks open and Husniya pokes her head in. "Are you going to sleep all morning? Bilgi is up if you want to talk to him."

"Give me a minute," I moan, rubbing my eyes.

"What happened to you?"

"Dreamy Clouds."

"What?"

"Forget it. Just—can you find me some krig?"

The girl takes a step closer and mumbles something to herself.

I try to raise my eyes, but the light is killing me. "Huh?"

She shakes her head. "I'll see if I can find some. Here." She hands me a stack of clean clothes and a warm basin of water from Filly. "I picked out stuff I thought you'd wear."

"Thanks, Hus. Go find Bilgi. Tell him I'll be at command in a few."

"Okay." Husniya disappears, pulling the door shut.

I'm clean and halfway through getting dressed when I hear the familiar chirp of a waiting PED message. I rifle through my satchel and pull the old janky piece of Gracile tech out. It chirps again. Clicking down to *new messages*, I hit the enter key and it pops onto the screen; a response from Gil. "'Bout time," I murmur. At least he's alive.

Mila. There's no time to explain. The stockpile is compromised. Bad things are happening here. I need your help. Now. ~ Gil

That's it? I scroll back. Did I miss something? Nope. That's the whole message. Damnation. Always cryptic. Since when did Gil ever want or need my help? Sard. Do I go after the stockpile or Faruq? If I don't move on Faruq, I may lose him again. But if Kapka gets to the stockpile, we're in trouble. Need to talk to Bilgi first.

I finish dressing and head out to the meeting room connected with command, dropping my soiled garments with Filly in the boiling room along the way. A man rewiring one of the lights greets me with hope in his eyes.

"Paladyn. What good will you do for the people today?" he says.

"Whatever I can." I fake a smile. Did I mean that?

"Very good. Blessings upon your task, Paladyn," he says.

I push into the meeting room, the grinding of the old metal door heralding my arrival as it swings inward. At the dust-covered table sits Bilgi and Ghofaun as well as a handful of others, including that jackbag, Giahi. How is it he always manages to get invited to these things?

"You look exhausted," Ghofaun says as I take a seat next to him at the table.

"No thanks to you and your Dreamy Clouds."

"It's a little strong, especially for the uninitiated." Ghofaun bares a sly smile. "Here, this should help." The monk slides a cup of steaming krig in my direction.

"Thanks." My voice disappears into the tin cup as it rises to my lips.

"Where's Mos?"

"He had to leave early this morning. Overnight, a rival faction attacked his people," Bilgi says, his voice like sand grating beneath the wheel of a cart.

I nod and take another sip. "They're having a hard time of it."

The old man coughs into his sleeve.

"Feeling all right, Bilgi?" Yuri asks from across the table.

I turn my eyes back to Bilgi. Is he sick? After the loss of the arm, he recovered and had been in relatively good shape. But looking at him now, something's not right. His eyes are sunken into his pallid face and there's a sheen of sweat on his brow. He coughs again, harder this time and the group at the table shrinks away.

"Go rest, Bilgi. We can handle this," I say, setting down my krig.

"I'm fine," he says. "It's only a fever. We need to discuss what you found out on your trip."

The room waits for my answer, the anticipation palpable. Even Giahi sits with his hairy forearms crossed.

Where do I start? "There's more to all of this than we first believed. What's even more strange is it all seems connected." I take a sip of krig, the hot black liquid sliding down my throat like warmed engine oil.

"Please continue," Bilgi says, coughing again.

Start them off easy, Mila. "The butchered people. That's not Kapka's doing, nor is it the Rippers. It's something else."

"Yes," Bilgi says. "But we still don't know what?"

"No. The bodies are cauterized at the wound site as though by flame. No weapon I know of can do that and no one I've spoken to has any answers. The sisters of the Vestal order said some of the Logosian people were taken, too."

Bilgi takes a moment to contemplate my words. "Hmm. And what else, Mila?"

Step two. "Kapka's threat has elevated. His people have upped the bombings and are now executing travelers in the Vapid. Kapka is near possessed, searching for an old-world Russian nuclear weapons stash. He knows if he finds it he'll have the power to bend everyone to his will. He's preparing for open war."

Whispered curses cascade around the table.

"Do we have any idea where this stash might be?" Yuri asks, his wizened eyes cool and calculating.

"Actually, we might. I got a message from Gil, my old information broker. He confirmed the stockpile Kapka wants is in Vel, but he also said something bad was happening and that he needed help."

"Then we need to move. We can't risk Kapka getting his hands on something like that or we're all doomed," Bilgi says, his tone resolute.

"There's something else." I pause.

The room grows quiet. Bilgi narrows his eyes. "Well, out with it, girl."

Here goes nothing. "Faruq is alive."

Giahi groans and others exchange glances and hushed words. "This again?"

I glare at Giahi. "You were there when we saw him in the Vapid. You know he could be alive."

"Yeah, I know, and you tracked him for days and found *nothing*. That was years ago," Giahi scoffs.

"Listen, I know you all don't believe me," I call out above the voices. "But I have good information on where he is this time. He's alive and if I can—"

"Enough of this sard," Giahi says, leveling a sausage-like finger at me. "You are not going to risk the lives of our people and waste our resources looking for some Musul you had a crush on. He's a corpse by now. Stop being a child and get over it."

I rocket to my feet, rage—pure and volcanic—bursting forth. "You don't get to interrupt me. You've never cared about anyone but yourself, which is why you're a coward who doesn't have the stones to be a leader. And I swear, Giahi, if you *ever* interrupt me while I'm speaking again, I'll stomp your sarding guts out!"

Ghofaun grabs me by the shoulders and Bilgi manages to stand between me and my opponent, bracing himself on the table. My friends urge me to sit.

Giahi reclines there, smirking, his stare traveling around the table to each and every person. "Is this the sort of rash, hot-tempered leadership we need around here? Do we really want this irrational cupcake gambling with

141

our lives?"

Bilgi's expressionhardens. "Giahi, do shut up."

"I'm just saying what everyone else is thinking."

"This just became your last command meeting." Bilgi forces the words through gnashed teeth. "Remove yourself or I'll have you thrown out."

Giahi stands, glowering. "My last command meeting? She's the loose cannon—kick her out. Oh no, but you couldn't do that to your pet—"

"Get out." Bilgi shouts, his frail body quaking with the effort.

Giahi locks stares with me, grinning devilishly as he moves to the door.

"I'll knock that stupid smirk right off your saucebox." I jab my finger around Ghofaun's shoulder at him. "Don't think so? Wait and see."

"Sure, Mila. You bet," he says, slamming the door on the way out.

"Mila, please. The billowing flame is only capable of destruction," Ghofaun says softly, his voice as calm as a flowing stream. "Please, sit." He motions to my chair.

Bilgi releases a sigh. He slumps back into his seat, looking even older and more sickly. "I'm sorry about that. I invited him because I assumed he could act like an adult."

Ghofaun gives me an earnest nudge. "Are you all right?"

"Yes." A deep breath swells in my lungs. "I'm sorry for the outburst, guys." I glance at the faces in the room. "This matter over Faruq is personal to me, as you all well know."

"Mila, dear." Yuri's tone is gentle, but it holds an air of pity. "It's been years since we had anything of substance to go on regarding Faruq."

His meaning isn't lost on me. I press my teeth together.

"Mila, I love your passion, I always have." Bilgi leans closer. "But you know we can't go looking for Faruq. We can't risk our people on a dangerous errand with little chance of success. I know you must understand this."

"Bilgi, I wouldn't consider it if I didn't think the chances were good—"

"The information, where did it come from?" Bilgi interrupts.

He's not going to like this. "A Gracile who traded me for it."

"A Gracile." He sits back, folding his arms. "After all this time, a Gracile appears and you actually believe the intel is reliable?" He pauses and clears his throat. "Please, everyone give us a moment."

Yuri gives me a patient dip of his head and Ghofaun pats my arm. Chairs scrape their legs on the floor. Mutters follow and the rest shuffle out, leaving Bilgi and me alone.

A stillness descends upon the room. Minutes pass.

"Okay, Bilgi. Speak your piece." I say, breaking the stalemate.

"Mila." Bilgi sighs. "You have to start thinking big picture. Look at me. I can't do this forever. If you are going to lead, you have to have everyone's best interest at heart when you make a decision. That's the only way people will follow you. We cannot sacrifice so much for one man, even if he were alive."

Don't you dare cry, Mila.

"I need you to focus on the threat Kapka poses in trying to find this arsenal. If he knows it's in Vel and he beats us there, we're done. You understand that? Kapka cannot be allowed to put his hands on nuclear weapons. Even if Faruq is alive, he won't be if Kapka blows us all to hell."

I hate it when he's right. "I get it, Bilgi," I say, staring at my lap.

The door dashes open, Bilgi and I look up.

"I'm sorry to interrupt," Ghofaun says, out of breath. "But Husniya is gone."

"What do you mean *gone*?" I say, standing.

"She must have slipped out earlier. Jape at the door said she left in full gear." The monk is already wearing his jacket and carrying my stuff.

"How long?" Bilgi asks.

"Hard to say. If she was listening in, thirty minutes. But if she left this morning, a few hours."

If she was listening, she heard what I said about having seen Faruq in the Vapid. She knows I kept it from her. I'm already moving to the door.

"Mila, wait. Think about this," Bilgi calls out.

"Bilgi, I will not stand by and allow something to happen to Husniya." Taking my sling bag and heavy jacket from Ghofaun, I pause long enough to hold the old man's stern gaze.

"I can't allow this," he replies, his voice full of anguish.

"Then designate whoever you'd like to try and stop us—" I look to the monk, whose expression is as hard as forged iron. "Just don't send anyone you want back."

143

CHAPTER NINETEEN

VEDMAK

The two-kilometer tunnel is narrow and dark. Dead, overhead glass bulbs no longer light the way. My scythe, crackling and alive, does the trick, bathing the rocky walls in cobalt light. Yet even my weapon's power source is fading, the white-hot blade sputters as the core nears the end of its reserve. It will need recharging soon.

Alongside, Gil—my pathetic stim-addicted prisoner—scurries with a hollow look in his beady eyes. A real fear of death and the allure of more stims has ensured his compliance. He will show me the way into Vel—the last great secret Etyom has to offer. He said the stockpile was not what we would expect and that it would need to be seen to be believed. On any other day, I would have shed his blood to gain the answer. But, after a string of such tiresome defeats, the lure of a game is too appealing.

The door before us is heavy, solid steel by the looks of it. It may even be hermetically sealed. Embedded in the wall is a key panel. Crude but effective. Depending on the length of the code, it would be impossible to guess. Lucky for me, I won't have to.

"Open it."

Gil scurries ahead and hovers around the keypad. "Are—are you sure you want to do this? It's not safe. Bad things happened in there—"

"Bad things are about to happen out here," I say, holding the scythe closer to his face. The plasma spits and chokes on the fading battery. "Open it."

He doesn't reply, but instead whimpers, tapping in a code. The relentless clicking of the keys begins to grate on my nerves. Just as I'm about to put him out of his misery for taking too long, the door pops open with a *clunk—hiss*. Through the crack, a stream of light flickers arrhythmically.

Fires? Is everything destroyed?

I click off my scythe and stow it on my belt beneath my cloak, then pull on the thick door.

144

What the hell?

For once, the peacock and I are aligned.

The passageway opens immediately into a flowing green hill that descends a kilometer or so in a gentle slope before leveling out into the floor of a U-shaped valley. At the gorge's center is a lake, wide and clear. Scattered throughout the grassy hills are houses and small dwellings akin to those owned by the farmers of old. And in the middle of each cluster of homes, great white struts formed of triangular lattices stretch up and support a huge glass ceiling also comprised of wedge-shaped panels. A fake blue sky, complete with clouds, is projected in each of the ceiling panes—though some flicker on and off, while others have gone black. It's as if Yahweh himself were controlling the heavens again. Slowly I step inside, inspecting the blades of green beneath these feet.

A hologram? This can't be real.

"What is this?" I spit.

The gaunt Robust sidles up. "It's Vel."

I've never seen a lake before. This is incredible. Is it manmade or natural? And the sky is so blue, I'd forgotten how it looked. Been down here so long—

Silence, peacock. Let me think. Everything still aches, and the stump of an arm throbs and burns. Must concentrate. I turn back to the emaciated Robust. "Don't mock me, runt. All this green is real?"

"Yes, it's a biome," he says, shutting the door behind us. It hisses as the seal is once again formed. "It is—was—one of the Gracile projects."

What is he talking about?

I pluck grass from the soil. On closer inspection, it's dry and beginning to brown. It doesn't actually smell like grass. Not how I remember it, anyway. Synthetic. "Start talking, Velian, or lose your tongue."

Gil rubs his hands together. "When the migration first happened, when the plague first took hold, it was the rich who arrived first. Those who would be Graciles." His gaze flits from one side of the valley to the next, his brow wet with worry. "We shouldn't be out here."

"Spit it out, Kozel."

Never thought I'd say this, but for the love of Yeos, do as he says.

"The story goes that Etyom as we know it, or knew it, wasn't planned this way," the Robust whispers. "The lillipads were never meant to be. The first people here tried to set up a power source and began building a biome, to escape the NBD. Vel was the first enclave built with the beginnings of the biome inside." Gil licks his cracked lips. "It was never finished. The power source didn't come online in time. Too many people arrived, mainly the poor. Those infected with the plague already. It's why the Creed were used in the first place. To defend Vel. But with the biome a failure, the Graciles switched tactics. They began building the lillipads to escape the dying—using the Creed as a security force to ensure they weren't interfered with. They sealed off Vel from the outside world, hoping one day to return to it. It forced the newcomers to build their own enclaves. The poor, the Robusts, chose to construct them around lillipads because they were promised trade agreements. They were lied to."

"The biome is working now, or was," I say, motioning to the flickering fake sky above.

How did no one find this? It's entirely below ground level? But something overhead would have been able to see.

He can't hear you, idiot. Let me ask the questions.

"They started with solar power, but eventually someone brought or invented two fusion reactors," Gil says.

Nikolaj and I worked on those.

"The Graciles ensured they were used for whatever they wanted up in the sky," the Robust continues. "But once they were done they immediately turned back to Vel to finish the biome. And armed with knowledge of the fusion reactors, were able to complete the power fission source in Vel." Gil motions to a long, white, squarish building with two stacked chimneys banded in red, sat on the shore of the lake. Nearby is a small, but deep quarry with sizeable steps cut into it where machines have stripped away the precious metals.

It's not a stockpile—it's a uranium-refining plant and power station.

"Why a nuclear power plant? Why not use a fusion reactor down here?"

Because the Leader was using them to power the lillipads, as well as my research.

"Oh, you mean the research he used to create a black hole?"

"What?" Gil says.

I grab him by his tattered shirt. "What was this place for?"

"Agriculture, mainly," he splutters. "Food. Vegetables. For the Graciles. We gave them most of what we grew, and they let us keep our way of life."

He means hæven. Imagine if the other Robusts found out?

I don't care about any of this. "Is the power plant functional? And where the hell are the Rippers you talked about? How did they even get in here? You better not be lying to me, you little snake."

"I don't know," Gil whimpers. "The Rippers are here, I swear. They killed almost everyone and took over like a bunch of damn squatters. I don't know how they got in."

"And the plant?" I ask.

He shakes his head. "There's some power because the sky is still on. But it looks damaged. No telling if it's a problem in the grid or the plant."

"Then let's find out." I grab the Robust by the armpit and haul him to his feet with an audible groan. Pain shoots through this body and into my consciousness. "There must be a command center in here. Show it to me."

He points at the largest abode, which also happens to be the closest.

Do you not think there'll be Rippers in there? It's the biggest building besides the plant. It's suicide.

Suicide? Make up your mind, peacock. First, you want us dead, then you want to live. Your lack of conviction is exhausting.

The weakling is silent and it satisfies me greatly.

***

Keeping low to the ground, we move silently toward the governor's house. The constant fading and reappearance of parts of the heavens casts Vel into temporary shadow and impedes our progress. The further inside we venture, the more obvious it is that Rippers do inhabit this place. Patches of blood-stained grass and soil punctuate the otherwise picturesque landscape. Dried innards and connective tissue webs across distant shrubs. But no bodies. No attire. No weapons. The victims have been stripped of furnishings and flesh.

Disgusting. I know it's not possible, but I think I'm going to be sick.

Don't be so pathetic. It's called survival. Dog eat dog. The way it's always been and always will be.

Gil rounds the corner of the low wall surrounding the house. Up close, it's easy to see it's been based on the old Soviet *gosdachas*—mansions for the rich and elite. Stalin himself had one, the filthy dog. This monstrosity was clearly built by new Russians with their *new* money. The ugly eclectic design in no way representing the grace of the original *dachniks*. Look at it. Can't even decide what it is. Two floors, in a shape that makes no sense, built entirely of red brick. The bars across the white-framed windows did little, the glass all but broken and now barricaded with wood.

"There's a remote, control station in the annex," Gil says. "Most is controlled from the plant itself, but in case there was a meltdown, this place could perform emergency tasks."

"How many Rippers are inside?"

"How should I know?"

"Take a guess, you little fool," I hiss back.

Gil is physically shaking. "Hey, you got those stims like you promised? Maybe some Easy, to take the edge off?"

I wrap the only hand I have left around his feeble throat and squeeze. "How. Many?"

"Maybe thirty?" he chokes out. "Rippers squat, and cram themselves in. But too many and they'll in-fight. Please ..."

I release him and he tumbles backward, wheezing and clutching at his scrawny neck.

"We go in quietly, through the rear to the annex. If there are Rippers there, you get fed to them first. If not, you get your fix."

Gil's eyes are wide, but he knows he cannot refuse. He climbs to his feet, and with the occasional shove in his back, we make it to the annex door.

A light rattle of the old-fashioned handle and the portal clicks open. No security here.

Inside, the décor clashes so much even these pompous Gracile eyes are offended. A mix of Soviet-style wallpaper and marble statues line the walls, while an array of technology is lumped on a table in the middle of the

148

room—monitors and keyboards strewn over it.

"Make it work," I rasp. "Tell me if the grid or the plant is faulty."

The Robust does as instructed, all the while glancing up to check for danger.

Vedmak, this doesn't feel right. Where are the Rippers?

Quiet, kozel. You should be grateful. Without the Rippers, I'll have to rethink my strategy for dealing with that little *suka* you're always crying about.

You only want the power plant. You won't even need to modify the tokamak. You can move your operation here. Just leave her be.

Don't try and placate me. You do not wish this to come to fruition. You fight me at every turn. Besides, killing your god-fearing friend is as important to me as the plan itself.

But why?

It's chess, boy. Everyone needs a suitable opponent. You will never be it. But she, yes, she can present me with a challenge.

"You're not going to like this," Gil whispers.

"Spit it from your lips."

"It's the reactor," Gil says, rubbing frantically at his arms. "There's a breach of some kind. It's leaking radiation. Slowly, but it's happening. It won't melt down, but the emergency shutdown is in process. It takes a while, but it will happen. At least that's what the readout says."

Guess you won't be moving your operation here after all. Or laying a trap for Mila.

You divide the pelt of a bear not yet killed, stupid child. I can still take the fuel, already purified in neat little packages directly from the core. And as for the bitch—

The door at the other end of the room flies open. Gil hits the floor and in the same instant, my scythe is aflame. I coil in readiness. A Ripper child bounds in, hair in knots, clothed in a cut-up fabric likely stolen from the original residents of this *gosdacha*. It's a female no more than five. She stands wide-eyed in front of me, staring up. Seconds later, two women rush in after her, gabbling something in a language I don't understand.

Ripper women and children? Is this a nursery or something? The men roam the Vapid, like hunter-gatherers. They must hide their women somewhere else normally ... but this place. This would have been perfect.

One of the Ripper women grabs the child and drags her back into the fold of clucking females. She barks something at me in what sounds like garbled English.

Need to get the attention of these chickens. "Gil, you have served me well. I believe there is no more you can do for me is there."

From his knelt position, the Robust stares at me with fearful eyes. "I have done what you asked, right? You'll give you me my stim and release me?"

"Release. Yes ... Debt is beautiful, but only after it is repaid."

"Wait—"

Gil's head leaves his shoulders and bounces across the floor, before coming to a rest at the feet of the savages. They shriek and kick it away. Apparently, they do not share their males' obsession with bloodlust.

"The greatest stim is the split second between life and death. An eternity in the most infinitesimal moments. Then, the great release. Everything I promised."

My scythe crackles and spits.

You're a bastard, Vedmak.

Actually, I knew my father. Unlike you. Now, quiet your mouth.

I wave my scythe in their direction, and then at the child. The horror in their eyes tells me they understand. These animals still fear for their young. They'll do as they're told.

You can't do this, Vedmak. I won't let you.

"Oh, but I can, and I will," I say aloud. "I think it's time we sent my Rat some more instructions, don't you?"

Giahi. I forgot about Giahi.

"But first, to ensure safe passage to the power station." I step forward, the overhead lights casting my shadow across the worried face of the grubby child. My scythe's blade sputters white-hot plasma. The women pull her closer to them.

Vedmak, no ...

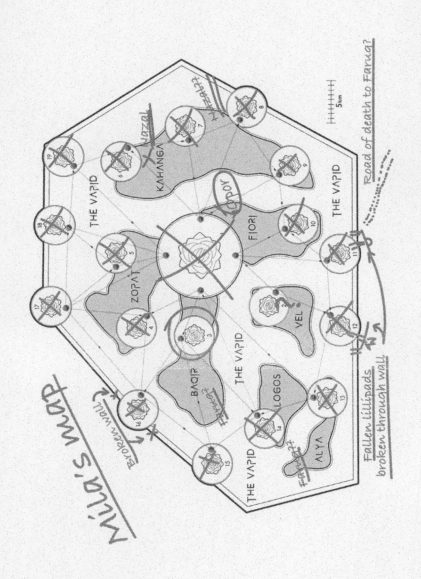

Milla's map

THE VAPID

HAZAL

KAHANGA

COPOY

FIORI

ZOPAT

THE VAPID

BAQIR

VEL

LOGOS

THE VAPID

ALYA

THE VAPID

Broken wall

Fallen lilipads
broken through wall

Road of death to Farxa?

5 km

CHAPTER TWENTY

MILA

Her tracks are long gone, lost in the deluge of snow. For a kilometer we've walked on anyway, hoping she didn't deviate from Oksana's instructions—find the Road of Death to the southeast; bear right at every fork. Up to the point where the teen's tracks became too filled-in to follow, she had done just that.

Damnation, it's cold. The landscape is smothered in fresh powder, deep and crystalline. I hug my arms against my body. So focused on catching up to her before she got too far, I'd forgotten to put on enough layers. Movement means warmth. Keep moving, Mila.

How did I miss she was so on edge? Husniya told Jape at the door she was running out on an errand. When we asked him about it, he told us she'd been fully geared up. Unbelievable, the nerve on that girl. What does she think she's going to do alone against a troop of Kapka's men, other than get herself killed—or worse—captured?

"Why couldn't she wait, for once?" I mutter, concern twisting with anger in my gut.

"If she overheard our conversation, she knew where it was going. You did too, I think," Ghofaun replies. "You never told her you'd seen Faruq once before and were unable to rescue him?"

"No, I didn't. And now to top it all off she's found out anyway, gone off on her own, and forced us to defy Bilgi's direct orders. The old man will have my head for this."

"All the more reason our mission must be a success," Ghofaun says.

Another kilometer disappears beneath our boots as we follow the desolate road that seems to lead nowhere. The Road of Death; the name is appropriate. We could lie down and be covered by the ever-falling snows, our bodies sinking into the eternal drifts, and there we'd remain, forgotten forever.

Ahead another fork in the winding path.

How many splits is this now? Five? Six? "Ghofaun, I don't think we're gonna find—"

"Mila." The monk grabs my jacket sleeve. "Look."

Beyond the gloom of gray and floating precipitation, a glow emanates from beyond the bend. Without a word, Ghofaun and I slink from the road, hiding in the frozen landscape. Out here, away from the decaying urban backdrop, my black leather jacket isn't doing me any favors in the way of concealment. Maybe if I needed to I could crouch down and look like a rock. Yeah, right, Mila. Let's not try that.

Between the sparse, dead shrubbery, we skulk. A combination of low crawling and low running across danger areas keeps us out of sight. Ghofaun slides like a wraith from one point of concealment to another, visible yet invisible, a specter in human form. I feel clumsy in comparison.

On either side of the road we wait, watching Kapka's sentries at the forward barricade as they laugh over some vulgarity. A nod from Ghofaun and we move as one. My left arm snakes around the neck of the closer man, my right foot pressing flat on the back of his knee, buckling his legs. A muffled groan is all that escapes him as I twist the man to the ground and lock my arms down. A moment of vise-like pressure and he gurgles, his eyes rolling back, his body slumping to deadweight in my arms.

"Goodnight." I release him, and his head thumps against the icy road.

The monk is standing over his felled guard, like he's been waiting on me to finish. "Whenever you're ready," he says, just above a whisper.

I grab the Draganov autoloading rifle from the ground where the sentry dropped it. Might come in handy. Missing its scope, the long rifle has iron-sights only, but otherwise, it's in great shape. Never shot one of these, but thankfully the action appears similar to the Kalashnikov. Tabbing the magazine free, it's packed full of gleaming brass. What are the odds? Kapka must have found a sealed ammo cache. I pilfer two more loaded ten-round mags from the felled guard and shove them into the pockets of my jacket.

Leaving the men where they lay, we advance on our hands and knees to the perimeter of the encampment. Lying prone with Ghofaun on my left, I take in the visible assets and movements of the enemy camp.

"Damnation," I say under my breath.

Inside the perimeter of eight-foot-long wooden stakes jutting from the snow at angles designed to maim, there's easily twenty-five fighters. At least half are armed with some sort of old-world firearm. And that's only what we can *see*. There's probably another ten who will come running as soon as the action kicks off.

Where the hell is she? "Can you see Husniya?"

Ghofaun shakes his head. "No. But the girl is as vulpine a creature as I've seen. She's more than capable of remaining undetected. It's her judgment I'm worried about."

"You can say that again." What are you planning, Husniya?

The larger tent must be Kapka's personal quarters. Of course, the tyrant of Baqir won't still be here. What reason would he have to remain? Yet, the tent looks occupied, complete with a small fire inside its heavy canvas walls. A shiver crawls up my spine at the thought of facing off with that maniac again.

"If Faruq *was* here, where would they keep him? Any thoughts?" I ask.

"Your guess is as good as mine. Maybe in the back near where that low awning is. Are those cages?" Ghofaun says.

"I can't tell from here. And can't see a good way to do this."

"Which is why we shouldn't."

"I agree, Ghofaun, but we're here at an encampment that's not supposed to exist. The information was good. Faruq could be here. We have to at least— "

"Oh no, Mila." Ghofaun tosses his head toward my right, his eyes wide. "We're too late."

Inside the outermost edge of the camp, creeping from one point to another, there she is. A guard passes and Husniya strikes like a coiled snake, the edge of her hand landing hard across his neck. The man falters and she drags him to the ground. Another strike to the face sends him out. She hauls his body behind a nearby woodpile.

"Foolish girl," I hiss. "She's going to get herself killed."

Ghofaun is already shrugging out of his heavy clothing. "I need a diversion," he says without looking up.

My stomach roils. "I'll go. Let me go."

"No. It is a matter of honor. She's my pupil. I will go after her. I won't argue this." He snugs his kukri blade into his belt and raises his hardened gaze to mine. "Give me a distraction."

My teeth press together, the muscles of my jaw tightening. "I can do that," I say, pulling the Draganov over.

A panicked shout from the camp. Dread crawls its way across the length of my body. One of the guards has raised the alarm. They've found the body.

"Ghofaun, we've got to—"

The monk is gone.

Sard it all. I scramble to the bottom of the rise and head for the main gate, the massive rifle in tow. Let's do this.

Shouts fill the snow-laden air, hanging with the drifting flurries, as I step onto the road. The gate is open, held only by three men armed with rifles. Their attention is diverted to the ruckus inside the camp. One catches me in his peripheral and spins around, jabbering in his native tongue.

The Draganov snaps up, sights aligned. A bark of fire and the barrel blazes hot three times in succession. The heavy rounds do what warmongers manufactured them to do, tearing ragged red holes into the stupefied guards even as they fumble with their weapons. I keep my eyes up, away from the gasps and groans of the dying men, my feet carrying me through the gate and into the encampment.

They chose this side. If that means they have to die, so be it.

The heavy rifle swivels left and right, tracking with my line of sight. My mouth forms the words carved into the hidden corners of my heart. "Be here, Faruq. Be alive."

Bullets streak overhead and whine past. I stumble, my momentum pitched forward into a roll that takes me to the kneeling position. There's a sharp sting in my left forearm and thigh. Sard. Pivoting hard to the left, I brace the rifle and lock on a group of radicals trying to take potshots at me from behind a wooden platform. Idiots. The weapon I carry, their own equipment, is meant for busting light cover.

The long rifle gushes fire and the screams of my enemies sing in my ears as the jacketed rounds shred the barrier in a spray of splintered wood and blood. I strip the mag free and insert the second, whip the charging handle back and let it fly forward with a satisfying *crack*. I forge ahead, my head filled with the violence of war. Where are my allies? Know your target and what's beyond, Mila. Don't hit your friends by accident.

The men without firearms charge me with their blades. My arms shake, my back protesting as the rifle comes up again, hellfire pouring forth. They die like the others, tumbling into the shallow ditches that will be their frozen graves. But their numbers are too great. No time to reload. Damnation.

Releasing the bayonet, I flick it free and hear it snap into position. "Where is he? Where is Faruq?"

From the right, there's a flash of movement. My heart soars as Ghofaun and Husniya, side by side, leap into the charging ranks of angry terrorists, creating a wild melee of furious screams and clanging blades. Ghofaun moves with the born grace of a dancer, feigning left and spinning right. The flying heel of his foot connects with the chins of three attackers in succession, knocking them back. At close range, the deadly curved kukri blade in his grasp is more formidable than all the bullets in the world. The warrior monk intercepts a blow meant for Husniya, lopping the attacker's hand from his wrist with a single strike. Another swipe inside and he's severed a man at the neck, blood issuing into the snow at their feet. He ducks and rises again, the blade flashing as he completes a handless cartwheel into a group of the men. Shrieks of mortal terror fill the air.

Beside him, young Husniya is no wallflower. Fighting tooth and nail, she dashes forward, intercepting a machete. She strips the weapon from the fighter's grasp and sweeps the man's legs out from under him—knocking his skull against the frozen earth, before leaping into the air—her whole body a battering ram as she crashes into the next man with a brutal double knee strike.

With a ragged scream, I launch into the fray, swinging the cumbersome Draganov rifle that now feels like lifting a plank of steel. Parry, dodge, duck. I drive toward my friends, shoving the sharpened bayonet spike into the chest of a wild-eyed fanatic. Blood spurts from his mouth. I kick him free and turn, ready for the next.

A gunshot like the sound of a cannon blasts into the air.

"Enough," a heavily accented voice screams out ahead of us.

I tear the empty magazine from the Draganov, numb fingers fumbling with the last mag in my pocket. I yank it free and snap it into the well, charging the rifle's action in one fluid movement. Together, backs to each other, Ghofaun, Husniya, and I face down the handful of remaining terrorists.

"Logosian!"

I turn, my rifle rising. Ahead is the maddened countenance of Kapka. My stomach contorts. Enclosed in the warlord's fist is the dark shaggy hair of a disheveled man. Kapka holds an antique gold-plated revolver to his head. Though emaciated, there is no mistaking him. It's Faruq. The angle of his jaw, the long nose, his eyes as dark as a winter river. His hands are bound in front and he's clothed in a burlap sack. My heart cramps.

"Faruq!" I shout.

There is no response, not a single shred of recognition on his face.

Tears well.

"Faruq! It's me, your sister!" Husniya shouts.

The fanatics gasp for breath, grunting curses as they plot their next move.

Kapka grins, his teeth a jumble of pale yellow and shimmering gold.

"I'll kill you, monster." I shake with the words.

"So, you've finally come for this traitor? Why now? You've wasted your pathetic lives." He shuffles farther behind his hostage. "I'll execute him and my men will finish you where you stand."

My back muscles scream and my arms quiver under the weight of the long rifle. I can't close the fingers of my left hand. Rivulets of blood drip from my forearm and off my elbow. Down the sights, the barrel wavers. No shot.

"Can you kill me from there before I do him? Are you that good?" He taps Faruq on the head with the barrel of the old wheel gun.

Husniya steps forward, her hands up, tears streaming down her face. "Faruq, it's me. It's Husniya. I've come for you, brother. Please. Look at me. I'm here."

The scene stirs an earthquake of such fury in my chest, I feel I might explode.

"You are an utter disappointment to me, daughter, but I am glad you are here for this." Kapka grins. "I wanted you here to see me finish this traitorous brother of yours." He cocks the hammer on the pistol and presses it to Faruq's temple.

"No!" Husniya shouts.

I've only got one shot. Any deviation and Faruq is dead. We all are. My body quakes with fear and adrenaline. I draw the sight picture and squeeze the trigger.

The Draganov round rips through Kapka's arm.

Faruq explodes to life, grabbing the pistol in Kapka's hand. He wrenches it from the warlord's grasp.

The men around us converge. I bare my teeth and unload the full capacity of my magazine into them. Ghofaun and Husniya plow into the ranks of the few fighters that remain.

The big-bore revolver booms again, blasting a hole through Kapka's groin. The tyrant shrieks and drops to his knees. Above him, Faruq levels the wheel gun at Kapka's head and cocks the hammer.

The last of the fanatics falls to the ground, dead or too wounded to fight.

"Your stranglehold on my people"—Faruq can hardly form the hoarse words with his cracked lips—"is over."

Kapka begs, his bloodied hands full of the fragments of his own mangled genitals. His pleas for mercy are unheard. Faruq pulls the trigger. The blast strikes Kapka through the eye, the boom of the hand cannon exclaiming the final moment of the despot's reign.

"Faruq!" I cry as Husniya and I run forward.

My emaciated friend turns toward us, the horrors he's endured at the hands of his own people stitched like a permanent scar into his face. He raises the revolver and points it at my chest. His hate-filled stare never wavers.

I slow, stumble, and finally collapse. My knees hit the slush.

"Faruq? We searched for so long. We never lost hope, Husniya and I. You're safe now."

Husniya stands with her mouth open. "Faruq?"

His gaze sticks to me, penetrating. "You left me. You had the chance to save me once and you left me."

Helpless, I raise my hands. "I couldn't. I had to protect the children.

I followed, tracking you for five days until the trail ended in the wilds of the Vapid, and I lost you … again." My head hangs, tears dripping from pinched eyes. "Please, come home."

"I am home," he says. "With my people is where I belong."

"I know it's hard, but you're confused. Please," I beg.

"Four long years you left me to rot in this hell." He shakes his head. "Leave. You're dead to me. Both of you."

"Faruq." My eyes flood. "They hid you from us. We did everything we coul—"

The revolver explodes, the bullet smashing into the ice before me. He points it at my chest again.

"Get out. Next time I won't miss."

Husniya breaks into a fit of sobbing. "How could you?"

Faruq says nothing. His face concealed in shadow, his weapon trained on us as the snow falls in clumps over the battlefield and covers the dead.

I can't breathe. Deep inside, a light flutters and grows dark.

"Leave. I won't ask again," Faruq rasps.

After all we went through, this is how it ends? I give a slight bow of my head but cannot seem to find the words as I stand on shaking legs, cradling my oozing forearm. I put my good arm around Husniya and motion for Ghofaun to join us.

On our way to the gate, I give one last look toward the embattled Faruq who lowers his head and his weapon.

"I meant something to you, once," I say, my voice trembling with emotion. Turning away and pulling a weeping Husniya along, we venture forth into the bleak, foreboding storm of unrelenting snow and ice.

CHAPTER TWENTY-ONE

VEDMAK

The youth stumbles along, crying incessantly. The cobbled-together chain is not enough to choke her but still cuts into her soft flesh.

The other end of the shackle is attached to the leather strap that usually holds my scythe, jangling against these ever-weakening legs. Just above her throat, the crackling plasma scythe hovers.

The Ripper women follow me like a herd of cattle, mewing for their offspring. It's garnered the attention of the males, who have come out of hiding. A tribe of them—some thirty strong—encircle me but never approach. They keep their weapons trained, moving as I move, yet none have the fortitude to make their move. Who knew these creatures were so sentimental? The power of parenthood overpowers their animalistic nature. Pathetic. To think I once held a glimmer of respect for these goblins. If it were me, I would have taken the shot, and risked the whelp.

Not even Rippers are as evil as you Vedmak, you realize that? What does that make you?

Better. It makes me better.

A larger male, adorned in all manner of bones and leather—presumably made from Robust skin—makes a move toward me. My scythe coughs plasma, leaving black pockmarks on the child's face. The girl wails again and the women shriek.

The male holds my gaze, his piercing blue eyes full of fury and fear. There's no telling when my weapon will cease to function, the battery all used up. Now, it's a game of poker. Who breaks first?

Just stay away. He'll do it.

The Ripper backs off, but never breaks his stare. Coward.

Slowly, but steadily, I shuffle toward the large entranceway to the power station. The closer I become, the more distance the Rippers put between us. They waddle and squirm, chattering among themselves. Stepping backward to the door, I nearly trip over something. A brief stumble, but manage to regain balance. There in the grass is a dead Ripper, his skin pale, blistered and weeping. He's not been eaten, his clothes still intact. Even his old revolver sits in a holster strapped to his chest.

Radiation poisoning. Gil said it was leaking. It's why they won't come closer. They know it makes them sick. It'll be the end of us.

Did you not design this body to be strong, Gracile?

I didn't design anything. And it is strong. It's still standing isn't it? But radiation poisoning is something different. It'll kill us, eventually.

I can repair the damage once we are back at the lab.

If you make it back.

Some pursuits are worth the risk, boy.

Backing into the doorway, and keeping the child close, I use the stump of this mangled arm to wedge against the handle and pull the door open. My scythe coughs a final time and snuffs out. There's a terrible moment of silence, all eyes on me. It feels like an eternity, as if I were once again trapped in the void. The Ripper who felt brave before now finds his courage and comes for me. I throw the scythe to the ground and dash forward. The child crashes down as well. In one smooth movement, I grab the handle of the dead Ripper's wheel gun and slide it out. The gun barks and the Ripper's thigh explodes. I spring to my feet, the gun pointed at the child's head as I back into the doorway yet again. The Rippers scream and yell. Once again, using the cauterized stump I open the door.

Let the child go, they won't follow us in. They're too scared.

A quick glance at the sniveling child, then at the bawling Ripper women. I raise the gun and fire. The bullet shatters the makeshift chain, freeing the girl. In unison, the women give a screech of relief and the child begins to run toward her hysterical clan.

Thank you, Vedmak. Thank y—

The second shot strikes the back of the toddler's skull and she falls, tumbling lifelessly into the grass. The anguished screams of the Rippers are deafening, at least until the door slams shut between us.

You sick, sarding, son of a bitch! Why? Why?

I need them suitably volatile, an appropriate welcoming committee for the so-called leader of Opor.

I hate you. I won't let you live. I'll kill us, I swear it to you.

164

Promises, promises, foolish boy. The bringer of death cannot be killed.

***

Navigating the inside of the station should be easy—but it's not. With the convenient directional signage and knowledge of Soviet nuclear reactors sponged from Demitri's consciousness, I should be able to move like a trained rat through a maze. Yet, my concentration wanes like the phases of the moon. I'm never fully in the light—in control. Without the Red Mist, the weakling in here with me fights, however feebly. His hatred for my deeds following the death of the child gives renewed resolve to his battle.

Sard off, Vedmak. You're sick. A monster.

I try to block out his incessant nagging and focus on the task at hand: contact the Rat; contact Merodach; find the uranium. Covering one ear, as if it will block out his piercing voice, I trudge on. The corridors are wide with high ceilings and feel distinctly industrial. I pass lockers and shower rooms, all stark and functional. Overhead, pipes of different colors line the walls and mounted boxes flash their individual strobing lights, but nothing is superfluous. Everything in its place, and a place for everything.

Through a double set of doors is an enormous gallery humming with activity. It's the Turbine Hall. The turbines sit in massive light-blue metal boxes, while the generator is the darker blue container next to them. The droning comes from super-heated steam, driving the rotor in the electrical generator. Why do I give a sard about this?

This is your mind, boring kozel. Full of useless information. No wonder you never lay with a woman.

I spit on the floor in disgust.

Because of you, I have laid with a woman. And because of you, I never will again.

You really are a miserable whining child. Now quit your braying, the control room is ahead.

Inside is a sea of indicators and actuators. A bench of instruments forms an inner circle, leaving a walking space between it and the dial-covered walls. Several monitors and keypads have been affixed to the bench and seem to supplement the reactor controls. I meander to the nearest monitor playing the same few frames in grainy black and white over and over. It's a camera feed from somewhere else. The entrance to Vel.

A few keystrokes, within increasingly itchy fingers, and the feed unfreezes. On the screen, the pressurized door to Vel pops open and through it streams a mass of panicked people, falling over one another like Siberian hamsters. I move closer, studying the pixilated video. No, not just people—Graciles.

Graciles? Graciles came to Vel?

The skinny addict said this was a Gracile facility. They probably fled for their sad little lives when the lillipads came down and this was the first place they thought of coming. Do you know any of these tragic wretches?

He refuses to reply.

A troop of Velian guards meet the Graciles, but the enhanced humans roll over the Robusts like a bovine stampede. They were scared of something. Seconds later, the mystery is revealed as hordes of Rippers pile in through the narrow gap behind the Graciles, crushing skulls, slicing bellies and breaking limbs. The damn fools left the door open, let the rabid animals in and sealed their own fate. In gritty flickering images, the slaughter of the Graciles and Velians plays out. The video skips back to the beginning and the massacre starts over.

There is nothing more to learn here. I turn away from the camera feed, searching the control panel. Demitri's knowledge bleeds into my own, though he is attempting to stem the flow and hinder my understanding. The readouts become blurred. Must focus. These instruments show that the shutdown procedure was initiated but ... something went wrong. It didn't complete. Internal radiation levels are at ten thousand rad. What does that mean?

It means we're already dead. Two days, two weeks. But soon. Of course, that's after our skin sloughs off, and we vomit and defecate ourselves into a dried-up husk.

The skin on the back of the only hand I have left is already reddening. Death is but an inconvenience to overcome. My lab can fix this body.

If we make it out alive.

There must be a way of reaching outside the enclave. A way the Graciles would have managed to communicate with the Velians. Think, must think. I need more stim to activate this brain …

Brain, yes. A neural link.

You don't have Merodach to act as your proxy.

No, but I have this.

A cord snakes out from the dash and hangs off the edge. I grab it up and bite down near the connecting end. I push up my sleeve with Demitri's cauterized stump, and awkwardly shove the connector into the port near his elbow, saliva drooling all over it.

There's a moment of nothing, but then my consciousness is alive. It's like being on a stim, the neurons in this skull firing rapidly as the brain connects to the web. In here, our consciences are more separated. Demitri's digital shadow, his *skygge*, the Graciles called it, stands before me—a glowing apparition set against a construct of hallways and portals no doubt designed to organize this digital world and prevent people from going crazy in a sea of information. This is why he was always afraid. Another Gracile seeing two digital shadows emanating from the same host. No one to worry about now. The neural-web is devoid of *skygge*. No other souls in here. After the lillipads fell, the Graciles abandoned it for fear of being located. Some Robusts jacked into it and became lost to the expanse, forever roaming until their biological bodies finally withered and died.

Opor still monitors for activity. They'll know you're here.

Not if I'm fast and use the backdoor.

I'll make enough noise in here for Yeos Himself to hear.

No, you won't. Your *skygge* is tied to mine—you're unable to make your will known. I remember the feeling well, when our roles were reversed.

In unison both my and Demitri's *skygge* place a hand on the nearest wall, which glows brightly with virtual neurons firing pulses back and forth. The cluster of digital cells around our fingers burns bright, until they migrate and reorder into a new rectangle—a new door. It flashes white and opens. We step through into the dark.

After a few moments, the gloom is burned away and our *skygge* fade, so that now we occupy a new host and see what he sees as if it were our body. The inner sanctum of Opor is before us.

"I am here, Rat," I say.

[Vardøger? No, no, now is not good—you can't be here].

167

The view darkens and only a rock-hewn wall greets me as the Rat hides in a corner.

"Where is the ugly sow?"

[She's not here. She went after Husniya, and the Musul Faruq. They received intelligence on his whereabouts].

"She's not on her way to Vel already? This actually works in my favor. Two chances to kill her. Now is the time to make your move. Remove the old man."

[Now? I'm not sure he's far enough along].

"Now, Rat. If fate is on my side, she'll die looking for her Musul pet. If not, when she returns urge her to come to Vel. And when she does, I'll be waiting. Make sure she brings a minimal party. She'll die chasing a doomed operation and you'll finally have Opor. Fail me on any of these points, and you'll watch your gizzards empty onto your feet."

[Yes ... yes Vardøger], he stutters.

A single thought to leave, and everything once again fades to black except for the doorway through which we came. Our *skygge* step through and we are once again in the corridor.

"Now to contact Merodach and bring my *Einherjar* here to collect our prize."

And you think you're going to be able to simply pull the uranium from the reactor?

Simple Demitri, your own consciousness has told me all I need to know. Lucky for us, the Soviets' design is simple and allows removal without a complete shutdown. Merodach will come and take me and the payload back to operations.

This broken Gracile shell suddenly convulses. I hack hard, coughing blood onto the console.

Like I said. If we make it out.

CHAPTER TWENTY-TWO

MILA

Dark descends like a bird of prey, in its talons a numbing cold that steals the last of the sun's life-giving warmth. The Road of Death will be our grave after all. Yet, at this moment, death is not a flame-wreathed messenger of evil, but a release. It calls to me, promising eternal respite if I just lie down in the snow.

"Come, Mila," Ghofaun says. "Lay down here and you will never return to us."

I don't respond or can't. Not sure which.

Ghofaun swivels in place, a shrunken Husniya wedged beneath his arm. "We have to find shelter or we'll die out here. This way."

Ahead and away from the road, a swath of black stone sweeps up, pushing through the ice in the form of a knobby outcropping.

Ghofaun points to it. "If we sit with our backs to the rock, that short overhang will provide a break from the falling snow."

"It won't … matter if this wind can still have at us," I manage.

Ghofaun wedges Husniya under the large, black rock and starts to rummage inside his pack. "That's why I grabbed this." The monk pulls a bundle of red canvas attached to interspersed wooden stakes.

"A windbreak," I mumble. We may live a while longer, though who knows if that's a good thing.

I grab one end and move in the opposite direction of Ghofaun, pulling the canvas break open. Ghofaun does the same. We jam the stakes into the hard ground with what little strength we have left.

In the dark, I slump to the ground next to Husniya.

"Stay with her." Ghofaun pats my knee. "I'll be right back."

Minutes pass, but it feels like an eternity. Unable to move, all I can do is watch the images behind my eyelids flicker like an old moving picture show. Memories I don't want anymore. Faruq and little Husniya crying for help in that dingy Baqirian alley. The way my Musul friend had smiled when he was into some bit of mischief. How my face flushed when he held my hand …

"Here we are." Ghofaun drops a pile of pitiful-looking sticks and dried dead brush. "It's not much, but it may hold a flame." The monk arranges a pad of dead moss and wiry scrub with a little tent of sticks over it.

I want to help but can no longer move my limbs.

From his pocket, he produces a single Draganov round and holds it up for me to see. Ghofaun pries the bullet open, pours the gunpowder onto the moss bed and braces the shell lip on a stick over it. Pressing the point of his knife to the primer, he manages the little balancing act for a moment before lightly striking the end of the knife with the latrine shovel.

There's a pop and a little shower of sparks from the bursting primer. With a *whoosh* the gunpowder takes. An involuntary gasp escapes my lips as I squint from the flash. Yet as quickly as it comes, the fire is gone, replaced by a smoldering pile of embers. Much like our brief time on this Earth—a flash of light, an opportunity for great good, immense evil, or worse, selfish nothingness. And just like that, our light too, for better or worse, goes out.

The monk leans close, whispering to the flame with gentle breaths, coaxing the sparks to live again. A small finger of fire takes hold on the moss bed. Rebirth. Renewal. The light begins again, feeble but growing. It knows nothing else, only the perpetual act of pressing back against the darkness. That is its only purpose. It knows not of the endless cold in which it exists and will never overcome.

Water drips away from my skin like thawing frozen meat. With great effort, I'm able to move my fingers again. Husniya sits unmoving, her eyes wide, hypnotized by the jumping and popping of the small fire. On the other side of the fire, the monk removes his wet overcoat and sets it aside to dry.

Ghofaun pulls some items from his bag. In a small bowl, he pours some almost-frozen water followed by a packet of medicinal herbs. Mixing furiously, the herbs soak up the water turning to a brownish paste. "Your arm," he says.

"It's fine." I pin the useless appendage to my body.

"No, it is not." Ghofaun levels his gaze at me. "The flesh will turn black and we will have to remove the limb. Let me see it."

Ghofaun gently pushes my sleeve back to the biceps. The wound is not large, but it does go all the way through.

He grabs a small flask of sloop from his bag. Ghofaun holds it up. It's not for drinking. A splash of sloop across the wound causes me to howl, fire coursing through my arm, my free hand clawing at the rock.

"It's okay, Mila. That's all," Ghofaun says, packing the wound with the paste. "You're lucky it was only a piece of the copper jacket and not a whole bullet that hit you." The monk finishes wrapping the wound with clean cloths, tying them tight and helping me back into my coat. "And your leg?"

I shake my head.

He eyes the bullet graze on my thigh and gives a slight bow, then takes a seat on the other side of Husniya.

Must sleep. It doesn't matter if I wake.

***

Cold light bleeds between my half-closed eyelids. The fire smolders, smoke rising, the last of the warmth fading. Without it, the early morning chill has invaded our shelter with cunning stealth, nipping at my face and sinking into my heavy garments. I heave myself from the ground but don't make it to my feet. Husniya still sleeps. But Ghofaun is already up, packing his belongings. Has he stood watch over us all night? Not that there's anyone out here beyond the walls.

I swing a bleary-eyed gaze across the horizon.

Panic fills my chest, stopping my heart. There's a man standing at the edge of the road, his long black robe lying in piles at his feet, a staff with a long sickle by his side. His heavy hood flops low, obscuring his face. His bony hand reaches out, beckoning me.

"Ghofaun, there's a man …" I start, my voice trailing away as I look to my friend and back to where the robed man had been.

"What is it, Mila?" Ghofaun says, his voice exhausted but full of patience.

The road is empty. "Thought I saw something."

"How are you feeling?" he says, pushing the last few items into his shoulder bag.

I grunt, checking the bandage on my forearm and flexing my fingers. "Still alive—thanks to you."

He says nothing.

"You held watch for us all night?"

Ghofaun dips his head. "I spent most of the night in the deepest levels of Chum Lawk meditation. It is not the same as sleep, but my chi allowed me to recover some while still remaining vigilant for threats."

"You joined in our fight, saved our lives from the elements, and watched over us as we slept." I bow my head to the warrior monk. "You are one, at least, whose loyalty knows no end."

Ghofaun sets his pack aside. "What happened yesterday injured me. I can't imagine how it wounded both of you."

His words are like a fresh slice into an unhealed wound, every ounce of pain newly remembered. There's a throbbing in the pit of my stomach. I'd rather die than feel this.

I can only grunt.

"Give it time." Ghofaun dips his head. "Time heals all wounds."

Not this wound. Need to change the subject. Turning, I place my hand on Husniya and give her a little shake. "Get up."

"I said I don't need you to treat me like a baby," she shouts, swiping my arm away.

I sit back with my hands raised.

The teen sits up, wiping the sleep from her eyes, her face becoming red in a deepening blush. "I'm ... that wasn't for ... Damnation, just forget about it." She starts to gather her things together.

"Master Ghofaun saved our lives."

"Thank you, Master," Husniya interrupts, blowing past both of us as she stomps her way down to the road.

The snow has stopped for now, but the sky has darkened with heavy clouds. Through the gray half-light of the early morning, we take off down the Road of Death back in the direction of Etyom, all the way following the tracks of the ornery teen. It takes Ghofaun and me longer than expected to catch up with Husniya moving with anger-filled purpose.

"Husniya, wait for us," I call out.

She continues to forge ahead.

Sard it all. She's going to walk right into a—

The girl stops dead in her tracks, hands raised above her head. Ghofaun and I pick up the pace.

Not far ahead is the female Gracile, Oksana, her Creed marching along with their weapons raised. The woman looks less than perfect. Her boots and cloak are muddy, her face so drained of life she almost resembles the troop of frozen Creed.

"You people again." I shake my head. "Don't worry, Oksana, I'm using the term *people* loosely. No need for any of you to be offended."

The Gracile says nothing, her gaze cold and tired.

"Lower your weapons," Zaldov says. "Mila Solokoff and her friends are our allies."

Husniya starts off again, prompting me to grab a fist-full of her jacket. "Wait, Hus."

The girl spins into me, her jab coming right up the center nearly striking my chin. Before I can stop myself, the flat of my hand lands hard across her face. The slap knocks her to the ice. She grunts and flails, wide-eyed.

My forearm throbs with waves of radiating pain. Ghofaun's gentle pressure on my shoulder pulls me back to reality.

"What is wrong with you?" I snap at the girl.

Ghofaun helps Husniya up.

My heart aches. Damnation, Mila. She's been through enough already without you slapping her.

"Me? What's wrong with *you*? How come you never told me? You had a chance to rescue him and you didn't."

Words fail to come.

"I don't need you. Any of you." Husniya shrugs Ghofaun off, tears running down her face. She turns and continues stomping down the road.

"Mila." Oksana takes a step forward. "I need to speak with you. The game has changed."

"Look, I don't know what you're talking about, but as you can see, I've got my own problems right now." I motion to Husniya.

There's an uncomfortable silence.

"I will look after Husniya." Zaldov's sterile voice breaks the stillness.

I stare at the strange Creed, then back at Oksana who nods.

"I am incapable of harming those with whose care I'm charged, Mila Solokoff," Zaldov says plainly.

"Go then and let us talk," Oksana commands.

"Affirmative," Zaldov echoes, marching away after Husniya.

Ghofaun stands with his arms folded, observing with narrow untrusting eyes.

"I take it you couldn't get out … again." I motion to her mud-soaked cloak.

The Gracile's eyes narrow. "And I assume your attempt to rescue your friend was a failure, since he's not with you?"

Heat flows from my scalp down my face. The desire to reach out and slap this Gracile is almost more than I can bear. "If you want to say something, you'd better get on with it."

Oksana steps to the side, revealing a woman, a Robust woman, who looks strangely like me. The athletic even boyish body-type, the short dark hair. This woman even has a scar across her eye that leads back towards her ear. It's like I'm looking at my reflection in a piece of cracked glass. But not a real reflection—there's something dark and distorted about her, as though she's been entangled with something evil for far too long.

The questions tumble out. "What is this? Why does she look like me? Who are you?"

"My name is Anastasia," the woman replies. Her voice even sounds a little like mine.

"I don't like this. Somebody better tell me what's going on. Right now."

"We encountered her on the road," Oksana says. "She said she'd gotten lost trying to get to Fiori."

"And?" I check the Robust woman over again. "Why did you care? Why should I?"

"She says she has a message for you from Demitri Stasevich."

"That's not possible."

"It is," Oksana says. "She wouldn't reveal much to me, but what she did—it could be bad, Mila. You should hear her out."

A wave of dread passes through my insides. He's coming. It takes me a moment to master myself. "Demitri isn't in control. How did he give you a message?"

"You are Mila?" Anastasia asks. Her voice is full of emotion, perhaps a longing to make sense of some madness her heart can't reconcile. "He told me to find you."

"Demitri did? Or—" I start.

"The Vardøger?" she offers. "He has two personalities, I know."

"Vardøger?" Oksana and I say in unison.

"Don't you mean Vedmak? Are you sure we're talking about the same person?" I press.

Anastasia looks confused. "That's what he demands to be called. The Vardøger."

"But you spoke to Demitri? He regained control?"

"For a time," Anastasia replies. There seems to be pain in her eyes. She's a bit slow, this one. "How did you *know* it was Demitri?"

"Because Demitri is soft and kind and gentle. Nothing like Vedmak, or the Vardøger, however you wish to call him. He was—is—trapped inside. Tormented. He promised to save me," she says, taking a moment to master herself. "He kept his promise. Vedmak was hurt. Demitri regained control. Cut off his own hand to free me."

Oksana looks to me for confirmation.

"Stress and injury do seem to shift the balance in his head," I say.

"Whatever this Vedmak is does not align with the Creator's work. Demitri is the angel sent to save me."

The Creator? "Are you Logosian?"

She shakes her head, a frown creasing her forehead. "I would not associate with those self-righteous zealots. They believe their rituals are the only way to worship Yeos, but He is everywhere and in everything, and—"

"Let me stop you right there." A deep breath in through my nose, the air cold and burning. Going to ignore that she called me a sarding zealot. "I don't need a lecture on religion from a *Soufreit*."

Anastasia crosses her arms and cocks her head. "You say the name of my people like we are not human. Like being wanderers and not having an enclave of our own makes us lesser. We are all creatures of Yeos. I may not be a Logosian, but I'd bet with that high-brow attitude, you are."

"Okay," Oksana interrupts. "We're getting off track. I'd like to hear the message before you two go to pulling each other's hair and scrambling around in the mud like a couple of rodents."

Anastasia and I both turn, staring at the unamused elite. Graciles. I might still break her nose before the week is out. No one says anything for a while. I cast a glance at Ghofaun, who simply shakes his head. He knows better than to interject himself in this boiler pot.

We are still alone, but we can't stand out here all day. My gaze falls back to Anastasia. She's feisty, I'll give her that. Question is, how did she end up with Demitri in the first place, and why were they in the Vapid?

"I don't get it," I start. "You say you know both Vedmak and Demitri, and your group was out on the road. If you really knew Vedmak, you'd be dead. What gives?"

A scowl darkens the woman's features. "Vedmak kept me in chains for the last three years. Shackled naked in the dark, cowering in my fear and shame, never knowing when he'll arrive to ..." She almost shakes with the words, her eyes welling up. "Demitri is the only reason I live at all. He fought Vedmak. For me."

Oh, Demitri, no. A familiar pain stabs at my heart. Faruq and now this. What has become of my friends? Maybe if I'd found them sooner. If I had not given up.

"Well done, Mila," Oksana says.

"Close your mouth, Gracile." I hate myself enough already.

"Look," Anastasia starts, wiping her face. "What's past is prologue. Do you understand? It's all part of Yeos' plan."

His plan. Does he truly have a plan for us? Am I part of it anymore?

"The Vardøger was headed somewhere," Anastasia continues. "Demitri told me to find you."

"So, she's here. Spit it out already," Oksana says.

Anastasia glares at haughty Oksana before continuing. "I didn't understand it all. Demitri told me what's happening is *worse than the Gracile Leader's plan*. He said the Vardøger is creating an army of Graciles *like him*."

"See," Oksana says, looking to me. "Bad."

"Wait, Vedmak is creating an army of Graciles with demons?" I ask.

Anastasia shrugs. "He said *like him*."

"There aren't enough adult Graciles to have an army that could take Etyom," Oksana offers. "At least there weren't before."

"Is there a way for him to create new Graciles?" I ask.

"We used to grow new Graciles from gene maps. But all the lillipads came down, and likely destroyed the body farms," Oksana says.

"Wouldn't that take years?" I ask. "To grow a mature human, I mean."

Oksana nods. "Yes, unless he's found a way to accelerate it. Though I'm not a bioengineer. I don't know how he'd do it."

"We've got to stop him—"

"Wait," Anastasia says. "There was one more thing."

Oksana and I stare expectantly.

"Something about a *VME*?" the strange woman says, looking to us for recognition of the term.

"Is that supposed to mean something to me?" I look to Oksana. The color is drained from her face. She understood all too well. "Well, what's a *VME*?"

Oksana licks her lips and shakes her head as if making intricate calculations internally. "It's complicated. I'll try to explain this in a way you might understand."

"Uh huh. Let's have it."

"A VME is a vacuum metastability event," she says. "It's a theory which suggests the universe exists in a fundamentally unstable state—that right now it's teetering on the edge of stability. Some scientists once theorized that at a particular point, the universe will tip over the brink."

"Okay, what the hell does that mean for us?" I ask.

"Well, when it happens, a bubble will appear. Think of it as an alternate universe. This alternate universe bubble will expand in all directions and wipe out everything it touches, destroying everything in our universe."

You've got to be kidding. "And Vedmak is, what, going to initiate this?"

"Vedmak or the Vardøger, or whatever you want to call this lunatic, may not even know he's doing it. Look, every time he creates a new clone, with the same abilities as Demitri's—as you've explained them to me—it's like making a crack in our universe. The more clones he creates, the more cracks until eventually the dimension or universe, from which this Vedmak comes, will come spilling into ours completely wiping it out."

I'm having serious *déjà vu* here. First a black hole, now this? "Is it even possible?"

"Demitri seemed to think so." Anastasia looks to me. "He was scared."

"What would Vedmak need to be able to create enough clones to tip the balance?" I ask, turning to Oksana.

"To create an army of clones large and fast enough for Demitri to be worried about an imminent VME?" The Gracile blinks several times, again making rapid computations in her pretty head. "A lot of energy. Something like that would require a huge power source, but there's nothing in Etyom that would be sufficient anymore. Nikolaj's fusion reactors were destroyed."

"When we were attacked in the Vapid, we were going to get something critical to continuing his work. He said it was in Vel," Anastasia says.

My skin tingles. Pulling my sling bag around, I rifle through it, snatch out my PED and read Gil's message again. I'd never responded to it. Sard. My eyes wide, I turn to Oksana. "Vel, Oksana."

The Gracile stiffens with the terrible epiphany. "The nuclear stockpile. He could use it as a power source."

Ghofaun touches my sleeve. "Mila, we have to get back and tell Bilgi and the others. Kapka may have wanted the nuclear stash, but if Vedmak has found it ..."

"We are all in grave danger," Oksana says, her voice as thin as glass.

I hand my PED to Ghofaun. "Send an advance message to Bilgi for me. Tell him the basics and that we're on our way back."

Without a word, Ghofaun starts typing.

"Mila, you'll need help. Scientific expertise for combating this, to be exact. Allow me to assist you," Oksana says, this time with no air of superiority in her tone.

"Why would *you* want to help *me,* your majesty?"

The defiance returns to Oksana's face. "How about I don't trust the fate of the universe to a Robust?"

You can't help but poke the bear, can you, Mila?

"And what about you?" the Gracile says, deflecting the tension to

Anastasia.

The Soufreit shakes her head. "No. I can't be part of this."

"You can't walk away now," I say. "What about Demitri? If you cared for him at all, doesn't he deserve to have the favor returned?"

Anastasia's gaze softens, her eyes welling. I can't tell if that's fear of facing Vedmak again or guilt for abandoning Demitri.

Oksana doesn't let the silence hang and opens her big mouth. "We can't let you leave."

"Let me?" Anastasia says, her face becoming a scowl. She turns, scanning the rolling hills of ice surrounding us. "Ussuri."

A growl, deep and menacing, echoes from the hills around us. Every one of us locks in place.

My blood turns to ice. "What in creation was *that*?"

Oksana, half crouching, looks absolutely terrified. The Creed regiment stands ready, their glowing metallic plasma rifles primed.

"Lower your weapons. He was only answering me," Anastasia says. "If he wanted to kill you, you'd be dead."

"What the *hell* is an Ussuri?" Oksana manages to squeak.

Anastasia stands proudly as a massive beast, auburn and black, slides from behind the snowdrift where it's been observing us this whole time. "Why does everyone keep asking that? Ussuri is his *name*."

CHAPTER TWENTY-THREE

FARUQ

Dirty fingers push a piece of dry cake along the bottom of the bowl, soaking up the remnants of taji stew. My tongue tingles with the sudden rush of salted broth. This sludge is a cheap way to feed large groups of soldiers, but after so long with so little it's nothing short of a feast. My stomach roils. Could easily eat eight bowls, only to throw it all up again. I set the dish aside and rub my distended belly.

This nauseated state isn't helped by sitting in Kapka's tent. Rugs and silks, bedding of the finest make, chains of pure gold, an antique set of Persian armor inset with silver and jewels. Who lives like this while others suffer? Is this my life now?

No, I am not Kapka. I am not a leader, good, evil or otherwise. Not even Ilah knows what I am.

Everything is changed. The clouded veil of youthful optimism that covered my eyes for so long has now fallen away to reveal the cruelty of this stone-gray world. It is an ugly truth hidden beneath the surface of Earth's last city since the beginning: even together, we are all alone, encircled and tormented by our demons. What is there for me now? A traitorous murderer with no allegiance to anything or anyone, except my own vengeance. And now, even it has left me unfulfilled.

The burlap sack clinging to my shoulders itches and burns my skin yet is contrasted by the soft heavy-pile rug enveloping my torn and blistered feet. An open-mouthed spice jar smokes on the desk nearby, sending its aromas swirling with snaking tendrils into the air. Just next to it is a wash basin, hand mirror, and the golden revolver I'd used to kill Kapka. I stand, the muscles of my legs emaciated but feeling stronger after taking food.

Unable to take the itching any longer, I shed the burlap sack and drop it to the floor. My heart falters. That old sack, my only possession for the past four years might as well be my own skin. Can I cast it off so easily? Can I make this wretched person I've become not exist?

With a grunt, I kick it away and move with careful steps to the basin to start the process of sponging the filth from my paper-thin skin. It is a painstaking process, the lashes and sores covering my body a constant stinging reminder of the abuse—delivered by my own people.

A haggard, bearded man with stringy hair and black pits for eyes stares back from within the glass of the ornate mirror lying on the table. With a snarl, I rake everything to the floor, the various accouterments clattering and splashing as they fall.

This is not me. This cannot be who I've become.

The tent flap moves. An attendant enters, his head bowed.

"Shapur, are you well?"

Shapur. A name for a prince. After a moment, I find my voice. "Don't call me that."

"Yes Sha ... um. Yes. I understand. What would you have me call you?" The attendant, a boy no more than fifteen, rubs his hands nervously. He was one of the few who did not take up arms and thus was not slain.

I shrug. "I don't care, boy."

The attendant licks his lips. "Sheikh ... a message arrived from Baqir. Before his death, Kapka called for a troop of reinforcements. They are set to arrive in the morning. What will you have us do?"

My teeth ache as I mash them together. More of his faithful to overcome. My body wavers, still too weak to be much good to me. I must rest. Must think on how to deal with these fanatics. Perhaps they will be glad to be free of his tyranny. Perhaps they'll murder me. "Leave me. I need time to rest," I groan.

"Yes, Sheikh."

"Dammit, boy. It's Faruq."

"Yes, Sheikh Faruq."

"No, just ..."

The young man is gone.

"I'm just Faruq."

I pick up the revolver and lie down on the bed. These plush quilts are made for entertaining whores. Too soft to be comfortable. But I can't summon the strength to crawl to the floor where I might feel ... anything but this.

In the darkness, they appear—Mila, then Husniya, both staring with those horrible looks on their faces. I turned them away. After they came to rescue me. The only people who ever cared for me and I sent them away to die in the storm. Just like Kapka said, I'm less than a pile of sard.

My fingers clamp down the wheel gun resting on my chest. "*No.* They left me to die. They abandoned me. What do I still owe them?"

Four years of my life. Gone. Years of abuse and humiliation. A tear slips down my cheek, running back to pool in my ear. I survived it—my only furious purpose to kill the madman who had ruined my life, prostituted my people, and made a mockery of my faith. Now it is done, but the death of that tyrant brought me nothing. No satisfaction. No further relief. What is left for me in this ugly world? Or the next? Surely burning in the fires of hell would be better than living in this place another day.

Time to finish this and end this miserable existence.

The barrel is cold beneath the floor of my chin. I thumb back the hammer. Eyes wide, I scream out to Ilah. "Where are you now?"

My index finger lurches against the trigger. The hammer falls with a snap like the rending of a dead branch. *Ftzzzz.*

The revolver, still clutched in my shaking fist, slips from beneath my chin. A small tendril of smoke wafts from the cylinder. A misfire. A failed primer in an antique round. I moan, the reckless sobbing catching and gurgling in my throat as the pistol falls from my fingers to the floor. Fate dooms me to live out this failed existence. Warm tears of misery and hate run heedlessly from the corners of my bruised eyes until exhaustion, slow and creeping, has its inevitable way with me.

CHAPTER TWENTY-FOUR

MILA

Not a soul stirs along the windswept streets of this place, once so colorful and vibrant. Beyond the usual desolation, there is something else hidden, waiting. A shroud of death hangs over the enclave of Fiori. A long trail of steam huffs from my mouth. Ghofaun and Oksana are two steps behind, hunched and forlorn. Trailing us, the squad of Creed *clumps* and *thumps* along without a word. Other than the fading tracks in the snow, there has been no further sign of Husniya or Zaldov, the Creed soldier who had resolved to care for her.

I shake my head with a grunt. "Hey, Oksana. What are the chances Husniya is still alive after being left alone with that death bot of yours?"

"The girl is safer with him than with us," the Gracile replies.

"Oh? How do you figure?" I glance at Ghofaun who meets my stare but remains silent.

"I told you. Zaldov is special."

"You're going to have to elaborate," I say, trudging along.

Oksana gives a sigh an exasperated parent might give a question-asking toddler. "He's not like any Creed you've ever known. Not even like these few, which are still highly advanced, I might add. He's also equipped with a tracking beacon I can follow to assist in locating him." She turns to the Creed behind her. "What is Zaldov's location at present?"

"Zaldov. Location." The nearest Creed soldier processes the information. "Northern Fiori enclave. Half kilometer radius of certainty."

"See? They're around here somewhere."

"Half kilometer certainty? That's not necessarily exact."

She shrugs. "It's something."

"Okay, I'm game. So, what else makes him special?"

"He's been modified."

I slow, turning. Typical elitist responses. Why does she have to be so difficult? "If I'm going to have to pry the answers from you, forget I said anything." I shake my head, turning forward again.

"Zaldov is unique because I fed him knowledge personally. Developed him myself to remind me of Nikolaj."

"Oh," I say. "I thought he looked familiar. You made him look like Nikolaj too, didn't you?"

There's a hint of sadness in the Gracile's face. "He is not Nikolaj, of course, but he does have my mate's loyalty—his strongest trait."

"I see, and you did this yourself?"

She gives a curt nod. "I have had an interest in cybernetics for a long time. That, combined with my advanced training in quantum biology, helped me to understand how to better engineer these Creed to be superior to any that came before them, to make than more ... human."

"I don't know if that's a good thing or not," I say, tucking my chin into my collar.

"It is a good thing. Though a machine, Zaldov's AI becomes more human every day. The irony is he's a better person than all of us. You'll see."

"If you say so." I shake my head again. "Seems unnatural to me, but I guess I'll give it—uh—him a pass. For now."

We cross the empty market, which is unusually quiet and empty this time of day. Where is everybody?

A lone man appears from nowhere, bustles past, and tries to disappear just as quickly.

"Hey, friend? What's the rush? Where is everybody?" I call after him.

"Ripper attack. They came last evening from the direction of Vel, while the market was still open. The guard couldn't hold them off. Nobody wants to be out here anymore. Too dangerous," he says, evidently not wanting to stop and talk.

"C'mon. Let's get back to base and hope Husniya beat us there," I say.

Oksana's pace slows, her brow knitted as she surveys the rubble of a fallen lillipad.

"What is it?" I ask.

"This was HAP One. I used to spend a great deal of time in this one ... with my friends."

There's no question the Gracile's wounds run deep. She turns to me, her eyes wet.

"I know you think of me as a typical cloud-dweller, haughty and entitled. But to have your whole world, everything you've ever known, literally come crashing down. To be one of the last of your kind in a world of chaos and fear and then find out one of your own is attempting to pervert what all Graciles worked so hard to perfect … It's not an easy pill to swallow."

We are not the same, Graciles and Robusts, but we share the loneliness of Etyom. I reach out and touch her arm. "Hey look, I don't know what lies ahead, but we'll face it together. All right?"

She nods and wipes her face, the tears forming small icy trails on her perfectly sculpted cheekbones.

I motion to the hidden tunnel under the wreckage of the Forgotten Jewel. "I'm going to take Ghofaun and go make contact with Opor. You can come, but your Creed will need to wait outside. I don't want to spook my people. Their experience with the Creed is less than favorable."

"I understand," Oksana says.

We march ahead through the ruins of the Jewel to the hidden entrance, an earthen ramp covered by rotting planks of wood descending into the dark.

"In there?" Oksana asks.

"Yeah," I say. "Come on."

She mutters something about Robusts under her breath.

After her little speech? Really? You can take the Gracile out of the clouds …

Pushing the planks aside, I step into the trench and start down. A silhouette waits in the shadows.

"Who's that? Identify yourself."

"It is I, Zaldov. I was asked to wait here by Husniya."

Zaldov. Never thought I'd be happy to see a Creed. "Is she inside?"

"She is. I ensured her safety as promised."

"Uh, yeah. Okay. I mean, thank you."

"I was my pleasure to be of assistance," Zaldov says, his movements a host of little clicks and whirrs.

Oksana greets Zaldov with a smile and touch. "Hold here on standby.

Only activate upon my remote command."

"Copy direct," Zaldov says, turning to the Creed with us. "Standby until remote activation."

Their postures all relax simultaneously.

Ahead, at the end of the dank tunnel, the heavy steel doors await. Ghofaun steps forward and knocks in the practiced manner. After a time, the door opens and we are met by Jape, who is still manning the door. A quick greeting and we're in, the door bolting behind us. At the far end of the dimly lit cavern-like room, Giahi steps from the command center doorway.

"So you retrieved the girl, but where's that Musul you can't help yourself over?"

I can't do this right now. "Where's Bilgi?"

Giahi stands unmoving, arms crossed.

"Giahi, where is Bilgi?" I say, my heart pounding.

"Bilgi was sick. You saw it."

"*Was*? You act like he's dead. He had a little fever." I step forward, unzipping my jacket.

"He was showing signs of the plague, Mila. I sent him away. Who's with you?" He motions to Oksana.

"No, hang on a second." I hold my hands up. "You don't breeze over that. Where *is* he?"

"Did you bring another Gracile here?"

"Giahi, I swear, you better not have done something to Bilgi. *Answer me.*"

"I told you. I sent him away. He was going to infect all of us."

Mos enters from the hall off to my right. His shirt is soaked; sweat glistens on his heavily muscled arms. He's been working on something. "Mila, is everyone okay? Did you find Faruq?"

"Hey, Mos. We're okay. Just hang on a second. Where's Bilgi, Giahi?"

Mos sighs. "He looked terrible, Mila. Everyone in command agreed he could have had the plague. We had to send him away."

My heart sinks. I look to Ghofaun, then back to Giahi. "Where did you send him? Tell me."

Giahi shrugs. "Zopat. To the clinic."

"The clinic? Giahi, that's where people go to die," I almost shout.

"He was old and sickly anyway. It was just a matter of time."

A lightning bolt of hate courses through me. That little troll.

Mos moves to intercept me. "Hang on, Mila. It's not going to help for us to fight amongst ourselves."

"Yeah, well it might make me feel better." I grit my teeth. Bilgi is gone. Cast out. What in creation do we do now? "Is Yuri here?"

Mos shakes his head. "You know how he is. We haven't seen him in days."

"What I want to know," Giahi interrupts, arms still crossed, "is why you brought a Gracile here again. That's a breach of our code."

"She's an ally. How is it a breach of our code?"

Giahi laughs. "An ally? You mean like the last Gracile you brought to us? The one who almost jeopardized our whole operation? Should I count the ways Graciles have wronged us?"

Oksana rocks her weight onto one leg, a hand on her hip.

"Giahi, I've got this. Thank you," Mos says, his brow stern.

Giahi scoffs. "That's all fine and good. But someone needs to keep Bilgi's little loose cannon in check. Most of us don't care to die for nothing just yet."

I swear upon the grave of my brother …

Mos gives my shoulder a squeeze, his attention still turned on Giahi. "I said I've got it."

Giahi shrugs and turns. "Sure, Mos. Sure you do," he says, and disappears into the dusty confines of the command center.

Mos forces a smile for me. "Don't listen to him. It's going to be okay. We'll send people to Zopat to make sure Bilgi is taken care of." He tosses his head at Oksana with a wink. "You going to introduce me, or what?"

"Uh, oh, yeah," I say, trying to clear my tangled thoughts. "Mos, this is Oksana. She knew Demitri, back before everything. She wants to help."

"Oksana." Mos extends a meaty hand. "The pleasure is all mine."

"Hello," Oksana says, staring at the offered hand. "What's that for?"

"Robusts shake hands in greeting. You guys don't do this?"

"Ah no, I'm afraid not." Oksana nervously wipes her hands on her jacket. "Doesn't that promote the transfer of germs?"

Mos lowers his hand and lets loose a good-natured chuckle. "I suppose it does. What do Graciles do instead? I'm always open to new things." He winks.

"Oh?" Oksana laughs nervously.

Mos, big for a Robust, is still a good bit shorter than Oksana, but he makes up for it by being more than twice as broad. That charmer has her so disarmed she's actually flashing a brilliant smile at him now. Good grief, I don't have time for this.

"Mos, a word?" I say, grabbing the Kahangan by the arm and pulling him from his eye-batting conversation with the Gracile. "Ghofaun, you too."

"Mila," Mos says, turning from Oksana. "Where did you find her? She's incredible."

"Yeah, I know. It's not an accident. She's engineered to look like that. Quit acting like a teenager. I need you to get your head right."

"Okay, yeah, sorry. What's up?" he says, his demeanor sobering.

"What's up?" Don't roll your eyes, Mila. "After we tried to rescue him, Faruq lost his mind and threatened our lives. It broke Husniya and it nearly broke me too. Now Bilgi has been sent away, and we learned Vedmak in Demitri's body may be making a play to claim the nuclear weapon cache in Vel—and you wanna know what's up?"

Mos motions for me to stop. "Wait, what?"

"It's true," Ghofaun says. "We are caught up in a most unfortunate turn of events."

"Yeah, that's what I'm telling you, lughead." I jab Mos in the chest. "Things are all messed up. So, I need you to stop fooling around."

"Yeah, whatever you need, Mila. You know that."

"Where's Husniya?" I ask.

"Resting, I think. She was all out of sorts." Mos rubs his chin. "I don't like that she came by herself."

"Look, I know. I tried to stop her. It wasn't going to work."

"The situation with her brother had a profound effect, no doubt," Ghofaun says.

"Yeah, I don't understand. Why would Faruq—" Mos starts.

"I can't even deal with that right now. We need to focus on the real problem here. Vedmak and the nuclear threat in Vel. He'll wipe us all out. He thinks he's the bringer of the apocalypse."

"The threat Vel conceals is unsurpassed," Ghofaun says. "Even without Bilgi's guidance, we need to act with all haste."

"I'm with you," Mos says. "In my absence, Kahanga is safe under the supervision of my sister, Ayodele. What do you need from me?"

I sigh. "I need you, Mos. You and Ghofaun. Now more than ever, I need your support."

He places a heavy hand on my shoulder. "You shall have it."

"How do you want to do this?" Ghofaun asks, fingering the Kukri blade tucked in his belt.

I inhale a deep breath of the musty underground air, the scent earthy and ancient. "We don't know what's going on in Vel. The last I heard was a message from Gil saying bad things were happening and that he needed my help."

"Okay, so we move on Vel with a sizable force," Mos says.

"Yes, logic would dictate. But we'll have to move fast and be discreet—two things we will not be afforded with a large group," I add.

"That, and Giahi will oppose our utilizing most of our people for this," Ghofaun says. "We don't need his approval, but there are those who are loyal to him. It will waste time trying to negotiate."

Mos and Ghofaun eye me expectantly. I glance at perfect Oksana, who's now fruitlessly trying to brush the grime from her jacket.

"There's something I need to know," Oksana says without looking up. The three of us turn, waiting. She glances at us. "Are you planning to kill Demitri? If so, a single bullet to the brain would end all of this. Demitri, Vedmak, as well as whatever madness he's attempting."

None of us respond. For the first time, I realize the terrible high stakes in this lethal game of cat-and-mouse. The easy path will require the killing of my Gracile friend in order to stop his demon.

I swallow hard. "I don't know if I can pursue that course."

Oksana gives a knowing look. "Then I will need to work on a suitable alternative."

"Such as?"

"Trust me, it's much more complicated than I can explain to you here.

Suffice it to say using Husniya's DNA, I'll try to isolate the protein she and Demitri share. If I can do that, there may be a way to cure it and, in the process, slam the door on Vedmak, shutting him out of Demitri's mind—this time for good."

"Is that possible?" I ask.

"Entirely," she replies. "But that will mean your mission is a rescue mission of sorts. I'll need you to bring Demitri here."

"Okay." I look at my friends. "Handpick fifteen of our best. *Anyone* but Giahi. Get them fed and geared up. This is going to be a hard push. That plus the three of us gives us almost twenty good fighters."

"And Husniya?" Ghofaun says.

"No." I wave him off. "She's been through enough already. Let her rest and assist Oksana with—"

"Now you're trying to cut me out?" Husniya says, entering from the long hallway next to command. She's geared up, her Mosin rifle propped over her shoulder. "This is my fight as much as yours. Demitri was my friend too."

"Husniya—"

"No," she says, pinching her eyes shut and tapping on her forehead, the way Demitri used to when trying to block out Vedmak. "No, you don't understand what I'm trying to do. You haven't understood for *years*."

Everyone stares at the girl, unsure of her meaning. Her face turns three shades of crimson. "Stop staring at me."

"Husniya, please listen. You've been under a lot of stress. Maybe you should—"

"This conversation is over and you aren't going to treat me like a baby anymore." She taps her forehead, harder now. "I'm ready to go. Will you all be coming or not?"

This is more than teenage angst. Margarida. That was the name of her voice. The soothing presence Husniya referred to as her childhood friend. She's not gone. Husniya is fighting Margarida's attempts to pacify her.

I take a deep breath and offer as gentle an expression as I can muster. "Of course we're coming, Hus."

"Good." She looks to Oksana. "And I'm going to need Zaldov."

What's with her and the Geminoid? The scowl on her face tells me she's not asking. Oksana shrugs. "He can go. At any rate, he's sworn to protect you."

"Good, it's settled," Husniya announces. "When are we leaving?"

How did she walk in here and start barking orders? I look the teen over; her countenance wavers, her composure a thing of glass. The others wait for me to answer. Even the chatter from the radio room grows quiet.

"Mos, Ghofaun. Get our people ready." I lift my chin. "We all leave for Vel in the morning."

CHAPTER TWENTY-FIVE

FARUQ

Morning breaks in a wash of soft gray light that slices through a gap in the tent flap. Shuffling to the edge of the bedding, I swing my feet to the floor and sit a moment, staring. The golden wheel gun lays on the floor where it fell. Like some holy saber, the weapon that took the life of the tyrant of Baqir, but refused to take mine, belongs to me now. Why am I still here? What can my miserable life be worth to anyone?

The attendant boy steps into the tent with a bow. "Sheikh Faruq, your breakfast." He presents another bowl of taji stew with a hunk of dry yellow cake.

It takes me a moment to gather my words. "Set it on the table there."

"Yes, Sheikh."

"What is your name, boy?" I ask. He's underfed and nervous.

"Baral."

"Okay, Baral. Why are you serving me? Why bring me breakfast? I killed Kapka, and most of the men in this camp died at the hands of …" I can't bring myself to say her name. "Well, they died."

"Ilah has sent you to save us," Baral says without hesitation. "Why would I not serve the last prophet of Ilah?"

It's as if I asked him *why do you breathe*? "I'm no prophet."

"I disagree," Baral says with a boyish innocence. "You have come to us in our time of need."

"All I did was put a bullet in Kapka," I retort.

"I do not refer to Kapka. He was always a pawn in the greater scheme. Used by those more powerful than him, and inflicting his own pain on others. Removing Kapka means you can now take your place as Prophet and lead us in the Judgment Day."

"Judgment Day? Do you not believe this has come and passed? Long ago, when Etyom was formed?"

"No prophet came in that time to guide us. Instead, Kapka's forbearers took our people. But now you are here. To lead us through the coming storm."

"What storm?"

"Against the false god. Against the Vardøger. They say he has an army. They say he can't be killed. But you can do it," he says. His eyes are full of hope. It's not something I've seen in a long time.

Vardøger. The name is familiar. I heard Kapka and his men talk about this man. Rumors and whispers of a demon. "You think this false god comes for us all?"

"A battle *is* coming," Baral says. "He will not take sides. Everything will be laid bare before him."

"If this Vardøger has an army, we stand little chance. Right now it's you, me, and a few of the men and women who worked this camp."

Baral bows low and, in a tone as respectful as he can, says, "I am sure Sheikh Faruq knows of the exploits of Mohammad. He was a warrior prophet. In less than ten years, his army grew from just three-hundred men at the Battle of Badr to ten thousand men marching on Mecca."

Warrior prophet? No, I can't let this happen. My people have suffered enough. Finally free of Kapka only to fight in someone else's war? My miserable life might not be worth much, but the lives of my people are. This boy's life is. If I must guide them, it will be to safety. Away from Opor, or this Vardøger, or anyone else who would do them harm.

"A group of Kapka's reinforcements arrives today?" I ask.

"Yes. They are arriving now."

I stand, supporting my weight. "See to it they are fed. You and the others as well. I will address everyone shortly."

"Everyone is to eat?" the boy asks, eyes wide.

"That's correct."

"Yes, yes Sheikh Faruq. It will be done," Baral says, disappearing through the flap into the cold.

Need to find something suitable to wear. The majority of Kapka's clothing is a mixture of luxury and old-world sophistication. A simple off-white tunic stuffed into rugged slacks with suspenders will do. The expedition boots are too large but will suffice if I layer up on socks. I throw on a heavy fur-lined jacket. I'm far too skinny for this garb, but there's no time to be picky.

I grab the wheel gun, break it open and eject all the empty casings—all but the misfired round. That one stays with me. I slip the token into my front pocket. Moving to the thick wooden dresser, I open it to reveal a crushed velvet-lined carrying case for the gun. Inside are rows and rows of large caliber, brass bullets with lead noses. I grab a handful, insert them into the cylinder and snap it closed, shoving the barrel into my waistband.

Here goes nothing.

Passing through the tent flap, the wind bites at the exposed areas of my flesh. I snug the jacket around me and walk past the groups of gathered men, newly arrived reinforcements requested by Kapka before his death. The attendants pass out bowls of taji stew, which the men hungrily accept. Their eyes dart back and forth, as the men chatter amongst themselves. Then they see me. Some say nothing, utterly confused, while others jabber and point dirty fingers at me. I'm sure I look like the risen dead.

With complete composure, drawn from some hidden reserve deep inside, I work my way past them, my chin up, my steps slow and surefooted. Secured in my left hand swings the large, blood-soaked cloth sack that contains my trophy. In a few steps, I'm up onto a short wooden platform. From here, I count about fifty men. They stare back, unknowing what transpired in this place.

Calm and discipline, Faruq. Be a rock. Hit them hard, then hold them fast. If you don't fill this vacuum, someone else will.

"Kapka is dead." The words rasp, hoarse and foreign across my vocal cords. "I killed him." I toss the bag from the platform. It lands with a clunk against the icepack, the bag sliding open to reveal the side of the madman's head.

A gasp ripples through the crowd.

"What is this treachery?" a burly captain on the front row shouts, his face twisted in anger. "Where are Kapka's men?"

"They chose their fate," I reply.

"This man has tried to seize the great Kapka's rule for himself," he shouts to the crowd. "He is not to be trust—"

The blast of my golden revolver causes everyone to flinch. Some of the closest men gnash their teeth and cup their ears. The captain stumbles back, staring at the small crater at his feet where the round struck the ice.

"My name is Faruq and I am here to tell you that you are free. I wish to rule no one."

The crowd grows still.

"Some of you no doubt believe in Kapka's dream, and have benefitted from it," I say, my voice on the verge of breaking. "Others were forced into his army. And yet others were treated as no more than slaves and whores to be used. Had Ilah willed, He would have made us a single community, but He wanted to test us. We should have competed with each other in doing good, not evil. Now is the time for change. Every one of you will return to Ilah and He will inform you regarding the things about which you differed."

"Don't think you can so easily bribe us with a hot meal and words stolen from our Holy Book," the captain says. "There is nothing to stop me from killing you where you stand, groveler-lover."

Groveler lover? He's referring to Mila.

The captain pulls a handgun from its holster and levels it at my head.

"Yes, you could kill me where I stand," I say. Breathe Faruq. Follow it through. "And then what?"

He stares at me, confused.

"Then you take over in Kapka's place? And perhaps it will be your head in a bag, and another man standing where I am now. If I have shown you anything, it is that even the weakest of men can overthrow a tyrant. This is the way of history."

The crowd murmurs, restless, volatile.

"Or," I continue, "we can find another way. I wish no more violence for our people. No more pain. The Graciles are gone. The enclaves are broken. We do not have to fight any longer. Come with me, and we can build a new way of life, together."

The captain's trigger finger twitches.

"Sheikh Faruq is the last prophet of Ilah," Baral interrupts. "I know this to be true in my heart. Kapka's own gun would not kill him. He will guide us through these end days."

The boy must have seen my suicide attempt.

"Blasphemer!" The captain swings his gun toward Baral.

195

My weapon bucks upward with a flash of fire and the captain's skull explodes in a pink mist of brains and blood. Again, I stoke the fire of the murderer hiding deep inside. When will it ever stop?

The crowd gasps. Several men grab up their knives and guns, their eyes flashing with anger.

"Threaten my life, if you must. But I will tolerate the oppression of the peaceful no longer." My words sound confident, but my chest aches.

"Fine," says another man. "Then we'll threaten *your* life." He and three other men rush me.

My blood runs cold and the specter of death casts a long shadow. Three more cracks of gunfire and my assailants tumble lifelessly into the snow. This time, it's not my doing.

One of Kapka's men steps forward, smoke spiraling from the barrel of his rifle. "I never wanted to join," he says. "Kapka forced me. Threatened my family. My name is Amir, and I will follow Faruq, the last prophet of Ilah."

No wait, that's not who I am. I'm not a—

"Kapka made good on his threat against my family," says another voice. It's one of the camp's cooks. Standing at the edge of the crowd, she holds a smoking revolver. Several more of the camp's women are with her. Each brandishes a weapon. "We too will stand with the prophet."

"No, you're not listening—"

A second captain steps forward to the short platform and turns to face the crowd. "Kapka's ways were not the ways of our forefathers. I will stand with the prophet."

"And I." Another man steps forward.

"I too."

"I will not."

This is getting out of control.

A crescendo of curses and shouts sweeps the crowd. A small melee ensues. But it's short-lived as the last of Kapka's loyal followers are pulled to the icy ground. Ruling through hate and fear only leads to more hate and fear. Few men were as loyal as Kapka hoped.

Still, this is not how I wished it. I am no prophet.

Baral sidles up next to me. "Not all men are born great," he whispers.

196

I swallow and cut my eyes at him. "Some have greatness thrust upon them," I whisper. My father used to say that to me.

Baral smiles.

This is not how I wanted it. Or is it? What did I expect? An icy-wind whips by, grabbing at my coat. I stare at the golden revolver in my hand then at Kapka's clothes hanging from my bones. Am I like Kapka? Or can I use this new power for good? To rescue our people from the hell of oppression and war?

The crowd stares at me, their hot breath misting the cold air. I can't even make out their faces, each person blurring into the next. An electrical sense of expectation grows to an unbearable tension. I started this. Now, I must finish it. I thrust my golden wheel gun into the air.

There's an instant of windswept silence. The throng of people before me erupts, cheering and pumping their fists.

"Fa-ruq! Fa-ruq! Fa-ruq!"

CHAPTER TWENTY-SIX

MILA

Through the screen of lashing wind and swirling snow, the black barrier surrounding Vel juts from the ice and into the sky. Oozing a sense of dread and foreboding, there's good reason why this, one of the last enclaves still intact, carries such a mysterious reputation. No one from the outside has ever entered this place. At least, none has done so and lived to spin the tale of it. What barren hell awaits us if we enter into this dark fortress? Is there even anyone alive in there?

I approach the wall and remove a glove, my bare fingers sliding over black steel, smooth and bitter cold to the touch. What secrets lie within? Why would Gil reach out to me after all this time? Too many questions to entertain. We have a duty to act on the information we have. Gil is here and he knows something about the nuclear stockpile all of my enemies seem to desire—Vedmak chief among them. He, most of all, cannot be allowed to access an object of such unnerving power.

"What are we doing?" Husniya asks.

I slip my glove back on. "We've got to find a way in. Do you see anything?"

The teen twists, her feet sliding in the slush as she examines the towering fortress wall. "No. Nothing but the wall. There aren't even seams. It's as if it is formed from one solid continuous sheet of metal."

"Exactly." I huff a cloud of steam into the air. "Which means we have to look for something out of place." I appraise my small but determined group of well-equipped fighters. "Mos, you and Hus take eight with you and go left. Ghofaun you and I will take the rest to the right." I pull two tarnished but functional emergency flare pistols from my satchel, handing one to Mos. "Shoot your flare if you find something. Hold until the rest of us can catch up. Assuming we can get in, we only move on Vel together. Everyone clear?" The group responds in kind. "Good, let's do it."

"No," Husniya says as if to herself. She mumbles something

indiscernible under her breath but leaves alongside Mos before I can question her.

I don't know what she's going through and I can't help her. Not if she won't confide in me. The loss of her brother was the final straw. She's cracking under the strain. A snowflake sticks to my eyelash. I wipe it free and touch the old photo of my brother and me, tucked neatly inside my pocket. Don't lose your resolve now, Mila. "You ready, Master Ghofaun?"

He gives me a thumbs up.

Minutes tick past as my boots plunge again and again into the fresh powder. We scan the dark foreboding monstrosity that surrounds Vel. There is nothing of note. Just an unending and unyielding barricade of cold black steel. Who made this, anyway?

A pop echoes in the distance. Ghofaun gives me a nudge. High above the fortress wall, Mos's flare arcs across the sky with a brilliant red glow. At its zenith, it drops, fading and fizzing as it falls back to Earth.

"That's it, guys. They've got something. Double time it back the way we came."

It takes longer than expected to make Mos and his team, but the slog is worth it. He's standing in what looks like the doorway to an external bunker, a couple of clicks out from the wall. It seems to be made of the same steel.

"What is it?" I ask. My heart flutters with anticipation, lungs still burning from the cold and double-time marching through knee-high drifts.

"It's a door." Mos shrugs. "To what, we don't know yet."

"It was cracked like this? Or did you do something?" I ask.

"We haven't touched it," Mos replies.

We push in through the door, guns up, scanning every inch for danger. But there's nothing inside save a small table, chair, and an old-fashioned stove with a cooking pot. A heavily armed bunker to protect *this*?

Mos holds up a couple of used auto-injectors.

"Stims," I say. "So, where's the user?"

"Do Velians even use stims?" Mos asks, eyeing the thread of pinkish liquid in the bottom of the injector.

"Some do," I say, my mind drifting back to my scheduled meetings with Gil. He was always stoned.

"Yes, I see it," Husniya says to no one in particular, as she pushes past me.

"See what?" I grunt.

"The opening in the floor," she replies.

My eyes widen. There's no way I should have missed that, but I had. Right smack in the middle of the room it sits, still ajar.

"It has a keypad next to it," Mos says, crouching down. "And it's already been opened. Without force."

I wave over a couple of our men who point their guns at the hatch.

Mos whips it back and for an instant, everyone stops breathing.

Only a square black hole stares back.

"I got this," Mos says.

Before I can protest, he's already dropped down inside.

"It's a tunnel," he calls up. "Pretty narrow. We can make it through side-by-side."

I sling my weapon and climb in after him. The cold, damp tunnel is dark and oppressive but thankfully empty. Everyone drops in with ease—all but Zaldov. He takes a moment to calculate the movement, then hops over the edge, landing with the thud-hiss of mechanical parts absorbing the impact of the short drop. The loud noise in this confined space causes my breath to catch in my lungs.

"Want to make some more noise?"

"I do not believe making more noise would be advisable," he says.

I expel a breath. "No, Zaldov, it's definitely not advisable."

We trek along in relative silence. The only sounds are the light swishing and jangling of gear, Zaldov's marching, and Husniya's soft murmurings, presumably to herself. The incline increases. Myself at the fore, we trudge up the hard-packed earthen ramp to a ladder extending through another hatch above. We scale the ladder entering into another jet-black chamber, the only identifiable way forward, a crack of light in the opposite wall. Another door left open? It looks immensely heavy. I wait for the others to make the top of the ladder.

"Zaldov, pull it open," I say, my eyes wide, prepared for anything.

Zaldov heaves, his mechanical fingers peeling back the heavy door. The growing brightness seems to sear my retinas.

"That's not possible," Mos says, his voice but a whisper.

Stepping through the opening and beneath an arched alcove, sunlight shines down upon my face. Before us lay sweeping hills of green, gently rolling down to a lake that shimmers and glints. Mouth open, eyes wide, I wander out onto the magical sunlit hillside. Pulling my gloves off, I sink to the ground, tiny blades of grass—real grass—slipping between my numb fingers. There is a sweet smell in the air I can't place. It fills my throat and sticks in my nostrils.

Mos is belly-laughing. "In all my years, I never thought I'd see such a thing."

The Kahangan and I make eye contact and I can't help but release an incredulous chuckle.

Ghofaun and Husniya follow, then one by one my fighters trickle in, awe and wonder written on their dirty faces. It's as if we were given a taste of heaven.

I dig past the grass, through the roots and into the soil and push the moist brown clumps through my fingers. "It's real, I can't believe it. Some sort of self-contained environment or greenhouse. All this time, hidden right before our eyes."

"No wonder it's built like a fortress," Mos says. "Who wouldn't want to live here?"

"How is this possible?" I ask. "Robusts wouldn't have had the tech or resources to pull this off. The Velians must have had help. And this sort of tech only comes from one place." My gaze drifts upward.

"Why would Graciles build this for the Velians?" Ghofaun says, his narrow eyes becoming knife-like slits.

"I don't know," I whisper. "But Gil's been holding out on me."

Ghofaun takes a small step back. "I'm not sure I like this, Mila. Something doesn't feel right with this place."

"What's not to like?" Mos replies.

"No, he's right," I say. There's a tinge of smoke in the air, a hint of decay. And not a single sound other than us. I rise to my feet, my brow knitted together. "Where are the Velians?"

"Mila Solokoff, may I be of service?" Zaldov approaches, his boots leaving deep impressions in the grass.

"Yes, tell me about this place. Make it the short version, Zaldov."

"One moment, searching outdated Gracile information archives," his monotone voice buzzes, his head twitching. "Formed when the first people fled to Etyom from all over the world, Vel is the first and oldest enclave. Sealed off from the rest of the survivors, it was initially a haven for the rich and powerful, intended to be the home of the future Graciles. That was before the creation of the lillipads. After the Graciles moved their people above the clouds, a small segment of middle-class Robusts were left in charge of the enclave. The Graciles allowed them to live here and cultivate the land in autonomy in exchange for seventy-five percent of all the food and energy they could produce. This arrangement lasted for a long time."

"Unbelievable." I force out a coarse laugh. "I knew there was something weird going on in this place."

"The Graciles got all their food?" Husniya asks.

"Almost, yes," Zaldov replies, turning to her. "Transferred to them through the lillipad stem via a high-speed magnetic rail elevator." Zaldov motions to the lillipads' support structure rising from the earth on the other side of the lake where it disappears through the fake sky above us.

"Wait, energy? What energy?" I ask.

"Nuclear," Zaldov replies, pointing to the building with high walls and smoke stacks down in the valley ahead.

"Son of a—" Mos starts.

"There's no stockpile," I say. "It's a full-on nuclear power plant. Zaldov, have you known this all along?"

"No, I had to perform a search of the archives via the neural web—"

"No, I mean you could have told us this all along," I interrupt.

"Yes, but you did not inquire until now, Mila Solokoff."

I cross my arms, flicking a strand of hair from my face. "Okay, find out everything you can on Vedmak. His location, his plan, base of operations, anything."

"Technically, Vedmak does not exist."

"Demitri Stasevich, then."

The Creed's head twitches. "There is nothing, Mila Solokoff. Only an old surveillance video feed from Zopat. That was days ago."

Damnation.

"So, where's Gil?" Mos interjects.

I unzip my jacket and survey the unusual space again. "He didn't say. He's gotta be here somewhere. Let's head down into the valley and start looking. Keep an eye out. If Vedmak is here, he won't come quietly. Trust me."

**

Down the hills of sweeping green, we march toward the lake. The blue sky above, though littered with unlit panels, seems to mesmerize everyone—everyone but Ghofaun. He looks worried. I can't blame him. We've yet to see another living soul.

Husniya giggles from behind.

A quick glance and there she is with a smile on her weary face, staring up at Zaldov.

"What? Did I make a joke?" Zaldov says, searching her features.

"No." She stifles another giggle.

"Then what? I want to learn," Zaldov says.

"You said, 'hopefully the Rippers won't *do us*.'" She snorts and adjusts her rifle. "I think you meant: do us *in*."

"Oh," Zaldov says, blinking.

When was the last time she laughed like that with me? But, then who am I to her? Mother? Big sister? Teacher? Don't be so selfish, Mila. She needs the outlet and a robot is better than no one. Even if the thing is just a soulless pile of walking junk.

Reaching the edge of the first cottage-style house, I raise a flat palm to the team. They fan out and take up kneeling positions of security on the corner of the house. The doorframe is cracked, the simple wooden latch distorted and hanging loose.

"Mos, Rinji, Jape." I point to each of them. "On me. Use caution, the door's been forced."

They fall in behind me as we slip into the small dwelling. Dust and decay hang in the air of this place like the soured memory of something that had been good once. Simple tables and chairs lie broken and scattered. The remnants of old produce and foodstuffs rot on the cluttered floor.

"Ransacked." Jape glances at me.

"Check the back room," I say, plucking an old black and white photograph from amidst the garbage at my feet. It's a family of four. They're smiling, the father dressed in miner's gear. The look of optimism on his face like the one my brother used to wear. Zevry …

"Mila," Mos interrupts. He waves me to the back, his hand covering his mouth and nose.

Renji steps out of a room, gagging and sputtering. I peer around the edge of the door. There they are, three of them, pinched into the back corner on the opposite wall from the splintered door. The mother's horrified eyes are locked open, her mouth hanging wide in a silent scream, her arms clutched around her children in a state of frozen rigor. All of their throats have been slashed. Dried blood, black and mottled, clings in congealed rivers down their fronts.

"Sweet Moses." I gasp and turn from the room. There's no longer any doubt—Rippers were here. Maybe still here. "Come on, we got to keep moving."

"You don't have to ask me twice," Mos says.

Renji pukes outside the door.

Ghofaun looks to me. "Everything okay?"

"They've been dead a while. Definitely the work of Rippers and it looks like they sacked this whole place. Everyone, stay on your guard and don't take any chances. They're probably still around."

"I think that's a fair bet." Husniya points to the largest structure closer to the lake. Smoke pours from the chimney of the regal-but-dilapidated abode. Straining my ears, I hear something, like a low chorus of moaning coming from the place.

"What is that?" I step past Husniya.

"I don't like it," Ghofaun says, his voice low. "Mila, what are we doing here?"

"Everybody, keep it together. Stay low, weapons ready," I reply.

In pairs of two, we dart forward from building to building, crossing the false idyllic countryside. We crouch at the edge of the closest building. The moaning and wailing has grown unbearable, the sound of wounded souls seeking escape. The hairs on my arms prickle. What in creation is going on here?

We round the front of the house, but stay low and huddle in the shadow of a few nearby trees and bushes.

"What sort of deviance is *this*?" Mos says.

Our people cry out in disbelief, exchanging worried glances.

Nailed to the wooden exterior are the body parts of a man. The legs, torso, arms, and head are aligned to form a grotesque jigsaw puzzle, ultimately resembling a whole person. But it's not just any person. It's Gil. His eyes are wide, staring blankly into space. A metal stake protrudes from the wooden panel and out through his open mouth.

"Bastards," I mutter under my breath.

Two Ripper warriors exit the front doors and with howls of rage, sprint off in the direction of the power plant.

"They've made this place their home." My stomach clenches in anticipation of what's to come. We won't get another chance at the element of surprise.

I check my weapon, my fingers twitching. "Okay, listen up. We can't circumvent this. We have to eliminate the Ripper presence here." All eyes turn to me. I swallow, the saliva sticking in my throat. "We press forward in wedge-formation. Once we have our ambush set, we hold until there's a threat. Don't give them the upper hand and don't hesitate to take them down if they try to secure weapons."

"Mila." Ghofaun touches my sleeve. "Look at the body. The parts are sliced too cleanly—"

I pull my arm away. "Is everyone clear?"

My comrades acknowledge, ready their weapons, and secure extra magazines.

One last check of my gear. The stubby old-world sub-machine gun feels heavier than ever. I disconnect the drum magazine, check that it's full and the rounds are properly seated and reattach it with a *snap*. "Husniya, get a clear line of sight. Take security with you."

"Yeah, I got it. I don't need you to tell me," she says, tapping her forehead and moving with Zaldov to another simple two-story building off to our right.

With everyone ready, I urge part of my forces to flank the right side of the building. But, before they can get in position, the door swings wide and a Ripper exits. He stands there, face-to-face with us, broken teeth bared in rage. A shot rings out and the creature tumbles back, clutching a mortal chest wound.

"I got 'em," Jape calls out.

Screams, shrill and terrible, erupt from inside.

A wild stomping of feet fills the air, the sound like the beating of many drums as the Rippers inside surge for the door.

"Get ready!" I shout.

Firebombs made with old glass bottles filled with sloop and stuffed with rags are lit by my anxious fighters.

"Burn them out." Jape yells out, lighting a bottle.

"Wait!" I cry.

But the fighters are deaf to my call. The flaming bottles fly through the windows, breaking with flashes of fire. The screams inside intensify into a bawling wail of madness as the mass of deranged creatures pours from the house toward us.

I hold my weapon at the ready, but can't bring myself to fire. Something isn't right.

A blaze of metallic rattling fills the air as my people fire on the emerging Rippers, the concussion drowning out the death screams of the ragged people. Tumbling and spinning, their bodies fall into piles forward of the threshold.

Oh, Yeos no. "Stop, we have to stop," I say, though the words are barely audible.

Flames lick from the windows, curling into black fingers of twisting smoke. Faster now, the blazing inferno envelops the large building, tongues of fire gushing from the doors and windows.

"Mos," I yank on his arm. "Make them stop!"

"Cease fire," Mos calls. "Cease fire, right now!"

As the cacophony subsides, it is replaced with the sound of terrified screams. A wave of nausea hits me alongside the realization. They are the screams of children.

"What have we done?" Ghofaun shouts.

Oh, Yeos, no. It's not possible. It can't be. I scan the warriors on the ground before us, except not a single one of them carries a weapon and … My stomach clenches and vomit spews from my lips.

"Oh, by the heavens," Mos says, his eyes full of pain. "These are unarmed women. Their children must be inside. We have to get them out. Ghofaun, help me get them out."

Our fighters back away, looking to each other for reassurance. But there is none to be found as the last of the child's screams fades into the crackling flames of the collapsing structure. This can't be happening. Rippers don't have children—do they? I vomit again into the grass, littered with shining brass cases. What have we done?

A furious sound born of the depths of hell fills the air. On the peak of a nearby hill stands a pack of Ripper males, screaming and rattling their melee weapons. They hurtle down the hill toward us, crossing the distance with reckless abandon.

Mos seizes my arm. "Mila."

Can't see. Can't move. Everything is numb. "Mos, I didn't know there were children. I didn't mean to …"

"Mila, we've got to go now or we're all dead."

I'm being shoved toward the nearest dwelling, the one where Husniya now leans through an upper window, taking precision shots at stray Rippers as they barrel forward. Through the doorway and into the musty abode I stumble. The door slams shut and the crossbar comes down with a thud. Mos barks commands. Our team opens fire through the windows.

Mos turns to me, gripping my shoulders in his meaty hands. "Go. Find Husniya."

"O-okay," I say, swallowing back bile.

"Mila!" Mos yells, inches from my face. "Snap out of it."

"Yeah … Yeah, okay."

Ghofaun, his face covered in shadow, pushes past me with a group of fighters and heads for the stairs.

The rickety door to the house creaks and flexes as the Rippers slam into it again and again. They howl with a lust for blood, hellbent on taking our heads. Resistance fighters shout and clamor as the savages crash through the dusty glass windows of the cottage. My people lock in hand-to-hand combat with the encroaching mob. The entrance door cracks and gives way and, with a wild battle cry, Mos charges into the midst of the invaders.

"Move your ass, Mila," Mos calls from somewhere within the scrum.

I jerk to life and make it to the top of the stairs in a few strides. "Husniya."

"Here," calls the teenager from a room at the end of the narrow hallway. "Where's Mos?"

"He's coming. Mos!" I shout.

The Kahangan reaches the top step, spins and kicks the closest Ripper in the chest. The force sends the brute tumbling into the pack that follows but they keep coming. Mos falls into the room and we slam the door shut, shoving a barricade of furniture against it.

Gasping for breath, Mos leans against the wall. "If they keep at it, they'll get in. Sooner or later."

Ghofaun can only nod.

I can feel my dismay turning to anger. My furious gaze rests on Jape, lungs heaving, leaning against a wall across the room.

"What the hell?" I say, squaring off. "I told you to wait."

"No," Jape says, his eyes resolute, "you said not to let them get the upper hand. That's what we did."

"There were children in there, Jape. Children!" My eyes well and I step forward, separated from Jape by a few fighters who try to hold me back. "You know better. You should have waited for my command."

"You didn't seem too eager to stop us, Mila. You knew what had to be done." Jape looks down and checks his weapon.

"I tried to tell you." The words fade from my lips and I wipe at my eyes.

The burning building filled with dead Ripper children calls to me through the room's only window. *Innocents, Mila.* My lungs tighten and eyes sting with bitter tears. *You're a murderer, Mila.*

Thick black smoke billows from the torched building. It snakes out and away on a light breeze, pointing like some terrible, shadowy finger. Directing my attention to something moving on the horizon. A man, exiting the power plant with a large lockable trunk propped on his shoulder.

No, it's not a man—it's Vedmak. He twists his head left and right, searching for danger. Apparently satisfied, he lurches from the building and hobbles toward the abandoned quarry beyond.

Before I can reconcile my actions, the butt of the sub-gun crashes through the glass of the window.

"Mila, what are you doing?" Husniya shrieks.

"Listen to me." I throw the gun to the floor. "Get clear of this place. When you do, come find me in the quarry."

"Where are you going?" Mos clenches his teeth. "You're leaving us?"

"I have to, Mos. I have to try and stop him."

Stepping through the window, I launch myself from the ledge and just barely snag the rim of the place across the lane. Pulling myself up, the brittle clay shingles crack and crunch beneath my boots. A few uneasy strides and I'm at the roof's apex.

"Mila, wait," Husniya calls out the window.

Can't talk now. Vedmak must be stopped. It's the only thing that matters.

Before she can protest further, I vault from the edge of the roof and land on the lip of the adjoining structure with a crack of disintegrating shingles. A spear whips past, almost causing me to lose balance. Below, a small group of Rippers track my movements. Damnation. From roof-to-roof, I jump, balancing across the narrow peaks of rounded shingles only to jump again. The Rippers howl in pursuit.

An ear-shattering *boom* erupts from the false sky overhead. Powdered glass floats to the ground in a shower of tiny diamonds. A Creed strike-ship drops through the blasted hole, its engines whining. The vessel banks hard, circling around to land close, on the edge of the quarry. Vedmak hobbles faster.

Sard it all to hell, he's going to escape.

The Rippers' attention is newly occupied. The group tracking me now runs screaming toward the deranged Gracile. Vedmak shoves the crate on board through a sliding side door. Then, on his command, six Graciles wearing Creed exo-skeletons exit the ship's rear loading-ramp and open fire on the Rippers with their plasma rifles. Wicked blue bolts rocket from the sleek metallic weapons. The energy projectiles knife through the air, obliterating the screaming Rippers.

This is my chance.

Another leap and I land on the last roof of this row. Ahead, a spiraling road descends into the dark quarry beyond. Sprinting to the edge, I reach into my satchel, draw out the emergency flare gun, and cock the hammer back. Flying from the roof, I extend my arm, aiming with one eye pinched, the flare firing forth with a popping sound. Landing with a grunt I toss the pistol and roll to my feet, my stride steady. The red flare streaks over the heads of the Gracile combatants, bounces off the loading ramp and flips straight into the cab of the strike ship. The pilot loses his mind, swatting and stamping as Vedmak makes for the door, but he's not in time. The strike-ship lurches forward, spinning off into the quarry, red-tinged smoke billowing from the open rear gate.

Abandoned, Vedmak spins, his eyes furious. He doesn't see me until it's too late. A scream of fury on my lips, I slam into his side, hitting him low in his pelvic axis.

His eyes widen as I drive him back. "There you are, you little bitch!"

"*Everything* is your fault. I'll destroy you!" I scream.

Vedmak's feet slip on the rim of the crater. He grabs a fistful of my hair and tumbles, shrieking, into the mineshaft below. Together we fall suspended in the dark until, with a sickening jolt, my breath is knocked from me.

CHAPTER TWENTY-SEVEN

FARUQ

The Baqirian warlord's palace holds no comfort. Inside this place, too many dreams of hate and abuse rise from within the depths of my heart. They mingle there, intertwined with images of my mother, the sound of her voice as she soothed the wounds of a troubled boy. But it's all replaced by the constant driving ache radiating from the center of my chest, a remembrance of other good things now gone—a whispered promise to Husniya as we crouched huddled on the street, the way hope once swelled in my chest at the sight of Mila.

No, damnation. Enough of that.

Silks and silver adorn the walls alongside suits of ancient armor, weapons and other military tokens from the world before. Kapka was a fanatic for everything warfare and by the looks of his palace, it was more lifestyle than political interest. An ancient stationary machine gun, complete with cases of ammunition and a tripod that locks into position, sits in the corner. Does that hateful monstrosity even function?

Two mornings ago, I'd marched with my new army through the gates of my home enclave. We were met with caution and general suspicion, but little resistance. Few people here remember their freedom, or at least, what their lives looked like before Kapka or his forbearers rose to power. When we returned without him, the looks of fear on my people's faces told me they were preparing for the worst—another, maybe even more despicable, power-hungry despot to fear. It will take time, but I will show them who I am. That our future is one we must claim together.

There is just one problem.

Word travels fast to friends and enemies alike in a place like Etyom, and time is of the essence. With Kapka gone, Baqir will be considered vulnerable. The danger lies not with Kapka's army or even his elite palace guard. They are more loyal to their bellies than any one ruler. And Kahanga was already sacked, so I'm told. No, Baqir's sister enclave, Alya, is our biggest threat. There, loyalists under the leadership of Governor Abd Al Jabbar, Kapka's cousin, are planning a coup. When they will strike is anyone's guess. We must remain ready.

I sit up from my bedroll on the floor in the main hall, my gaze roving across the sleeping bodies of my men, all but the faithful Baral. The young boy sits nearby, reading some old text on our long and turbulent history. He must have watched over me as I slept.

Baral sets his book aside. "Sheikh Faruq. You are awake. Let me fetch your breakfast."

There is hope in his eyes, a strange glimmer of something better to come. I'd nearly forgotten what it looked like. "No. I can get my own food, thank you."

"Nonsense," he says, already moving toward the kitchen. "The prophet does not fetch his own food."

Standing, I rub my hands and arms and follow Baral, using friction to push the early chill from my limbs. Does he believe such a thing? Do the others? How long can I draw out this fantasy before they refuse to follow the bastard son of one of Kapka's wives? A man who is more ghost than prophet.

"Sheikh." A well-built man with ribbons of silk sown to the breast of his sand-colored shirt approaches from my left. He was one of those who had first supported me back at the encampment.

"Yes? Captain Kahleit, correct?"

"It is I, Sheikh." He gives a salute. Do I salute back? Probably not. "Seven of the men deserted overnight."

"Deserted? To where?"

He opens his hands with a shrug. "To Alya, Sheikh. Abd Al Jabbar is a ruthless tyrant, like his cousin, but he holds the loyalty of many who supported Kapka."

"Our people are deserting us?"

"A few of them, Sheikh. They're scared. They don't believe in our cause. They do believe in the brutality of Al Jabbar."

"What can we do?"

Captain Kahleit frowns. "We can capture their families. Show them the error of their ways."

Is this all they know? "No, Captain we do not do that anymore."

"Then what will you have from us?"

The question is earnest. The support of even those who are behind me is thin. What am I supposed to do now? I'm no warlord.

"We will fill their ranks with those who wish to join us."

As I answer, Baral rounds the corner, a steaming bowl of baked tajis in hand. When he speaks, he does so around a bulbous lump in his cheek.

"I taste it first, Sheikh. Make sure it is safe." He winks and hands me the bowl.

The wafting aroma of a spoonful of taji beans and spice rises to my nostrils, the warmth gracing my cold lips. Baral coughs, sending a wad of half-chewed beans onto my tunic. He coughs again. The rest of the beans fall from his tongue as he grasps for his throat.

Lightning fast, Kahleit slaps the bowl from my hands and catches the boy attendant as he slumps. Baral's eyes loll white, blood and foam squeezing from between gnashed teeth.

"Baral, no," I shout.

The boy convulses uncontrollably.

"Poison," Kahleit says.

"Poison?"

Baral's fit is short-lived. A final spasm and he exhales loudly, relaxing into Ilah's embrace. I slide the young boy's eyelids closed, leaving my fingers resting on his still warm cheeks.

"He's dead," Kahleit confirms. "Those beans were meant for you."

Before I can reason myself from it, I'm dashing for the kitchen. A man I don't recognize bursts through the back door. "That man, who was he?" I shout.

The head cook appears stupefied. "He arrived this morning, Sheikh. Said you sent him to work under me."

I crash my shoulder into the metal door to the street. It swings wide, squealing on old hinges. Down the steps two at a time, I nearly slip on the thick ice but manage to keep straight and head toward the courtyard—the only way he could have gone.

"Stop that man! He is an enemy of the cause!"

By the time I round the corner, my men already have him. Held fast, he's spitting curses.

Must remain calm. I nonchalantly flick the remnants of poisoned food from my tunic and strut forward. The man continues to struggle and spit in my direction.

"You would make an attempt on my life?" I say, trying to keep composure—though my fists are balled, blood pulsing hot and furious through my veins. "You killed an innocent boy to get to me. Have you no shame?"

"Baqir has become impotent," the man retorts. "The faithful in Alya will lead the way forward for our people now. You are but a dog who bit his master. You are no prophet."

"I never said I was anything but a man who wants what is right for his people. You and your fanatical brood are the heathens. You mock our people and our faith."

"You whine like a woman," the attacker says then spits at my feet. "That is all you are good for. Words."

I'm so tired of his kind. The only thing they understand is violence. So be it. "I will stamp you out like an insect," I say through clenched teeth, my nose almost touching his.

A wicked grin is plastered on the man's face. "Good luck," he whispers.

Click.

No.

"Bomb!" I yell and fling myself in the opposite direction. My men swell around me, forcing me back as the device detonates in a concussion that seems to split my skull and tear its way through my eardrums.

Lying on the ground, I cough and blink away the dust. A severed arm, still oozing blood, lies crooked across my ankle. I kick it away, my ears ringing, the screams of the dying muffled and muted beneath a constant whistle. I was so close. I should be dead. How am I not dead?

Hands snake under my arms and pull me to my feet.

"Sheikh, you are alive? Ilah be praised. I must get you to safety." It's the muffled voice of Captain Kahleit.

"No." I wrench from him and stand on shaking legs.

The broken bodies of my men lay strewn about the courtyard like wind-tossed trash. So much senseless death and carnage. First the boy, now these loyal souls who used their bodies as a buffer between me and the blast. Stepping forward, I kneel to apply pressure to the flayed chest of one of my men, an open wound that will surely be fatal. Blood pumps in gouts through my fingers. The man grasps my sleeve, bubbles of blood and spittle on his lips.

"We believe. Lead us to victory, Prophet," he says with a final gasp.

What do I do? What would Mila do? "Don't compare yourself to some Logosian," I hiss through a clenched jaw.

Some Logosian? How far I have fallen. She cared for me, maybe even loved me.

"Stop it." I pinch my eyes. "Stop." Shaking, I cry out, raising a blood-soaked fist into the air. My anger pouring through a voice amplified by the blast, now too loud in my own ears. "Al Jabbar! I'm coming for you!"

CHAPTER TWENTY-EIGHT

DEMITRI

Every inch of my skin burns as though what's left of this abused corpse is set ablaze. My stomach convulses with waves of nausea and my ghost appendage throbs with phantom pain in time with the beating of my heart. An absolute blackness covers everything, enveloping me in a cold, heavy cloak. Am I finally where I deserve to be, in the bowels of Hell? Is this what damnation feels like? Or perhaps this is the dimension to which Vedmak was cast for his sins.

Now, for mine. I am trapped here too. Vedmak. Vedmak, are you there? Nothing. I'm once again in control. At least for now, but I know all too well he will return. There's no escaping him.

Slowly, the blackness eases—the weakest of light now detectable. The narrow shaft through which I fell extends above at least twenty meters. The sounds of battle are faint overhead. There's no way I can go back the way I came. The small cavern has at least a couple of openings that disappear into the dark—tunnels perhaps. A way out? If I even want one, perhaps it's better to die here. The flesh of my remaining hand is blistered and weeping. My scarred face is wet with fluid from broken skin and blood. Radiation poisoning. My death will be long and painful but fully deserved.

There's a faint scratching in the gloom.

"Is someone there?" I say, the vibration of my words making my head ache.

Only the scraping click of a rusted wheel gun hammer cocking answers me.

"You know who it is, don't play games, Vedmak," a familiar female voice says.

It takes a few seconds for my eyes to adjust, the shadowed outline of her face appearing, centered behind the stovepipe barrel of the hand cannon she has trained on me.

"Mila?" Of course, Mila. She pushed us into the shaft.

"Don't act like you don't know," she rasps.

Gradually, her form becomes clearer. She's huddled against a rock wall, knees drawn up, clutching her midriff with one arm and holding the gun with her free hand. The hate in her stare cuts to the bone. My once-friend knows all too well what I've become.

"Mila, it's me. It's Demitri."

She wipes her free arm across her nose and sniffs. "Why should I believe you?"

Can't blame her. I wouldn't believe me either.

"This is all your fault," Mila says, her voice unusually frail.

My chest cramps.

"*Everything*. Everything is your fault," she repeats. "Do you know how many people have died because of you? How many innocents? I know it's you, or Vedmak, or whoever's been butchering my people. I saw the weapons your soldiers carry."

"I … Mila … it wasn't … Please, it's me." I mumble.

"Stop talking." She jerks the wheel gun at me. "Let's say it is you, Demitri. Let's entertain this lie. It doesn't change anything. Do you know how many men I lost looking for you and Faruq?"

Faruq, yes. He was in the Vapid. "I saw him. Kapka had him."

"Kapka's dead," she replies. There's no relief in her voice.

"Then you found Faruq?"

She holds my shadowed gaze, pain, abhorrence, and sadness burning in her tear-filled eyes. She wipes her nose again. "Yeah, I found him. And he sent me away. He'd been tortured. He's not himself anymore. And now he's is gone. Because of you."

"Me?"

"If I'd not been trying to stop you, I could have had more time and resources to find him." She coughs, wincing in pain and grips her ribs again. "All because you can't control that damn voice in your head. And now, everyone else is going to pay the price of your cowardice." Loathing pours from her, venom now flowing from her lips like a stream. "I murdered children. Do you know that, Demitri or Vedmak or whoever the hell you are right now? *Children are dead because of my orders.*" Her voice echoes around the narrow chamber.

"The Rippers."

"All because I wanted to try and save you. I defied Bilgi and everyone in the resistance by looking for you and Faruq." Her voice trails off and she stops, swallowing her words before her tears can fall.

"I'm sorry."

"Sorry?" Mila spits back, her eyes so welled up a flood may escape them at any moment. She raises the gun and points it at my head. "Everything I've done has been wrong. Bilgi, Faruq, Gil."

From this angle, the muzzle looks like a massive stove pipe. I focus on it—Mila's face now nothing but a blur in the background. I feel empty. Before the lillipads fell, I'd wanted to live more than anything at any cost. Since Vedmak had taken control, death has more than once seemed preferable. Now, I feel nothing.

"I have to do one thing, the one thing that matters," Mila says, her wet eyes burning a hateful stare into me.

I don't have any words.

"Say something, damn you." She lurches forward and presses the cold metal of the weapon to my forehead.

"There's nothing left to say, Mila. You should do it." A tear slips from the corner of my eye.

Mila screams in my face and the gun's hammer slams down, a brief fireball illuminating the space between us.

A moment passes. I open my eyes and am greeted by the familiar dark of the mine shaft. Mila's pallid face, close to mine, is etched in panic. Above my head, she has the gun in both hands, pointing it toward the sky. Smoke wafts from the barrel into the dark.

Staring at me the whole time, she slowly lets go of the gun and it clangs to the rocky floor. Defeated, I slump against a large boulder and cry.

For a long while, neither of us speaks.

"We'll cure you," Mila says, finally. Shuffling forward, she places a cold hand on my face.

Her touch sends a fresh wave of guilt through me and more tears fall. "I'm sorry, Mila. I'm so sorry."

"It's okay. I found you, now."

"You don't understand. The things he made me do …"

Mila takes a deep breath, as if she wants to say one thing, then changes her mind and switches the subject. "We may have a way to rid you of Vedmak. Oksana said she knows how."

Did she just say Oksana? Vedmak had never found her. She's still alive, after all this time. I wipe my face. "Oksana is with you?"

"She's with the resistance," Mila says, rubbing her ribs again. "Or I should say, she's agreed to help."

'Sana is helping Robusts? I can't believe it. If anyone could help, it would be her. For the first time in years, there's a glimmer of hope. The pebbles roll and slide beneath me as I shuffle on my butt trying to sit more upright. "You would take me to her? But you need to know, Opor has been compromised. Giahi is working with Vedmak. They have a neural link. Vedmak is using him to overthrow you and Bilgi."

Mila sighs and stares at me again. "How did I not see it? I should have but I didn't. So blinded by my own demons. I couldn't save Bilgi from exile. Or Faruq from Kapka. Or even keep Husniya close, for that matter. She hates me."

"I'm sorry," is all I can muster.

Her face hardens. "I can't fail again. I'll get you back to Opor and figure out how to deal with Giahi."

"You're not a failure. You're the strongest person I know."

Mila's resolve breaks and she hangs her head. "Demitri, it's been so long. How did this become our lives? The things we've done."

She searches my eyes as if I have the answer. As if somewhere in this Gracile head is the solution. Is her faith so broken she hopes for answers in me now, instead of her Yeos? What am I supposed to say? If Yeos exists, he'd surely smite me before Mila. At least she'd tried. At least what she did, she believed it was for the right reason.

The sound of gunfire and plasma rifles way above us breaks the silence.

"We have to find a way out of here," she says, her face hardening. "Can you walk?"

"Yes, but, I don't know how long Vedmak will stay gone," I say.

With a grunt, I force myself to my feet and offer Mila my hand. She grabs it, and I hoist her up, wincing with a fresh streak of pain that shoots up my arm.

219

"What's happened to you?" she asks, studying my blistered skin.

"Radiation poisoning. If we don't get to Oksana, I'll die anyway. Just more painfully than by a bullet," I say.

She squints at me then wraps my severed arm around her neck. "Come on, we better get moving."

With slow limping movements, we trudge on through the maze of musty earthen underground tunnels, which are lit only by the occasional clanking generator. For a while, we don't speak, the crunch of pebbles beneath our boots echoing softly in the endless meandering dark.

"Did you hurt yourself when we fell?" I observe her hand clutched against her ribcage.

"Yeah. I don't think they're broken. Bruised maybe? It hurts to breathe." She looks me over, my stump of an arm hanging about her neck like a cannibal's necklace. "What happened to your hand?"

"I had to cut it off … to keep him from hurting someone," I manage.

From under my arm, Mila looks up to meet my gaze. She simply gives my forearm a pat.

My heart aches.

As we continue on, I offer fragments of the last four years. Vedmak, and his army of Graciles who he sends out on raiding parties to kill off Robusts using plasma weapons. Scare-tactics against Opor. His plan to grow more Graciles and link them to souls like his, using the nuclear fuel rods for power. The fact that if he links too many, it'll generate a VME and kill us all. But eventually, it comes back to the simplest issues. The pain inflicted on those we care for. What I was forced to do to Anastasia. What Vedmak does to anyone who crosses his path. The Gracile children whose growth has been accelerated but their minds underdeveloped, so Vedmak murders them. Mila recounts Faruq's torture and mental break, Husniya's worsening condition, and Bilgi's exile. These are the things that haunt us both and, in the end, what really drives us. Mila seems hellbent on saving me as if it might redeem some horrible misstep. The more we talk, the more I can't decide if that is a good thing.

Another bend, another choice of dreary tunnels. It feels like hours, but I know it hasn't been. A battle still rages above us, the muffled zip of plasma rifles firing and *whump* of homemade grenades penetrate the thick rock.

"Sard," Mila groans. "How do we get out of here?"

I shake my head. "I don't know. We need to find a way up. There must be an exit. A ladder or winch or something."

Perhaps you should pray to the little suka's false god.

My arm spasms, jerking to life, seized by some invisible presence. "Oh no."

"What's wrong?" Mila searches my face, before answering own her question. "It's Vedmak, isn't it?"

I can only nod, swallowing a lump from my throat.

"Fight him Demitri," she says, her face stern.

"I can't. He's too strong."

"You have to be stronger." She jabs a finger in my chest, her expectant stare boring holes into me. "Believe you *can be.*"

I avert my eyes. "I'm sorry, Mila."

"Damnation, c'mon we have to get you help," she says yanking me farther down a tunnel.

"Wait," I say and pull away. My head swarms, goose-bumped flesh tingling hot. "He's coming back. You have to go. He'll kill you. Run, Mila. Get as far from me as you can."

I don't wait for an answer, and instead shove her to the ground, buying precious seconds. Vedmak's maniacal laugh swells in my head until I can no longer hear my only friend's footsteps, or her shouts for me to stop, far behind in the labyrinth of twisting dark.

CHAPTER TWENTY-NINE

MILA

"**D**emitri!" My echoing scream disappears into the depths of the passage ahead. The black rock walls seem to amplify the air of oppression in this place. "Demitri, let me help you," I shout in frustration, fingernails digging into my palms as I clench my fists.

He's gone.

I've got to get out of this tomb and warn the others. If Vedmak is taking back over, he's going to try to get out of Vel again with the nuclear power cells. I wheel around and jog in the opposite direction, a fragment of hope at a possible way out stuck in my mind. I'd passed an alcove while chasing my deranged friend. Can't say for sure it's what I think it is, but it bears checking out.

Retracing my steps, I slow my heart rate by controlling my breaths. My thoughts stretch in so many directions I fear my mind might shatter, the pieces of the person I used to be scattered and forgotten. Demitri is going to be the death of us both.

Why can't he face his demon? Don't have time for this. Damnation, my ribs ache.

An old wooden platform with a section of rail track leading up into another tunnel at an angle appears from the dark. My legs feel like lead, the muscles full of acid after all the running and jumping, not to mention the fall. My boots clunk up the steps to the short platform. There's a cable attached to the front of the railcar. Of course. Maybe I can get in and it will winch me to the surface. Only one way to find out.

The rusted generator at the foot of the shaft silently collects dust. In the dim light of the single incandescent bulb hanging above the platform, I unscrew the gas cap and peer inside. Bone dry. Sard. "Great." I huff, disgusted with my fortune. This generator hasn't been used in ages. That should have been obvious since there's no way to refine petrol anymore.

Most machines run on electrical turbines or …

Or, a nuclear power plant. Of course. The power is *piped in*.

Crouching, I check the console and brush away the thick dust coating. There. From under the box snakes a long hose, the black rubber coating flaking with dry rot. It runs up the wall and is bundled with a host of other cables running the length of the tunnel above my head. I follow the hose. Each winding turn looks the same as the one that came before it, a mind-numbing maze of serpentine rock walls lit only by the occasional hanging bulb.

I stop abruptly, my boots slipping on the gravel beneath their treads. Above, at the junction, there's a main power cable. At its end are a series of outlets designed for a plug. But, there's one too few. The end of my cable hangs with no female pairing for its prongs. I grab a wooden crate and drag it over. Stepping up onto the corners, it creaks and wobbles but holds. Straining up, I grab the nearest plugged-in cord and yank it free. The tunnel around me plunges into a darkness. Panic rises in my chest, the anxiety at the thought of being lost down here smothering. I swallow and fumble with the free cords.

"Damnation. Come on, already," I curse, my fingers blindly securing the new plug. There's a disorienting flash as the prongs sink in. And, way back from where I came in the dark of the tunnel, there's a *peep* and the soft hum of something electrical.

"Yes. Okay, Mila. Hurry up. You've got this."

I make my way down the wall toward the sound, groping the irregular stones in the wall like a blind person. Beyond the black, a faint red light grows brighter as I near the platform. A second time, my boots clunk onto the wooden platform.

Flicking the power breakers on, the winch hums to life. It's about five meters to the rail car. Looking back to the console, I mash the green button labeled *winch engage* and in two strides, vault from the platform to the car. Crouched in the cold steel bucket, it makes its slow, steady ascent to the surface.

A tiny square of light begins to grow and widen in the distance. I wince at the squalling grind of the cart's wheels beneath, their axles in desperate need of grease. But there's another sound now—the *pop-whiz* of gunfire and the *zap-thud* of plasma bolts slamming into flesh and bone, rendering people to windblown ash. My people.

A knot forms in my stomach, my hands searching for the Makarov pistol, a knife, something. I come up empty. The knot tightens as the square of false-paneled sky grows wider, the sounds of war, louder. Unarmed, I am to be thrust into the heat of battle with nothing but my wits.

The Creed strike-ship screams overhead, its engines pivoting for a vertical landing. Now clear of the flare, it swings in a wide arc, circling the maw. He must be looking for a place to land. You're running out of time, Mila.

Scrabbling from the cart, I realize I'm not out of the quarry just yet. An earthen wall inset with a series of short wooden ladders stands between me and the rim of the mining pit. Running forward, I leap for the ladder. My feet catch the rungs, the pressure snapping them. Another hop before they give way and I snag hold of a rung halfway up and start to pull. After what feels like an eternity, I make it up the series of short ladders to the lip of the mining quarry.

A handful of Gracile soldiers, twisted grins of pleasure on their perfect faces, blast holes in the meager cover the remaining resistance fighters cower behind. But they're not advancing. They're holding their position behind a makeshift bunker of junk. Above them, the strike-ship slows, twisting in midair. They're protecting the ship for an extraction. They're expecting *him*.

"Mila," the wheezed sound of my name is barely audible.

A young man lies nearby, clutching at his pelvis. From the hips down nothing remains but the ashen stumps of protruding pelvic bone.

"Jape," I call out, scrambling on all fours over to him.

Jape's arms shake involuntarily, his eyes stuck wide, white spittle in the corners of his mouth. Dragging him behind the edge of a nearby dwelling, I pull a medical stabilizer from his jacket and press it against his neck. With a hiss, the hypodermic needle delivers the cocktail of painkillers, anti-shock, and slow-stop for hemorrhaging.

A plasma bolt strikes the edge of the building and showers us in a sheen of powdered brick. I pull him a little farther behind cover. Jape's shaking has slowed, his eyes glassy.

"I'm sorry, Mila. Back at the house—I should have listened for your orders. I just …just …" Jape stutters, spittle clinging to his lips.

"Don't think of that now, Jape." I grab his hand.

"Can …" He manages. "Can I have another?"

I clench my teeth to fight back tears. "No. Another cocktail will stop your heart."

"Please, Mila. This is killing me, like my insides are all dried up. I don't want to die in pain. Not like this." He pats the ashen turf where his lower half used to be.

"Jape, lay back and—"

He struggles to swallow. "Just one more hit."

Tears fill my eyes as I pull a second auto-injector from his jacket. I press the nozzle to his neck and give him a second dose.

He raises a hand and grabs my arm, the squeeze weak. "Thank you, Paladyn," he says. His breathing slows, his eyes dim until the spark of life in him fades and is gone.

There's that name again: Paladyn. Do they still believe in me? Does a protector of the people commit murder? Do they get all their people killed?

A scream, high and shrill, brings me back to the conflict. Sard it all.

"Lead, Mila. That's your job. Do your job," I say through clenched teeth.

I grab Jape's sub-machine gun, a cobbled-together thing that looks like it belongs more in a welding shop than on a battlefield. Pulling two old Soviet grenades from Jape's vest, I sling the sub gun and move to the edge of cover for a better view.

Husniya is cowered behind a low wall currently being shredded by the blue flashes of plasma bolts striking home. The girl screams again, covering her head.

I've got you, Hus. I pull the pins on both grenades, odd lemon-shaped devices with little posts on top that fit well in the hand. The spoon on the first one ejects from the body with a *ching*. I hurl it toward the Gracile position. I let the second grenade fly, the spring-loaded spoon flipping into the air. Both grenades in flight, I raise my hands high. "Hey jackbags, make you feel strong to shoot down a woman?"

They swing their rifles on me and it takes everything I've got inside to not dive for cover. Their faces seem to glow in anticipation of the kill when the first grenade detonates. There's a flash and the Graciles scream as shrapnel finds its way through the spaces in their exo-suits. The second grenade explodes in their confused midst. Howls of pain and terror drift from the gray smoke.

"Go," I scream at my men behind the bunker. "Don't let them escape."

The sound of my voice stirs my people to action. They open fire, rising and running toward the confused elites. Through my fear I drive forward, heedless of the stabbing pain in my side.

The remaining Graciles stumble from the smoke. holding their wounds, their arms clawing for purchase amidst the ash. My friends, Mos, Ghofaun, and Husniya, lead the resistance forward with bold strides.

Someone lands a lucky shot and a Gracile is hit in the neck. His muscled frame tenses and a jet of crimson shoots through his fingers as he chokes on his own blood. The last few stumble back toward the gunship.

"They're falling back," I shout above the melee. Beneath my arm, the sub-gun chatters away in a predictable staccato.

The last few Graciles fall back to the rear of the ship. One of them collapses, sprayed with bullets that riddle his body and ping off the Creed vessel. The others scramble flat to the icy ground.

The strike ship's engines whine, preparing for takeoff.

"Target the engines. Don't let them leave," I scream.

A fusillade of bullets looses upon the strike ship, but this time they don't rattle on the hull. Instead, they hit an invisible barrier that ripples like a pool of water. A chill descends upon me, the fine hairs at the nape of my neck prickling. The Gracile soldier who'd laid flat reappears looking smug. A portable plasma shield. It's large enough to cover the strike-ship and prevent us from circumnavigating it. Damnation.

"Mila," Ghofaun calls across the battlefield. "Look."

The monk is standing with Mos and the rest of our people. His gaze is fixed beyond the plasma shield, near the nose of the gunship. And there, probably originally trying to flank our enemies, are Husniya and Zaldov. But now, they're trapped behind the energy wall. And there's not a damn thing I can do.

The enemy soldier starts to stride toward Husniya, but he hasn't made it two paces when his smug grin slackens and blood spurts from his lips. A huge leaf-shaped blade lances through his neck. It's yanked free, and he drops lifelessly to the ground.

From the shadows, the form of my Gracile friend appears. Demitri?

My men unleash a volley of gunfire.

"No, wait," I shout

The bullets disintegrate into the shield.

"It's Demitri!"

Demitri drops to the ground, apparently exhausted, but forces himself to his knees, using the Ripper's spear he's holding as a crutch. He looks to me, pain in his eyes, then to Husniya.

Husniya's face lights up and she takes a step forward. When Zaldov moves with her, she stops him with an upheld index finger. I can't hear what she says as she shakes her head and lays a flat palm against his chest. The Creed looks down at her, then back at the Gracile. Zaldov nods, lowering the plasma rifle in his hands—its digital display blinking red from an empty power cell.

Husniya walks forward, wiping tears from her face. She's begging something of her old friend.

Demitri offers a gentle smile and opens his arms to her.

Mos and Ghofaun can only watch in silence.

Husniya breaks into a fit of sobbing as she enters the arms of her friend and buries her face in his chest. He responds by wrapping his severed arm around her, tears forming in his eyes.

"Demitri?" I whisper.

As if he heard, Demitri looks straight at me. His lips peel back over perfect teeth in a sadistic grin. Husniya gasps as the twelve-inch spear tip erupts through the taut muscles of her back.

My legs give out, knees driving against the turf, my fists balled, a ragged scream tearing from my throat.

Husniya coughs, flailing, blood splattering on Vedmak's chest as he hoists her up, the weight of her body sliding her down the shaft of the spear.

"Husniya!"

Screaming curses, Mos empties his weapon, the shield rendering his attack useless.

There's a shriek, high and piercing. It is the sound of absolute pain. But it's not Husniya. Zaldov launches forward, crossing the divide in a single leap.

Vedmak dumps the wounded girl to the side and tries to brace, but he's not fast enough. Zaldov drives down with a hammer fist blow to the bridge of the nose, laying it flat against Vedmak's face in a spray of blood. Another shrill scream and Zaldov hits Vedmak again, this time with a precision hook to the ribs, followed by an uppercut, then a cross to the chin.

I bolt upright, my eyes wide, my fists clenching handfuls of my jacket. "Yes, Zaldov! Do it!"

Vedmak falters, crawling to all fours, a look of panic on his blood-smeared face. Rising, he yanks the spear free of Husniya and jams it through Zaldov's left shoulder, wrenching the robot's arm free of the socket. His severed mechanical appendage dangling, Zaldov lets loose a fearsome cry, utilizing a cross body block with his right arm that shatters the spear shaft. Zaldov grabs Vedmak by the throat, lifts him up and slings him against the ground the way a frustrated child would discard a doll.

Absolute terror now envelops Vedmak's pale, beaten features.

The gunship's thrusters engage. Vedmak forces himself to his feet and kicks Zaldov in the chest, knocking him back. He grabs the hydraulic piston attached to the liftgate as it whines closed. With a burst, the ship accelerates into the sky. Vedmak swings himself up and into the hatch, the ramp sealing shut behind him. A thunderous boom echoes as the thrusters launch the strike-ship upward, propelling it through the hole in the roof and out into the swirling storm.

After a moment, the translucent blue wall of the plasma barrier flickers and fades. I sit on frozen knees, mumbling through tears, hands clutched to my chest. My companions rush forward, administering a medical stabilizer and trying to apply compression bandages to Husniya's terrible wound. Beyond them, arm dangling, Zaldov paces back and forth like a lost pup, his gore-covered fist clenched.

"Mila, we have to go," Mos shouts to me. "We have to get her back to Opor if she's going to have any chance."

"I can't … I …" My body refuses to stand.

Demitri was right. I should have killed him when I had the chance.

But I was too weak. I couldn't, and now Husniya has paid the price.

"Mila, we are leaving," Mos shouts as he heaves the girl up and they all run toward the enclave's entrance.

Ghofaun grabs my elbow and attempts to lift, but I yank it free. "Just leave me."

"Mila, please." He reaches for me again.

"She was with you. Where were you?" I clench my fist and shake it at him.

"No, Mila, where were *you*?" The monk's face is hard.

I can only shake my head. "I'm done. Leave me alone."

Ghofaun stares at me, his eyes boring into me for what feels like an age, but says nothing and eventually leaves.

I failed everyone who ever needed me or called me friend. Better that I never existed at all than to have become the unwitting instrument of so much misery. I slump back into the dying grass, the weight of my failures, my faithlessness, and my shame a millstone of anguish and self-loathing pressing down on my chest.

Snowflakes flutter and swirl through the hole in the false sky above, falling lower and lower until they come to rest on my face like the cold kiss of death.

CHAPTER THIRTY

VEDMAK

You killed her, you bastard. She did nothing to you.

"Be silent, petulant child. I have no time for your mewing." A hacked cough turns to agonizing pain. It's hard to breathe, the shell all but dead now. The radiation poisoning eats away at these last living cells. The rescue attempt, the Opor attack—everything took far too long. "Just hold your tongue."

Or you'll do what? Demitri spits back. *Huh, Vedmak? What more can you possibly do? You've taken everything from … from everyone. You murdered Husniya. You murdered one of your own, just to get to her.*

The gunship shudders, its engines whining as the power reserves dwindle.

"So? I killed the little rodent. As I should have done the first time we encountered her." Another hard cough and blood spatters the metallic floor.

She was my responsibility. She was my friend. I dragged her into all this. She was only a girl! The Gracile's voice grows loud in this aching head, the rising decibels sending pain into the depths of my soul.

"And now she's a *dead* girl."

You're going to regret this. I promise you.

Ignoring the peacock's empty threats, I force myself from the floor and prop against the bulkhead with the only hand I have left to use. With painful steps, bones aching, skin burning, head ringing, I hobble toward the cockpit. The ship drops suddenly, nearly sending me sprawling. "Damn it all to hell, Merodach!"

My Gracile warrior merely grunts. Beyond the fractured glass of the windshield, a violent storm stirs in the dark. The whipping of sleet and snow obscure the way ahead while strong gusts of frozen wind batter the hull and threaten to force us off course.

"Just get us to the lillipad," I bark my last order and slide to the floor, back pressed to the doorframe of the cockpit. "Once there, everything will be well again. And I can take revenge on that little whore. Her and her damnable Creed attack dog." The robotic puppet attacked while I was unprepared.

Demitri laughs like never before. It's a crazed, maniacal sound.

"Something funny, *kozel?*"

Between fits of laughter, he answers, *You didn't recognize that Creed?*

"What are you blithering on about?"

Nikolaj. He shouts. *It was Nikolaj. I mean not him, but a Creed that looks like him. Oksana is with Mila. She must have built him.*

Nikolaj? The useless neo brother? And Oksana would be the whore he kept as a mate. She still lives? "This is funny why? You simple idiot."

There's a fresh bout of laughing. "*Nikolaj kicked my ass. Well, your ass. Nikolaj. There's poetic justice there, don't you think?*"

"You've lost your mind."

Demitri's laughing halts abruptly and he answers in a tone deep and as cold as the grave. *Oh no, I am saner than I've ever been. You know why, you sick sarding son of a bitch? Because for the first time in my life, I have true purpose: to destroy you.*

"And how do you propose to do that? In all these years, you've not managed to do anything worth talking about. Don't waste my time."

That's your weakness—arrogance. You messed up by killing Husniya. You're done, you piece of sard. I only need a moment. A split second to take full control. It might be while you sleep, while you eat. Just a single momentary lapse. I'll take control and kill us both. You're mine, you bastard.

There's a resolution in his voice. An undeserved certainty.

You'll see, Vedmak or Genrikh or whatever your damn name is.

The ship sways from side to side then judders violently as we head into the eye of a storm. The nuclear power cells sit in the corner of the hold, glinting in the low lights. It won't be long now. I have what I need to draw my brethren from their purgatory and into waiting Gracile shells. I'll have the power to reap the souls of men. I'll be death incarnate and nothing will stop me.

I try to shove from the floor, but can't move. Another attempt and still these legs won't obey.

Something wrong, Vedmak? Demitri's voice is hard as stone.

231

If he had lips, I swear to Yahweh he'd be smirking.

"What are you doing, puppet?"

I think it's you who has become the puppet.

"You can't control me."

I may not be able to control you, but I can pull on your strings. Every damn thing you want to do I'm going to fight, tooth and nail. Taking a piss will be like moving the heavens.

"You, you can't do this." I heave again and fight for a few inches. This already flayed body screaming in pain as his consciousness battles mine for control. "You. Won't. Beat. Me," I say through gnashed teeth, gradually rising.

Watch me, Vedmak. Watch me.

CHAPTER THIRTY-ONE

MILA

Dawn lances across the endless horizon in a streak of red that seems to set the whole world aflame. It's like I'm seeing something forbidden, something perfect and unspoiled. A visual treat reserved for the eyes of Yeos alone, not the likes of some selfish, faithless, coward. Long after the death of all things on this planet, the sun will still rise and set. Or will it? Will even the sun cease to exist after Vedmak's apocalypse erases us?

Something stirs in my chest—a nudge reminding me of some critical thing undone, forgotten in a dark corner of my heart. How long has it been, Mila? How long has it been since you called the creator's name from down on your knees?

From behind the window's glass, the broadening blades of orange light expand into the fading purple of night. The image is one of victory, of the light pushing back eternal dark for one more day. But the darkness always returns. Light simply keeps it at arm's length for a spell. Still, one last time, I'll finish watching it.

That's what I tell myself at least.

But every day for the last however many months I've risen in my stolen abode, five kilometers up on one of the last remaining lillipads, and I've watched the sun rise. Here above the orange-tinged tufts of clouds the world is a different place. Simple. Serene. Unlike a single spoiled human life; a thing that can be so ugly and used up it's no longer recognizable to its owner.

Who have you become?

Damnation. I slap my own face a few times; the last one leaves a lingering sting. Life is pain and I am, somehow, still among the living. I watch as a spike of light, the topmost edge of a giant burning ball of gas millions of miles away, crests the horizon. I turn my gaze down until the light dims, muted by the automatic sun-shades.

Moving without thought, my legs take me across the sterile Gracile chamber, all gleaming metal and glass and endless white. I stop at the counter and palm a silver bag of the squishy tasteless gel. Tearing the end open and squeezing the contents into my mouth, I swallow the glob. These carboprotein packs, as they are labeled, provide no satisfaction but they do keep hunger at bay. I run my fingers over the last box. Won't last much longer.

And then what? Starve to death up here alone? A coward's way out. I'm not brave enough to end it. To be judged by Him. Not like the Graciles I'd found here on that terrible day when I first rode in the magnetic rail elevator from Vel up to this place. I'd found them, all of them, in the common area in the center of this lillipad. A huge group, all lying in a heap, their bodies cold and stiff. A mass suicide. When the rest of their kingdom fell from grace, they must have known their time was over and the clock was ticking. They could never go back to what existed before and instead of trying to survive in the arctic hell below, they took the easy way out. I have no idea how they did it. There wasn't a scratch on their perfect bodies. Perhaps suicide is easier when you don't fear eternal damnation.

An exasperated huff whistles through my teeth. Do something. Anything.

I make my way to the bank of monitors and flick them on one by one. The camera feeds wink to life, each providing a different visual on locations inside the walls of Vel. The Velians thought they were free, but they were caged animals just like the rest of us. Worse, their daily movements appear to have been strictly monitored to make sure they were producing according to the deal with their masters above.

An active movement sensor is triggered and one of the monitors switches its feed. Rippers. I watch them move from one screen to the next, carrying a bundle of clothes and sewn garments, harvesting produce from one of the many orchards, tending to the ... children. I swallow several times in succession. The lump in my throat stays.

These are people, Mila. You saw yourself as above them, the same way the Graciles treated you. No matter how much you try to convince yourself otherwise, they are human and they want the same things all people want—safety, plenty, community. The Rippers were initially criminals, outcasts from the various enclaves. But now? What about those children? Are *they* criminals? Do *they* deserve to be treated like animals or exterminated because of their parents' and grandparents' failures?

I rub sweaty palms against the cloth of my shirt. This is my atonement. To see their humanity, and my lack of it. Is the way of the Lightbringer lost to me, now only the distant memory of someone who could have been? Someone better than the miserable wretch I've become.

"I'm sorry." The words mumble from my lips. My knees shake. I lower to the ground. "I'm sorry for who I've become, Yeos." I gasp a pitiful sob, my face burning with shame. "Momma, Papa, Zev, I'm sorry." I raise a trembling hand to my mouth, and the dam breaks, my shoulders slumping as I lie to weep on the floor.

CHAPTER THIRTY-TWO

FARUQ

"They'll never surrender." I heave a sigh loaded with the pressure that has continued to build after six long months of vicious deadlock. At every turn, the insurgents embedded in the enclave of Alya under the rule of Abd Al Jabbar defy me.

"We will be victorious, Sheikh," Captain Kahleit says from over my shoulder. "But it will take some time to root out this madness."

My fingers tent before my face. "Of course, Captain. And how is everything else? Baqir? Our people?"

He clasps his hands behind his back. "The people are well. Their faith in you has grown. They now know you have their best interests at heart, Sheikh. Life is still difficult for them, food is in short supply, but spirits seem to be up. There is an air of relief since you arrived to liberate the people from oppression."

"Good," I say. "That's good, Captain." I pause, looking over my weathered confidant. I have watched my attendants, captains, and fighting men be murdered over the long cruel months. Kahleit is one of the few who has remained since the beginning. A stalwart, black-bearded man with thick shoulders and air of earned confidence. He is now the closest thing I have to a friend.

Who's fault is that, Faruq? Who denied his friends and his blood when they came to rescue him?

The crack in my resolve widens, thoughts drifting back to the snow-covered encampment littered with the bodies of Musul men. The look of terror on Kapka's face when he knew his death was at hand. The sound of Mila and Husniya's strained voices as they trembled, crying out for me to return to them. A pit of blackness grows inside. A place without light or sound or touch. It is here I must store these things. They cannot be allowed to injure me any longer. My people need me. That is my only purpose, now.

Captain Kahleit waits, his face questioning.

"And you, Captain? How are you holding up?" I ask.

"I believe that is a question I should ask you, Sheikh," he replies. "Are you sure you are content here?" He gazes around the small clay-walled room adorned with simple wares, silks, and a few hand-woven rugs from the community marketplace. In the corner a small fire glows, heating the space and casting comfortable shadows.

"The ornaments of the palace are not for me. You know that. This was my mother's home. It was good enough for her."

"Of course, Sheikh."

The room hums with memories of my mother and sister. We lived here in this house on the back side of the palace for a time. I hated it—being anywhere close to the man who'd had my father murdered. Even worse when he claimed my mother as one of his wives—but what was she to do? Deny the tyrant of Baqir? No, she'd done what she had to so Husniya and I remained safe. But when mother had slipped into the black sleep and eventually away to Ilah, Kapka had my sister and me thrown from this place and into the frozen streets, forced to live like animals. It was then I knew we had to stick together. Husniya was the only thing left that mattered.

And how much do you care for her wellbeing now, Sheikh Faruq? I rub my forehead, trying to press the poisonous thoughts from my mind.

"Are you all right?" Kahleit asks.

"Yes, just a passing headache," I lie.

"May I fetch you some water?" He moves to the nearby clay basin, dips a cup and hands it to me.

"Thank you, Captain." I toast him with my mug. "Your presence is a comfort to me."

He gives a slight bow.

I raise the cup to my lips.

"Captain." A young, slim framed man knocks on the wooden door, peering, but afraid to stick his head in.

"What is it?" Kahleit says.

"There is a group outside the gate. They say they are here to see the Sheikh."

"They asked to see the Sheikh in person?" Kahleit asks.

"Yes—no, not exactly." The man appears nervous. "They asked to see him, but they used the name Faruq."

Kahleit looks to me. "It could be another attempt on your life."

I stand and meet the young man's eyes. "What does this group look like?"

"Very strange, Sheikh. An old man, a Zopatian, a Kahangan …" He licks his chapped lips.

"And?" Kahleit says, the mounting irritation evident in his voice.

"They say they have news of your sister, Sheikh."

A sudden vigor fills my body.

"Sheikh, maybe I should screen them first—" Kahleit begins.

"No, I will see them without delay." I pat the gold-plated big-bore revolver tucked in my waistband.

"Very well, Sheikh." Captain Kahleit steps to the side, motioning for the nervous messenger to do the same. He knows I will not be swayed.

Crossing the compound with lengthening strides, I whistle to two squads of guards who appear to be betting on a game of carved dice. At the sound of my call, they snap to attention and fall in line marching in my wake, not even bothering to pick up the dice spinning on the icy cobblestones. Though I've never harmed or threatened a single one of them since the day I rose to power, they still call me the tyrant killer. I don't know if they follow me out of loyalty to my cause or a residual fear from Kapka's reign of terror. I may never know.

With my hands thrust into the deep pockets of my heavy coat, I slow my gait as we approach the eastward-facing gate in the enclave wall. Controlled breaths exhale in plumes of steam. I give one last glance over my shoulder at Captain Kahleit and the men who trail behind me.

With a jerk of Kahleit's finger, the men fan out on either side with their pikes in hand and flank the strange visitors who stand between the heavy double doors to the enclave.

I knew in my heart who these visitors were but now, suspicions confirmed, my throat tightens. They look old, haggard, and aged by the cruel machinations of fate. For a spell, we just stand there, my gaze roving from one to the next. There is no joy in my chest at this reunion. Only regret and sadness, the spoiled memories of a broken family.

"Where is Husniya?" I rasp.

"She's not with us," Bilgi replies.

"What have you done to my sister, you cowards?"

Mos hangs his head, his stare to the ground, but he remains silent. Are those tears? Ghofaun, the monk, holds my gaze, his narrow eyes full of pain and loss. I turn my attention past the giant Creed with mismatched arms that must have been repurposed to the old man who stands at their center, his hands clasped together. Bilgi.

"Answer me, old man. What. Have. You. Done?"

Bilgi opens his hands with a helpless shrug, his demeanor contrite. "Faruq— "

"He is Sheikh," Kahleit calls from behind me. "You will address him by his title, foreigner."

I hold up my hand to Kahleit.

Bilgi gives a slow bow. "Sheikh, she is gravely injured. She fought because she wanted it, because she believed in her friends and in the cause of freedom, as you once did, when you walked alongside us."

"She was brainwashed to believe in your cause. Just as these men—" I motion to my guards "—were brainwashed to believe that killing in the name of Ilah was just. You are no different from Kapka. You are sly, and your methods are more concealed, but you are not different. Sending young people to die for your cause. You don't care for them."

"That's not fair, Faruq," Bilgi replies.

Captain Kahleit bristles at the lack of title and takes a step forward.

"If you cared so much, why did you leave me to rot? Answer me that." My face burns, the old hate welling up.

"We couldn't find you. We tried—" Bilgi starts.

"No, you know what? I don't care anymore. Just bring me my sister," I say, my words edged like a well-sharpened blade.

"She was impaled on a spear. She barely made it. We were forced to hide her. Even Logos and Fiori are no longer safe. She has received treatment for nearly half a year, but I fear she may not live much longer."

"Who did this?" I pull the revolver from my waistband. "Tell me who must die for this."

Mos meets my gaze for the first time. "It was Demitri, Faruq. Demitri did this. Or, at least, the demon that has claimed him did. Demitri called it Vedmak. Others call it the Vardøger."

"You should come with us, Faruq. See your sister before it's too late. Then fight with us—"

I shake my head. "We are finished. Do you understand?"

"And Husniya?" the old man asks.

"Do not use my sister as leverage, old man. She … she chose you. Brainwashed or not." I almost choke on the words. "My people, the enclave of Baqir will not be party to your warmongering. Leave us in peace."

"There will be no peace, not with Vedmak on the loose," Bilgi says.

"You would say that." I motion to the pitiful group. "Rally your fighters and storm the gates. I'm sure you and …" Her name has to be forced from my lips. "… and Mila will find a way to kill and betray those who remain faithful to your cause."

"You would speak of Mila this way?" Bilgi cocks his head.

"What of it? She couldn't be bothered to come here today herself, I see."

"Mila is gone," Ghofaun says flatly.

"And what should that mean to me?" I ask.

Bilgi sighs. "We are divided. Giahi has taken over the Opor headquarters and exiled us on threat of death if we ever return. Mila never returned from the mission where Husniya was wounded. She could be dead for all we know. And as we lay broken and scattered, Vedmak is raising an army of deranged Graciles that he means to use to murder and enslave the rest of us. When they reach their full potential, nothing will stop them. You and your people will not be spared the onslaught, Faruq. Death will come for us all."

"Let him come. The Musul nation will not go quietly," I say, crossing my arms.

"Vedmak's arrogance will kill us all before we ever have a chance to raise a blade," the monk says. "To build his army, he's opening a gate to another place full with demons like him. If the rift is too wide it will engulf us all."

So, he will open the way to *an-Nar*? Unleashing the seven levels of

Hell upon the Earth?

"That's why we need your help," Bilgi interrupts. "We have to do something. We can't stand by and wait for oblivion."

A mirthless laugh bubbles up from inside. "You fooled me with that line once, Bilgi."

Bilgi's eyes search mine. "Please."

"No," I say, holding his gaze.

"The Faruq I knew was a noble man. He was the best of us." Bilgi rubs at his sunken face, eyes tired and rimmed with red. "That man still lives inside you. I know he does."

"You're wrong. That man was murdered by your betrayal. Now, if you value your lives leave my enclave."

"You doom us all, Sheikh Faruq. Every last remaining vestige of humanity," Bilgi says.

"So be it. You all shall go to your graves with innocent blood on your hands, but I will not." I motion to my guards to force them out.

The men with pikes advance. Bilgi does not raise his arms this time.

"You will. Your inaction drenches your hands in blood, Sheikh, the blood of Etyom. But nonetheless, we will stand against this evil in your stead." Bilgi turns alongside those I once called friends and brothers and passes through the heavy wooden enclave doors.

CHAPTER THIRTY-THREE

MILA

The rail elevator jolts and I instinctively reach out to the slick shiny metal panels of the wall. A whooshing sound accompanies my descent. For the first time in as long as I can remember, I have clean clothes, hair tied back out of my face, and fresh skin after taking a turn in one of the Gracile bathing chambers.

Leaving the lillipad is foolish, but I'm out of options. The Graciles' stash of bland carboprotein packs in their little eight-ounce square packages have run out. I could hold my position, tucked safely away in my tower in the sky, watching the sun rise on each new day until my body fails me and I waste away. But death is too easy. A gift I do not deserve.

After a few minutes, a chime sounds and the single door slides back. I stand there flat footed, peering out, waiting for a spear to hit me in the chest. Nothing. It's significantly colder than I remember. I shrug into my heavy leather jacket and raise my head to peer at the blasted hole in the ceiling, dark clouds churning above. That would be the reason. I take a cautious step from the concrete loading platform onto the turf. The grass makes a crinkling sound beneath my feet. The little green blades are turning brown. Paradise is dying.

The closest orchard isn't far.

Ripened red fruits I don't recognize hang from the branches in clumps. I pull one from a bunch and pinch it, the juices and seeds squirting from the busted skin. Saliva pools beneath my tongue. I pop one into my waiting mouth. It's the most delicious thing I've ever eaten in my life.

Plucking several bunches of the little red fruits, I place them in my satchel and move to the next row. One of the hard, yellow fruits comes free from its branch with a *snap*. Looking it over, I raise it to take a bite when a tickle at the back of my neck makes every muscle freeze. My heart skips a beat at the sight of a Ripper child. She can't be more than four or five years old. We stand there staring at each other. The moment feels heavy, bloated with expectation. Any second now she's going to run screaming and I'll be as good as dead.

Slowly, I continue to move the yellow husk of the fruit toward my lips, when the child grunts at me and shakes her head. I stop again, brow furrowed. With a deliberate slowness, I extend the fruit toward the child and give it a little shake.

"You can have it."

She takes a step forward. Then another, casting a glance over her shoulder.

"I won't hurt you," I say. Am I reassuring her or myself?

The child takes another step, now just feet away. She's beautiful, if dirty, with little chocolate curls of hair that hook around her ears and frame dark, curious eyes. She reminds me of Husniya. Or myself. Or perhaps any innocent child in this hell we call home.

"Here, it's yours," I say.

In a flash of movement, the girl snatches the fruit from my hand and wheels to run, but then stops. Looking back to me, she giggles and pops the fruit against her knee, busting the thick husk open. The inside is rotten and putrid. She smiles, her eyes, mischievous yet proud of her knowledge. She tosses the poisonous fruit away.

I release a held breath, tension draining from my shoulders.

"Hey," I call after her.

She stops and turns to me, confusion etched into her little face.

"Here." I grab a handful of the red fruit in my bag and toss it to the ground a meter from her feet.

She scoops them up, and immediately scarfs one—the juice spilling down her chin. Then, with a giggle, she turns and runs back through the orchard, disappearing through the rows of trees.

That fruit might have killed me. Saved by a Ripper child. The irony.

CHAPTER THIRTY-FOUR

VEDMAK

The stone walls of the mountain stronghold stretch up into the night sky. These cows have lived in conceited safety for far too long. Their belief in some paltry god cannot protect them from me. But it isn't for my own pleasure that we will sack their sanctuary. No, it's because this place is important to *her* and I know she'll hear of it.

The newest additions to my army of *Einherjar*, driven by the Alchemist's latest concoction of Red Mist, shuffle in adrenaline-fueled anticipation at the foot of the peak. The miniaturized nuclear powerplant I had constructed accelerated the screening process for *dushi* like mine pure, driven toward the one truth. Though the ratio of *dushi* to whining, sad, pacifist sheep-like souls is still poor, in less than six months I have been able to harvest enough to build this army of several hundred adult, Gracile-bound warriors and grow another thousand youngling shells ready to accept my brethren. Still, I need more to secure my triumph, and grow impatient. So, tonight, we slake our thirst for blood; another piece knocked from the chessboard in this war.

This is no victory, Vedmak. Unarmed Vestals? The cutting down of innocent women? You've become good at that, my Gracile demon says. *You're only doing this because you're bored and petty. What a sad little imposter you are.*

His tone has grown in volume and confidence over these months. Demitri's mouth has not stopped running day or night.

"Innocent? These braying donkeys spout off about love in the name of a god that does not exist." I spit on the snow-laden ground.

Demitri scoffs. *You're a monster in the bedroom of a scared child. But all children soon grow up. And the children of Etyom will rise against you. Murdering these Vestals will only elicit the rage of the Logosians. They'll come for you. Or maybe I should summon that Creed to beat the stuffing out of you once more.* He laughs, coarse and remorseless.

"Be silent, stupid *kozel*."

If you're so powerful, force me. Oh, but that's right. You can't, can you? Demitri's voice is cold and mocking. *Every damn stim the Alchemist tried didn't work did it? You're stuck with me. And the beauty of being trapped in this place of endless dark is that I never need to sleep. In this place, time is irrelevant. But you—trapped in my body—are bound by the laws of the physical world. How long has it been since you slept, Vedmak? Weeks? Months? Stimmed to the eyeballs, afraid of letting go.*

"Enough of this." I turn the valve screw another quarter inch, letting yet more Red Mist filter in through the breathing apparatus. The lungs sting, the muscles of this body tensing in anticipation of the violence yet to come.

That's not going to help you much. What did you say to me once? Can't outrun your shadow.

Killing these Vestals will help. Yes, a worthy distraction. Flaying these mindless sheep and silencing their lies will bring me peace. I clang the metal of my unfired scythe against the thick steel of the sword-like blade that now adorns the stump of an arm. It is an efficient, if not barbaric implement of war.

My *Einherjar* roar long and loud, their own weapons enflaming; maces, swords, and double-bladed axes setting the cloudless night sky aflame with the glow and crackle of blue plasma. "Var-dø-ger! Var-dø-ger!" Their chant echoes in the cracks and crevices of the mountain the Vestals of the Word call home.

A lone figure appears in the open spire window, peering out at those who will deliver her death. She screams and turns to flee, but a plasma bolt strikes her true and her body evaporates in a puff of ash. Her scream is brief and horrible.

"Glorious!" I yell. "Attack!"

The *Einherjar* charge the stone footsteps leading up to the heavy double doors.

Yet these feet will not move.

I scream again, willing this shell to capitulate. The muscles burn and feel as if they will tear.

You might command your army to do this, Vedmak, but you won't enjoy it. Not one single moment, Demitri says as if through imaginary gritted teeth.

"You damn fool," I shout aloud and give the valve to the Red Mist a full turn.

The legs struggle to obey and, though weighed down as if wearing lead chainmail, I trudge forward. By the time I've reached the top, Merodach has used a long, plasma broad sword to hack flaming gashes into the hardwood doors. Another swing and burned splinters explode from the portal, shattering across my mask. With a mighty grunt, Merodach kicks into the barricade, the door cracking and splitting.

"Again," I shout.

Merodach snorts. Rearing back, the thick muscles of his leg coil. The heel of his boot lands with a satisfying crack against the joint. Bursting inwards, the doors swing wide in a spray of splinters.

We stream through, pouring into the torch-lit corridors.

"Leave nothing in your wake!" I shout.

The *Einherjar* power off into the temple, kicking in the doors of praying women and cutting them down. The Vestals are dragged from their rooms—the pretty ones are raped and left to bleed, the old and useless are beheaded on the spot. There will be no mercy for these cows.

A veiled woman streaks past and I swing my scythe first, followed by my stump-sword. But my attempt is slow and clumsy, the blades never coming close. She runs as fast as her cumbersome attire will allow, only to be seized by Merodach. He lifts her and smashes her skull into the wall, painting it in her blood, then tosses her lifelessly down a twisting set of steps.

Was that a miss, Vedmak? Such a shame.

"Quiet, *kozel*," I demand and shove off toward the steps. "Down. Go down. They're hiding in the bowels of this place."

Without a force to stop them, my *Einherjar* cut through the religious zealots with little effort. Yet my blade tastes no blood. Every swing, every thrust of my scythe is evaded as if I were telegraphing my intent long in advance. Each time, the crimson-clothed vermin are picked off by one of my Gracile soldiers.

I told you.

"Damn you, Gracile!"

Merodach shoots a quizzical stare and, without breaking his gaze, casually lops off the head of yet another woman. Her disfigured corpse slumps to the ground. He lets his glare linger before stomping off into the last tunnel. I make chase, lumbering along behind as fast as these damned limbs will allow.

The final door is thrust open.

Inside, five or six Vestals kneel on the floor encircling something. They pray in whispers to a false god who will not save them. Their leader, the Mother Vestal, a young well-made woman, wearing some kind of headpiece, stands in front. One of them breaks her litany, crying out at my coming and runs for the door. I turn the valve screw wide open, letting a maximum dose of the Red Mist filter into the mask, filling the burning tissues of these laboring lungs.

With considerable effort, I manage to grab her by her habit and drag her writhing to the floor. "Yes." I scream with glee. "My blade will taste your blood." I raise my scythe above, which crackles and spits blue plasma. Her tear-filled eyes are afire with the reflection of my weapon and the orange light of the torches that fill this room.

"Yeos, save us," she whispers.

"Damn your false god!" I cry. "I am the Vardøger. I am Death!"

The scythe comes down with all the force I can muster.

"Genrikh, please."

My attack falters. What did she say?

"Genrikh, don't do this," the Vestal says.

But it's not the Vestal. My wife stares back at me from under the headdress of the habit, her face panicked.

I loosen my grip on the scythe. "Ida? No, no it can't be."

"Genrikh, my love, don't kill me," she says.

"No, no this isn't possible," I shout, scrambling off the woman. "Make it stop."

Demitri's laugh is incessant in this skull, growing louder and louder.

The woman clambers to her feet and makes for the door, but Merodach snatches her up by the throat and brings her back to me. The Vestal, who appears exactly as my beloved stares at me, her eyes bulging, her face turning blue through lack of air.

"Please," she hisses through Merodach's grip. "Genrikh …"

I raise the plasma blade high, but it won't come down.

Merodach's expectant stare bores holes into me.

What's the matter, Vedmak? Can't get it up?

Another scream of frustration pours from these stolen lips, yet still the image of Ida haunts me.

"I will kill you, Demitri."

Will you now? How exactly? Kill yourself. Destroy my body? Please, be my guest.

Enraged, I turn back to the Mother Vestal. She and her braying sheep will pay.

It may be so but not by your hand, Vedmak.

The Mother Vestal clutches a heavy tome to her chest and appears to pray; her lips moving but no sound issues forth. My soul burns with the desire to cut her limb from limb, but every fiber of this stolen body fights me.

"Reams of paper will not save you," I hiss.

She slowly opens her defiant eyes, her chin thrust upward. "But it brings a peace you shall never know, demon. Even so, I pray for you—"

Merodach grunts, more urgently than normal.

"What the hell is it?" I snap.

He swings his arm to point behind the huddling Vestals.

I push past them to see. A chuckle erupts from within. "Well, well, well. I would have had no luck, if not for misfortune. And I thought only cockroaches couldn't be killed."

Husniya? Oh no.

"The whelp lives," I say, giving her barely breathing corpse a nudge with my boot. The Musul girl groans. "Her friends abandoned her here for what? Healing?"

"She's dying," the Mother Vestal says. "There's no saving her. Let her pass to the Lightbringer in peace."

"The Lightbringer?" I say, nearly choking on my own snort. "Those Opor morons brought a Musul girl to the followers of Yeos? The irony. Her pathetic brother will likely kill you for that."

"Yeos loves all His children. It does not matter by which name the people are known," the Mother Vestal replies, clutching the tome to her chest even tighter.

Merodach raises a boot to stamp on Husniya's skull.

No, don't. I won't let you kill her.

Fear not, whining child.

I motion to Merodach, halting his attack. His already foul mood at my inability to kill darkens.

"She is more use to me alive. Give her a stabilizer," I say. "We take her to the Poisons Lab."

Merodach pulls an autoinjector from his pocket and presses it to Husniya's neck. The girl moans.

"You can't have her," the Mother Vestal insists. She stands stoic, unflinching. A slight twitching at the corner of her mouth, the only tell of the fear in her heart. "If you take this girl, the one you fear will come to stand against you, bearing the light."

I force this body to lurch forward, seizing the mother Vestal by her robes. "*She* is nothing. I have defeated that insolent Logosian whore at every turn. She cannot—she *will not* defy me." I shove the Vestal back and turn from the wretch, the fire of my life force burning in a white-hot, all consuming, fury. A few heavy-footed steps toward the door and I stop by Merodach's side. "Leave them alive to tell of what we did here. Let it be a battle cry. But burn the book. Leave no comfort. Then bring the Musul cockroach."

Merodach nods, though apparently frustrated at not being able to finish his slaughter of these women.

I turn back long enough to see him seize the Vestal by the neck, her feet kicking and fingers clawing at his thick hands. The tome clunks to the floor. There's a wonderful shriek, long and sustained, followed by the unmistakable smell of burning paper and flesh as the doors close behind me.

Fenrir, one of my better soldiers, runs up in the dark corridor, his blood-covered armor clanking. "Vardøger, you must come. You must see."

"What is it, boy?"

"There's something, like nothing I've ever seen, coming from Zopat—from the lab."

I follow Fenrir back to the spire window and search the sprawling horizon. Logos, broken and burned, lies stretched out below. Vel, its secrets now spilled, sits on the hill to the east. And beyond Baqir, in the North, the bright lights of Zopat seem to once again burn brightly. But it is not Zopat. A large, glowing dome of green fire rises from the ground.

Yes. The door is open. More of my brethren will come.

CHAPTER THIRTY-FIVE

MILA

I have no idea how many weeks have passed since first coming here. Time has lost all meaning. Attempting my practiced Chum Lawk meditation for the thousandth time since I've been here does nothing. The usual serenity and strength to be drawn from my connection to the Creator is gone. Why does it feel as though He no longer speaks to me? Tears once again cut a worn path down my cheeks. This open wound never seems to heal. Am I to forever bleed for my sins?

"Husniya. I wasn't there when you needed me. I failed you … and Faruq, and Demitri … Bilgi, Ghofaun, Mos … and Denni … and you, dear Yeos." Another sob shakes my shoulders. "I was told I was something, could be something more. I let it blind me … Forgive me."

The motion sensor beeps, again.

I sniff and turn my attention to the monitors. On the corresponding screen, the little Ripper girl I'd encountered scurries around the orchard. But she's not picking up fruit. For the last few days she's come back, searching for me. She wouldn't return if she knew the truth.

"You carry the weight of the world on your shoulders, dear Mila." The words of the sister Vestal, Katerina, emerge from some darkened tomb inside me, as if I too had another spirit dwelling within. I watch the little girl skipping around without a care in the world, trying to dredge up the words that once gave me strength. *"There is one way to endure the path of the Lightbringer. Every step, every single act must be one of love. Not pride, nor strength, nor self-righteousness. Love and faithfulness are the only weapons that will overcome such evil."*

Not pride.

Nor strength.

Nor self-righteousness.

Love. Like that of the little girl in the orchard. She knows no other way. No hate. No ugliness.

Katerina's words are pointed, exposing how far I've fallen from the way. But the pain of realization feels right, like the hand of a surgeon cutting to remove a spreading infection. I grow still, deep breaths swelling in and out, the beating of my heart slowing, tears dripping from a chin tucked close to my chest.

Yeos, speak to me. Please.

A mechanical whir, nearly imperceptible to the untrained ear, rises in pitch. I try to focus, to stay in this moment of reflection. But I can't. Now that I hear the distracting noise, curiosity drowns out all else. The whine grows, morphing into a pulling grind that slows with motorized precision.

The magnetic rail elevator is coming.

That can only mean one thing—someone has accessed it and is on their way up. I had to use my PED to hack the access terminal. It wasn't easy. Not just anyone is coming up. It's either a Gracile with the correct biometric profile, or it's someone who deliberately hacked it, the same as I did. What it isn't is a mistake. What it might be is my demise.

I rise from my kneeling position on the crushed white fabric pillow, my legs stinging as blood re-enters them. I turn to face the elevator, though can't decide if I should run or fight or let whoever it is kill me.

With a chime and a squeak, the polished metal door of the elevator slides open. A man stands in the shadows stoic and unmoving. He's Gracile, wearing a small pack on his back. My skin prickles. With a slow sweeping movement, the Gracile pulls the stop lever, locking the elevator in place with the door open. But he remains where he stands. What keeps him from entering? Does he even see me standing here?

"Mila Solokoff." The voice reaches out from the sterile metal box.

I know that voice. "Zaldov?"

"It is I."

Relief washes over me from the top of my scalp to the bottom of my feet. I roll my shoulders and exhale a breath I didn't realize I was holding. "Zaldov, what are you doing? Are you trying to give me a heart attack?"

"No. My intentions are not hostile. A scan of your vitals reveals that you are in good health."

"That's not what I … never mind. You can come out of the elevator, you know."

Zaldov takes a few clunking steps forward from the shadowed confines of the elevator. The arm Vedmak took has been replaced, though it looks somewhat immobile and cobbled together from junk parts. Am I actually happy to see this stupid bot?

"How did you find me?" I ask.

"I monitored the surveillance from Vel and saw you exit and reenter the elevator here." His head adjusts with little jerking tilts. "Why did you leave us, Mila?"

I hug myself, squeezing away at the ache radiating from deep inside. "I couldn't face the things I'd wrought. You all had lost faith in me and I ... I'd lost faith in myself."

"But you are needed again," Zaldov says, his movements accompanied by little buzzes and whirrs.

"No one needs me."

"Bad things are happening."

I pull on the back of my neck. "It's Etyom. Bad things are always happening."

"Not like this."

"What is it? What aren't you telling me?"

The silence in the room draws out, Zaldov's lack of an answer more disturbing than anything he could have said.

"Well?"

"The one called Giahi has taken over Opor. Oksana, my benefactor, is his prisoner. Her other Creed were disabled and your friends were exiled."

I clench my teeth. "Demitri said Giahi intended to overthrow Bilgi and me. Said the little power-hungry troll was in league with Vedmak. That they had a neural link. With us both gone, he succeeded."

"If this accusation is correct, Mila Solokoff, their interaction may still be traceable through the neural web."

"Are you sure?"

"There is a twenty-seven point six percent—"

"Yes or no?"

"I am not sure, Mila Solokoff. But we can try."

"If there was proof, someone could take back control," I say, now pacing. "If only Bilgi hadn't contracted the NBD."

"Bilgi is recovered."

I stop dead in my tracks. "What? How do you know?"

"When we were thrown out, he found us. He did not have the plague, as you suspected. As best he could determine, he had been poisoned to mimic the effects of the NBD."

"Giahi."

"Yes," Zaldov says.

I huff out an irritated breath. "So, who's *we*? Who's left?"

"The monk, the Kahangan, Husniya, a few others. Bilgi approached Faruq about helping but he turned us away—"

"Wait, what? Husniya? Husniya is *alive*?"

He hesitates. "Bilgi took her to the Vestals."

My stomach knots. "But she's alive, right?"

"We believe so," Zaldov says.

"She is or she isn't."

"She was barely alive when he left her with the Vestals. That's why I am here," he says.

The irritation prickles across my skin, the familiar hot-headed Mila creeping back. Can't do it like this. Got to remain calm. I exhale my frustration. "What happened?"

Without a word, Zaldov removes the small pack from his back. He sets it on the ground and unzips it, reaching inside. A ripple of fear courses through me as he draws a heavy tome from the bag, the cover charred by flame. The Writ.

Suddenly, I'm lightheaded, the air caught in my lungs, "Where did you get that?"

"Mila—"

My stare hardens. "Don't screw with me. Where?"

"Vedmak sacked the Vestal's temple. Few were left alive." He extends the priceless volume to me. "I found the body of the senior Vestal, burned. She was still clutching this."

My body shakes, tears welling in my eyes as I reach for the holy book. "Katerina." I clasp the tome, bits of ash and charred leather flaking away beneath my fingers. "You and your sisters did not deserve this." A terrible sadness pools within. "And Husniya?"

"We did not find her body. Bilgi believes Vedmak took her."

Demitri, how could you allow this?

"Mila?"

"Give me a second," I say sniffling and turning away. The storms of fate have returned this treasure to me one last time. The thought of revenge is all consuming. Yet, holding the book, Katerina's words seem more powerful than ever.

Love and faithfulness are the only weapons that will overcome such evil.

Zaldov waits as still as a statue, his soft clicking the only tell he's still operational. After a few moments I grab my old sling bag and insert the Writ, the weight comfortably familiar inside.

"All right, Zaldov," I say, grabbing a bag from the counter and stuffing my remaining stash of fruit into it. "We go."

"Yes, Mila Solokoff. We must. Time is running out," Zaldov replies as I brush past him, step into my boots, grab my jacket and make for the elevator.

I turn to face him. "Time is running out. Did I miss something else?"

"Yes." Zaldov's joints squeak. "Something is emanating immense power from Zopat. The energy signature confirms the VME you and Oksana feared is on the brink of occurring. We must stop Vedmak."

I swallow the lump of fear from my throat. "Of course it is. If the VME is on the brink, that means he's been pulling in evil souls to attach to Graciles here. He has an army. We'll need one too. You said Bilgi went to see Faruq. It was to ask for his help? Faruq is in charge now?"

"Yes. He controls Kapka's forces. But he is caught in his own feud with Alya and does not wish to be drawn into a battle he does not view as his."

"That's unfortunate. We need more fighters," I say.

Zaldov cocks his head. "Of all tools used in the shadow of the moon, men are most apt to get out of order."

"What?" I say.

"It is a quote from a book called *Moby Dick*," he replies.

"*Moby Dick*?"

"It is a story of obsession, Mila Solokoff. Of reaching beyond human limits to achieve something no matter the cost. Oftentimes, we must enlist others to help in these quests, but it is oftentimes these same people who cause us more harm."

Such wisdom from a machine, it's almost as if Yeos were communicating through him. I put a hand on his shoulder. "The responsibility is mine, Zaldov. But I can't do it alone."

He seems to consider my words, then bows his head.

Another idea forms. It's crazy. But what choice do I have? "C'mon. We have to move."

"One moment, please." Zaldov clomps past me to a seam in the wall. Scanning up and down, he stands there, his nose inches from the surface. He places his hand over a sensor plate set into the wall.

"What now?"

Unseen bolts slide free with several repeated *thunks* and a heavy, Gracile-sized section of the wall pops open and swings outward. Without a word, Zaldov steps inside. I peek inside at the small selection of plasma rifles and other armaments.

"Gracile weapons? How'd you know this was here?"

"It is in my stored memory. Every lillipad has an armory for the Creed to access in the event of an attack." He stops stuffing weapons into a duffle bag long enough to tilt his head at me. "I thought we could use them?"

"How? Robusts can't utilize Gracile weapons."

"Oksana's Creed can," Zaldov says, standing and hoisting the ungainly bag of weapons over his shoulder.

"Good thinking, Zaldov. Let's do this."

***

The elevator door shunks open. I pull the lock and step onto the concrete platform beneath the stem that rises through the fake flickering blue sky above.

"Zaldov," I say, "can you get back out?"

"Out?"

"Of this enclave. Unseen."

His head bobs. "Yes, of course. I am equipped with stealth capability."

256

"Good," I say, casting a glance over my shoulder. "I need you to do something for me."

"Yes?" the Creed says, tilting his head.

"Take my satchel. In exactly one hour, meet me outside where we came into Vel the first time those many months ago. Do you remember the outbuilding?"

"Yes."

"One hour. If I'm not there, take my bag and go back to Bilgi. He'll know what to do."

"Why should I not wait for you?"

I take off my jacket and re-shoulder the food bag. "Because I'll be dead. Now go. No more questions."

Zaldov reaches into his bag and lifts out a plasma rifle. Pulling a cable from his arm, he jacks it into a small square port in the weapon's stock. His eyes flash, flickering for a moment before returning to normal. He unplugs the port and extends the rifle to me.

"It is now unlocked. You will need protection."

"Thank you, Zaldov, but I'm all right," I say, refusing the glowing metallic rifle. "No more guns for me. Now go."

He looks like he wants to probe further, but without another word, Zaldov steps away with light footfalls until he disappears around the corner of a nearby building. Maybe Oksana was right. Synthetic or not, he's nearly as human as the rest of us. Could a Creed have a soul if the Creator willed it?

Enough. No time to ponder the mysteries of the universe. I need my head clear for what comes next.

At a brisk pace, I cross the top of the orchard, the clear well-groomed rows only now starting to show the first signs of neglect. Pulling one of the red fruits from the branches of a nearby tree, I sink my teeth into the pink juicy center. Minutes pass.

From behind a nearby tree, a little face framed in dark curls looks back. I outstretch the other half of the fruit, smiling. The little girl creeps to me then cautiously accepts it, a curious laugh cresting her lips.

With deliberately slow movements, I rise and shoulder my bag. "Come on."

There is neither sight or sound of any inhabitants, but I know better. This is Ripper territory, and we are being watched. The child wanders along three or four paces behind, focused on sucking the last bit of juice from her fruit. Our gazes meet for a moment as she registers the direction we're walking. She picks up a stone and with a grunt throws at my legs.

"It's okay, little one," I say in a tone as soothing as possible.

Is it okay? Or am I a complete fool?

The child grunts again, this time grabbing my jacket and tugging. There is fear in her large eyes. I kneel to face her, "Don't worry for me—"

The blow lands against the side of my head. The world spins and my vision narrows as the child screams, pulled away by a young mother. I crash against the brittle, dry grass. The air fills with hoots and shouts as scores of Rippers flood from the buildings into the narrow lane. I'd hoped perhaps having her with me would offer some kind of protection, a message that I came in peace. Guess not …

"Yeos protect me," I mumble, pushing myself to my knees. My jaw throbs with each beat of my hammering heart. I rise and take a few steps, my hands raised. A young male runs at me from my left. He strikes me in the stomach with the heel of his spear, doubling me over. The small crowd goes wild with approval. Gasping, I straighten and continue forward as another male shoves me from behind. A stone hits me in the ribs, then one in the thigh, the burning sting lancing into my hip.

I grit my teeth. Come on, Mila. You can take it.

Two more males approach. One knocks down my hands and punches me in the face while the other shoves me to my knees. The metallic taste of blood fills my mouth.

They're going to kill me.

I raise my hands again as I'm kicked in the back, face down into the grass again, dust in my eyes and nose. The pack is wrenched from my shoulders, the zipper popping as it's torn open. A second later, the contents are dumped over my head. I flinch as a knife slips beneath my neck and my hair is yanked back.

This is it, you fool. You asked for this. I pinch my eyes shut. "I mean you no harm," I whimper.

The Ripper who holds a fistful of my hair jabbers in a rough dialect I can only partially understand. But two words stand out: *baby killer*. The others around us jump up and down and thrust their spears at me. They want my blood emptied onto the grass. I don't blame them.

I do my best to show my palms again, the strain on my scalp excruciating. "Please. I come in peace."

Another savage jerk of my hair shuts me up. Yeos be merciful.

There's a squeal from behind. I can't lower my head to see, but feel small arms wrap around my legs. It's the little girl. She's jabbering something at my captors.

Ahead, the hysterical crowd parts to reveal a large Ripper, muscled and bare chested. He approaches and the crowd quiets, waiting for their leader to speak my judgment.

"Please, I—" My hair is jerked again.

"Don't speak," the Ripper chief says, his words difficult to understand. "You have no voice here, woman."

The insult might normally set me on fire, but in this moment, my life hangs by a thread.

He jabs a finger at one of his subordinates. "Take the child."

The girl is grasped and peeled from me, kicking and screaming like a feral animal.

The large Ripper chief looks me over and picks up a bunch of red fruit. "And this is … what?"

"It's a peace offering," I say, my chin high, hair pulled up at a miserable angle.

He throws the fruit against my face. The crowd laughs. "You think we can't pick our own fruit?" The words growl from his throat. He squints and looks to the one with a death grip on my hair. "Open the child killer's throat, then put her head on a stake."

My body shakes with wild tremors.

The blade starts to pull when a *crack* splits the air. A blue bolt flashes against the ground, scorching the grass black beside the Ripper chief.

"Let her go," the monotone voice calls out from beyond my field of vision.

It's Zaldov.

A tiny stream of blood runs from my neck to the collar of my jacket.

259

The Ripper chief stands, his lips pulled back over broken teeth in a snarl. He looks to me then to where Zaldov must be standing. "And if I don't?"

"Kill her then," Zaldov replies. "But you die next, reduced to a pile of ash, followed by as many of your people as I can deconstruct or pummel to death before you tear me apart. Your choice."

Oksana really has done a number on this Creed. He sounds almost … emotional.

The Ripper chief casts a disgusted look at me. The moment grows heavy with anticipation. I swallow, the knife pressing.

The grip on my hair releases. The muscles of my neck and back scream at the sudden relief. Zaldov stands in the open, dividing the crowd, a plasma rifle extended in one hand.

"Mila, are you okay?" the Creed asks.

"Yes. Did you deliberately go against my directive?"

"I did. It was in your best interest."

I rise to my feet and nod gratefully. "Now you're thinking like a human."

The Ripper chief crosses his arms. "What do you want, Logosian?"

I take a moment to compose myself, brushing the grass and dust from my clothes. "A truce."

"A truce?" He laughs. "And why would we care to hold a truce with the murderous resistance leader who burned our nursery to the ground?"

"I'll never be able to atone for my mistake." I suck in a breath and hold it a moment before releasing. "I know you think me a monster. Hell, I feel like one. But there's someone, something, far worse out there."

He doesn't respond.

"Have your people encountered a deranged Gracile? He wears a full cloak and carries an energy weapon that is curved like this." I draw a crescent in the air with my fingers. "We all fought with him months ago in this same place." I point to the blasted hole in the false blue sky above.

There is a flare of recognition on the chieftain's face.

"He's doing something that will destroy us, maybe everything," I continue. "It's complicated, but he has triggered something cosmic."

He stares blankly at me.

"Think of it this way. He's a demon. And he's opened the gate to Hell to bring more like him into the world. It doesn't matter how much you hate me. If I don't stop him and close the gateway, we're all going to die. Including your children."

There's a groan of discontent from the crowd.

The Ripper chief works his jaw back and forth. "Then why come back here? Why are you not fighting this demon?"

"I can't do it alone. We could use some help against him. He's set up his base near Zopat."

The Ripper chief casts a menacing glance at Zaldov, who still holds a bead on him. "And you want us to die for your cause?"

"Not my cause. *Our* cause. Like I said, we're all doomed if he carries this out. Besides, why wouldn't you want to kill a bunch of Graciles?"

"I don't make deals with your kind."

This was always going to be a long shot. I must have been mad to think they would help. "Fair enough." I raise my hands. "But let me go, at least. I have to stop him."

The Ripper chief takes a step forward, the muscles of his jaw tightening. From either side, Rippers approach, pushing spears into my ribs. Zaldov tightens his grip on the plasma rifle.

"Then go," the chieftain growls. "Stop him if you can. If you are successful, your head still belongs to me. There will be nowhere you can hide, no escape from the wrath of our blades. You are marked for death."

I push a spear point aside and brush past the scowling Ripper on my right. "Aren't I always?"

CHAPTER THIRTY-SIX

VEDMAK

The luminous green fire is hypnotic. Tendrils of energy pass over one another, connecting and dissipating with a crackle, like neurons being fired in some ethereal brain. It has engulfed half the base now. The equipment, furniture, walls, ceiling and even the ground are now gone. The bubble's incandescent surface blocking my view to anything that may exist on the other side. Yet I feel a kinship with this thing, a sense of belonging. Almost as if I can hear my comrades calling from the great beyond. Yes, this is the gateway to enough *dushi* to finish what I started those many long years ago. The last great purge.

It seems to me, you should have stayed where you came from, Vedmak, Demitri chides. *Not that it matters now. You've caused a rift in space-time. A VME is all but inevitable. We're not even going to Hell. Who knows what will happen when it tips over the edge and devours everything at the speed of light.*

Hold your tongue, boy. Can I not finish a thought without the intrusion of your whining voice?

Why should I let you? What did you ever do for me? Besides, these will likely be the last moments I get to say anything at all, before that bubble swallows everything.

I can control this. I am one with the universe.

No, you're one with me. And you're exhausted, Vedmak. Weary to the core. You should rest. Take some much-needed sleep. My Gracile demon's voice is dripping with sarcasm.

He knows I can't sleep. The Red Mist the Alchemist created, more powerful than anything before, is the only thing keeping the whining *kozel* at bay and from seizing this body back. The Alchemist is still working on something stronger, if the old goat doesn't die first. No, sleep is not an option. I cannot rest until my task is complete. The Logosian will come soon with her band of misfits. And I will be ready.

Oh, she'll come. It was a mistake to raid the Vestal temple and take

Husniya. Now you've given Mila purpose, Demitri says. *And even if I can't kill you, I'll make sure she gets the chance.*

I ignore my demon and turn to face what is left of the cage-filled dungeon. Where once terrified Graciles huddled, there is only the ever-growing green dome. It matters not. My legion of Gracile warriors, all endowed with a *dushi* like mine and controlled by the Alchemist's stim, will die for me. Several hundred Gracile adults and perhaps fifty more adolescent warriors. Still, I need more.

"Where are we on the youngling warriors, Sergei?" I ask, approaching the trolley on which lays a Gracile boy just fourteen years in biological age.

The cowardly Gracile servant scurries back and forth from the trolley to his desk. He's dragged half his equipment from the Poisons Lab into the dungeons to finish my army.

"It's still not optimal, Vardøger," he whimpers. "The ratio of souls you want to souls you don't is still too low. And even when we do find one, the Gracile child we've rapidly grown has to be developed enough to bind with it. Most don't have the mental capacity. We're running out of specimens."

"Then start attaching *dushi* to the Rippers too. I need as many as I can get."

"I can't guarantee the transplantation will take in the Rippers."

I grab the sniveling man by his throat. "Did I ask for your opinion?"

He shakes his head, a stream of urine soaking his clothing.

Leave him alone, Vedmak.

My grip involuntarily weakens and Sergei slips against the trolley, which clangs and clatters into the wall, spilling surgical instruments to the ground.

Damn you, Gracile.

I turn to Sergei. "Get the last of the cells. Put them in the Rippers. Only keep the violent ones. Understand?"

Merodach bursts into the room, shoving the female Gracile engineers forward. They nearly tumble to their knees, but manage to keep their balance. There is true fear in their eyes. They know something.

"Spit it out, sheep."

"The reactor, it's unstable," Alyona says.

Told you, Vedmak.

"Speak up. What are you whining about?"

"The reactor," Nadezhda interjects. "It's not built for what you're trying to do. We … we had to patch it together based on an old submarine reactor from the mid-twentieth century. The power conversion is too low. There wasn't enough shielding and it's spewing radiation. If it doesn't melt down, we'll die of gamma radiation poisoning anyway."

I tried to warn you, but you wouldn't listen. You've doomed us all.

"How close are we?" I spit.

"The plasma rifles are fully charged, but the gunships are not at full capacity," Alyona says, her eyes downcast.

"Your embryo room is taking up too much power," Nadezhda adds.

Not to mention you've triggered a VME which you can't control and will swallow us whole. Nice work. Death by nuclear meltdown, radiation poisoning or being converted into nothing by a VME. Or maybe Mila will come and kill us first. What to choose, what to choose?

"Shut up, shut up!" This Gracile voice reverberates off the rock-hewn walls.

The women cower.

I step to Alyona. "I need those gunships ready before the little *suka* gets here, do you understand?"

She understands, it's you who doesn't.

"Yes, yes Vardøger. It's just there's not enough liquid water to cool the reactor and—"

"Merodach."

The lumbering mute warrior steps forward and runs her through with an efficient thrust of his dagger upward and into the chest cavity. She struggles with little gasps for a moment before slumping to the ground, her lifeless eyes lolling back in her skull.

Are you insane, you sarding fool? You just had one of your engineers murdered. You never think ahead, Vedmak, and it's going to be your downfall. She's dead, and for what? Now you're down a valuable asset. What happened to the great strategist?

You want to see strategy, puppet? Let me show you.

I already know what you're doing, Vedmak.

It's one thing to know—it's another to taste.

264

Always with the words and the riddles. But come on. Let's go. Show me what your inferior mind has cooked up. Impress me.

The Gracile releases his relentless hold over these muscles, allowing me to roam a little more freely. I push past Merodach, but stop in front of Nadezhda long enough to instruct her to push the reactor as hard as it will go, then march up into the lillipad proper, through the white halls and sterile foyer out into the bitter cold.

Wind and sleet bite at this skin and sting these eyes, but I don't even bother pulling on my mask or wrapping my cloak around. Only my unignited scythe helps push this body toward the glassy ice battlement ahead. I grab one of the rope ladders nailed to the inside of the ice wall and climb, hand over frozen hand until I reach the summit. From here to my rear, I can see the whole lillipad and the dome of green fire consuming the rear half of the structure.

I make my way along the wall, through the pressing wind, to an outcropping of pure ice protruding from the top of the battlement. Affixed to it by ropes and iron nails, spread-eagle for the world to see, is the Musul girl. She's clad in thick furs, the skin on her face blistered and red from the cold. At her feet is the Alchemist. The old woman's tiny frame barely withstands the weather; a tether holds her to the ice lest she blew away like the twig in the wind.

Husniya, I'm so sorry.

"Is she ready, wench?" I shout over the growing storm. "It is installed?"

The Alchemist looks up, her lips blue and quivering. "She … she's ready."

"And she won't die of the cold or her injuries?"

The woman shakes her head. "She's st-stimmed up good. Between that and the f-fur, she won't freeze."

I peer over the edge of the twenty-meter-high ice wall to my soldiers, who stand in regiments, wearing roughly hewn armor. Unflinching. Uncomplaining. I can't see from here, but know their almond-shaped Gracile eyes are filled with hate and an unparalleled lust for blood. On either flank are several gunships, charging their cells for the final confrontation. And of course, rows upon rows of stimmed-up Rippers driven to madness through liberal application of the Alchemist's cocktail.

Yes, this battle will be glorious.

"Good," I say, turning back to the old woman. "Can't have her dying now, can we?"

"N-no," the woman stutters through chattering teeth.

"And the final stim for me? You have it?"

The woman looks up and deep into these eyes, as if searching for the Gracile that hides inside. Holding my gaze, she fishes around in her pocket, extending a bony hand clutching a glass cylinder filled with sloshing crimson liquid. "Here," she whimpers. "It is complete, as you asked."

"Oh, I'm aware it is, you old bag of bones. Did you think I would take an untested stim?"

She bows her head, "Vardøger, I would never—"

"Sabotage me? Of course you would." I snort. "Which was why I had Merodach test it first. Just to be sure."

I'll never let you get that anywhere near my body.

No, but you can't stop *her* from doing it.

"You attach it," I say.

My demon fights for control, but our wills are equal, neither being able to make a single muscle move. Our internal battle rages, hot and vicious, the sinewy fibers of this body straining to breaking point as the withered crone slowly climbs to her feet. She approaches, her steps unsteady on the ice, then unscrews the casing to the vial that will deliver the stim. She clips in the vial and twists on the casing.

"The mask," I say.

She pulls the mask from my belt and slips it over my head and attaches the hose. One last hopeful gaze through the round windows and into these eyes, and she opens the valve. Thick reddish mist hisses inside and I feel my control of this body coming back, like blood returning to a limb.

A massive inhale and a forceful exhale. Yes!

Damn you, Vedmak. I'll stop you.

Try and stop this, boy.

"You have been useful, Alchemist," I say, turning to the old Robust woman. "This is simply your finest work."

There's a moment of pride in her eyes that is quickly replaced by the fear of realization.

"But I'm afraid if you have reached your zenith, you have also outlived your usefulness."

Stop!

These Gracile hands, more powerful than ever, grasp her by the throat. She's lifted into the air with ease, flapping in the wind like a flag at half-mast. Without another word, I fling her screaming from the battlement, her wail fading into the storm until not even the impact of her frail body on the icy ground below is heard. I grunt in satisfaction, stomping with renewed energy and confidence to the unconscious, splayed Musul girl. I lean in close so the mask is touching her ear.

"Let the daughter of the star breather come," I whisper. "You and I have a little surprise for her."

CHAPTER THIRTY-SEVEN

MILA

Standing on the side of an ancient ramshackle abode, snow-laced crossbeams jutting from the first floor through the fallen in roof, I survey the entrance to Opor. At least six guards with old, long-rifles are visible; three occupying the entrance while another three patrol the ruins of the Forgotten Jewel on foot.

"Patrols everywhere. That's Giahi, for you. Never one to do anything subtly," I say.

"What is it you plan to do?" Zaldov asks in a hushed tone.

I hunch my shoulders and zip up my jacket to my throat. "I'm going to walk right in the front door."

"Oh." Zaldov's parts whir as he searches the snow-covered landscape. "Do you think that is a good plan?"

"Yeah. I'll go straight for Giahi. They'll be so focused on me you can do your part. You *can* wake the other Creed remotely, can't you?"

"Once I'm within thirty meters."

"Good. Focus on freeing Oksana. If you encounter trouble, try not to kill anyone. These are our fighters after all."

"Understood," Zaldov says.

"You have the captured audio ready for delivery?"

"Yes."

"Good. That's our ace. Be ready when I call for it."

"I understand, Mila Solokoff. Good luck."

I wink. "Luck's got nothing to do with it."

Breathe it out, Mila. They're not guards at an enemy outpost. They're your people. They don't want to be working for Giahi—they're just stuck and have to go with whoever is in charge.

I step from the shadow, clutching my ribs, and head for the hidden entrance to the hideout of Etyom's ever-volatile resistance group.

A few crunching steps across the hard-packed ice and they see me.

Immediately, they tense, rifles raised.

"Who is that? State your business," one of the men says.

It's Gustov, the machinist. On his left is Elene from the armory. The third man I don't recall. Damnation. How do I not know his name?

"Gustov, it's me," I call out.

"Mila?" He lowers the rifle. "Where've you been?"

"It's a long story. Escort me inside, please."

He fires a worried glance at Elene. "We've been given orders to shoot you on sight if you ever returned."

"The others too," Elene says, lowering her weapon.

The third man continues to cover me with his rifle. Probably one of Giahi's loyalists. I lock stares with him.

"Okay, do it," I say.

No one makes a move.

Gustov licks his lips and shrugs like a kid in trouble. "Mila, we don't want that."

"Good, me either," I say, still locked on the third man. "But, what about this guy?"

"Me?" the third guard says, his voice wavering.

Time to double down.

"No," I say through clenched teeth, "the other jackbag still holding me at gunpoint." With two steps, I walk into the end of his weapon, the cold steel of the muzzle burying in my chest. "Locate your potatoes and pull the trigger or get out of my way."

Don't make me do this.

His eyes grow wide. He adjusts his hold on the rifle and jabs me. "I'll do it. I will. Get back."

"You're one of Giahi's idiots, huh?" I say.

"Don't do it, Alexei," presses Gustov.

"You always were a stuck up bitch," Alexei fires back.

He shoves again. I slip to the side, redirect the barrel up and yank the weapon from his grasp. The steel muzzle whips across his face, breaking his front teeth in half.

The man lets loose a childlike cry and falls back.

"Eewe sarging bitssh." He gurgles.

269

Handing the weapon to Gustov, I lean in toward the bleeding man. "You chose the wrong side, doughboy. Here's some free advice. Don't point a weapon at someone who's got deeper resolve than you do. That's a good way to get hurt."

Alexei cries, blood running between his fingers.

"Listen close." I rap my knuckles on the top of his head. "You don't want to still be here when I come back out. Do we understand each other?"

He whimpers and gives a feeble nod.

I look to Gustov and Elene. "Are you guys with me?"

"We're with you, Mila," Elene pipes up, checking the action on her weapon.

"Good. Don't kill anyone. These people are our friends. We're taking back what belongs to us. Now tie my hands loosely behind my back and escort me in to see Giahi. Make it real."

After a few moments, with my hands behind my back and looped with rope, we head into the tunnel leading down beneath the wreckage of the old miner's dive. At the door, Gustov bangs his fist against the riveted steel in a rhythmic pattern.

"Who is it?" a muffled voice says from behind the door.

"Gustov and Elene. We've got a priority prisoner. Giahi is gonna want to see this."

"What prisoner?"

"Just open up and you'll see," Gustov says and looks to me, his eyebrows raised.

"Shove me inside when the door opens," I whisper.

The rusted steel of the latch unbars from the other side and the door squeals open. A widening shaft of light enters the tunnel. As the portal opens, Gustov shoves me into the room.

The doorman, another of Giahi's goons, hocks a laugh. "You weren't kidding. Didn't you have orders to shoot her?"

Gustov gives me another push. "Yeah, but she has information Giahi needs to hear."

"Suit yourself," the man says, turning to the door. "He's going to be ripe when he sees her—"

A fist snaps through the closing gap in the door, catches the guard across the chin—knocking him unconscious. But the guard doesn't hit the ground. With lightning speed, the hand grasps him by the tunic and drags him back into the tunnel. A moment later, Zaldov tiptoes through, then shuts and bolts the door behind him.

I stifle a chuckle.

Gustov and Elene glance at each other but say nothing.

"Keep going," I say. "The charade's not over yet."

Zaldov steps back into a nearby shadow and an instant later, he's gone.

***

Gustov jerks me this way and that making a good show of my capture. A few of my people are standing in the corridor. Their faces slacken at my coming and they part, pushing their backs against the rock-hewn walls. Their murmuring draws more people into the passage. My gut knots at the thought of their hating me. Yet, as Gustov shoves me past, some of them whisper: *Paladyn.*

Never thought I'd be happy to hear that word again. Keep your face hard, Mila. Sell it.

As we near the double doors, my gaze lands on Filly, the girl who always takes care of my clothes. There's a hint of desperation in her gaunt face.

"Mila?" she says longingly as I approach.

I wink but say nothing, trudging forward, my boots crunching on the gravel floor of the walkway.

"Right here." Gustov gives a firm jerk on my bonds.

The doors to the command center swing wide and Giahi steps out, shaking his jug head, his thick forearms crossed across his chest. "Well, well, well. Even with additional security, the rats still get in."

"Speaking of rats, Giahi, what's the meaning of—"

Without warning, he lunges forward and slugs me in the stomach. The impact knocks the wind from me and I fold in half. Wheezing on my knees, I struggle for breath.

"Get her up," he orders.

I gasp as Gustov hauls me to my feet.

271

Giahi leans in close. "That was for speaking out of turn. Do it again and see what happens."

"Nice." I take another breath. "Taking cheap shots while I'm tied up. I was worried you might have developed a spine while I was gone. Glad to see that's not the case."

The second punch lands home and though I clench my abdominal wall at the last moment, it still knocks the wind from me again. Sarding coward. I'm hauled to my feet again. Gasping, I lower my eyes. Let him think he's won, Mila.

"Anything else to say?" Giahi smirks, "No? Tell me why I don't put a bullet in your head, traitor. Where have you been?"

"On the mission to Vel, I was led into a trap. There was no way for me to come back from what happened. You should know. You set me up."

"Lies." Giahi laughs, appraising the crowd. "Who actually believes that?"

My gaze wanders across the familiar faces. Some bear looks of confusion and pity.

Giahi turns back to me. "You deserted us."

"Deserted? You exiled the rest of the leadership, so don't pretend like I left you hanging. You wanted this as much as your puppetmaster did. Don't for a second act like what you've done was for anyone's benefit but your own," I say.

"Yeah, I took control. Someone had to. This place was a mess. Opor was completely impotent. But I'm going to make it strong again."

"How? By subjugating everyone? You know that's not what this place was about. They do too." I toss my head at the gathering crowd. "You're part of the problem, Giahi. Vedmak is going to destroy everyone and everything and you've been all too eager to help him do it."

Giahi steps forward to punch me again.

"Yeah, that's right. Hit me to shut me up, because you can't risk the truth getting out."

"You don't know anything." Giahi spits at my feet.

"No? Let them hear it, Zaldov."

There's a pause, audio crackles through the speakers in the room. Giahi's voice loud and clear is heard conversing with another.

"Now is the time to make your move. Remove the old man." Vedmak's voice echoes off the red rock walls.

"Now? I'm not sure he's far enough along." The reply is distinctly Giahi.

"Now, Rat. When she returns, with the old man gone, she'll receive yet more intelligence. A reason to come to Vel. And when she does. I'll be waiting. Make sure she brings a minimal party. She'll die chasing a doomed operation and you'll finally have Opor. Fail me on any of these points, and you'll watch your own gizzards empty onto your feet."

"Yes … yes, Vardøger."

Giahi's eyes grow wide as he draws a small chrome pistol from his waistband and racks the slide.

"You're dead." He presses the gun to my forehead.

"Not so fast." An old woman behind Giahi draws a pistol from under her cloak, leveling it at him. Immediately two of his henchmen turn their rifles on the old cripple.

"Shoot them," Giahi says. "And shoot anyone who gets in the way."

"I would advise against that," Zaldov says, the crowd parting to reveal several Creed armed with glowing plasma rifles.

Giahi's confident façade drains away. "What's the meaning of this?" he says turning, his men jerking their rifles back and forth at too many threats to cover.

"Yes. I think that's an excellent question." Oksana steps forward, a tired and overworked version of the perfect woman I'd first met.

"Oksana," I say. "I can't believe I'm saying this, but, I'm glad to see you."

"Took you long enough to get here," she fires back. "This Neanderthal has kept me locked up working on his pet projects for the last six months."

"It's a long story, but you can thank Zaldov," I say.

The Gracile pats Zaldov on the shoulder.

"This isn't a sarding family reunion," Giahi barks, pushing the pistol flush to my face. "Flinch a muscle and I'll blow this cow's brains out."

"You'll be dead before her body hits the ground." The old woman drops her cloak, stands straight, and pushes her hair back.

"Yuri?" I almost laugh. I've never seen the master of deception with his silver hair down.

"I've been watching things spiral out of control here. Under Bilgi's orders I was supposed to sabotage the entire operation. But now you've come back from the dead." He smirks.

"I'm in charge here," Giahi shouts. "I call the—"

My hands come free from the loose bonds and intercept Giahi's wrists, driving them upward. The concussive blast rings in my ears as he squeezes off a round. Shots ring out from Yuri's weapon and Giahi's riflemen drop to the floor, clutching their thighs.

Giahi grunts, attempting to pull back his hands but before he can adjust, I've pivoted beneath him and yanked his arms down. He flips over my bowed back and hits the ground hard. With a jerk, I strip the gun from his grasp.

"Everyone hold your fire," I call out, catching Yuri's nod that he's okay.

I point the pistol at Giahi's head.

"Do it." His lips curl back in a snarl. "You don't have it in you."

Pressing my teeth together, I hold his stare. "You're right," I say, lowering the weapon, dropping the magazine and disassembling it in front to him. "I'm not you and I'm done with the killing." I toss the broken down pistol parts off to the side. "Get up."

Giahi laughs and makes his way to his feet. "You wanna go a few rounds, you salty little bitch?"

"It won't take that long," I say, raising my fists.

"Everyone stand back. No one interferes," Yuri calls out.

The crowd widens. Without warning, Giahi lurches in with a barrage of punches. Parrying the first two, the third grazes my chin as I step to the outside and deliver the hardest palm strike I can muster straight to his ear with a satisfying smack.

Giahi stumbles back, rubbing the side of his head.

I've been waiting years for this.

"I'll kill you with my bare hands, you rotten whore," Giahi swears.

I say nothing, my focus absolute. He comes again, a snarl of fury melted into his ugly face.

I sidestep, deflect down and deliver a kick of my own hard and fast to the groin. The strike doubles him over. An uppercut to the jaw and an elbow strike to the back of the head sends him to the floor, wheezing.

"What's the problem? I thought you were a tough guy? Should I let your men tie me back up?"

Giahi groans and raises himself shaking to his feet. This time he says nothing, his chest heaving.

"Surrender and I'll leave you some dignity."

"Sard off." He charges in with a scream.

He grips my shoulders and shoves me back against the wall. He slips his meaty hands to my throat. Madness flares in his eyes.

The crowd presses in, gasping.

Enough of this.

I gouge deep into his ocular cavity. With a piggish squeal, he releases me, his hands flying to his ruined eye. A sweeping low kick takes his balance, followed by a knee strike to the face that sends him down.

Giahi makes it to his knees, trembling, blood and fluid streaming from the wounded socket. "Kill me."

Without breaking eye contact with Giahi, I extend my hand to Yuri, who fills it with his pistol. I accept it and turn the handgun over. "I will spare your life, but your eye and your teeth are to remember your treachery."

"Teeth?"

I whip the slide of the weapon across Giahi's face with a crack, sending three bloodied teeth scattering across the floor. He slumps back, gurgling through split lips, and pitches to the side, unconscious in a pool of gathering blood.

"Yeah, you can live without your teeth." I hand the weapon back to Yuri. "Thank you, friend."

He gives a short bow. "Time is short, Mila. Bilgi is gathering everyone to meet the coming storm head on."

"And we will join them, but first, please see that Giahi's wounds are treated and he is confined to lockup."

Yuri gives a little bow and alongside two others, drags Giahi away. The crowd breaks into cheers and applause.

With a sigh, I hold my hands up to the crowd. "Everyone. I know some of you must be very confused. Just know that we all have been deceived. As we speak Vedmak, in the body of my friend Demitri, is doing something terrible. Something far worse than the Gracile Leader ever dared. The whole world, maybe even the known universe, is at stake. I'm sure you've all seen the growing green dome of green fire?"

Whispers of the terrible gateway ripple through the crowd.

"That's it. That's what will kill us all. We have to stop him. We have to try. I'm not going to lie to you. He has an army. An army of Graciles bonded to demons like Vedmak. But if we stop him, we stop annhilation."

"By stop, you mean kill, right?" Yuri says.

I shake my head. "I know you don't understand, but I have to try to save him. I have to."

"Mila, you can't save him," Yuri says.

"Oksana's been working on an antidote. Right, Oksana? To remove Vedmak forever," I say.

The Gracile smirks. "Lucky for you, the tasks this troll had me working on were menial." She waves at the unconscious Giahi. "I have it. I think."

"Good."

Yuri steps forward, pity etched into his features. "Mila, this doesn't make sense. Why save one Gracile? If Oksana has a cure for the madness, why are we not curing all of them? Hmm? Because we can't. Because this is war."

He speaks with words that could easily have come from Bilgi. Their wisdom cuts deep. I hadn't thought of that. We're going to war against her people, and she has never once argued the point.

"Oksana," I say, my voice but a whisper.

The Gracile gives the saddest smile I think I have ever seen. It quickly fades and she clears her throat. "Sun Tzu once said: *'a kingdom that has once been destroyed can never come again into being; nor can the dead ever be brought back to life.'* We Graciles have had our time and we squandered it. I would like to tell you to spare my kind, to avoid killing them, but they won't spare you. Or whatever resides inside them won't. I don't have enough of the antidote yet to cure all of them. The VME feeds on the connections between the Graciles and the … demons. Without enough cure, and no time, the only way to stop it is to kill them. Do what you must to save us all."

"And sparing this monster who leads them?" a woman calls out.

Oksana turns to the crowd, though addresses no one in particular. "Mila's need to save Demitri is logically flawed, perhaps selfish even. But a more human desire I have never seen. And if we aren't fighting to save our humanity, imperfect as it is, then we should just let the VME take us all."

The room grows quiet.

My mind is suddenly filled with the horrific thought that we are about to commit genocide to save the universe. It's paralyzing.

"Mila?" Yuri presses. "Did you hear me? If you don't succeed, I'll kill Demitri myself. It's nonnegotiable."

I can only wave him off.

I clear my throat and address the crowd. "I won't force you to fight, but if you have a mind to stand with us in this, get yourself ready. Time is short."

The small throng disperses and heads off to their individual tasks.

"Oksana," I start, though I have no idea what I'm supposed to say.

She shakes her head. "Don't."

I exhale away any speech that was brewing inside.

"The delivery system," she blurts out. "You'll have to be close enough to manually hit him with an auto injector. There's no other way."

"That part could prove difficult," I reply.

"There something else though, Mila."

"Something else?"

"I think this antidote may also be a cure for the NBD."

What did she say? "What? How is that possible?"

"I stumbled upon it. I'm not one-hundred percent on this but the antidote works by editing his genes inside his own body. It's like a virus that will instruct his cells to stop making the protein that allows quantum entanglement. This same tech can be used to instruct bacterial cells to self destruct. NBD bacterial cells. It's a tech worked on a couple of hundred years ago, but the plague took hold so quickly it was never fully explored."

I can't even fathom what this could possibly mean right now. A cure?

A world free from the fear of the NBD?

"Back up everything you've got and get ready to go. We can deal with that later. Right now we focus on saving Demitri and Husniya—" I shake my head. "As well as everything else any of us have ever known."

Yeos give me strength.

CHAPTER THIRTY-EIGHT

DEMITRI

Dark clouds, heavy with snow, gather on the horizon. A deep roll of thunder and a flash of jagged, forked lightning in the distance foretells the impending sounds of war. Pushed directly toward us by a brutal Siberian squall, the saturated vapors move with malevolent intent. Harbingers of death, they bring darkness—and Mila.

Vedmak stands on the battlement, impatiently waiting for his mortal enemy to appear so he can slaughter her and her friends. Wind batters my body, the body he stole from me, but I can't feel it at all. Not even a remnant. He paces back and forth, restless like a caged animal. He seems to be deep in thought but I have no connection to him, pushed back into the recesses of my own brain. Locked away where I can't meddle.

This is the worst it's ever been. The potency of this cocktail—his red mist the alchemist cooked up—is incredible. I'm so far away, a vignette of numbness permanently obscures the world. He has complete control now. Though I fought as hard as I could, it just wasn't enough. He was one step ahead. He's always one step ahead. And because I failed, everyone will die. Either by his hand, the hands of those he controls, or the VME.

Perhaps it's the best course, to let him finish what he started; to let the universe collapse and finally rid itself of the disease that is the human race. We have brought nothing but death and destruction from the moment we appeared on the planet. Nature, mother Earth, Yeos—whatever force one believes in—has tried to cleanse the planet before with little success. Natural disasters, famines, plagues, all seemingly sent like Earth's immune response to a virus. Only the NBD almost succeeded. Yet somehow, like cockroaches, we survived.

It begs the question: is Vedmak really the enemy? What if he was right all along and he's the answer. Earth's final cure. Better to shake the universe like a child's magnetic drawing board and start over.

The demon spins on a dime again, trudging the worn path, ice crunching underfoot. In front of him, Husniya is fixed, splayed out, to the icy outcropping. A particularly violent gust whips sleet and her jet-black hair about her face. Little Husniya. Mutilated by my hand once already, and now this. Vedmak's final insult to Mila. He hovers next to her for a moment, stroking her face with a gloved hand, apparently admiring his ingenious idea.

This is all my fault.

She is innocent, yet forced to be something she's not to survive. Molded and bent out of shape simply for being born into a world she had no hand in creating. Suffering for the mistakes of our ancestors. She, all the children of Etyom, deserves a chance to make it better.

I can't let this happen. I can't let him win.

Mila will never be able to stop Vedmak, not with his little trick. But I can from the inside. I have to—it's my responsibility. Evgeniy and Mila, they had faith in me and so far, I have failed miserably. Well no more.

Do you hear me, Vedmak? No more!

The monster cocks his head, as if listening to the storm speak his name, but then leaves Husniya and returns to his angry pacing. You heard me, you bastard. No stim works permanently. You told me once you can't outrun your shadow, Vedmak. It's true. I will defeat you, one way or another. Even if I must die doing it.

The Ripper battle, radiation poisoning, that Creed's attack, sleep deprivation, and my own mental assault have driven him to the brink. This can be used to my advantage, if I can just break through. Perhaps… It's cliché to suddenly feel the need to believe when everything comes apart at the seams. But what can it hurt?

Yeos, I don't know if you're real. Anastasia and Mila believe in you. Maybe I've been the one who is wrong all along. If you can hear me—prove me wrong. Show me you're real. Give me the chance to stop Vedmak and save Mila and Husniya, and Anastasia and all the children of Etyom. Take me if you have to. Just allow humanity one more chance.

I focus, drawing what energy I can from the ether, my consciousness coalescing into an imaginary ball of light that sits at the center of my own body, ready to explode outward, destroy Vedmak, and finally reclaim the flesh.

Concentrate, Demitri.

Concentrate.

Ayúdame …

What was that? Is someone there?

Ayúdame … por favor … ayúdame a rescatar a la niña," a voice says from the void.

Margarida?

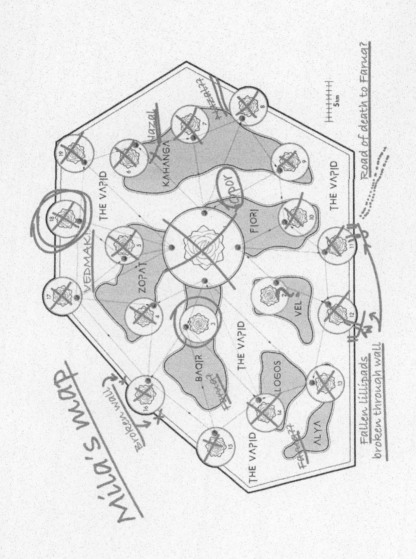

Milla's Map

CHAPTER THIRTY-NINE

MILA

In the distance, the stacked stone walls of the Zopatian enclave loom, high and impenetrable. Behind it, our destination calls to us, the emerald-green glow emanating into the sky like manmade *aurora borealis*. We round the northernmost edge of the enclave, keeping a good few kilometers' distance as we circle back west.

Two lillipads once stood over Zopat; both fell inside the walls. Meaning Zopat remained one of the few enclaves not breached. We scoured it, looking for both Demitri and Faruq, but found nothing. But the great green beacon strobing up into the atmosphere behind Zopat jogged all our memories: there was a third, to the north near the outer wall. Since few ventured that far, it was all but forgotten. That surely is where Vedmak hid all these years, and where we are headed.

I adjust the bulky cylindrical launcher hanging from a worn canvas strap on my shoulder. It was recovered after the battle for the Gracile Leader's rocket ship. After digging through the armory for a few minutes, I'd found it under a pile of old flack jackets. A quick oiling of the breach break mechanism followed by a function check and everything appeared to be in working order. I even found eight lead-filled beanbags and an extra canister of compressed air for it.

"You may not be here in the flesh for this one, Denni. But you're with me nonetheless," I say, remembering the way my little friend's vivid sky-blue eyes twinkled when she had one last trick up her sleeve.

"Here, take this." Oksana hands me a thin white rectangular device with a glass viewing port and a safety cap covering a short needle. Pinkish liquid sloshes in the loaded syringe. "You know how to use it—just don't forget to remove the safety cap in the heat of the moment."

"Thanks," I say, accepting the auto-injector and clipping it to my belt. "Hope it will work."

"It's too late for hope. We'll have to try it and find out."

"I don't like the sound of that."

She shrugs. "It's all we've got."

"And you know your part? Can you pull it off?"

She sidles up and we stare at frozen battlement which stands twenty meters high in the distance. "I'm the only one who can."

Without another word, Oksana touches my arm, slings a bag over her shoulder, and sets off at a brisk pace to the west.

Behind, a rumble in the heavens rolls out, long and deep. A winter storm is fast approaching. I turn back to our target. I'm not sure how I didn't see if before, but a force has gathered and is standing in solidarity, perhaps half a kilometer before the frozen barricade. And at the center, gesturing to the left and right, is an old, stooped figure, one arm missing.

"Oh, by the hands of Yeos," I say, taking off toward the amassed crowd at a trot. The rhythmic crunch of my boots impacting the ice falls in cadence with the banging of my heart. "Bilgi!"

The old man turns as I run up, a smile creasing his weathered face. I crash against him, squeezing him in a crushing embrace.

"You were gone, and I wasn't sure I was going to see you again," I say, my words muffled in his heavy clothing.

He pulls me close with his good arm. "I had to go. Giahi convinced everyone I was sick."

"I know. Praise the Maker you're not. What happened?"

"As soon as I left, I went to the body ranch in Zopat."

I scowl. "It's a clinic, Bilgi. They do the best they can with nothing."

"Don't scold me." He laughs. "That's what everyone calls it. Anyway, they told me I had something in my system, but it wasn't the plague. But by then it was too late. The others had been exiled by Giahi and our influence over Opor was lost." He raises my chin to gaze into his wizened face. "Where were you?"

"I had to get myself figured out." I don't want to hold his gaze.

"And did you?" he asks, though he seems to know the answer.

"Yeah, I did."

"Some said you were dead. Not me, I knew you'd return to us." He hugs me again. "It warms me inside to know you found your way." He extends his arm, distancing himself again, and his face turns serious once more. "Tell me you have a plan, Mila."

"More of a theory than a plan, Bil. Oksana thinks she's found the cure to Demitri's psychosis. I'm going to hit him with this and hope it does what she thinks it will." I unclip the injector and hold it up for him to see.

Bilgi shakes his head. "Are you crazy? You know how close to him you'll have to get?"

"We have a chance to rescue Demitri from his demon. Don't we owe it to him to try?"

He looks at me long and hard, his gaze a withering blast of cold. "*You* might owe it to him. The rest of us don't harbor the same allegiance for that deranged Gracile. What has he done for us?"

Now it's my turn to glare. "Oh, I dunno. Maybe he helped me take down the Gracile Leader and save the world—the human race—from extinction. The stress of which, I might add, crushed him and allowed Vedmak to take control." My voice rises, shaking with an intensity I didn't anticipate. "So I don't want to hear anyone questioning what we owe him, because we owe him everything."

"Okay." Bilgi shrugs. "You're right. I'm sorry. I wasn't there for much of that. All I know is what he's cost us over the last few years since the rise of this Vardøger. And now, we're faced with another cataclysmic event—one that could be averted by putting a lead slug between his eyes."

My frown deepens.

"But, if you are determined to choose the hard path, have at it, my little krogulec. After all, who can stop you once your mind is set?"

Mos and Ghofaun approach.

I don't have the words, my chest tight. "Mos." We step forward, slap our hands together and pull each other in. The broad-shouldered Kahangan and I touch foreheads. "I'm so glad to see you, friend."

"And I you. We were worried," he says.

I turn to the wizened monk dressed in traditional red Lawkshan robes, a sash of gold across his midsection. He wears a pleasant expression. I place a hand on his shoulder and he reciprocates. "Ghofaun, I'm so sorry, I—"

He waves his hands. "No apologies. The past is the past. It is a blessing to see you return to us, Mila."

Yuri and Zaldov march up with the rest of our fighters walking warily alongside the small contingent of Creed.

"Yuri," Bilgi calls out, "you brought our people."

"Mila brought our people, Bilgi."

"What happened? How did you get free of Giahi?" Bilgi asks.

I wave my hand. "Long story. What you need to know is Giahi is out of the picture."

"You killed him?" Mos asks, his heavy brow creasing.

I shake my head. "No, that's not who I am anymore. Maybe I never was deep down, and it messed me up. That's why I had to leave for a while, I had to remember." I touch the worn picture in my breast pocket. "I needed to reconnect with what's important."

Bilgi's face sobers. "You know Vedmak has Husniya. He captured her from the Vestal temple. I'm glad you didn't have to see it. It was terrible. The Vestals' dying act was to try to shield Husniya from that monster."

"And yet, he still took her." I swallow. "Zaldov briefed me on all of it." I try unsuccessfully to put the innocent face of Sister Katerina out of my mind. "Their sacrifice to protect Hus and the Writ will not be forgotten." I pat the heavy tome in my bag. "It's time for us, *all of us*, to come back."

My friends respond in agreement.

"This isn't going to be easy," Yuri mutters.

"It never is," I say. "What have we got in the way of support?"

"I've brought two-hundred of my best from Kahanga." Mos smacks a closed fist against his chest. I look over his shoulder to the lines of his men standing ready, their machetes and rifles poised, their clothing mismatched and multicolored—the visage of a cobbled together militia.

"And I have rallied a dozen Zopatian monks. They are each worth fifty trained soldiers." Ghofaun bows.

"Mos, Master Ghofaun." I bow. "You are both true believers in the cause. Always have been. Thank you."

Bilgi grunts an approval. "Plus the Opor fighters and few Creed you brought, we're in better shape than I first thought." He surveys the gathering masses. "But, who's this?" He points to a group of shadows drifting from the gray haze in the West.

I stare, trying to get a fix on the individuals materializing from the frozen swirl of shifting smog. First one rank appears, then another, followed by a third, marching in formation toward our position. The man in front, leading the sizable group, comes into focus and all blood drains from my limbs.

Faruq.

"Baqirians," Yuri says.

"We approached Faruq for help," Bilgi says. "He refused us. Looks like the winds of fortune may have changed."

I wait in silence, unsure of how this exchange will go. Mustn't blow too hard upon the spark of hope glowing in my chest.

After crossing the expanse, a man with an eyepatch behind Faruq shouts out a few commands and the various Baqirian men come to a halt. They coolly eye the Kahangans, the monks, and the resistance fighters. Faruq marches up, wearing tan expedition pants, boots and a heavy fur-lined coat. His gait is steady and sure, the strict confidence of the man I once knew is visible again. He stops several meters away and surveys us.

He won't make eye contact. My heart aches.

"Sheikh Faruq," Bilgi says with a courteous dip of his head.

"Let us get something straight. I am here for my sister." Faruq's eyes are as hard as steel.

His few words are crushing. He's not here for me. All I want to do is wither up and blow away in the endless Siberian wind. It isn't fair for him to continue to punish me. It isn't fair and there's nothing I can do but take it. Yeos be the strength of my heart.

"Very well, Sheikh. We welcome your support in any way you choose to give it. What are your terms?" Bilgi asks.

"I am here to rescue my sister and that's all—do not get in my way."

"Of course." Bilgi bows again. "We have a condition as well—try not to kill Vedmak. We believe Demitri is still trapped inside. We will save him if we can."

"That's a fool's errand," Faruq says. "You want to spare the fiend that maimed my sister?"

"Not spare. Cure, if possible," Bilgi says. "Demitri would never deliberately harm Husniya. You know this. He's as much a prisoner as you once were—"

"Enough," Faruq says.

"Please," Bilgi says, his tone soft.

"No," Faruq says, touching the gold-plated wheel gun in his waistband. "If that's what you want, you'd better reach him before I do."

Faruq moves to leave.

"Faruq." I can barely choke out his name.

He stops, but still will not meet my gaze.

"May I suggest you take Ghofaun and his monks with you? They will be nothing but an asset on your mission to rescue Husniya."

No one moves, feathers of sleet floating between us.

"Please," I say, and look to Ghofaun, who winks for me to continue. "We want to see her safe as well. Accept this help as a token of our good will."

Faruq does not reply, but simply bows his head in acquiescence and rejoins his men.

Ghofaun squeezes my arm as he passes. He signals to his monks—short Zopatians clothed in sashes of gold and carrying staffs and kukri blades. Together they head off to join with Faruq's force.

For the first time, I notice a group of women, clad in heavy-hooded robes of crimson and cream, standing behind the outermost edge of the massing troops. Some of them are only girls, even younger than Husniya. The last of the Vestals. They came to war? I watch as these mighty women form into rows, their lips moving in unison, hands pushed toward the sky.

"They pray for us, Mila," Bilgi says, touching my arm. "It is a sign. Yeos is among us."

"I never thought I'd see something like this. Any of it," I say.

Bilgi looks to me, his eyes sad and knowing. "This is it. What's the play, my girl? I'm not so sure brute force will win the day this time."

"I know. I've been working on a better way to do this."

Mos shifts his heavy bulk. "My scouts have told me there's not any other way in than through this gap in the ice wall here." He points to the entrance to the concealed lillipad.

"Yeah, I know, so, here's what I'm thinking—"

An ear-piercing screech of static drowns my words. I squint my eyes, cupping my palms over my ears. Then, as abruptly as it came, the sound is gone. Another heavier rumble, the churning storm above closing in.

"Do I have your attention?" Vedmak's amplified voice seems to rise from the ice itself. "Are all the miserable wretches lying on my doorstep listening to the voice of their conqueror?" Demitri's body steps into view on the upper left portion of the ice wall.

A small army of Graciles adorned with armor step to the rim of the enormous barrier, facing out, their shouldered plasma rifles glowing with intense blue light. At the same instant, a powerful force of armored Gracile warriors carrying swords, battle maces, and barbaric horned axes marches through the gap in the ice wall and fans out five ranks deep.

"He's got us dead to rights out here in the open," I say to Bilgi.

My stoic mentor says nothing.

"I am the Vardøger," Vedmak continues. "Accept your place beneath the heel of my boot. You will not win this day." His voice booms across the ice. "And this is my insurance." He steps over to a vertical jagged crop of ice jutting upward from the top of the wall. Grabbing a section of canvas tarp, he snatches it down to reveal a young woman lashed to the ice. It has to be Husniya.

While still slumped unconscious, she appears to be wearing some sort of metallic headgear and is secured by rope and spikes driven into the ice.

Faruq cries out something in Baqirian.

"We are now interconnected via the neural web," Vedmak announces with glee. "If I die, *she* dies."

"This is not good, Mila Solokoff," Zaldov says.

My heart sinks. No. How could an impossible task be made even worse?

"He cannot stop us!" Bilgi shouts. "We will stand against this, Gahhhggg—" His words are cut short in a gurgling scream. A hole opens in his chest, bands of flesh peeling off like the red petals of some prehistoric flower. Warm blood sprays across my face as Bilgi stumbles.

The lingering crack of a rifle hangs in the air.

"The old one talks too much." Vedmak laughs lowering an old Mosin-Nagant bolt-action rifle propped over his deformed arm. "Not anymore."

"Bilgi, no," I cry, pulling his sagging body against mine. "Bilgi, oh come on. No. Hang on." Tears seep from between pinched eyelids as I sink to my knees, cradling the wheezing old man close.

His lifts a hand and taps my chest, his gaping blood-filled mouth forming soundless words.

"Bilgi … I can't. I don't understand," I say, my stomach coiling in knots. "I can't lose you."

He jabs me in the chest again, his eyes wide. "You are the one, Mila. You are … destined for the path …" He gurgles and the last glimmer of life escapes him.

I scream, my body shaking with a terrible vigor, spittle clinging to my lips, tears dripping from my chin. I clutch Bilgi to me.

"The rest of you vermin are next," Vedmak says. "Kill them all."

The air erupts with sound and fury. The Graciles on the wall open fire with their plasma weapons, eviscerating the ranks of my people—rendering friends and comrades to ash.

Vedmak points at me. "Kill the little *suka* once and for all."

The Graciles wheel on me, taking aim. This is my miserable end. I swallow and take a deep breath, pinching my eyes even tighter. The rising prayer song of the Vestals like a chorus of the saints to my ears. I am who I was meant to be. I am ready.

Yeos, my life is yours to forfeit.

The building storm above us ruptures, a blast of ice and wind snapping across the battlefield, whipping waves of snow from the ground. Crystals of ice sting the skin, the gusts cutting through layers of clothing like a score of thrown blades.

The glowing rifles snap, the first bolt striking left of me and the second buzzing overhead to plunge into the snowbank behind with a hiss. They fire again. This time, with my stinging eyes wide open, I will them to hit me. Both shots veer wide, striking the snow. I lower the body of my adopted father to the ground and rise to my feet, blood drenching my clothes. Vedmak snatches the glistening metallic rifle away from one of his soldiers. Bracing it as before, he fires a blistering string of shots that gouge at the ground before me, throwing chunks of mud and ice into the air.

Is the rifle malfunctioning? The storm throwing off his aim? Or could it be … "Stand up and fight! Yeos is with us!" I scream, thrusting my launcher into the air.

With an electrifying shout, the resistance rises from where they lay prone behind bush and rock. Some fire upon the entrenched Graciles while others charge for the gap. The squad of Creed soldiers opens up on the regiment of Gracile defenders standing atop the ice wall. I charge forward, my gaze locked with that of my old friend up on the ice wall.

Demitri. I'm coming for you.

CHAPTER FORTY

FARUQ

My vocal cords strain as I call out to the splayed form of my little sister high above on the wall of ice. What have those fiends done to her? Is she even still alive?

"Sheikh, we must fight!" Captain Kahleit shouts.

The blue streak of a plasma bolt cuts the air between us.

I throw myself against the ground as another rips past. Gasping frozen air into my lungs, the wind and sleet sting my exposed face. Time seems to stall and lose its meaning, the battle blossoming around us. My people, the Kahangans, and resistance fighters are cut down in full measure by flying projectiles and plasma bolts. These mad Gracile titans show us no quarter. They do not differentiate between our ways, our skin color, or our beliefs—we are, all of us, beneath them, worthy only of death.

Then I see her, rising from the snow. Talons of fear clutch at my heart shattering its icy facade as I watch Mila stand, defiant in the face of certain death. Bolts zip past her, missing their mark again and again. It's not possible she will survive this.

"Mila!" I cry out.

For a moment, the whiteout obscures everything, the terrible possibilities of her fate driving my mind toward insanity. Then, through a break in the sleet, I see her again. How can this be? With a scream she charges forward, her weapon—the tubular one Denni had once given her—thrust upward into the air.

A flood of memories assaults my senses, sights and sounds and smells. Mila and I fighting together side by side against the forces of the Gracile Leader. Shared purposes, destinies intertwined. The visage of this fearless woman strikes a chord within, the immeasurable depths of my own weakness and selfishness laid bare. A stroke of anguish courses through my heaving chest.

What sort of man have I become who would refuse the only ones I ever loved?

A roiling wave of nausea causes my mouth to flood with saliva. And then, Kahleit is there, dragging me to my feet as my men begin to run.

"Onward, Sheikh! We will show them all the nature of our fortitude."

"Yes," I manage, dragging my ice-covered sleeve across my mouth and swallowing back the bitterness.

Pulling my arm free, I run toward the towering wall of ice before us, the only way in a narrow pass filled with armor-clad brutes, and beyond a hoard of ragged men. Are those Rippers?

An ear-piercing blast followed by a growing whine intercepts my thoughts. I wince, scrunching my brow as I focus on the source of the growing cacophony.

A repurposed Creed strike-ship rises from behind the towering wall, its suspended plasma cannon pivoting to lock on us. My men scream and shout, running, falling, and diving for anything that may provide them cover. I just run, vision blurred, tears streaming down my cheeks. We're doomed.

With a crack like lightning, a blue bolt fired from the strike-ship tears its way through the ranks of the Kahangans. Their screams distort as their bodies come apart, bursting into gray clouds like the handmade confetti poppers Kapka forced everyone to fire off at his parades. The human ash hangs there for a moment, dissipating into the ranks of bawling survivors.

Another bolt looses from the massive strike ship, this time rending some of my men to dust.

A Kahangan rocket-propelled grenade screams upward, loses its thrust, and drops over the wall.

That's it. I've seen strike ships taken down with these weapons before. "Kahleit," I scream. He looks up at me from behind a bush. "Fire all of the rockets."

"But Sheikh— "

"Fire them all at the strike ship. That's an order."

Kahleit makes it to a knee, then swings an arm overhead. "Loose the rockets! Fire upon the strike ship!"

The men pull the launchers forward, casting confused looks at each other.

"Fire!" Kahleit screams. "All of them."

The men jolt to action, a barrage of rockets firing off from different positions, whining into the air in unison.

"Follow me," I shout, rising and running once again. I draw the golden wheel gun from my waistband and forge ahead, the rallying shouts of my men ringing in my ears.

CHAPTER FORTY-ONE

MILA

"Kahanga!" Mos shouts, his voice sending his soldiers screaming and running with him. "What's the plan?" he yells at me.

"There is no plan," I shout back. "Don't stop moving. Take down Vedmak any way you can—just don't kill him and watch your fire. Husniya's life is at stake."

Above, Vedmak throws down the plasma rifle in favor of the old-fashioned bolt-action weapon. Working the action one-handed, he shoulders and braces across his forearm, taking aim on me. The rifle cracks once. The round zips past. He works the action and fires again, but I keep running, fearless, a heart full of reckless purpose.

Vedmak shatters the old rifle on the ice barrier at his feet and flings the parts over the wall. With a wave of his arms, more men pour from the gap—but the others now loosed upon us are not Graciles.

Dear Yeos, he's using stimmed Rippers like mindless attack dogs.

Far to the left, Faruq leads his Baqirians forward. A host of old Soviet RPGs whistle from their launchers, whining toward the humming strike ship. The Gracile pilot jerks the ship left and right, dodging the rockets, but there are too many and he's not fast enough. The ship receives a blow to a wing and spins out of control, crashing low through a portion of the ice wall.

Husniya is above that section.

The craft distorts with the screech of tearing metal and comes apart in a ball of flaming debris. Vedmak severs Husniya's bonds with his plasma blade and hoists her into the crook of his stumped arm. He jumps from the wall as it disintegrates beneath his feet. Snagging a section of severed support cable, he falls. It snaps tight as he drops out of sight on the far side of the wall.

How the hell was he able to do that?

I focus on the formation blocking our approach, a veritable wall of armored biological perfection.

"Carve your blades into them. Do not stop!" Mos shouts.

His men howl their response, machetes in the air. The few rifles they have pop, well-taken shots dropping the last of the deranged Graciles still carrying plasma weapons.

The launcher snugs into my shoulder and fires. A tattered blue cloth beanbag sails from the muzzle, laying a Gracile's nose flat. The armored soldier sinks to his knees, his hands flying to his blood-drenched face. Then I'm on him with a spinning back kick that catches him right in the same spot. With a howl, he crashes against the snow, clutching his disfigured features.

The lines of Kahangans, Baqirians, and Resistance collide with the possessed Graciles, screams of fear and death filling the air.

A Gracile comes at me headlong. Not toe-to-toe, Mila. Work to their disadvantage.

I deflect a sword meant for my head with the barrel of the launcher, slip beneath, and rise again. A crippling stomping kick to my attacker's knee breaks it inward with the sound like snapping firewood. I follow with a crucial blow, slamming the barrel of my launcher into the base of his skull, sending him tumbling into the snow. Immediately, another is there, attempting to smash me into the ice with a cudgel. Deflecting the strike, a roundhouse kick to his ribs yields nothing but a grunt. I give him another in the same target area. This time he winces and steps back, his face twisting with fury.

From seemingly nowhere, Zaldov drives into the armored Gracile. The Creed clubs him to the ground, then pivots and engages multiple Graciles at close range with his plasma rifle. Their gray powder is snatched away by the wind.

"Thanks," I huff.

Zaldov's rubbery lips stretch into a smile.

Forging ahead, I load another bag into the breach, shoulder, and fire. The lead shot-filled projectile drops the Gracile charging Mos. My friend grins at me before drawing Svetlana, the .44 magnum, from his belt and blasting a Ripper through the chest.

The Gracile ranks are powerful and they leave their mark in blood, but our sheer numbers are superior. The lives spent here are the terrible price we must pay for victory. Splitting the ranks and driving the few remaining Gracile warriors to the outside where they are isolated, we clear a path to the gap in the wall.

A second strike-ship slings snow in all directions as its jets whine, preparing for takeoff. Before I can scream for someone to take it out, a thin cloaked figure runs from beneath the belly of the aircraft and disappears into the whiteout of the storm.

Was that …? A fiery flash precedes an incredible concussive blast that rends the strike-ship in half.

Oh, Yuri, I could kiss you right now.

Inside the wall, the short incline opens up. Faruq's forces and the monks flood in through the breach left by the fallen strike ship, the Kahangans and my people fan out.

There's a host of screaming. More Rippers. But these are different.

Through the blizzard and the sounds of war, the Ripper chief from Vel appears. Are they here to help?

His minions yelp and howl, flying onto the battlefield to our left and into both Faruq's ranks and the ranks of Vedmak's forces. A stone sinks in the pit of my stomach. Good job, Mila. I invited them here and they're going berserk—on everyone. It's a bloody free-for-all.

Vedmak's Rippers and the chieftain's Rippers clash and spill each other's blood, Faruq's Baqirians drive into them with the full weight of his forces. A section of the Rippers breaks free—some are Vedmak's and some aren't, but they're not fighting each other anymore. They're coming at us. At *me*. There's still a mark on my head. They won't stop until it sits on a pike. The distance between us vanishes as they close.

"We're trapped," I call out.

I can't seem to move, my body frozen by the sheer madness of war.

"Not yet," a strange voice calls back.

Past us charges a massive blur of orange and black, a whirlwind of flying claws and fangs. The Rippers shriek the sounds of terror and death.

"Ussuri!" I shout.

The massive tiger swings his head in my direction, jowls foaming with blood. Mounted atop the great tiger's back is Anastasia, wearing a strange headdress of colored silks and black feathers.

"What are you doing?" I shout.

"Buying you some time. The Vardøger must be stopped." She pivots on the tiger's back, facing off against a band of regrouping Rippers.

"How did you know to come?"

She flashes a wild grin. "Logosians aren't the only ones with whom Yeos speaks."

Even in the throngs of war, she can throw a veiled insult. One I perhaps deserve. "May His hands be upon you, Soufreit."

The wanderer bares her teeth and yelps wildly. Grabbing a handful of Ussuri's fur, she sends him leaping into the front lines of the Rippers with astonishing speed and breathtaking power. The Ripper chieftain and his brood are stalled. Many of them drop their weapons and run screaming. The chieftain backs away, mouth agape, as the great beast savages another section of his men.

My head won't go on a pike just yet.

There's a crackle of electrical white noise, and the shimmering VME bubble growing from within the lillipad undulates and swells. It's growing fast. No time to waste.

Between us and the fallen Gracile fortress beyond, Vedmak stands defiant. There is lust for blood in his eyes as his sputtering scythe lops heads and limbs from the first resistance and Kahangan fighters to reach him. He points his weapon at me with an evil sneer.

Behind him, a huge Gracile darts into the lillipad, Husniya flopped over his massive shoulder.

Don't stop, Mila. Don't you dare stop now.

CHAPTER FORTY-TWO

VEDMAK

The Alchemist's final gift courses through me turning my blood into a burning lake of fire. I am a god of war. Reaping souls is my harvest—and the harvest is plentiful. My senses tingle with another inhaled breath of the nebulized concoction. These whimpering cowards come and bring war to my house. I will give them what they so desire.

Twisting, I grind the toes of my boots into the bloody slush at my feet searching for a more stable position. The open-mouthed head propped against my ankle draws a cruel smile across these lips. Let them come and share his fate. The plasma scythe ignites with a crackling sound then fizzles as it steadies. It pops and sputters a few times and catches again. The power cell won't last much longer.

I lift the stump of an arm, now adorned with a crudely welded war hammer. A crimson wash, the blood of my foes, drips from its square edges. I am battle born, made to bring the end that haunts all men.

The little *suka* fights her way through the throngs of warriors to reach me. She is an aggressive creature—there is no shame in admitting that. I hate the bitch down to Demitri's very bones but admire the tenacity with which she comes. Pure, driven, dauntless. It will make emptying her blood upon the snow that much more satisfying.

"Come on," I shout, pointing my scythe at her. "Come and taste of death."

But she cannot. Instead, she's swarmed by a swath of my Rippers.

A group of the Kahangan fighters breaks through the lines and gallops toward me, their mouths filled with the last words of dying men. The neural link activates, connecting with the optical nerve in Demitri's head. The battlefield stutters, slowing to a crawl. I have all the time in the world to take these fools apart.

I sidestep a clumsy swipe from a machete. My scythe buzzes as it swings upward, cleaving the shocked man vertically from groin to sternum.

He cries out, falling and fumbling with his guts as they empty into his hands. Glorious. The single frames of action come one at a time and I take the second attacker head on, the iron hammer crashing down into his clavicle and folding his chest inward. The third and fourth would have had a good shot had they not hesitated. The scythe crackles as it sweeps clean through the lower half of one man, his gawking upper end toppling awkwardly into the snow at his own feet. I turn on the last man, who is just registering the carnage I have wrought upon his comrades. His feet slide as he tries to change direction.

And the flame of my weapon sputters out. Sard it all to hell.

No matter. I lunge, crossing the distance in a fraction of a second, swinging the heel of the scythe upward, catching him hard under the chin. The sound of his teeth breaking against each other is sweet music. His body, straight as a board, flops backward into the snow, unmoving.

With a gasp, the world around me regains its composure. A stream of blood rolls from my host's left nostril. I am beyond the human weakness that plagues this flesh.

A fury still boils over inside my chest, at the turning of the tide of battle. The cockroaches brought their forces to bear this time, and no matter the superiority of my Graciles or the madness in these stimmed-up Rippers. Not even the *dushi* of my brethren or the mind-altering chemicals are enough—my army is still being forced back.

The Logosian's resistance and their allies keep pushing forward. This is not how it was supposed to be. This body quakes with pent up rage.

Charging forward, I seize a resistance fighter by the neck and sling her back against the ice at my feet, her skull breaking upon impact. Another two fall from critical blows from the iron hammer attached to my arm.

A roar freezes me in place.

No. It can't be. I turn to see the source of the primal sound, knowing full well from what it comes. The massive tiger stalks its way toward me, and riding on its back is … is … "You!" I scream, vocal chords straining above the chaos. "You would come to challenge me? Desire me to break you again, do you? Did you enjoy it that much?"

"Give up, demon. Give back what you have stolen," my former captive says with confidence, her headdress blowing in the storm.

"I will not. I'll kill that tiger and choke the life out of you!"

"Don't make me hurt you," she calls into the wind.

Infernal bitch. I try to ignite the plasma scythe. It would give me a strong advantage against the beast. But no, the worthless garbage sputters, the power cell extinguished.

She notches an arrow to her bow and draws on me.

"Do it," I screech. "You can't because you know the weakling Demitri who set you free still lives trapped inside this body."

She hesitates, staring into the eyes I've stolen. The bow twangs. I can't even turn before the shaft strikes, penetrating deep into the thigh muscle. A spike of searing pain flares through this engineered shell.

"No, but I can slow you down," she says.

That bitch! She shot me. Flinging the used-up scythe into the snow, I grab the arrow shaft and yank the barb from the meat. Blood streams down the thigh of my Gracile war horse.

The tiger roars and there's another twang of the bow. The arrow strikes me in the shoulder, stopped by the plate armor I wear.

"I'll kill you all!" I scream, sprinting as fast as this injured shell will allow toward the lillipad entrance, now being barricaded by Merodach.

"You can't stop it, Vardøger," the wild woman calls out, her voice swarming my brain. "Fate is coming for you."

CHAPTER FORTY-THREE

FARUQ

Pleas for life and howls of death fill my ears. A hastily thrown trip mine detonates beneath the swarming band of Rippers on our left, shearing a whole section of them off at the knees. Another three of my men go down, thrown spears protruding from their chests.

"Kahleit," I shout, turning and blasting a hole through the chest of a charging Ripper. "Kahleit, where are you?"

Advancing forward, Captain Kahleit parries a spear point with his gleaming saber. The polished steel flashes as he jams it into the gut of another painted man. "I'm here," he calls back, slicing a Ripper's head from his shoulders.

"He took my sister through there," I yell, turning my attention through the giant hole in the ice wall made by the fallen gunship toward the barricaded entryway to the lillipad.

The predatory roar of some unknown beast penetrates the snowstorm. What was *that?* No time to find out. We've got to get inside or we're all going to be lying dead out here. But how?

A rocket-propelled grenade screams past. The projectile slams into the makeshift barricade, blowing a ragged hole of flying glass and splintered wood right through the middle of it. I turn to see Ghofaun, who drops the RPG launcher to the ground.

"Kahleit, now!" I shout.

"Yes, Sheikh," Kahleit yells back. He orders a squad with him while the rest of my men shove forward, working to stave off the swarming army of Rippers.

One breaks through the lines, a wild scream upon his lips as he comes for me. With numb fingers, I break the cylinder of the revolver open and fumble with the loose large caliber rounds jangling in my pocket. I pull one free from the fabric pouch, drop it into the cylinder and snap it shut with a flick of my wrist. The hand cannon rises fast, my frozen index finger clenching the trigger. A fireball erupts from the barrel. The large round obliterates the Ripper's skull in a shower of blood and bone. The headless corpse falls at my feet. My stomach rejects the meal I consumed hours ago, taji beans and roasted Chiori splashing into the snow and across my boots.

Fate, you are a cruel mistress. I was not made for this. I drag the sleeve of my jacket across my mouth with a groan.

Kahleit grabs my arm, his fingers digging against flesh. "We must move, Sheikh. Now."

"What?" I manage before seeing the answer to my question. The Rippers with their barbaric savagery are not stopping. My men cannot hold them. Mortal terror claims my limbs. Ilah, be merciful.

There's a flash of golden silk, then another, as two Zopatian monks whirl past, one armed with an eight-foot ashwood staff, the other with the curved blade. The Rippers come, but they cannot land a single blow. The monks twist and spin, their feet dancing on cushions of air. Again and again, their weapons land true, the battered and broken bodies of Rippers piling at their feet.

"With me, Faruq," Ghofaun's voice calls out from the madness. He dodges the thrust of a Ripper's spear and executes a handless cartwheel. The monk's kukri blade slices through the air and clean through the Ripper's neck. "Now," he yells.

Through the blood and the screams, I climb the remains of the hill and run for the opening in the lillipad entrance. The lillipad is enormous and within it, rising out of the rear, is a huge dome of green fire.

Ghofaun clears the way, while Kahleit covers my hasty ingress. I glance down to align the cold brass in my hand with the holes in the cylinder of my wheel gun. My forearm aches from a death grip too long engaged against the rosewood handle of the heavy pistol. I secure four rounds, the fifth dropping into the snow at my feet. No time. I snap the cylinder closed and raise the weapon back to the high ready position.

Mila has destroyed the makeshift barricade and charges through alongside Mos and several Creed—their faces lit by the shimmering green thing beyond.

"Husniya? Where is my sister?" I shout.

Into the inner sanctum we race, but immediately grind to a halt a few meters inside. In our way stands a wall of Graciles, but not just any Graciles. These monsters wear armor plating and carry melee weapons that burn with blue fire. On their backs are cylindrical tanks with hoses that loop over the shoulders and vent with a red steam beneath the nose.

The emerald sphere creeps into the room, dissolving the walls centimeter by centimeter. The gate to unspeakable damnations is still growing.

A voice from the shadows speaks. It's Vedmak. "Kill them, Merodach."

The biggest one of the Graciles, the one called Merodach, swings a fiery mace above his head, his eyes wild with rage.

I stare down the monstrous Gracile abomination before me. No more games. "Bring my sister to me and I won't destroy you all." My voice shakes with anger, the words bolstering my resolve.

Merodach grunts and bares a sadistic grin as he steps forward.

Mila and Mos glance at each other, then me.

Ilah give me strength.

The towering, armored mute and his brethren come for us. My gold-plated hand cannon levels upon his bulk and fires, the first shot striking low and staggering him. With a scream of rage, he rushes me. My finger jerks against the trigger again and again, each blaze of fire threatening to topple the mad Gracile. One large round left in the cylinder. I dive to the left to avoid a crushing blow from his flaming weapon.

To my side, Kahleit and Ghofaun work together to take down one of the titans with their blades. On my right, the lead Creed with mismatched arms slams into an armored Gracile with a crushing blow to the skull.

There is swirling dust in my nose and eyes. I roll to the side to get a fix on my attacker. His breathing labored, a thirst for death in his eyes, he turns on me. But the monster is slowing, blood pouring down from the holes in his plate armor. He struggles to heft the fiery mace again.

Rolling to my back, I point and fire. The recoil bucks the heavy revolver high. Wide-eyed, the furious Gracile shudders, blood spraying from what must surely be a fatal neck wound. Groaning, bulging muscles shaking, he lifts the mace over his head to pulverize me against the floor. I fumble with the big bore revolver's cylinder, dumping hot brass across my sweat-soaked shirt. There is no time to ready my weapon. Frozen in terror, my heart slamming against my breast, I wait for the death blow.

There's a loud smack. A tattered blue beanbag slams across the chin of the brute. He stumbles, dropping the mace, which flickers and eventually quenches. His eyes wide, searching, he grabs at his neck wound, the blood pumping through his fingers. He drops to his knees with a groan and rolls to his side.

There's someone standing over me. A beanbag launcher hangs in her hand. I should have known.

"Come on," Mila says, panting. "Let me help you."

I shake my head.

"Faruq. Look at me."

I raise my eyes to meet hers, an avalanche of emotion crushing down upon me.

"Give me your hand," she says, her voice gentle. "We're out of time."

Slowly, I reach up, my fingers encircling the warmth of her wrist, my heart surging at her touch. She pulls me to my feet and our gazes connect. I can't stop the tears from building. In a different life, a better life free from the bonds of expectation, bias, and hate, we could have had something special. The thought twists like a knife buried to the hilt and meant to kill. I struggle to push back a wave of bitter anguish. The words I want to say to this woman refuse to come, though I want so desperately to utter them.

"Mila, I … I'm …"

She shakes her head, squeezing my wrist. "You'll tell me when this is over."

I swallow back my mumbled words, her stare boring into my soul.

"Faruq." She holds my gaze. "Will you give me the chance to save Demitri?"

I manage a feeble nod.

"Thank you." She squeezes my hand. "Now go. Save Husniya. She needs you."

"Yes," I say, reluctantly releasing her hand. "I will."

Mila turns and separates from me, her stride full of purpose as she crosses the room.

There's a scream as a force of Rippers slams against the pikes of my men blocking the entrance to the lillipad.

"Kahleit, hold them off until this is done," I shout.

"Yes, Sheikh," my captain replies.

Ahead, the fallen bodies of his Gracile guard at his feet, Vedmak appears from the shadows and shrugs free of his cloak. Hidden behind some kind of mask, his breathing sounds heavy. He is no longer the meek, kindhearted Gracile I met those many years ago.

Just beyond him, the green orb of pulsating energy swells, enveloping more of the room.

Something hollow grows in the pit of my stomach as Mila, Mos, and the Creed close in on Vedmak, their bodies poised for action. I ease the hammer back down to the safety position and sprint off into the maze of lillipad corridors beyond. I must find Husniya.

CHAPTER FORTY-FOUR

MILA

The hate in his eyes as he paces back and forth like a trapped predator chills my blood. I hold his withering gaze. He does not look at my companions, jeer, or make idle threats. His silence is foreboding. There's a pensiveness, excitement even, at my arrival, as though he's waited his entire life for this moment.

"Demitri, we're here to help you," I say, lightly touching the auto injector on my belt to make sure it's still there.

The Gracile laughs, breathing deep the vaporous mist that hangs curling about his mask. "The whelp can't hear you. He's locked out. It's just us now. Are you ready for me to visit upon you what you fear most, little one?"

Don't play his game, Mila. Resist. It's what you do. I swallow the dry lump from my throat.

Beside me, Zaldov shifts, little whirs and clunks sound as he adjusts his combative stance.

"You do not scare me." Vedmak looks from me to Mos and finally to Zaldov. "You honestly believe it will be a problem for me to defeat all three of you at once?"

"What about four?" Ghofaun says, stepping in line with us.

Vedmak rolls his shoulders. "What is it you hope to achieve? You cannot save the girl. You cannot wrest this body from my grasp. You can't stop the machinations of destiny. I was made to rule, and in this perfect shell, I will. You all are nothing more than a momentary inconvenience."

"No," I say, "your scythe is gone. You're vulnerable without your tech."

He raises his severed arm. Secured to the stump with a series of heavy leather straps is a cruel-looking, crudely welded iron hammer the size of two fists. It's still wet with the blood of his victims. "Worry not. This will serve me well." An evil grin spreads across his lips.

Yeos give me the strength to stay true to the path.

I huff out a breath. The image of my brother smiling and Bilgi's bloodied fingers tapping my chest flicker in my mind. I touch the edge of the worn picture sticking from the edge of my pocket.

"Mos, Ghofaun, Zaldov, we hit him in waves. Time it perfectly. One of us right on top of the next. Wear him down. Give me the chance I need." I take a step forward. "Demitri, if you can hear me, fight back. We don't want to hurt you more than we have to."

"We are with you, Mila Solokoff," Zaldov says, his posture locked and ready.

"'Til the end," Ghofaun says.

"Quit your braying and make your play, woman," Vedmak rasps.

Zaldov launches forward, crossing the gap between us in a blur of movement.

"Ahh, the protector. We have a score to settle." Vedmak dodges Zaldov's initial swing.

Knocking away a second punch, and deflecting a thrusting kick, Vedmak belts Zaldov across the face with the hammer. Shooting in low, he secures the Creed by the waist and twisting, flings him backward against the far wall in a stunning display of strength. Zaldov crashes and slides to the floor.

Master Ghofaun beats Mos and me to the punch and whips into the air with the natural grace of a carnival performer. Landing three successive kicks, the monk staggers Vedmak back. The Gracile grunts and shakes his head, then repeatedly slaps himself in the face.

Demitri is trying to come through, I know it. *C'mon, Demitri.*

My Kahangan ally seizes the moment and sacks the Gracile from the left, pinning his arms to his sides as they fall tumbling to the floor. In a deft movement bereft of weakness, Vedmak hip-tosses the bulky Kahangan, rolls on top of him, and stretching high, drives down swinging the iron hammer with astonishing fury. Mos is only able to provide a flinch response, his arms seizing to cover his face as the heavy head cracks down on bone. There's a shrill scream as Mos's arm crumples beneath the blow. A look of terrible glee fills Vedmak's face as he swings down again, Mos defenselessly clutching his deformed arm.

"No!" Jumping into the air and planting both feet into Vedmak's chest, my sheer momentum knocks him from my friend. I land hard on my back and roll back over my shoulder and onto my knees. Scooping a moaning Mos beneath his armpits, I drag him from the fight. "Hang in there, Mos."

"He ... he got me, Mila."

I draw Svetlana's chrome from the holster on his hip and place the heavy magnum in his good hand. Squeezing his shoulder, I meet his eyes. "Fire on him only if you have no other choice, okay?"

He nods with a grimace of pain. "Go get 'em."

Across the room, Ghofaun slams into Vedmak with another barrage of blows. Ducking a backward swing, he defeats an attempt to smash him with the great hammer, rising fast to the inside of the Gracile's guard with a flurry of open-handed blows, chops, and elbow strikes.

"Argh, no. Silence, fool child!" wails Vedmak.

"Fight him, Demitri!" I scream. "Ghofaun, it's working."

With a feint, Vedmak tricks the monk, seizes him by his robes and flings him overhead against the cold hard floor in the same manner a person would bust a block of ice.

I collide once again with the huge frame of the Gracile. He grabs for me, swinging the hammer down hard where I was an instant before. With a crack, the heavy bludgeon slams against the floor.

"C'mon Demitri!" I shout, rising outside Vedmak's guard and deliver a swift elbow strike to his ribs, followed by a strong one-two scissor kick combination to his midsection.

"Demitri is dead. I killed him!" Vedmak shouts, his eyes wide with fury.

He catches me in the stomach with a strike that sends me sliding across the floor. Rising to my knees, I watch as Zaldov and Ghofaun together collide with our foe, systematically landing blow after blow. But something is wrong—the Gracile is letting it happen, or ... can it be he's having trouble reacting?

Demitri.

With a wild scream, Vedmak skillfully sidesteps a would-be crushing blow from Zaldov and lands a brutal stomping kick that doubles Ghofaun over. The hammer lands hard against Ghofaun's back and sends him into a heap against the polished floor. Swiveling his focus, Vedmak jumps into the air, and slams down with the full weight of the bludgeon into the top of Zaldov's head. The Creed hits the ground hard and tries to rise when Vedmak jams him back against the ground with his boot.

"Can you feel pain, puppet? Let us find out."

"Get up, Zaldov!" I shout.

The Creed flails and tries to push up, but to no avail. "Mila Solokoff, help me."

But I'm unable to reach him in time. I watch in horror as Vedmak shoves his hand under Zaldov's chin and begins to pull. Zaldov's neck makes a popping sound as it elongates.

Vedmak cackles with glee. "Let's see what you're made of."

"No. Please. I'm not ready to d-ahhhh!" The Creed's voice screams in a wash of electronic distortion.

"Zaldov!"

Wrenching, Vedmak pulls Zaldov's head from his shoulders. The Creed's mouth hangs open, shock frozen on his rubbery features.

There's an emptiness in my chest, a sudden rush of loss. "Zaldov."

Vedmak stands and tosses the head to the side. He laughs—a terrible guttural sound. "Such profound weakness—to think you trusted this thing, even treated it as though it were human. Disgusting."

The Creed was a loyal ally. He didn't deserve that. I struggle to keep a swell of hate from filling my heart. Hate is not the way, Mila. Stay focused.

Vedmak looks to the headless Creed, then Mos, his ruined arm clutched against his body, the other outstretched weapon shaking, then to Ghofaun's crumpled form, unmoving on the floor. He bares his teeth in a wicked grin as his eyes connect with mine. "All alone are we now?"

"No," I say fixing my eyes back on the twisted form of my old friend, resolve swelling in my chest. "I'm never alone."

CHAPTER FORTY-FIVE

FARUQ

The cracked plate glass windows slide past, each one only different from the next in the pattern. My head snaps left and right as I careen down the hallway, which is all polished steel and shimmering glass. Each room offers only glimpses of the chambers beyond, most of which appear to be laboratories of some sort.

"Husniya?" I stop short in the hallway, listening, the hand cannon raised. I crack the cylinder and assure the last round is still aligned in the staging position—ready to fire with one last cock of the hammer.

There's a muffled cry from somewhere down the hall ahead, the sound lost in the ruckus in the main chamber behind me. I hear a scream high and shrill. It's Mos. They're getting killed back there.

"Husniya, where are you?" I shout.

There's another crash ahead, the sound of instruments falling to the floor. I take off at a sprint. Damnation. Where is she? All these rooms appear the same.

On the floor ahead, a Creed soldier twitches, his head jerking spasmodically, a diamond-shaped hole the shape of a well-sharpened blade in the place where his right eye should be.

"Defend ... the principal ... must ..." Its distorted voice chitters, sparks popping from the gaping hole.

The principal? There's another groan. Rounding the doorway to the left, I enter a strange room with glowing glass eggs. On the floor another Creed lies still, its head twisted backward. And beside it ...

"Husniya!" I cry, crouching next to the shrunken form of my little sister.

Something shuffles in the dark, knocking metallic trays from the counter. The glass eggs clack together, shining their pink light on the scuffle. It's a Gracile, bearing down on his prey. A woman. The tall one who was with Mila.

"Hey. Let her go." I level my weapon at the brute.

My gun bucks upward with a blast of fire.

The Gracile flinches, his right arm dropping to hang limp. He glares at me and starts to come. The female Gracile, wild with fury, erupts from beneath him. Clenching a piece of jagged glass from the counter, she swings upward, jamming it through the floor of the Gracile's chin and into his brain. He convulses, a spray of blood peppering the nearby wall, before crumpling to the floor.

With the threat gone, I set the empty hand cannon on the floor and reach for the metallic headgear clamped against my sister's skull.

"Don't," the woman gasps, rubbing at her throat. "Sever the connection now and you'll kill her."

I press my teeth together. "I cannot leave her like this."

The woman approaches, kneeling on Husniya's other side. "No, we take her with us. Once Mila has done what she needs to do, we remove it," she says, still rubbing her throat. "Thank you, by the way."

"I'm just here for my sister."

"Regardless, you didn't have to help me, but you did."

"What are you doing back here?"

She swallows and looks over her shoulder toward the strange glass enclosure on the far side of the room. It's a much larger space than I'd initially thought, the walls extending into the darkness on either side. The little glass light bulbs come into focus. Except they're not lights. Inside each egg is tiny life.

"It's an embryo chamber," the Gracile woman says as though reading my thoughts. "It's the fuel source for the VME."

"The what?"

She seems flustered, her hands shaking. "The fiery green bubble out there. If we don't stop it right now, it's going to wipe us all out."

"Okay, so what do we do?" I say.

"We destroy the embryos. All of them," she says, revealing a small pouch with a brick of putty labeled COMP B. Strapped to the brick is an old windup timer with wires leading to a thin tube shoved into the putty. The wires run from one brick to another and another.

"How many do you have?"

"Enough. But I need your help placing them. They have adhesive backings so we can place them straight on the glass. Then we set the timer and we get the hell out of here.

Another scream from the main chamber, followed by the maniacal laughing of the deranged Gracile we all once called friend. This has to stop. I have to finish it. This is why I suffered. All of it brought me to this critical moment.

Now choose, Faruq.

I lower my sister to the ground and meet the Gracile's eyes. "I will help you. My name is Faruq, and I am a man of my word."

"I'm Oksana," she says. "There isn't much time, Faruq. Help me with the satchel."

Standing, I lift the bag and move with her to the far wall, the glass eggs glistening in the pale light. She pulls the primary brick and I lift the second, unravelling the wires as I move away. I watch her peel the glue pad's cover and slap the brick against the glass. I move to follow suit, stopping when my eyes focus on the tiny form inside the glass globe before me. Though young, it is undoubtedly human. My heart skips a beat.

Is this murder? Is this all that is left of the Graciles? Will I be dammed for committing such genocide? I swallow, hesitation paralyzing me.

Mila cries out, her voice echoing down the empty corridor. She's pleading. It's a sound that turns my blood to ice. Stay alive, Mila.

I exhale and slap the charge against the glass. It must be done.

"Good. Remain focused, Faruq," Oksana says. "Now affix the next. We'll not make it out of here if we delay."

I do this for you, Husniya. It's all for you.

CHAPTER FORTY-SIX

VEDMAK

"What is this supposed to be?" I say, watching her as she stands poised in the strange semi-crouched position, waiting. She lunges to the side, stripping the weight from my front leg. I stumble, my footing unstable as she strikes me in the gut with two open palms, then rises, hovering in the air. The blur of her twisting body preceeds a spinning kick that whips across this face like a twirled lariat. I fall back, rolling to my knees, where my hand moves to the radiating soreness of this jaw.

"Tricky move."

"It's called the sparrow hawk," the little rodent says, baring her teeth at me. "Come have some more."

Bouncing and skipping, she throws strike after strike designed to injure but never deals a fatal blow. First a hooking punch glancing the jaw. Then a kick that feigns for the groin as she switches feet and spins, catching me square in the stomach. Like some little irritating bird, she pecks. "Stand and fight. Are you so afraid to engage me in real combat?"

She comes again and I aim to smash her with the hammer, but it sails in an arc over her head as she drops low and throws an open hand against the knee, a spike of pain firing into my spine as my balance falters. Dammit all to hell.

The time-dilation protocol installed into this mask has failed. I'm too slow with this heavy garb. Even this damn Red Mist fails me. I can feel the Gracile pushing through—forcing his way to the surface. He pulls on these muscles, clawing at the inside of this skull for a foothold.

I suck in another deep lungful of the nebulized stim, but it seems to offer no advantage. Damn the Alchemist. A fleeting glimpse at total control only for it to wear thin too soon. Should have known better than to trust that wasted hag. Another roundhouse kick skims too close and I near tumble over Merodach's lifeless corpse. Everything—everyone—fails me. I am surrounded by constant failure.

You are the failure, a voice whispers.

Demitri. No.

Frustrated, I tear the mask free and cast it aside. Beads of salty sweat pour into these eyes, blurring my vision. The Red Mist hisses freely from the dangling nozzle. "Sarding piece of dog meat." I grab the hose and yank it away from the tank on my back, shrugging off the heavy cylinder. It clangs to the floor.

"Come at me, whore," I scream.

She doesn't flinch. There's an unnerving serenity in her movements. She floats in and out, the punches and kicks landing precisely in the solar plexus or the inside of a thigh, or against the chin.

"Worthless insect. Be still!"

She pauses, her chest heaving. "Demitri, if you're in there give me a sign, please."

"He's not coming back, you stupid bitch. He's de—"

Every fiber of this engine freezes. I'm seized, unable to bend the flesh to my will. And then, these lips move on their own.

"Mila, I'm here."

No!

"Demitri!" Mila cries back. "I knew you were still with me. Fight him. You have to fight!"

"I'm trying. You have to kill us. Kill us befoggg—"

The jaw we both struggle to control locks, the tongue rolling in this throat as I push his consciousness back. "Not this time, boy." I reclaim the body, tearing it from his ethereal grasp and stomp toward the Robust bitch. Her weakness is the soul that resides in here with me. Showing his presence has only stupefied her.

I lean back to deliver a devastating pressing kick to her scrawny chest, but in that moment the little *suka* is gone. Instead, the pallid and tortured face of Ida stares back, the bullet hole in her forehead once again oozing blood.

"No. This is you Demitri. I will dig you out of this skull if it's the last thing I do."

Do it Vedmak. Dig me out. Kill us both.

I slap at this Gracile face, trying to block out the image of my beloved. *Run, Mila. Why aren't you running?*

I howl with a lust for death and draw all of the strength I possess to turn this earthly vehicle against her, focusing on what Demitri noticed. The whelp clasps a small syringe. "What is it you have there, child? Show it to me."

"Why don't you come find out," she wheezes.

"A stim won't help you, stupid *kozel*. Go ahead. Stick yourself. Show me the best of the creature in which your Yeos has put so much faith."

But she doesn't inject herself. Instead, she rushes for me.

It's not meant for her.

I ignore my Gracile demon to perfectly time the backfist strike. Hardened knuckles catch her across the jaw. Her tiny Robust body crashes into the cold floor and her precious stim clatters about until coming to rest a hair's breadth from the emerald green dome of energy. With fevered determination, she crawls on her belly toward the syringe, bony fingers outstretched, the skin blistering as the energy wall crisps her flesh.

There's the click of an old hand gun hammer cocking. The Kahangan. He's got me. I spin and charge him. As he pulls the trigger, the deafening crack of the weapon is drowned out by a resounding boom that shakes the foundations of the lillipad.

What the hell was that? An explosion?

I turn back to the Kahangan. A burning gouge is seared into this Gracile cheek where the bullet grazed. "You missed," I hiss. With the room still shaking, I raise the great hammer to strike the death blow.

But it will not fall.

I told you, I'm going to stop you.

Si, Nunca ganarás, another voice says.

What? What new foe stalks me?

Husniya's guardian haunts you too. You inadvertently let her in when you connected with the girl. You're finished, Vedmak.

Si, vuelve al Infierno, demonio.

"Arghh!" I scream, frozen in mid swing, unable to move as I wish.

The ground beneath shakes with one quake after another. The room starts to come apart, the heat of the energy dome licking at exposed skin, leaving behind the unmistakable stinking odor of charred hair.

This lillipad is coming down, and we're going to die in it together.

Juntos, Margarida says.

As I stand there, arms raised high, the ever-approaching dome of fire crackles and pops, then fizzes and seems to choke as if starved of its source of power. No, that's not possible. The green light increases in intensity until it becomes a blinding white. Suddenly, it collapses, imploding on itself with a high-pitched sound that scrapes the inner ear. Bitter cold Siberian air is sucked into the void left behind, whipping debris and mutilated bodies with it. And then, nothing.

Snowflakes and dust motes dance in the air.

They did it!

"The embryos. My legacy!"

Rage fills whatever fragment of a soul is left in here. Power surges to the muscles of the stolen engine and I'm free as the whore comes again, fearless determination in her dark eyes. I parry away strike after furious strike, my own speed matched play-for-play by this insect. She dances and spins, edging ever closer into my circle of death.

I've got you now.

Mila. Don't, please, I'm not worth it.

"Silence your wailing. She dies," I reply aloud.

"You first, Vedmak," Mila says, and steps full into me.

Foolish woman. She's left herself wide open, an undeserved look of victory plastered across her wretched face. The moment slows to a crawl, allowing me to savor the sweetness of my victory. The blood-soaked hammer catches her across the side of the head. Her skull cracks and her eyes roll back, her feet lifting from the floor as she parts from me.

There's a tug in the stomach of my Gracile form. I look down to see her hand gripped tightly around a syringe, the needle of which now slides from this stolen flesh. What is *this*?

She crashes into the floor and grows still. The empty syringe tilts from her limp hand and clatters free.

"Mila, no!" screams the Baqirian as he stumbles back into the room, the flaccid body of his sibling in his arms, the pretentious Oksana at his heels.

The Musul's bawl melds with the wild screaming of the Gracile inside this skull. Yet, something else is wrong. My very soul feels as if it is untethered, flapping in the cosmic wind, no longer anchored to this world. "What did that little bitch do to me?"

Demitri hasn't stopped bawling.

"No, this can't be. I am Death. I cannot be undone."

My Gracile demon's hatred burns me away like the flash of tinder. His consciousness, hot and bright as the sun, swells inside until I can only see an arresting light. His soul consumes this corporeal shell and forces me back into the void. I flail in the dark, twisting, grabbing, but touching nothing. The emptiness is absolute. There's a roaring blast of absolute pain the likes of which I've never experienced before. I fall, hurtling back to my prison. Back to Hell—and this time, there is not even a thread of the living world on which to hold.

CHAPTER FORTY-SEVEN

DEMITRI

"Mila! Oh, Mila, no."

I crash to my knees at her side, my fingers trembling and outstretched for her face, but I can't bring myself to touch her. What have I done? This can't be. It isn't supposed to be how it ends. Mila, get up, move, anything, please. You can't die. It should have been me.

She lies there, unmoving, sprawled awkwardly. Blood runs freely from her nose and mouth, her skull indented from the devastating blow Vedmak bestowed. My insides feel liquified, my heart a heavy stone that threatens to tear its way through my body and slap against the cold hard floor.

Vedmak, you bastard. Where are you? Vedmak!

He doesn't answer.

"Vedmak!" I scream, but my voice is lost to the rumbling concussions shaking the lillipad.

Metal squeals and electrical wires fizz and spark as the structure comes apart. In a fit of anger, I tear at the leather straps holding the killing device strapped to my arm. They break, the hateful thing knocking to the ground.

I grab Mila by the old leather jacket she's always wearing. "You stupid Robust, you did that on purpose. You knew what would happen. You did it ... to save—" Tears cut a path through the grime on my cheeks and I choke on my words. I bury my head in her chest and cry harder than I've ever cried in my miserable life. My shoulders shake, the sobs uncontrollable, the tears soaking her shirt to the skin.

Can't breathe. Can't make it stop. My heart burns with a thousand things I need to say but will never get the chance to. "Mila... Mila, no."

She stirs under me, eyes fluttering.

"Mila?"

"D-Demitri, is it you?" she croaks.

My lungs falter and for a moment I have no breath to speak. "Yes, Mila it's me, I'm here."

Her face is ghostly white, her head lolling. "I can see Him now. He's waiting for me."

"What? Who?" I ask, stroking the hair from her face.

"The Lightbringer. He's—" She slips into unconsciousness again.

Another quake rumbles through the lillipad and chunks of the ceiling fall away, exploding into clouds of dust all around. Faruq approaches, a terrible slack expression on his face. In his arms he cradles his sister.

"Stay with me, Mila, c'mon." I sniff hard and remove the damn cloak Vedmak had me wear and lay it across her. My arms slip under her head and knees and I brace to lift.

"Demitri?" Oksana's voice reaches out. My tear-filled eyes take in her beautiful face. "Is it you?"

I can only gasp, my body trembling. "What have I done?"

A moment passes and a hand touches my shoulder. "It worked," she whispers. "I can't believe it worked."

"I couldn't stop him before he ..." I mumble.

Oksana regards the headless form of the Creed, who looks so much like my brother Nikolaj, with a sad pursing of trembling lips. She turns back to Mila and gives my shoulder a gentle squeeze. "She's gone. We have to go, Demitri. This place is coming down."

Mila sputters back to consciousness, blood oozing from her nose and ears.

I recoil and brace to take her weight. "No, I won't let her die here alone."

Mila's gaze rests firmly centered with mine. "I'm not alone, Demitri," she whispers, her words slurred. "Never was." Her tongue moves to wet her lips, "You saved us all. You ... didn't know that, did you?"

"You're concussed, Mila. It's bad. You need help."

Slowly, Faruq kneels beside us, lowering Husniya to the ground.

"No, Demitri." Her cold fingertips rise to touch my face. "I got to see my friend one last time. I got to make a difference." She swallows, her stare growing distant.

Faruq reaches out and grasps her fingers. "Mila?"

"Tell Faruq," she mumbles, her eyes far away.

"Yes, Mila, I'm here," Faruq says, tears running down his face. "I'm here."

"Tell Faruq I loved …" Mila's body relaxes with a sigh, her pupils dilating as a whispered breath caresses my cheek.

Faruq's head drops, his shoulders shaking.

"Mila?" My scream fills the room, long and loud, becoming hoarse until only a barely audible hiss escapes my throat. I clutch her as close to me as I can. Lungs burning and empty, I can't even cry.

My gaze drifts from Faruq to Oksana, and to the battered monk and the broken Kahangan who have gathered around us in silent disbelief. Each one of them ignores their own injuries and the devastation all around, as if dying here with her were the only just thing to do.

"Demitri," Oksana says as softly as she can, "Mila is right, you saved us all. I need you now, to help me. I'll explain, I promise. Right now, you have to come. Don't let her death be in vain."

No one says anything.

"Up. Everybody up, c'mon." Oksana stands and tugs at me and Faruq. The ceiling rumbles long and low.

Pressing Mila to my chest, I rise. My eyes burn with tears of hatred for Vedmak and guilt at my own impotence. "I'm not leaving her behind. If I die carrying her out, so be it."

Faruq climbs to his feet, holding Husniya. Ghofaun shoulders a broken but mobile Mos. I'm sure they wish me in her place. For now, the vengeance in their eyes is replaced only with despair. Both men dip their brow. Oksana simply motions us forward and leads the way out of the crumbling lillipad.

I follow her out, Faruq, Ghofaun, and Mos at my heels. We stumble through the smoke and debris and out into the hostile Siberian cold. The battlefield before us is a wasteland of bodies and blood. Few are left standing and fewer have any fight left in them. They wander around, lost, probing the now cold bodies of friends and brothers in arms. At our approach, Baqirian, Kahangan, Zopatian, resistance fighter, all become still and silent, fixated on Mila's lifeless body hanging in my arms.

A small group of Rippers, still furious with rage and led by a large Robust adorned with a necklace of skulls, approach. There's a roar and I flinch. It's the tiger. Anastasia is atop the beast, a notched arrow drawn.

Together, they form a formidible shield against those who would do us harm. The Rippers stall, fear and doubt upon their blood-stained faces.

The tiger roars again.

The chieftain glares at Mila's broken form long and hard but finally turns and, with a wave of his arm, his Rippers disband, dissappearing with him through the broken wall of ice. I am sure it will not be the last we see of him.

Anastasia lowers the pulled bowstring and takes note of Mila's limp form hanging in my arms. She stares deep into me. "Demitri?"

"Yes," I whisper. "Thank you."

She closes her eyes and exhales, her cheeks wet with tears.

A screech of twisting metal echoes from behind us and the broken lillipad finally collapses in on itself, sending a rush of ice and snow against our backs. We don't even acknowledge it. Instead, we trudge out from the shadows of this hell and onward to, well, who knows where. Forward, I suppose. The only way for us now is forward.

EPILOGUE

DEMITRI

I should say something, but I can't.

A bitter wind bites at my cheeks and stabs at my eyes. The icy blast only serves to remind me that I'm alive and she's not. The hollow space inside, once filled by Vedmak, feels deeper than ever. And without my friend, I fear it is a wound that will never heal.

The faces of friends who knew—no, *loved*—her longer and better than I, are withered and cold. They flick the occasional glance at me, the bringer of so much death. What right do I have to be here, to send her on to wherever she believed she would go after this life? She's dead because of me. Her life was given to save me. I gaze at the headstone, a meager boulder, bearing her name and carved with an inscription. Perhaps they entertain me simply in fear of Anastasia's tiger, sat at my side now. I turn to the Soufreit, searching her eyes for that look—the one that told me I'm a good person. Anastasia rests a hand on my lower back in a comforting gesture and gives me a nod. I offer a weak smile, but it quickly fades.

Ghofaun, Mos, Oksana, Yuri, and a gathering of Robusts of all races and religions shuffle back and forth to keep warm. The Vestals encircle everyone, holding silent vigil, standing strong against the Siberian wind. Here in the ruins of Logos, there are few walls left to shield us—but this is where Mila would want to be buried. This was her home.

At the back of the crowd, though still in front of a few hundred Graciles who huddle like lost sheep, stands Faruq with Husniya who grips his side, sobbing gently. I catch his eye for a moment. Still warring with Alya, he came anyway. Put his troubles aside to say a final goodbye, though I doubt he will utter a word. He carries perhaps more guilt over her death than even I do.

Say something, damn you.

That's what Vedmak would snarl at me. Despite the fact he's gone, I find myself wondering how he would handle this situation. His evil knew no bounds, and yet I take strength from the lessons he taught me—a fact I'm sure he would despise.

I clear my throat, unable to make eye contact with anyone.

"Mila was my friend," I start, my voice barely audible. "Perhaps my only friend. A thing I never thought I would have. Something I was unsure even existed. My pain, my anguish at her passing is unbearable. Still, I know compared with your pain, it is meaningless. After what I've been party to, I don't feel I have any right to speak to you today, though … here I am." I suck in a frigid breath. "But it's not about me. It's not even about you— her loved ones and comrades in arms."

They stare at me, brows furrowed.

I wait for a gust to die down, and clasp Anastasia's hand in mine for the strength to carry on. "I spent my life in relative luxury. Free to read books and learn all there is to learn about the universe. All Graciles did. We had it all figured out. Except we didn't. Mila had lived through pain and loss that I can't imagine. It made her tough, and sarcastic and difficult and, well, very special."

From the crowd, there's a cough followed by the sniffing away of tears.

"Despite her hardship," I continue, "she chose to live every single day for the benefit of others. She never gave up hope there was a light at the end of the tunnel for humanity—for me. It cost her her life to prove it. She told me I saved her. That I saved everyone. I didn't understand what she meant, at least until now. Oksana has told me the antidote she created for me can be used to fight the NBD. Without me, or Vedmak, even, we would perhaps never have considered such an approach. Maybe this is true. Maybe it isn't. But how did *I* save *her*? She died. Because of me."

Tears well in my eyes and the stone in my throat threatens to choke my words to silence. I try to swallow it away and fail miserably.

"Mila wanted to make a difference, to do something with her life. She believed saving me was a great thing because I was worth more to the universe than her. She was wrong." I sniff hard, swallowing over and over, working to be able to make it through this. "I haven't saved you. Mila's love did. If she hadn't fought with everything she had to come for me, to bring me back from the demon who stalked me, there would never be a cure for the NBD. You all would not have banded together in battle. You would not stand here together now. Because of her, you all united. And because of her, we have a chance to *stay* united."

Snow blusters though the graveyard, picking up debris and flinging it between our feet and against Mila's headstone. The rattling noise draws everyone's attention to the simple monument. Below her name, seven words are carved deep into the rock. I drop to my haunches next to the shiny black sarsen.

"I don't know if you're with Yeos now," I say to my friend, who now lies buried beneath the earth at my feet. "I don't know anything but this—" I turn to the mourners. "If we are to rebuild the human race, it will take time and patience and an understanding many of us will struggle with. But we have to try. We have to follow Mila's lead. Sometimes we have to make great sacrifices to get to our destination." My fingers run across the engraved words I once saw beneath a painting in Evgeniy's apartment. "Indeed, it may well take death to reach a star. To die quietly of old age would be to go there slowly on foot. That was never Mila's way. She went in with everything she had, a heart full of belief in something greater. And so should we."

ACKNOWLEDGEMENTS

We humbly thank all those who have helped us bring this world to
life.
It takes a village to create a book.
Italia Gandolfo, Renee Fountain, Liana Gardner, Jason Kirk, Holly
Atkinson, Justin Paul,
Chris Rapier, Chris Currenton, David Jones, Kat de Sousa, Tess
Burnside and Marina Diner.

ABOUT THE AUTHORS

 A veteran law enforcement officer, **Stu Jones** has worked as a beat cop, an investigator, an instructor of firearms and police defensive tactics and as a member and team leader of a multi-jurisdictional SWAT team. He is trained and qualified as a law enforcement SWAT sniper, as well as in hostage rescue, close quarter combat and high-risk entry tactics. Recently, Stu served for three years with a U.S. Marshal's Regional Fugitive Task Force - hunting the worst of the worst.

Known for his character-driven stories and blistering action sequences, Stu strives to create thought-provoking reading experiences that challenge the status quo. When he's not chasing bad guys or writing epic stories, he can be found planning his next adventure to some remote or exotic place.

Stu lives in Alabama with his wife, two children, and a golden-doodle who thinks he's human.

www.StuJonesFiction.com

Gareth Worthington holds a degree in marine biology, a PhD in Endocrinology, an executive MBA, is Board Certified in Medical Affairs, and currently works for the Pharmaceutical industry educating the World's doctors on new cancer therapies. Gareth is an authority in ancient history, has hand-tagged sharks in California, and trained in various martial arts, including Jeet Kune  Do and Muay Thai at the EVOLVE MMA gym in Singapore and 2FIGHT in Switzerland. His work has won multiple awards, including Dragon Award Finalist and an IPPY award for Science Fiction. He is a member of the International Thriller Writers Association, Science Fiction and Fantasy Writers of America, and the British Science Fiction Association. Born in England, Gareth has lived around the world from Asia, to Europe to the USA. Wherever he goes, he endeavors to continue his philanthropic work with various charities.

www.GarethWorthington.com
www.ItTakesDeathToReachAStar.com